THE
OUTCASTS
AND OTHER STORIES

THE OUTCASTS
AND OTHER STORIES

MAXIM GORKY

This edition published in 2019 by Arcturus Publishing Limited
26/27 Bickels Yard, 151–153 Bermondsey Street,
London SE1 3HA

Cover design: Peter Ridley
Cover illustration: Peter Gray

AD006512UK

Printed in the UK

CONTENTS

INTRODUCTION

BORN ON 28 MARCH 1868 in Nizhny Novgorod, Russia, Gorky grew up knowing Russian working-class life all too well. When he was five, his father died, forcing him to live with his grandparents while his mother remarried. At the age of eight, Gorky had to leave school and work full-time, as his grandfather could only afford a few months of school fees. Despite taking on numerous jobs, such as those of assistant shoemaker, errand boy and dishwasher aboard the *Volga* steamer, he found himself constantly hungry, with ragged clothing, and was often beaten by his employers. However, the cook aboard the *Volga* introduced him to reading, a passion he would never lose.

While working odd jobs in the city of Kazan, Gorky encountered the Populist movement and their ideals pitting the people against the élite. At first, it just made him more depressed about his own plight. He attempted suicide at the age of 21. After failing to take his own life, spurred on by misery, Gorky took to the life of a hobo as he wandered across southern Russia.

These tragedies of his early life were hugely influential on his later success as a writer. Looking back on those memories, he adopted the pen name 'gorky', the Russian word for 'bitter'. His tales drew on his personal experiences and his hatred of the atrocious working conditions and unfair treatment he had observed. His first story, 'Makar Chudra' was published in 1892.

Yet it was not until three years later, when 'Chelkash' was published in the St Petersburg journal *Russkoye bogatstvo*, that Gorky began to receive recognition for his work. It is the tragedy of a brash thief who recruits a naïve young peasant to his cause. Like many of his tales, it featured low-class, rugged and forsaken characters, their daily struggles and the intelligence and grit they needed to survive. His enlightening perspective and storytelling prowess won him critical acclaim and the hearts of many readers.

While his strengths lay with short fiction, Gorky also tried his hand at play- and novel-writing. *Foma Gordeyev* (1899) was his first novel, but like a number of his early attempts, he struggled to sustain a compelling narrative. His most significant longer work, *Mat* (1906), dealt directly with the Russian revolutionary movement, but lacked the emotional pull of his shorter fiction.

His later years were dominated by politics. He joined the Marxist party, only to leave it after observing Lenin's controversial tactics. In 1921, he fled the country and settled in Italy. By the 1930s, Gorky's sins had been forgiven by the Communist Party and Stalin went to great lengths to entice him to return home. The Russian leader went so far as to rename Gorky's home city after him. After a decade-long absence, Gorky was only too willing to return home, and to celebrate his return, he was appointed as the leader of the newly-established Union of Soviet Writers in 1932.

He died at the age of 68 on 18 June 1936. As the father of Soviet revolutionary literature, Maxim Gorky stands above his Russian contemporaries for his sympathetic portrayals of tramps, thieves and outcasts by providing an unsurpassed level of intimacy – made possible only through his personal experience.

MAKAR CHUDRA

(tr. Margaret Wettlin)

A COLD DAMP WIND came out of the sea, wafting over the steppe the pensive melody of the waves breaking on the shore and the rustle of dry bushes. Now and then a gust would lift up some shrivelled yellow leaves and throw them into our camp-fire, causing the flames to flare up; then the darkness of the autumn night would shudder and start back in fright, giving us a glimpse of the boundless steppe to the left, the limitless sea to the right, and in front of me – the form of Makar Chudra, an old Gipsy who was keeping watch over the horses belonging to his camp pitched some fifty paces away.

Heedless of the cold wind that blew open his Caucasian coat and struck mercilessly at his bare hairy chest, he lay facing me in a graceful and vigorous pose, drawing regularly at his enormous pipe, emitting thick clouds of smoke through his nose and mouth, gazing fixedly over my head into the silent darkness of the steppe, talking incessantly and making not the slightest effort to protect himself from the vicious attacks of the wind.

'So you go tramping about the world, do you? Good for you. You have made the right choice, young falcon. That is the only way. Go about the world seeing things, and when you have looked your fill, lie down and die.'

'Life? Your fellow-men?' he queried on hearing my objections to his 'That is the only way.' 'Why should you worry about that? Are not you life itself? And as for your fellow-men, they always have and always will get on famously without you. Do you really think anybody needs you? You are neither bread nor a stick, and so nobody wants you.

'Learn and teach others, you say. Can you learn how to make people happy? No, you cannot. Wait until your hair is grey before you try to teach others. What will you teach them? Every man knows what he needs. The wise ones take what life has to offer, the stupid ones get nothing, but each man learns for himself.

'A curious lot, people: they all herd together, trampling on each other, when there is this much space—' and he made a sweeping gesture out towards the steppe. 'And all of them work. What for? Nobody knows. Whenever I see a man ploughing a field I think to myself: there he is pouring his strength and his sweat into the earth drop by drop, only to lie down in that very earth at last and rot away. He will die as big an ignoramus as he was born, leaving nothing behind him, having seen nothing but his fields.

'Is that what he was born for – to dig in the soil and die without having had time even to dig himself a grave? Has he ever tasted freedom? Has he a knowledge of the vastness of the steppe? Has his heart ever been cheered by the murmur of the sea? He is a slave – a slave from the day of his birth to the day of his death. What can he do about it? Nothing but hang himself, if he has the sense to do that.

'As for me, at fifty-eight I have seen so much that if it were all put down on paper, a thousand bags like the one you have there would not hold it all. Can you name a land I have not seen? You cannot. I have been to places you have never even heard of. That is the only way to live – moving from one place to another. And never stop long in one place – why should you? Just see how day and night are always moving, chasing each other round the earth; in just the same way you must chase away your thoughts if you would not lose your zest for life. One is sure to lose it if he broods too much over life. Even I did once; I did indeed, young falcon.

'It was when I was in jail in Galicia. "Why was I ever born?" I thought in my misery. It is a great misery to be locked up in jail – ekh, what a misery! My heart was gripped as in a vice every time I looked out of the window at the open fields. Who can say why he was born? No one can, and one should never ask himself such a question. Live, and be thankful to be alive. Roam the earth and see what there is to see, and then you will never be miserable. Ah, but I almost hanged myself with my belt that time.

'Once I had a talk with a certain man. A stern man he was, and a Russian, like you. A person must not live as he likes, he said, but as is pointed out in the word of God. If a man lives in obedience to God, he said, God will give him whatever he asks for. He himself was dressed in rags and tatters. I told him to ask God for a new suit of clothes. He was so angry he cursed me and drove me away. But just a minute before he had said one ought to love his neighbours and forgive them. Why did he not forgive me if I had offended him? There's your preacher for you! They teach people to eat less, while they themselves eat ten times a day.'

He spat into the fire and was silent as he refilled his pipe. The wind moaned softly, the horses whinnied in the darkness, and the tender impassioned strains of a song came from the Gipsy camp. It was Nonka, Makar's beautiful daughter, who was singing. I recognized the deep throaty timbre of her voice, in which there was always a note of command and of discontent, whether she was singing a song or merely saying a word of greeting. The haughtiness of a queen was frozen upon her swarthy face, and in the shadows of her dark eyes glimmered a consciousness of her irresistible beauty and a contempt for everything that was not she.

Makar handed me his pipe.

'Have a smoke. She sings well, doesn't she? Would you like to have a maid like that fall in love with you? No? Good for you. Put no faith in women and keep away from them. A maid gets more joy out of kissing a man than I do out of smoking my pipe. But once you have kissed her, gone is your freedom. She holds you with invisible bonds that are not to be broken, and you give yourself to her heart and soul. That is the truth. Beware of the maids. They always lie. She swears she loves you above all else, but the first time you cause her a pin-prick she will tear your heart out. I know what I say. There are many things I know. If you wish, I will tell you a true tale. Remember it well, and if you do, you will be as free as a bird all your life.

'Once upon a time there was a young Gipsy named Zobar – Loiko Zobar. He was a fearless youth whose fame had spread throughout Hungary and Bohemia and Slavenia and all the lands that encircle the sea. There was not a village in those parts but had four or five men sworn to take Zobar's life, yet he went on living, and if he took a fancy to a horse, a regiment of soldiers could not keep him from galloping off on it. Was there a soul he feared? Not Zobar. He would knife the devil himself and all his pack if they swooped down on him, or at least he would curse them roundly and give them a cuffing, you can be sure of that.

'All the Gipsy camps knew Zobar or had heard of him. The only thing he loved was a horse, and that not for long. When he had tired of riding it he would sell it and give the money to anyone who asked him for it. There was nothing he prized; he would have ripped his heart out of his breast if he thought anyone had need of it. That was the sort of man he was.

'At the time I am speaking of – some ten years ago – our caravan was roaming through Bukovina. A group of us were sitting together one spring night – Danilo, a soldier who fought under Kossuth; old Nur; Radda, Danilo's daughter, and others.

'Have you seen my Nonka? She is a queen among beauties. But it would be doing her too great an honour to compare her with Radda. No words could describe Radda's beauty. Perhaps it could be played on a violin, but only by one who knew the instrument as he knew his own soul.

'Many a man pined away with love for Radda. Once in Moravia a rich old man was struck dumb by the sight of her. There he sat on his horse staring at her and shaking all over as if with the ague. He was decked out like the devil on holiday, his Ukrainian coat all stitched in gold, the sabre at his side set with precious stones that flashed like lightning at every movement of his horse, the blue velvet of his cap like a patch of blue sky. He was a very important person, that old man. He sat on and on staring at Radda, and at last he said to her: "A purse full of money for a kiss!" She just turned her head away. This made the rich old man change his tune.

'"Forgive me if I have insulted you, but you might at least give me a smile," and with this he tossed his purse at her feet, and a fat purse it was. But she just pressed it into the dust with her foot, as if she had not noticed it.

'"Ah, what a maid!" he gasped, bringing his whip down on his horse's flank so that the dust of the roadway rose in a cloud as the horse reared.

'He came back on the next day. "Who is her father?" he asked in a voice that echoed throughout the camp. Danilo came forward. "Sell me your daughter. Name your own price."'

'"It is only gentlemen who sell anything from their pigs to their consciences," said Danilo. "As for me, I fought under Kossuth and sell nothing."

'The rich man let out a roar and reached for his sabre, but someone thrust a lighted tinder into his horse's ear and the beast went flying off with its master on its back. We broke camp and took to the road. When we had been on the way two whole days, we suddenly saw him coming after us. "Hey!" he cried. "I swear to God and to you that my intentions are honest. Give me the maid to wife. I will share all that I own with you, and I am very rich." He was aflame with passion and swayed in his saddle like feathergrass in the wind. We thought over what he said.

'"Well, daughter, speak up," muttered Danilo into his beard.

'"If the eagle's mate went to nest with the crow of her own free will, what would you think of her?" said Radda.

'Danilo burst out laughing and so did the rest of us.

'"Well said, daughter! Have you heard, my lord? Your case is lost! Woo a pigeon – they are more docile." And we went on our way.

'At that the rich man pulled off his hat and hurled it down on the ground and rode off at such speed that the earth shook under his horse's hoofs. That was what Radda was like, young falcon.

'Again one night we were sitting in camp when all of a sudden we heard music coming from the steppe. Wonderful music. Music that made the blood throb in your veins and lured you off to unknown places. It filled us all with a longing for something so tremendous that if we once experienced it there would be no more reason to go on living, and if we did go on living, it would be as lords of the whole world.

'Then a horse came out of the darkness, and on the horse a man was sitting and playing the fiddle. He came to a halt by our campfire and stopped playing, looking at us and smiling.

'"Zobar! So it is you!" called out Danilo heartily.

'This, then, was Loiko Zobar. His moustaches swept down to his shoulders, where they mingled with his curly hair; his eyes shone like two bright stars, and his smile was the sun itself. It was as if he and his horse had been carved of one piece. There he was, red as blood in the fire-light, his teeth flashing when he laughed. Damned if I did not love him as I loved my own self, and he had not so much as exchanged a word with me or even noticed my existence.

'There *are* people like that, young falcon. When he looked into your eyes your soul surrendered to him, and instead of being ashamed of this, you were proud of it. You seemed to become better in his presence. There are not many people like that. Perhaps it is better so. If there were a lot of good things in the world, they would not be counted good. But listen to what happened next.

'Radda said to him: "You play well, Zobar. Who made you such a clear-voiced fiddle?"

'"I made it myself," he laughed. "And not of wood, but of the breast of a maiden I loved well; the strings are her heart-strings. It still plays false at times, my fiddle, but I know how to wield the bow."

'A man always tries to becloud a girl's eyes with longing for him so that his own heart will be protected from the darts of those eyes. And Zobar was no exception. But he did not know with whom he was dealing this time. Radda merely turned away and said with a yawn: "And they told me Zobar was wise and witty. What a mistake!" And she walked away.

'"You have sharp teeth, my pretty maid!" said Zobar, his eyes flashing as he got off his horse. "Greetings to you, friends. I have come to pay you a visit."

'"We are glad to have you," replied Danilo.

'We exchanged kisses, chatted a while and went to bed. We slept soundly. In the morning we found Zobar with a bandage round his head. What had happened? It seems his horse had kicked him in the night.

'Ah, but we knew who that horse had been! And we smiled to ourselves; and Danilo smiled. Could it be that even Zobar was no match for Radda? Not at all. Lovely as she was, she had a petty soul, and all the gold trinkets in the world could not have added one kopek to her worth.

'Well, we went on living in that same place. Things were going well with us, and Loiko Zobar stayed on. He was a good companion – as wise as an old man, and very knowing, and able to read and write Russian as well as Magyar. I could have listened to him talk the night through, and as for his playing – may the lightning strike me dead if there ever was another his equal. He drew his bow once across the strings and the heart leaped up in your breast; he drew it again and everything within you grew tense with listening – and he just went on playing and smiling. It made you want to laugh and cry at the same time. Now someone was moaning bitterly and crying for help, and it was as if a knife were being turned in your side; now the steppe was telling a tale to the sky – a sad tale. Now a maid was weeping as she said farewell to her lover. Now her lover was calling to her from the steppe. And then, like a bolt from the blue, would come a gay and sweeping tune that made the very sun dance in the sky. That was how he played, young falcon! You felt that tune with every fibre of your body, and you became the slave of it.

'And if at that moment Zobar had called out: "Out with your knives, comrades!" every man of us would have bared his knife against anyone he pointed out. He could wind a person round his little finger, but everyone loved him dearly. Yet Radda would have nothing to do with him. That was bad enough, but she mocked him besides. She wounded his heart and wounded it badly. He would set his teeth and pull at his moustache, his eyes deeper than wells, and at times something would flash in them that struck terror into your heart. At night he would go deep into the steppe and his violin would weep there until morning – weep for his lost freedom. And we would lie and listen and think to ourselves: what will happen next? And we knew that when two stones are rolling towards each other, they will crush anything that stands in their way. That was the way things were.

'One night we sat for long round the fire discussing our affairs, and when we got tired of talking, Danilo turned to Zobar and said: "Sing us a song, Zobar, to cheer our hearts." Zobar glanced at Radda who was lying on the ground not far away gazing up at the sky, and he drew his bow across the strings. The violin sang out as if the bow were really being drawn over a maiden's heart-strings. And he sang:

Hi ho, hi ho! My heart is aflame,
The steppe is like the sea.
And like the wind, our gallant steeds
Are bearing you and me.

'Radda turned her head to him, propped herself up on one elbow and laughed in his face. Zobar flushed crimson.

Hi ho, hi ho! My comrade true,
The hour of dawn is nigh;
The steppe is wrapped in shades of night,
But we shall climb the sky.
Spur on your horse to meet the day
That glimmers o'er the plain,
But see that lovely Lady Moon
Is touched not by its mane!

'How he sang! No one sings like that nowadays. But Radda murmured under her breath: "I would not climb so high if I were you, Loiko Zobar. You might fall down into a puddle and spoil those lovely moustaches of yours."

'Zobar threw her a furious glance, but said nothing. He was able to control himself and go on singing:

Hi ho, hi ho! If daylight comes
And finds us both asleep,
Our cheeks will burn with crimson shame
As out of bed we leap.

'"A splendid song," said Danilo. "Never have I heard a better one; may the devil turn me into a pipe if I have!"

'Old Nur stroked his whiskers and shrugged his shoulders, and all of us were pleased with Zobar's brave song. But Radda did not like it.

'"Once I heard a gnat trying to imitate the eagle's call," she said. It was as if she had thrown snow in our faces.

'"Perhaps you are longing for a touch of the whip, Radda," drawled Danilo, but Zobar threw down his cap and said, his face as dark as the earth:

'"Wait, Danilo! A spirited horse needs a steel bridle! Give me your daughter to wife!"

'"A fine speech," chuckled Danilo. "Take her, if you can."

'"Very well,' said Zobar; then, turning to Radda: 'Come down off your high horse, maid, and listen to what I have to say. I have known many a girl in my day – many, I say – but not one of them ever captured my heart as you have. Ah, Radda, you have enslaved my soul. It cannot be helped – What must be will be, and the horse does not exist that can carry a man away from himself. With God and my own conscience as witness, and in the presence of your father and all these people, I take you to wife. But I warn you not to try to curb my liberty; I am a freedom-loving man and will always live as I please." And he walked up to her with set teeth and blazing eyes. We saw him stretch his hand out to her, and we thought: at last Radda has put a bridle on the wild colt of the steppe. But suddenly Zobar's arms flew out and he struck the ground with the back of his head.

'What could have happened? It was as if a bullet had struck him in the heart. But it was Radda who had flicked a whip about his legs and jerked it. That was what had made him fall.

'And again she was lying there motionless, a scornful smile on her lips. We watched to see what would happen next. Zobar sat up and held his head in his hands as if he were afraid it would burst, then he got up quietly and went out into the steppe without a glance at anyone. Nur whispered to me: "You had better keep an eye on him." And so I crept after him into the steppe, in the darkness of the night. Think of that, young falcon.'

Makar scraped the ashes out of the bowl of his pipe and began to refill it. I pulled my coat tighter about me and lay back, the better to study his aged face, bronzed by sun and wind. He was muttering to himself, emphasizing what he said by shaking his head gravely; his grey moustaches twitched and the wind ruffled his hair. He reminded me of an old oak which has been struck by lightning but is still strong and powerful and proud of its strength. The sea went on whispering to the sand, and the wind carried the sound to the steppe. Nonka had stopped singing. The clouds that had gathered made the autumn night darker than ever.

'Loiko dragged one foot after the other as he walked, his head drooping, his arms hanging as limp as whip-cords, and when he reached the bank of a little stream he sat down on a stone and groaned. The sound of that groan nearly broke my heart, but I did not go near him. Words cannot lessen a man's grief, can they? That is the trouble. He sat there for an hour, for another, for a third without stirring, just sitting there.

'I lay not far away. The sky had cleared, the moon bathed the whole steppe in silver light so that you could see far, far into the distance.

'Suddenly I caught sight of Radda hurrying towards us from the camp.

'I was overjoyed. "Good for you, Radda, brave girl!" thought I. She came up to Zobar without his hearing her. She put her hand on his shoulder. He started, unclasped his hands and raised his head. Instantly he was on his feet and had seized his knife. God, he'll kill her, I thought, and was about to jump up and raise the alarm when I heard:

'"Drop it or I'll blow your head off!" I looked: there was Radda with a pistol in her hand aimed at Loiko's head. A very daughter of Satan, that girl! Well, I thought, at least they are matched in strength; I wonder what will happen next.

"'I did not come to kill you, but to make peace," said Radda, pushing the pistol into her belt. "Put away your knife." He put it away and gazed at her with fuming eyes.

'What a sight that was! These two staring at each other like infuriated beasts, both of them so fine and brave! And nobody saw them but the bright moon and me.

"'Listen, Zobar, I love you," said Radda. He did nothing but shrug his shoulders, like a man bound hand and foot.

"'Many a man have I seen, but you are the bravest and handsomest of all. Any one of them would have shaved off his moustaches had I asked him to; any one of them would have fallen at my feet had I wanted him to. But why should I? None of them were brave, and with me they would soon have gone womanish. There are few brave Gipsies left, Zobar – very few. Never yet have I loved anyone, Zobar. But I love you. And I love freedom, too. I love my freedom even more than I love you. But I cannot live without you any more than you can live without me. And I want you to be mine – mine in soul and body, do you hear?"

'Zobar gave a little laugh. "I hear," he said. "It cheers my heart to hear what you say. Speak on."

"'This is what else I would say, Zobar: do what you will, I shall possess you; you are sure to be mine. And so waste no more time. My kisses and caresses are awaiting you – and I shall kiss you passionately, Zobar! Under the spell of my kisses you will forget all the brave life of the past. No longer will your gay songs, so beloved by the Gipsies, resound in the steppe; now shall you sing soft love songs to me alone – to Radda. Waste no more time. This have I said, which means that from tomorrow on you will serve me as devotedly as a youth serves an elder comrade. And you will bow at my feet before the whole camp and kiss my right hand, and then only shall I be your wife."

'This, then, was what that devilish girl was after. Never had such a thing been heard of. True, old people said that such a custom was held among the Montenegrins in ancient times, but it never existed among the Gipsies. Could you think of anything more preposterous, young man? Not if you racked your brains a whole year.

'Zobar recoiled and the steppe rang with his cry – the cry of one who has been mortally wounded. Radda shuddered, but did not betray her feelings.

'"Good-bye until tomorrow, and tomorrow you will do what I have said, do you hear, Zobar?"

'"I hear. I shall do it," groaned Zobar and held out his arms to her, but she went away without so much as glancing at him, and he swayed like a tree broken by the wind, and he fell on the ground, sobbing and laughing.

'That was what she did to him, that accursed Radda. I could hardly bring him back to his senses.

'Why should people have to suffer so? Does anyone find pleasure in hearing the groans of one whose heart is broken? Alas, it is a great mystery.

'When I got back to camp I told the old men what had taken place. We considered the matter and decided to wait and see what would happen. And this is what happened. In the evening when we had gathered about the fire as usual, Zobar joined us. He was looking downcast, he had grown haggard in that one night and his eyes were sunken. He kept them fixed on the ground and did not raise them once as he said:

'"This is how things are, comrades. I searched my heart this night and found no room in it for the freedom-loving life I have always lived. Radda has taken up every corner of it. There she is, the beautiful Radda, smiling her queenly smile. She loves freedom more than she loves me, but I love her more than I love freedom, and so I have decided to bow before her as she ordered me to, that all shall see how her beauty has enslaved the brave

Loiko Zobar who, until he met her, played with women as a cat plays with mice. For this she will become my wife and will kiss and caress me, and I shall lose all desire to sing songs to you and I shall not pine for the loss of my freedom. Is that how it is to be, Radda?" He raised his eyes and looked at her grimly. She nodded without a word and pointed to the ground in front of her. We could not imagine how this had been brought about. We even felt an urge to get up and go away so as not to see Loiko Zobar throw himself at the feet of a maid, even though that maid be Radda. There was something shameful in it, something very sad.

"'Well?' cried Radda to Zobar.

"'Do not be in so great a hurry. There is plenty of time – time enough to grow tired of me," laughed Zobar. And his laugh had the ring of steel.

"'So that is how things are, comrades. What is left for me to do? The only thing left for me to do is to see whether my Radda's heart is as strong as she would have us think. I shall test it. Forgive me."

'And before we had time to guess what he was up to, Radda was lying on the ground with Zobar's curved knife plunged into her breast up to the handle. We were dumbstruck.

'But Radda pulled out the knife, tossed it aside, held a lock of her black hair to the wound, and smiled as she said in a loud clear voice:

"'Farewell, Zobar. I knew you would do this." And with that she died.

'Do you see what the maid was like, young man? A devilish maid if there ever was one, so help me God.

"'Now I shall throw myself at your feet, my proud queen," said Zobar in a voice that rang out over the steppe. And throwing himself on the ground, he pressed his lips to the feet of the dead Radda and lay there without stirring. We bared our heads and stood in silence.

'What is to be said at a moment like that? Nothing. Nur murmured: "Bind the fellow," but nobody would raise a hand to bind Loiko Zobar; not a soul would do it, and Nur knew this. So he turned and walked away. Danilo picked up the knife Radda had tossed away and stood staring at it for some time, his grey whiskers twitching; there were still traces of Radda's blood on the blade, which was curved and sharp. Then Danilo went over to Zobar and plunged the knife into his back over the heart. After all, he was Radda's father, was the old soldier Danilo.

'"You've done it," said Loiko clearly, turning to Danilo, and then he went to join Radda.

'We stood looking at them. There lay Radda, pressing her hair to her breast with her hand, her wide-open eyes gazing up into the blue sky, while at her feet lay the brave Loiko Zobar. His curly hair had fallen over his face, hiding it from us.

'For some time we stood there lost in thought. Old Danilo's whiskers were quivering and his thick brows were drawn. He looked up at the sky and said not a word, but hoary-haired Nur had thrown himself on the ground and his body was shaking with sobs.

'And there was good cause to cry, young falcon.

'The moral is, let nothing lure you off the path you have taken. Keep going straight ahead; then, perhaps, you will not come to a bad end.

'And that is the whole story, young falcon.'

Makar stopped talking, slipped his pipe into his tobacco pouch, and pulled his coat over his chest. A fine rain was falling and the wind was stronger. The waves broke with a dull angry rumble. One by one the horses came up to our dying fire, gazed at us with big intelligent eyes, then ranged themselves in a ring about us.

'Hi, hi!' Makar called to them affectionately, and when he had patted the neck of his favourite black, he turned to me and said: 'Time to go to sleep.' He wrapped himself from head to foot in his Caucasian coat, stretched out on the ground and lay still.

I had no desire to sleep. I sat there gazing into the darkness of the steppe, and before my eyes floated the image of Radda, so proud, so imperious, so lovely. She was pressing the hand with the hair in it to her breast, and from between the slender dark fingers oozed drops of blood that turned into fiery stars as they struck the ground.

And behind her floated the brave figure of Loiko Zobar. Locks of curly black hair covered his face, and from under the hair streamed big cold tears.

The rain increased and the sea sang a solemn dirge to these two handsome Gipsies – Loiko Zobar and Radda, daughter of the old soldier Danilo.

And the two of them whirled round and round, soundlessly, gracefully, in the darkness of the night, and try as he might the handsome Zobar could not overtake the proud Radda.

AT THE SALT MARSH

(tr. Margaret Wettlin)

I

'GO TO THE SALT marsh, mate. You can always get a job there. Any time at all. Because it's such damned hard work nobody can stick it long. They run away. Can't stand it. So you go and try it for a day or two. They pay something like seven kopeks a barrow. Enough to live on for a day.'

The fisherman who gave me this advice spat, gazed out at the blue horizon of the sea, and hummed a dreary tune to himself. I was sitting beside him in the shade of a fishing shack. He was mending his duck trousers, yawning and mumbling cheerless observations about there not being enough jobs to go round and what a lot of work it took to find work.

'When it gets too much for you, come here and have a rest. Tell us about it. It's not far away – about five versts. Hm. A queer life, this.'

I took my leave of him, thanked him for his advice, and set out along the shore for the salt marsh. It was a hot August morning, the sky was clear and bright, the sea quiet and gentle, its green waves running up on the sand of the shore one after another with a mournful little plash. In the blue mist far up ahead of me I could see white patches on the yellow sand of the shore. That was the town of Ochakov. Behind me the shack was swallowed up by bright-yellow dunes tinted with the aquamarine of the sea.

In the shack where I had spent the night I had listened to all sorts of preposterous stories and opinions which had put me in a very low mood. The sound of the waves was in harmony with my mood and served to intensify it.

Soon the salt marsh came into view. Three plots of land, each about 400 metres square and separated by low ridges and narrow ditches, represented the three phases of salt-digging. The first plot was flooded with sea water which, as it evaporated, left a layer of pale-grey salt tinged with pink. On the second plot the salt was being gathered into piles. The women with spades in their hands who did this stood knee-deep in glistening black mud without talking or calling to one another, their drab grey forms moving listlessly against the background of the thick, saline, caustic *rapp*, as this mud is called here. On the third plot the salt was being removed. Bent in two over their barrows, workmen plodded numbly and dumbly ahead. The wheels of the barrows scraped and squeaked, and the sound was like a rasping, mournful appeal to Heaven sent up by the long line of bare human backs. And Heaven poured down an insufferable heat that scorched the parched grey earth spotted with salt-marsh grasses and glittering salt crystals. Above the monotonous creaking of the barrows could be heard the deep voice of the foreman cursing the workmen who emptied their barrows of salt at his feet. His job was to pour water out of a pail over it and then build it up into an elongated pyramid. He was a tall man, dark as an African, and wearing a blue shirt and full white trousers. From where he stood on a heap of salt waving his spade in the air, he kept shouting at the men who were pushing their barrows up the planks:

'Empty it to the left! To the left, you hairy devil! Damn your hide! What you want's a good jab in both eyes! Where you going, you scorpion?'

Viciously he wiped his sweating face with the hem of his shirt, grunted, and, without interrupting his swearing for a minute, undertook to level the salt by striking it with the back of his spade with all his might. The workmen automatically pushed up their barrows and as automatically emptied them in obedience to his commands: 'To the right! To the left!' This done, they would straighten up with an effort and turn back for another load, walking with uncertain steps down the shaking planks half-buried in thick black ooze, dragging their barrows that now creaked less noisily but more wearily.

'Put some pepper in it, you bastards!' the foreman would shout after them.

They went on working in the same cowed silence, but sometimes anger and resentment was evinced in the twitching of their sullen exhausted faces smeared with dust and sweat. One of the barrows would occasionally slip off the plank and sink in the mud; the forward barrows would move away from it; the barrows behind would come to a halt while the ragged and grimy tramps holding them would stand gazing with dull indifference as their mate struggled to lift the sixteen-pood load and put it back on the plank.

Out of a cloudless sky the sun blazed down through a haze of heat. It pressed its torrid attentions upon the earth with increasing ardour, as if this day of all others was the one on which it must prove its devotion.

When I had taken this in, I decided to try my luck at getting a job. Assuming a nonchalant air, I walked over to the plank down which workmen were dragging empty barrows.

'Greetings, mates. Good luck to you.'

The response was utterly unexpected. The first workman, a sturdy grey-haired old man with trousers rolled to the knee and sleeves to the shoulder, exposing a sinewy bronzed body, did not hear me and walked past without paying me any notice. The second workman, a young chap with brown hair and grey eyes, threw me a hostile glance and made a face, throwing in a coarse oath for good measure. The third – evidently a Greek, for he was as brown as a beetle and had curly hair – expressed his regret that his hands were occupied and therefore he could not introduce his fist to my nose. This was said in a tone of indifference inconsonant with the desire expressed. The fourth shouted at the top of his lungs: 'Hullo, glass-eye!' and tried to give me a kick.

If I am not mistaken, this was what in refined society is called getting 'a cold reception,' and never before had I been given it in such striking form. In my chagrin I unconsciously took off my glasses and put them in my pocket, then made my way to the foreman to ask him if he could give me work. Before I had reached him he shouted at me:

'Hey, you, what do you want? A job?'

I told him I did.

'Have you ever worked with a barrow?'

I said I had hauled dirt.

'Dirt? That don't count. Dirt's a different story. We haul salt here, not dirt. You can go to the devil and stay there. Come on, Funny-Bones, dump it right here at my feet.'

And Funny-Bones, a limpish Hercules with trailing moustaches and a pimply purple nose, gave a tremendous grunt and emptied his barrow. The salt poured out. Funny-Bones swore, the foreman out-swore him, both of them smiled approvingly and turned to me.

'Well, what do you want?' asked the foreman.

'Maybe you've come to get some salt for your pancakes, *katsap*[1],' said Funny-Bones, winking at the foreman.

I urged the foreman to take me on, assuring him that I would soon get used to the work and keep up with the others.

'You'll break your back before you get used to this work. But

---

1 *Katsap* – derogatory nickname for a Russian – Tr.

what the hell, go ahead. But I won't pay you more than fifty kopeks the first day. Hey there, give him a barrow!'

Out of nowhere appeared a half-naked boy, his bare legs bound to the knee with dirty rags.

'Come along,' he muttered after glancing at me sceptically.

I followed him to where some barrows were heaped one on top of another and set about choosing the lightest for myself. The boy stood scratching his legs and watching me.

When I had made my choice he said: 'Look what you've took. Can't you see the wheel's crooked?' – and with that he walked away and stretched out on the ground.

I selected another barrow and joined the other workmen who were going for salt, but I was oppressed by a vague uneasiness that kept me from speaking to my fellow-workmen. The faces of all of them expressed weariness and annoyance that was very definite, though as yet disguised. The men were worn out and furious: furious with the sun for mercilessly scorching their skin, with the planks for sagging under their barrows, with the *rapp* – that vile ooze, thick and salty and full of sharp crystals – for lacerating their feet and then eating into the wounds until they became running sores – in a word, with everything about them. This fury could be detected in the overt glances they stole at each other, and in the curses that now and then came from their parched throats. No one paid the least attention to me. But when we entered the plot and moved along the planks towards the four heaps of salt, I suddenly felt a blow on the back of my leg and turned to have someone hurl in my face:

'Pick your feet up, clumsy!'

I made haste to pick my feet up, then put down my barrow and began shovelling salt into it.

'Pile it on,' ordered the Ukrainian Hercules who was standing beside me.

I filled it as full as I could. At that moment the fellows behind shouted to those in front:

'Get going!' Those in front spat on their hands and lifted their barrows with loud grunts, bending almost double and straining forward with their necks stretched out as if that lightened the load.

In imitation of their methods, I, too, bent over as far as I could and strained forward. I lifted the barrow. The wheel gave a screech, my collar-bone seemed about to snap, and the muscles of my arms quivered from strain. I took one faltering step, then another.... I was thrown to the right, to the left, jerked ahead... the wheel of the barrow ran off the plank and I went flying face down into the mud. The barrow gave me an edifying fillip on the head with its handle and then turned slowly upside down. The piercing whistles, the cries, and the shouts of laughter that accompanied my fall seemed to press me further down into the thick warm muck, and as I floundered in it, vainly trying to lift the bogged barrow, I felt a sharp pain in my chest.

'Lend a hand, friend,' I said to the Ukrainian who was standing beside me holding his sides and rocking back and forth with laughter.

'You mud-sucking bastard! Gone wading, eh? Hoist it back on the plank. Push down on the left side! Tch, tch! The *rapp* will suck you down if you don't watch out.' And again he laughed till the tears came, gasping and holding his sides.

The grey-haired old man in front glanced at me and dismissed me with a wave of his hand.

'Why the hell couldn't he keep to the boards?' he said, and went on with his barrow, grunting angrily.

The men in front continued on their way; those behind watched ill-humouredly as I struggled to extricate my barrow. The mud and sweat were pouring off me. No one offered to help me. From the salt-heap came the voice of the foreman:

'What's the hold-up, you devils? You dogs. You swine. Out of sight, out of mind, eh? Get a move on, God damn you!'

'Make way,' barked the Ukrainian behind me, almost striking me on the head with the side of his barrow as he lumbered past.

Left alone, I pulled the barrow out somehow, and since it was empty now and plastered all over with mud, I ran it off the plot with the intention of exchanging it for another.

'Took a flyer, mate? Don't mind; that happens to everybody at first.'

I glanced round to see a chap of about twenty squatting on a board in the mud beside a salt-heap. He was sucking the palm of his hand. He nodded to me, and the eyes that glanced through his fingers were kindly and smiling.

'I don't mind. I'll catch on soon. What's the matter with your hand?' I asked.

'Just a little scratch, but the salt eats into it. If you don't suck it out you might just as well quit the job – you won't be able to use your hand. But you'd better get back to work before the foreman starts shouting at you.'

I went back. I had no accident with the second load; I hauled a third and a fourth and then two more. No one paid the slightest attention to me, and I was deeply gratified by this circumstance, which ordinarily I would have regretted.

'Time for dinner,' someone cried.

With a sigh of relief the men went to have their dinner, but even then they displayed no enthusiasm, no joy in the opportunity to rest. Everything they did was done reluctantly, with suppressed anger and disgust. It was as if rest could bring no pleasure to bones racked by labour, to muscles exhausted by heat. My back ached, so did my legs and my shoulders, but I tried not to show it and walked briskly over to the soup pot.

'Hold on there,' said a grim old workman in a ragged blue blouse. His face was as blue as his blouse from drink, and he had heavy scowling eyebrows from under which flashed inflamed eyes, fierce and mocking.

'Hold on there. What's your name?'

I told him.

'Hm. Your father was a fool to give you a name like that. Maxims aren't allowed to go near the soup pot the first day. Maxims live on their own food the first day, see? It would be different if you was named Ivan or something else. Take me, for instance. My name's Matvei, and so I get dinner. But not Maxim. He can only watch me eat. Get away from that pot!'

I looked at him in astonishment, then walked away and sat down on the ground. I was astounded by such treatment. Never before had I experienced anything like it and certainly I had done nothing to deserve it. Dozens of times before this I had had occasion to join groups of workmen, and our relations had always been simple and comradely from the very first. There was something strange about all this, and my curiosity was aroused despite the insult and injury I had suffered. I made up my mind to discover the answer to this mystery, and, having resolved on this, I was outwardly composed as I watched the others eat and waited to go back to work. It was essential to find out why I had been treated so.

II

At last they finished eating, finished belching, and began to smoke as they strolled away from the pot. The Ukrainian Hercules and the boy with the bandaged legs came over and sat down in front of me, cutting off my view of the line of barrows left on the planks.

'Want a smoke, mate?' asked the Ukrainian.

'Thanks, I wouldn't mind,' I replied.

'Haven't you got any tobacco of your own?'

'If I had, I wouldn't take yours.'

'True enough. Here,' and he gave me his pipe. 'Going to keep on working?'

'Yes, as long as I'm able.'

'Hm. Where you from?'

I told him.

'Is that far from here?'

'About three thousand versts.'

'Oho! Pretty far. What brought you here?'

'Same thing as brought you.'

'So you were driven out of your village for stealing, too?'

'What's that?' I asked, realizing I had been trapped.

'I came here because I was driven out of my village for stealing, and you said you had come for the same reason,' and he burst out laughing, delighted to have caught me.

His companion said nothing, only winked at him and smiled slyly.

'Wait—' I began.

'No time to wait, mate. Got to get back to work. Come along. Take my barrow and line up behind me. Mine's a good dependable barrow. Come along.'

And off he went. I was about to take his barrow when he put in hastily: 'Here, I'll take it myself. Let me have yours; I'll put mine in it and give it a ride – let it rest up a bit.'

My suspicions were aroused. As I walked beside him I studied his barrow, which was lying upside down in mine, to make sure that some trick was not being played on me, but the only thing I noticed was that I had suddenly become the centre of attention. Efforts were made to conceal this, but I could tell it by the frequent winks and nods in my direction and all the whispering that was going on. I knew that I must be on my guard and supposed that, judging from what had gone on before, whatever was being schemed was highly original.

'Here we are,' said the Ukrainian, taking his barrow out of mine and pushing it towards me. 'Fill it up.'

I glanced round. Everyone was hard at work, and so I, too, began to shovel in the salt. There was no other sound but the rustle of the salt as it fell off the spades, and I found the silence oppressive. I was convinced that I would do well to get away from here.

'That's enough. Have you fallen asleep? Get going,' ordered blue-faced Matvei.

I grasped the handles of the barrow and with a tremendous effort pushed it forward. A sharp pain made me cry out and drop the barrow. This caused more pain, worse than the first: I had ripped the skin off both palms. Clenching my teeth in pain and anger, I examined the handles and saw that they had been split at the outer edge and chips of wood inserted to hold the crack open. So skilfully had this been done that it could hardly be detected. It had been calculated that when I grasped the handles tightly the chips would fly out and my flesh would be caught as the wood came together. The calculation proved correct. I raised my head and looked about me. Cries, hoots, jeers slapped me in the face, and all around me I saw ugly, gloating grins. From the salt-heap came the coarse oaths of the foreman, but nobody cared; they were too much taken up by me. I looked about me blankly, dazedly, conscious that I was seething inside with a sense of hurt, with hatred for these men, and with a desire to get revenge. The men crowded in front of me, laughing and swearing, and I wanted terribly – excruciatingly – to insult and humiliate them.

'You beasts!' I cried, shaking my fists as I advanced and cursing them as vilely as they had cursed me.

A tremor passed through the crowd and they retreated uneasily. But the Ukrainian Hercules and the blue-faced Matvei stood their ground and began to roll up their sleeves calmly.

'Gome on, come on,' murmured the Ukrainian with relish, not taking his eyes off me.

'Give it to him, Gavrilla,' urged Matvei.

'What did you do that to me for?' I cried. 'What have I ever done to you? Aren't I a man like the rest of you?' I shouted some other stupid, absurd, senseless words and trembled all over with fury, at the same time keeping a sharp eye out to see that no more tricks were played on me.

But the vapid faces turned to me were not so lacking in sympathy now, and some of them wore an expression almost of guilt. Even Matvei and the Ukrainian moved back a step or two. Matvei began to pluck at his blouse and the Ukrainian to rummage in his pockets.

'What did you do it for? What made you?' I insisted.

They maintained a blank silence. The Ukrainian toyed with a cigarette, his eyes fixed on the ground. Matvei walked off until he was farther away from me than anyone else. The others scratched their heads glumly and turned back to their barrows. The foreman came up, shouting and shaking his fists. All this happened so quickly that the women raking the salt, who had stopped work on hearing my cry, reached us only when the workmen had gone back to their barrows. I was left alone with a bitter sense that my wrong was undeserved and unavenged. This made it all the harder to bear. I wanted an answer to my question; I wanted revenge. And so I shouted:

'Just a minute, mates!'

They stopped and looked at me sullenly.

'Tell me why you hurt me so. Surely you have a conscience.'

Still they were silent, and this silence was their answer. More composed now, I began to speak to them. I began by saying I was a man like themselves; that, like them, I had to eat, and so had to work; that I had joined them as an equal, for we were united by a common fate; that I did not look down upon them or think myself above them.

'We are all equal,' I said, 'and we ought to understand one another and help one another in any way we can.'

They stood there listening attentively, although they avoided my eye. I saw that my words affected them, and this inspired me. A glance round at them convinced me of this. I was filled with a bright and poignant joy, and, throwing myself down on a heap of salt, I wept. Who would not?

When I raised my head I was alone. The working day was over and the workmen, in groups of five or six, were sitting near the salt-heap, forming big dark smudges on the rosy background of sunlit salt. It was very quiet. A breeze came from the sea. A little white cloud was sailing slowly across the sky; little wisps of mist broke away from it and dissolved in the blue expanse. It was all very sad....

I got up and went towards the salt-heap with the firm intention of taking my leave and going back to the fishing shack. Matvei, the Ukrainian, the foreman, and three other solid middle-aged rough-necks got up as I approached and came to meet me, and before I had a chance to say a word Matvei held out his hand and said, without looking at me:

'Here's what, mate: you'd better quit and go your way. We've collected a little sum to help you. Take it.'

Some copper coins lay in his hand, which shook as he held it out to me. I was so taken aback that I could only stare at them. They stood with hanging heads, silently, foolishly pulling at their rags, shifting from one foot to the other, glancing about furtively, jerking their shoulders, their every movement revealing extreme discomfiture and a desire to have done with me as soon as possible.

'I won't take it,' I said, pushing Matvei's hand away.

'Come, don't offend us. We're really not such a bad lot. We know we hurt your feelings, but, when you come right down to it, are we to blame? No, we're not. It's the way we live that's to blame. What sort of a life do we live? A dog's life. The sixteen-pood barrow, the rapp gnawing at your feet, the sun scorching your back all day long, and – fifty kopeks a day. It's enough to turn any man into a beast. Work, work, work, drink up your pay, and back to work again. And that's the beginning and the end of it. When you've lived like this for five years – well, there you are – nothing human left – a beast, and that's that. Listen, mate, we do worse things to each other than we did to you; and we're chums, so to speak, while you're a newcomer. Why should we be easy on you? So there you are. The things you said to us – well, what of it? You put it right – it's all true – but it don't fit us. You oughtn't to take it so hard. We were just fooling. And after all, we do have hearts. You'd better go away;

you think your way, we think ours. Take this little mite and good-bye, mate. We've done you no wrong, and you've done us none. It's true things turned out bad, but what do you expect? They never turn out good with us. And there's no point in your staying on here. You just don't fit in. We've got used to each other, and you – you're not our kind. Nothing will come of it. So you'd better go. Go your own way. Good-bye.'

I looked round at them. Clearly they all agreed with Matvei, so I tossed my knapsack over my shoulder and was about to leave.

'Just a minute, let me put in a word,' said the Ukrainian, laying a hand on my shoulder. 'If it was anyone but you I'd give him a punch in the jaw as a keepsake. But nobody's touching you, and we've even made you a present. You might say thank you for it.' He spat and began twirling his tobacco pouch, as much as to say: just see what a clever fellow I am!

Crushed by all this, I hastened to take my leave. Once more I set out along the edge of the sea, this time for the fishing shack where I had spent the night. The sky was clear and hot, the sea empty and majestic. Little green waves came rolling noisily over the beach. For some reason I felt unspeakably hurt and ashamed. Slowly I dragged my feet over the hot sand. The sea gleamed tranquilly in the sun, the waves murmured something sad and incomprehensible....

When I reached the shack the fisherman of my acquaintance got up to meet me.

'Not to your taste, that salt, eh?' he said with the satisfaction of one whose predictions have turned out to be correct. I looked at him without a word. 'A little too much salt,' he said emphatically. 'Hungry? Go and have some porridge. Don't know why they made so damned much – half of it's left. Get your spoon going. First-rate porridge, with flounder and sturgeon in it.'

Two minutes later I was sitting in the shade outside the shack, very dirty, very tired and hungry, eating a cheerless meal of porridge with flounder and sturgeon in it.

CHELKASH

(tr. Margaret Wettlin)

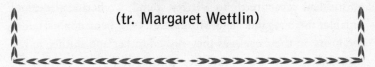

THE BLUE SOUTHERN SKY was so obscured by dust that it had a murky look. The hot sun stared down at the greenish sea as through a thin grey veil, and its rays found poor reflection in the water, churned up as it was by the strokes of oars, the propellers of steamers and the sharp keels of Turkish feluccas and other craft which ploughed the crowded harbour in all directions. The waves of the sea, crushed within their granite encasements by the enormous weights gliding over their surfaces, hurled themselves at the shore and the sides of the ships – hurled themselves growling and foaming, their flanks littered with all sorts of rubbish.

The clang of anchor chains, the clash of the buffers of goods cars, the metallic wail of sheets of iron being unloaded on to paving-stones, the dull thump of wood against wood, the clatter of carts, the whistle of steamships rising from a wail to a shriek, the shouts of stevedores, seamen and customs guards – all this merged to form the deafening music of the working day which surged rebelliously in the sky above the harbour, while from the earth below new waves of sound kept rising to meet it – now a rumble that shook the earth, now a crash that rent the sultry air.

The granite, the steel, the wood, the paving-stones, the ships and the people – everything was impregnated with the mighty sounds of this impassioned hymn to Mercury. But human voices could hardly be detected in the general chorus, so weak and even ridiculous were they. And the people themselves, they whose efforts had given birth to all this sound, were ridiculous and pitiable; their ragged dirty wiry bodies were bent double under the loads on their backs as they rushed hither and thither in the dust and the heat and the noise, and they were as nothing compared with the steel leviathans, the mountains of merchandise, the clanging railway cars, and all the other things which they themselves had created. The things of their own creating had enslaved them and robbed them of personality.

The gigantic ships lying with steam up whistled and hissed and heaved great sighs, and every sound they uttered was filled with mocking contempt for the drab and dusty creatures crawling over their decks to load their deep holds with the products of the servile labour. It made one laugh till the tears ran to see these long files of stevedores carrying thousands of poods of grain on their backs to be deposited in the iron bellies of the ships so that they themselves might earn a few pounds of grain to fill their own bellies. A poem of bitter irony could be read in the contrast between these ragged sweating men, stupefied by the heat, the noise, and the exhausting labour, and the powerful machines these men had made and which stood radiating well-being in the sunlight – machines which, when all is said and done, had been set in motion not by steam, but by the blood and muscles of those who made them.

The noise was oppressive; the dust tickled the nose and got into the eyes; the heat scorched and enervated the body, and everything seemed tense, as if the end of endurance had been reached and catastrophe was imminent, a tremendous explosion that would clear the air so that men might breathe freely and easily. And then silence would descend on the world and there would be no more dust and turmoil to deafen and irritate people and drive them mad; and the air of the town, of the sea, and of the sky would be fresh and clear and beautiful....

Twelve measured strokes of a bell were heard. When the last brassy vibrations had died away the savage music of labour was found to have subsided, and a minute later it turned into a mere rumble of discontent. Now the voices of the people and the plash of the sea were more audible. It was the dinner hour.

I

When the stevedores stopped work and scattered over the docks in noisy groups to buy victuals from the vendors and find shady corners where they could squat on the pavement to take their meal, Grishka Chelkash put in an appearance. He was well known to all the dockers, a confirmed drunkard, a bold and clever thief. He was barefooted and bareheaded, had on a pair of threadbare corduroy trousers and a filthy cotton shirt with a torn collar that exposed a bony chest covered by brown skin. The matted state of his iron-grey hair and the crumpled look of his lean and hawk-like face indicated that he had just waked up. A straw had become caught in his moustache, another in the stubble of his left cheek, while behind his ear he had stuck a sprig of linden. Long and lanky and a bit stooped, he sauntered slowly down the cobbled street, sniffing the air with his hooked nose and casting a glittering grey eye about him as he searched for someone among the dockers. His long dark moustache kept twitching like a cat's; beheld his hands behind his back and kept rubbing them together and twisting his crooked grasping fingers. Even here, among hundreds of other roughs, he instantly attracted attention because of the resemblance to a steppe-hawk conveyed by his predatory leanness and aimful walk, which, like the flight of the bird of prey he resembled, concealed a tense alertness under an appearance of poised tranquillity.

As he came up to a group of stevedores sitting in the shadow cast by a pile of coal baskets, a stocky young chap, with a blotched and vapid face and with scratches on his neck suggesting a recent fight, got up to meet him. He fell into step beside Chelkash and said under his breath:

'The seamen have discovered two bales of cloth missing. They're searching.'

'So what?' Chelkash asked, calmly running his eyes over him.

'What d'ye mean "so what"? They're searching, I tell you.'

'And you thought I might join in the search?'

'Go to hell!'

The chap turned back.

'Wait! Who gave you those beauty-marks? A pity to mess up your shop front like that! Seen Mishka?'

'Not for a long time,' called back the chap as he joined his comrades.

Everybody who met Chelkash greeted him as an old acquaintance, but he, usually so cheery and biting, must have been out of sorts, for his replies were all very terse.

From behind a pile of merchandise suddenly appeared a customs guard – dark-green, dusty, aggressively erect. He planted himself in front of Chelkash in a challenging pose, his left hand on the hilt of his dirk, his right reaching out for Chelkash's collar.

'Halt! Where you bound?'

Chelkash retreated a step, lifted his eyes to the guard's red face and gave a cool smile.

The face, wily but good-natured, tried to assume a dread aspect: the cheeks puffed out and turned purple, the brows drew together, the eyes rolled, and the effect on the whole was extremely comical.

'I told you once to keep away from these docks if you didn't want me to smash your ribs in, and here you are again!' he roared.

'Howdy, Semyonich! Haven't seen you for a long time,' said the imperturbable Chelkash, holding out his hand.

'I wouldn't cry if I didn't see you for another fifty years. Move on, move on.'

But he shook the extended hand.

'Here's what I wanted to ask,' went on Chelkash, holding the guard's hand in steel fingers and shaking it in an intimate sort of way. 'Seen Mishka anywhere?'

'What Mishka? I don't know any Mishka. Move on, man, or the packhouse guard may see you and then—'

'The red-headed chap I worked with on the *Kostroma* last time,' persisted Chelkash.

'That you *thieved* with, you mean. They've put him in hospital, that Mishka of yours – got his leg crushed by some iron. Get out of here, I tell you, get out before I throw you out by the scruff of the neck.'

'Listen to that, now! And you said you didn't know no Mishka. What makes you so nasty, Semyonich?'

'None of your talk! Get out!'

The guard was getting angry; he glanced about him and tried to free his hand, but Chelkash held on to it as he looked at him calmly from under bushy eyebrows and went on talking:

'What's the rush? Don't you want to have a nice little chat with me? How you getting on? How's the wife and kiddies? Well?' His eyes twinkled and his teeth flashed in a mocking grin as he added: 'Been wanting to drop in to see you for ever so long, but just can't seem to manage it. It's the drink—'

'Drop it, I tell you! None of your joking, you lanky lubber. I mean what I say. But maybe you're turning to house-breaking, or robbing people in the street?'

'Why should I? There's enough here to keep you and me busy a lifetime. Honest there is, Semyonich. But I hear you've snitched another two bales of cloth. Watch out, or you'll find yourself in trouble yet!'

Semyonich trembled with indignation and the saliva flew as he tried to give voice to it. Chelkash let go of his hand and calmly strode off on his long legs to the dock gates. The guard followed at his heels, cursing him roundly.

Chelkash was in better spirits now; he whistled a tune through his teeth, thrust his hands into his pockets, and retarded his steps, tossing off well-aimed quips to right and left. He was paid in his own coin.

'Just see what good care of you the bosses are taking, Grishka!' called out a stevedore who was stretched out on the ground with his comrades, taking a rest after their meal.

'Semyonich's seeing I don't step on any nails in my bare feet,' replied Chelkash.

They got to the gates. Tavo soldiers ran their hands down Chelkash's clothes and pushed him out into the street.

He crossed the road and sat down on the curbstone opposite a pub. A line of loaded carts came thundering out of the dock gates, while a line of empty ones moved in the other direction, their drivers bouncing in their seats. The docks belched forth a roar of sound and clouds of dust that stuck to the skin.

Chelkash was in his element amid this mad welter. He was anticipating a good haul that night, a haul that would cost him little effort but require a great deal of skill. He did not doubt but that his skill was sufficient, and he screwed up his eyes with pleasure as he reflected on how he would spend all his banknotes the next morning. He thought of his pal Mishka. He needed him badly, and here he had gone and broken his leg. Chelkash cursed under his breath, for he feared he could not handle the job alone. What would the weather be like? He glanced up at the sky, then down the street.

Sitting on the pavement, his back against a hitching post some half a dozen paces away, was a young lad in a blue homespun shirt and trousers, with bast sandals on his feet and a torn brown cap on his head. Beside him lay a small knapsack and a haftless scythe wrapped in straw and neatly tied with string. The lad was sturdy, broad-shouldered, fair-haired, his face was tanned by wind and sun, and he had large blue eyes that stared amiably at Chelkash.

Chelkash bared his teeth, stuck out his tongue, made a frightful face and stared back with popping eyes.

The boy blinked in astonishment at first, then he burst out laughing, calling out between spasms: 'Crazy as a loon!' Without getting up, he hitched along the curbstone to where Chelkash was sitting, dragging his knapsack through the dust and allowing the tip of his scythe to clank over the cobbles.

'Been on the booze, eh?' he said to Chelkash, giving a tug at his trousers.

'You're right, baby-face, you're right' confessed Chelkash with a smile. He was instantly drawn to this wholesome good-natured chap with eyes as clear as a baby's. 'Been haymaking?'

'Yes. Made hay, but no money. Times are bad. You never saw so many people! They all come drifting down from the famine districts. No point in working for such pay. Sixty kopeks in the Kuban, think of that! They say they used to pay three or four rubles, or even five.'

'Used to! They used to pay three rubles just to get a look at a Russian! That's how I earned a living ten years ago. I'd come to a Cossack village: 'Here I am, folks, an honest-to-God Russian!' They'd all crowd round, look me over, poke me, pinch me, oh-and-ah and pay me three rubles. Give me food and drink besides and invite me to stay as long as I liked.'

At first the boy opened wide his mouth, an expression of wondering admiration on his round face, but as he realized Chelkash was fabricating, he snapped his mouth shut, then burst out laughing again. Chelkash kept a straight face, hiding his smile in his moustache.

'A queer bird you are, talking talk as if it was God's truth and me swallowing it. But honest to goodness, it used to be—'

'Isn't that just what I was saying? It used to be—'

'Oh, come!' said the boy with a wave of his hand. 'What are you, a cobbler, or a tailor, or what?'

'Me?' Chelkash mused awhile and then said: 'I'm a fisherman.'

'A fisherman? Think of that! So you catch fish, do you?'

'Why fish? The fishermen here don't only catch fish. Mostly dead bodies, old anchors, sunken boats. There's special fish-hooks for such things.'

'Lying again. Maybe you're one of those fishermen who sing:

We cast our nets
Upon the shores,
In market stalls, in open doors.

'Ever met fishermen like that?' asked Chelkash, looking hard at the boy and grinning.

'No, but I've heard about them.'

'Like the idea?'

'Of people like that? Why not? At least they're free; they can do what they please.'

'What's freedom to you? Do you hanker after freedom?'

'Of course. What could be better than to be your own boss, go where you like and do what you like? Only you've got to keep straight and see that no millstones get hung round your neck. Outside of that, go ahead and have a good time without a thought for anything save God and your conscience.'

Chelkash spat contemptuously and turned away.

'Here's what I'm up against,' went on the boy. 'My father died without leaving anything much, my mother's old, the land's sucked dry. What am I supposed to do? I've got to go on living, but how? God knows. I have a chance to marry into a good family. I wouldn't mind if they'd give the daughter her portion. But they won't. Her old man won't give her an inch of land. So I'd have to work for him, and for a long time. For years. There you are. If only I could lay hands on, say, a hundred and fifty rubles I'd be able to stand up to her father and say: "Do you want me to marry your Marfa? You don't? Just as you say; she's not the only girl in the village, thank God.' I'd be independent, see? and could do what I liked." The boy heaved a sigh. 'But it looks as if there was nothing for it but to be his son-in-law. I thought I'd bring back a couple of hundred rubles from the Kuban. That would be the thing! Then I'd be a gentleman! But I didn't earn a damn thing. Nothing for it but to be a farm-hand. I'll never have a farm of my own. So there you are.'

The boy squirmed and his face fell at the prospect of being this man's son-in-law.

'Where you bound now?' asked Chelkash.

'Home. Where else?'

'How do I know? Maybe you're bound for Turkey.'

'Turkey?' marvelled the boy. 'What honest Christian would ever go to Turkey? A fine thing to say!'

'You are a blockhead,' murmured Chelkash, turning away again. Yet this wholesome village lad had stirred something in him; a vague feeling of dissatisfaction was slowly taking form within him, and this kept him from concentrating his mind on the night's task.

The boy, offended by Chelkash's words, muttered to himself and threw sidelong glances at the older man. His cheeks were puffed up in a droll way, his lips were pouting and his narrowed eyes blinked rapidly. Evidently he had not expected his talk with this bewhiskered ruffian tramp to end so suddenly and so unsatisfactorily.

But the tramp paid no more attention to him. His mind was on something else as he sat there on the curbstone whistling to himself and beating time with a dirty toe.

The boy wanted to get even with him.

'Hey, you fisherman! Do you often go on a bout?' he began, but at that moment the fisherman turned to him impulsively and said:

'Look, baby-face, would you like to help me to do a job tonight? Make up your mind, quick!'

'What sort of job?' asked the boy dubiously.

'"What sort"! Whatever sort I give you. We're going fishing. You'll row.'

'Oh, I wouldn't mind doing that, I'm not afraid of work. Only – what if you get me into trouble? You're a queer egg; there's no understanding you.'

Chelkash had a sensation as of heart-burn.

'Don't go spouting on things you don't know anything about,' he said with cold animosity. 'I'll give you a good crack over the bean, and then you'll understand a thing or two.'

He jumped up, his eyes flashing, his left hand pulling at his moustache, his right clenched in a hard and corded fist.

The boy was frightened. He glanced quickly about him and then he, too, jumped up, blinking nervously. The two of them stood there silently measuring each other with their eyes.

'Well?' said Chelkash harshly. He was seething inside, twitching all over from the insult taken from this puppy he had held in such contempt so far, but whom he now hated with all his soul because he had such clear blue eyes, such a healthy tanned face, such short sturdy arms; because he had a native village and a house there, and an offer to be the son-in-law of a well-to-do muzhik; he hated him for the way he had lived in the past and would live in the future, but most of all he hated him because he, a mere child as compared with Chelkash, dared to hanker after a freedom he could neither appreciate nor have need of. It is always unpleasant to discover that a person you consider beneath you loves or hates the same things you do, thereby establishing a certain resemblance to yourself.

As the lad looked at Chelkash he recognized in him a master.

'I don't really – er – mind,' he said. 'After all, I'm looking for work. What difference does it make whether I work for you or somebody else? I just said that because – well, you don't look much like a workingman. You're so – er – down at heel. But that can happen to anybody, I know. God, haven't I seen drunks before? Plenty of them, some even worse than you.'

'All right, all right. So you're willing?' said Chelkash in a milder tone.

'With pleasure. State your price.'

'The price depends on the job. How much we catch. Maybe you'll get five rubles.'

Now that the talk was of money, the peasant wanted to be exact and demanded the same exactness from the man who was hiring him. Once more he had his doubts and suspicions.

'That won't suit me, brother.'

Chelkash played his part.

'Don't let's talk about it now. Come along to the tavern.'

And they walked down the street side by side, Chelkash twirling his moustache with the air of a master; the lad fearful and distrusting, but willing to comply.

'What's your name?' asked Chelkash.

'Gavrilla,' answered the lad.

On entering the dingy, smoke-blackened tavern, Chelkash went up to the bar and in the off-hand tone of a frequenter ordered a bottle of vodka, cabbage soup, roast beef and tea; he repeated the list and then said nonchalantly: 'On tick,' to which the barman replied by nodding silently. This instantly inspired Gavrilla with respect for his employer, who, despite his disreputable appearance, was evidently well known and trusted.

'Now we'll have a bite and talk things over. Sit here and wait for me; I'll be right back.'

And he went out. Gavrilla looked about him. The tavern was in a basement; it was dark and damp and filled with the stifling smell of vodka, tobacco smoke, pitch, and something else just as pungent. A drunken red-bearded sailor smeared all over with pitch and coal-dust was sprawling at a table opposite him. Between hiccups he gurgled a song made of snatches of words which were all sibilant one minute, all guttural the next. Evidently he was not a Russian.

Behind him were two Moldavian women. Swarthy, dark-haired, ragged, they too were wheezing out a drunken song.

Out of shadows loomed other figures, all of them noisy, restless, dishevelled, drunken…

Gavrilla was gripped by fear. If only his boss would come back! The noises of the tavern merged in a single voice, and it was as if some huge multiple-tongued beast were roaring as it vainly sought a means of escape from this stone pit. Gavrilla felt some intoxication seeping into his body, making his head swim and his eyes grow hazy as they roved the tavern with fearful curiosity.

At last Chelkash came back and the two men began to eat and drink and talk. Gavrilla was drunk after his third glass of vodka. He felt very gay and was anxious to say something nice to this prince of a chap who had treated him to such a fine meal. But somehow the words that surged in his throat would not come off his tongue, suddenly grown thick and unwieldy.

Chelkash looked at him with a condescending smile.

'Stewed? Ekh, you rag! On five swigs. How are you going to work tonight?'

'Ol' pal!' lisped Gavrilla. 'Don't be 'fraid. I'll show you. Gimme a kiss, c'mon.'

'That's all right. Here, take another guzzle.'

Gavrilla went on drinking until he reached the point at which everything about him seemed to be moving up and down in rhythmic waves. This was unpleasant and made him sick. His face wore an expression of foolish solemnity. Whenever he tried to say anything, his lips slapped together comically and garbled sounds came through them. Chelkash twisted his moustache and smiled glumly as he gazed at him abstractedly, his mind on something else.

Meanwhile the tavern was roaring as drunkenly as ever. The red-headed sailor had folded his arms on the table and fallen fast asleep.

'Time to go,' said Chelkash, getting up.

Gavrilla tried to follow him but could not; he let out an oath and laughed idiotically, as drunks do.

'What a wash-out!' muttered Chelkash, sitting down again.

Gavrilla kept on laughing and looking at his boss with bleary eyes, while Chelkash turned a sharp and thoughtful eye on him. He saw before him a man whose fate he held in his wolfish paw. Chelkash sensed that he could do what he pleased with him. He could crush him in his hand like a playingcard, or he could help him get back to the solid peasant way of life. Conscious of his power over him, he reflected that this lad would never have to drink the cup it had been the fate of him, Chelkash, to drink. He envied and pitied the boy; he despised him, and yet he was sorry to think that he might fall into other hands, no better than his own. In the end, Chelkash's various emotions combined to form a single one that was both fatherly and practical. He pitied the boy and he needed him. And so he took Gavrilla under the arms and lifted him up, giving him little pushes with his knee as he led him out into the tavern yard where he laid him down in the shade of a wood-pile, he himself sitting beside him and smoking his pipe. Gavrilla tossed about awhile, gave a few grunts and fell asleep.

II

'Ready?' whispered Chelkash to Gavrilla, who was fussing with the oars.

'In a minute. The rowlock's loose. Can I give it a bang with the oar?'

'No! Not a sound! Push it down with your hands; it'll slip into place.'

Both of them were noiselessly busy with a boat tied to the stern of one of a whole fleet of barges loaded with oaken staves and of Turkish feluccas carrying palm and sandal wood and thick Cyprus logs.

The night was dark, heavy banks of tattered clouds floated across the sky, the sea was calm and black and as heavy as oil. It gave off a moist saline odour and made tender little noises as it lapped at the shore and the sides of ships, causing Chelkash's boat to rock gently. At some distance from shore could be seen the dark outlines of ships against the sky, their masts tipped by varicoloured lights. The sea reflected these lights and was strewn with innumerable yellow spots that looked very beautiful quivering upon the background of black velvet. The sea was sleeping as soundly as a workman who has been worn out by the day's labour.

'Let's go,' said Gavrilla, dipping an oar into the water.

'Let's.' Chelkash pushed off hard with the steering oar, sending the boat into the lanes between the barges. It glided swiftly over the water, which gave off a blue phosphorescent glow wherever the oars struck it and formed a glowing ribbon in the wake of the boat.

'How's your head? Aching?' asked Chelkash solicitously.

'Something fierce. And it's heavy as lead. Here, I'll wet it.'

'What for? Wet your insides; that'll bring you round quicker,' said Chelkash, holding out a bottle.

'Ah, God be thanked.'

There was a gurgling sound.

'Hey! That's enough!' interrupted Chelkash.

Once more the boat darted forward, weaving its way among the other craft swiftly and soundlessly. Suddenly it was beyond them, and the sea – the mighty boundless sea – stretched far away to the dark-blue horizon, from which sprang billowing clouds: grey-and-mauve with fluffy yellow edges; greenish, the colour of sea water; leaden-hued, throwing dark and dreary shadows. Slowly moved the clouds across the sky, now overtaking each other, merging in colour and form, annihilating each other only to appear again in new aspects, grimly magnificent. There was something fatal in the slow movement of these inanimate forms. It seemed as if there were endless numbers of them at the rim of the sea, and as if they would go on crawling across the sky for ever, impelled by a vicious desire to keep the sky from gazing down upon the slumbering sea with its millions of golden orbs, the many-hued stars, that hung there alive and pensively radiant, inspiring lofty aspirations in the hearts of men to whom their pure shine was a precious thing.

'Nice, the sea, isn't it?' asked Chelkash.

'I suppose so, but it makes me afraid,' said Gavrilla as he pulled hard and evenly on the oars. The water let out a faint ring and splash as the oars struck it, and it still gave off that blue phosphorescent glow.

'Afraid! You *are* a boob,' grunted Chelkash.

He, a thief, loved the sea. His nervous, restive nature, always thirsting for new impressions, never had enough of contemplating its dark expanses, so free, so powerful, so boundless. And he resented such a tepid response to his question about the beauty of the thing he loved. As he sat there in the stern of the boat letting his steering oar cut through the water while he gazed calmly ahead, he was filled with the one desire to travel as long and as far as he could over that velvety surface.

He always had a warm expansive feeling when he was on the sea. It filled his whole being, purging it of the dross of daily life. He appreciated this and liked to see himself a better man, hero among the waves and in the open air, where thoughts about life lose their poignancy and life itself loses its value. At night the soft breathing of the slumbering sea is wafted gently over the waters, and this unencompassing sound fills the heart of man with peace, crams away its evil impulses, and gives birth to great dreams.

'Where's the fishing tackle?' asked Gavrilla suddenly, glancing anxiously about the boat.

Chelkash gave a start.

'The tackle? I've got it here in the stern.'

He did not wish to lie to this green youth and he regretted having his thoughts and feelings dispelled in this abrupt way, it made him angry. Again he had that burning sensation in his throat and chest and said to Gavrilla in a hard and impressive voice:

'Listen, sit where you are and mind your own business. I hired you to row, so you row; and if you start wagging your tongue it will go hard with you. Understand?'

The boat gave a little jerk and came to a halt, the oars dragging and stirring up the water. Gavrilla shifted uneasily on his seat.

'Row!'

A fierce oath shook the air. Gavrilla lifted the oars and the boat, as if frightened, leaped ahead in quick nervous spurts that made the water splash.

'Steady!'

Chelkash half rose without letting go of the steering oar and fastened cold eyes on Gavrilla's white face. He was like a cat about to spring as he stood there bent forward. The grinding of his teeth could be heard, as could the chattering of Gavrilla's teeth.

'Who's shouting there?' came a stern cry from out at sea.

'Row, you bastard! Row! Shhh! I'll kill you, damn your hide! Row, I tell you! One, two! Just you dare to make a sound! I'll rip you to pieces!' hissed Chelkash.

'Holy Virgin, Mother of God!' murmured Gavrilla, trembling with fear and exertion.

The boat swung round and went back to the harbour where the ships' lanterns formed clusters of coloured lights and their masts stood out distinctly.

'Hi! Who's shouting?' came the cry again.

But it came from a distance now. Chelkash was reassured.

'It's you who's shouting!' he called back, then turned to Gavrilla who was still muttering a prayer.

'Luck's with you this time, lad. If those devils had chased us it would have been all over with you. I'd have fed you to the fishes first thing.'

Seeing that Chelkash had calmed down and was in a good humour, the trembling Gavrilla pleaded with him:

'Let me go; for the love of Christ, let me go. Set me down somewheres. Oi, oi, oi, I've been trapped! For God's sake, let me go. What do you want of me? I can't do this. I've never been mixed up in such business. It's the first time. God, I'm lost for sure. Why have you done this to me? It's a sin. You'll pay for it with your soul. Oh, what a business!'

'Business?' asked Chelkash sharply. 'What business?'

He was amused by the boy's terror; he took pleasure in contemplating it and in thinking what a ferocious fellow he himself was.

'Bad business, brother. Let me go, for the love of God. What do you need me for? Come, be a good chap—'

'Hold your tongue! If I didn't need you I wouldn't have brought you, understand? So shut up!'

'Dear God,' murmured Gavrilla.

'Stop blubbering,' Chelkash cut him off sharply.

But Gavrilla could no longer control himself; he whimpered softly, coughed, sniffled, wriggled, but rowed with a strength born of despair. The boat flew ahead like an arrow. Once more they found themselves surrounded by the dark forms of ships. Their boat became lost among them as it turned and twisted through the narrow lanes of water.

'Listen, you! If you get asked any questions, keep your mouth shut if you value your life, understand?'

'God!' breathed Gavrilla, adding bitterly:

'It must be my fate.'

'Stop blubbering,' whispered Chelkash again.

This whisper robbed Gavrilla of his mental power; he was benumbed by a chill premonition of disaster. Like one in a trance he dropped his oars into the water, threw himself backwards as he pulled, lifted them and dropped them again, his eyes fixed steadily on his bast sandals.

The sleepy plash of the waves was dreary and terrifying. But now they were in the docks. From the other side of a stone wall came the sound of human voices, of singing and whistling and a splashing of water.

'Stop,' whispered Chelkash. 'Put down your oars. Push with your hands against the wall. Shhh, damn you!'

Gavrilla guided the boat along the wall by holding on to the slippery masonry. The boat moved without a sound, the slime on the stones deadening the sound of its bumping.

'Stop. Give me the oars; give them to me, I say. Where's your passport? In your knapsack? Let's have it. Hurry up. That's to keep you from running away, pal. No danger of that now. You might have run away without the oars, but not without your passport. Wait here. And mind, if you blab, I'll find you even if it's at the bottom of the sea!'

And then, pulling himself up by his hands, Chelkash disappeared over the wall.

It happened so quickly that Gavrilla gave a little gasp. And then the heaviness in his heart and the fear inspired by that lean bewhiskered thief fell from him like a garment. Now he would run away! Drawing a free breath, he glanced round. To his left rose a black hull without a mast, a sort of gigantic coffin, empty and abandoned. Every time the waves struck it, it let out a hollow sound that might have been a groan. To the left was the slimy wall of the breakwater, a cold heavy serpent uncoiled upon the sea. Behind him loomed other dark forms, while ahead, in the opening between the wall and the coffin, he got a glimpse of the empty sea with black clouds banked above it. Ponderous, enormous, they moved slowly across the sky, spreading horror in the darkness, threatening to crush human beings with their great weight. Everything was cold, black, sinister. Gavrilla was frightened. And his present fear was greater than that inspired by Chelkash. It clamped him tightly round the chest, squeezing all resistance out of him and pinning him to his seat.

Everything was quiet. Not a sound was to be heard but the sighing of the sea. The clouds moved as slowly and drearily as ever, and so many of them rose out of the sea that the sky was like a sea itself, an agitated sea turned upside down over this smooth, slumbering one. The clouds were like waves whose foamy crests were rushing down upon the earth, rushing back into the chasms out of which they had sprung, rushing upon the new-born billows which had not yet broken into the greenish foam of savage fury.

So oppressed was Gavrilla by the austere silence and beauty about him that he was anxious to have his master come back. What if he should not come? Time dragged slowly – slower than the movement of the clouds across the sky. And the longer he waited, the more menacing grew the silence. But at last a splash, a rustle, and something like a whisper came from the other side of the breakwater. Gavrilla felt that he would die in another minute.

'Hullo! Sleeping? Here, catch this. Careful,' came the muffled voice of Chelkash.

Something square and heavy was let down over the wall. Gavrilla put it in the boat. A similar bundle followed. Then the lanky form of Chelkash slid down, the oars appeared, Gavrilla's knapsack fell at his feet, and Chelkash, breathing hard, took his seat in the stern.

Gavrilla gave a diffident smile of joy.

'Tired?' he asked.

'Ra-ther! Well, lay on the oars. Pull with all your might. You've earned a neat little sum. Half the job's over; all you've got to do now is slip past those bastards and then – collect and go back to your MashKa. I s'pose you've got a Mashka, haven't you?'

'N-no.' Gavrilla was putting forth his best effort, his lungs working like bellows, his arms like steel springs. The water gurgled under the boat and the blue ribbon in its wake was wider than before. Gavrilla became drenched in sweat but he did not let up on the oars. Twice that night he had a great fright;

he did not wish to have a third one. The only thing he wanted was to get this accursed job over as quickly as possible, set foot on dry land and escape from that man while he was still alive and out of jail. He resolved not to talk to him, not to oppose him in any way, to do everything he ordered him to, and if he managed to get away safely, to say a prayer to St Nicholas the Miracle-Worker on the very next day. An impassioned prayer was ready on his tongue, but he held it back, panting like a locomotive and glancing up at Chelkash from under drawn brows.

Chelkash, long and lean, was crouching like a bird about to take wing, his hawklike eyes piercing the darkness ahead, his hooked nose sniffing the air, one hand clutching the steering oar, the other pulling at his moustache, which twitched as his thin lips spread in a smile. Chelkash was pleased with his haul, with himself, and with this youth whom he had terrorized and converted into his slave. As he watched Gavrilla exerting himself, he felt sorry for him and thought he would offer him a word of encouragement.

'Ekh!' he said softly, with a little laugh, 'got a good scare, did you?'

'Not so bad,' grunted Gavrilla.

'You can take it easier now. The danger's over. There's just one place more we've got to slip past. Take a rest.'

Gavrilla obediently stopped rowing, and dropped his oars into the water again.

'Row softly. Keep the water from talking. There's a gate we've got to get past. Shhh. The men here can't take a joke. Always ready with their guns. You'll have a hole in your head before you know what's struck you.'

Now the boat was gliding through the water almost without sound. The only sign of its movement was the blue shine of the water dripping off the oars and the blue flare of the sea as the drops struck it. The night grew darker and stiller. The sky no longer resembled an agitated sea – the clouds had spread out to form a heavy blanket that hung low and immobile over the water. The sea was even more calm and black, its warm saline odour was stronger than ever, and it no longer seemed so boundless.

'If only it would rain!' murmured Chelkash.

'It would hide us like a curtain.'

Great forms rose out of the water to right and left of the boat. They were barges – dark and dreary and motionless. On one of them a light could be seen moving: someone was walking about with a lantern in his hand. The sea made little pleading sounds as it patted the sides of the barges, and they gave chill and hollow answers, as if unwilling to grant the favours asked of them.

'A cordon!' said Chelkash in a scarcely audible voice.

Ever since he had told Gavrilla to row softly, the latter had again been gripped by a feeling of tense expectation. As he strained ahead into the darkness it seemed to him that he was growing – his bones and sinews ached as they stretched and his head ached, too, filled as it was with a single thought. The skin of his back quivered and he had a sensation of pins-and-needles in his feet.

His eyes felt as if they would burst from straining so hard into the darkness, out of which he expected someone to rise up any minute and shout at them: 'Stop, thieves!'

Gavrilla shuddered on hearing Chelkash say 'A cordon.' A dreadful thought flashed through his mind and struck upon his taut nerves: he thought of calling out for help. He even opened his mouth, pressed his chest against the side of the boat and took a deep breath, but horror of what he was about to do struck him like a lash; he closed his eyes and fell off the seat.

From out of the black waters rose a flaming blue sword of light; rose and cleaved the darkness of night; cut through the clouds in the sky and came to rest on the bosom of the sea in a broad blue ribbon of light. There it lay, its rays picking the forms of ships, hitherto unseen, out of the darkness – black silent forms, shrouded in the gloom of night. It was as if these ships had lain for long at the bottom of the sea, to which they had been consigned by the forces of the storm, and now, at the wall of this flaming sword born of the sea, they had been raised, that they might gaze on the sky and on all things that exist above water. The rigging of their masts was like clinging seaweed that had been brought up from the bottom of the sea along with the gigantic black forms it enmeshed as in a net. Then once again this fearsome blue sword rose, flashing, off the bosom of the sea, and once again it cleaved the night and lay down again, this time in another spot. And again the forms of ships which had not been seen before were illuminated by its light.

Chelkash's boat stopped and rocked on the water as if deliberating what to do. Gavrilla was lying in the bottom of the boat, his hands over his face, while Chelkash poked him with his foot and whispered savagely:

'That's the customs cruiser, you fool! And that's its spotlight. Get up. They'll have it pointed at us in a minute. You'll be the ruin of me and yourself as well, you idiot. Get up!'

A particularly effective kick in the back brought Gavrilla to his feet. Still afraid to open his eyes, he sat down, felt for the oars, and began to row.

'Easy! Easy, damn you! God, what a fool I picked up! What you afraid of, snout-face? A lantern – that's all it is. Easy with those oars, God damn you! They're searching for smugglers. But they won't catch us. They're too far out. Oh, no, they won't catch us. Now we're—' Chelkash looked about triumphantly '—we're out of danger. Phew! Well, you're a lucky devil, even if you are a blockhead.'

Gavrilla rowed on, saying nothing, breathing heavily, stealing sidelong glances at the flaming sword that kept rising and falling. Chelkash said it was only a lantern but he could not believe it. There was something uncanny about this cold blue light cleaving the darkness, giving the sea a silver shimmer, and once more

Gavrilla was gripped by fear. He rowed mechanically, all his muscles taut as in expectation of a blow from above, and there was nothing he wanted now; he was empty and inanimate. The excitement of that night had drained everything human out of him.

But Chelkash was jubilant. His nerves, used to strain, quickly relaxed. His moustache twitched with gratification and his eyes sparkled. Never had he been in better humour; he whistled through his teeth, drew in deep breaths of the moist sea air, looked about him, smiled good-naturedly when his eyes came to rest on Gavrilla.

A wind sprang up, rousing the sea and covering it with little ripples. The clouds grew thinner and more transparent but the whole sky was still covered with them. The wind rushed lightly back and forth across the sea, but the clouds hung motionless, as if deeply engrossed in drab, uninteresting thoughts.

'Come, snap out of it, brother. You look as if you'd had all the spirit knocked out of you; nothing but a bag of bones left. As if it was the end of the world.'

Gavrilla was glad to hear a human voice, even if it was Chelkash's.

'I'm all right,' he murmured.

'You look it! Got no stuffings in you. Here, take the steering oar and let me row. You must be tired.'

Gavrilla got up mechanically and changed places with him. In passing, Chelkash got a look at the boy's white face and noticed that his knees were trembling so that they could hardly hold him. This made him more sorry than ever for him, and he gave him a pat on the shoulder.

'Come, chin up! You did a good job. I'll reward you well for it. What would you think if I handed you a twenty-five ruble note, eh?'

'I don't want anything. Nothing but to get on shore.'

Chelkash gave a wave of his hand, spat, and began to row,

swinging the oars far back with his long arms.

The sea was quite awake now. It amused itself by making little waves, ornamenting them with fringes of foam, and running them into each other so that they broke in showers of spray. The foam hissed and sighed as it dissolved, and the air was filled with musical sounds. The darkness seemed to have waked up, too.'

'So now,' said Chelkash, 'you'll go back to your village, get married, start working the land, raise corn, your wife will bear children, there won't be enough to eat, and all your life you'll work yourself to the bone. What fun is there in that?'

'Fun?' echoed Gavrilla faintly and with a little shudder.

Here and there the wind tore rifts in the clouds, revealing patches of blue sky set with one or two stars. The reflection of these stars danced on the water, now disappearing, now gleaming again.

'Bear more to the right,' said Chelkash.

'We're almost there. Hm, the job's over. A big job. Just think, five hundred rubles in a single night!'

'Five hundred?' repeated Gavrilla incredulously. Frightened by the words, he gave the bundles a little kick and said, 'What's in them?'

'Things that are worth a lot of money. They'd bring in a thousand if I got the right price, but I can't be bothered. Slick, eh?'

'Good Lord!' said Gavrilla unbelievingly. 'If only I had as much!' He sighed as he thought of his village, his wretched farm, his mother, and all those dear and distant things for whose sake he had set out in search of work; for whose sake he had undergone the tortures of that night, he was caught up in a wave of memories – his little village on the side of a hill running down to the river, and the woods above the river with its birches, willows, rowans, and birdcherry.

'How I need it!' he sighed mournfully.

'You don't say. I s'pose you'd jump straight on a train and make a dash for home. And wouldn't the girls be mad on you! Why, you could have any one of them you liked. And you'd build yourself a new house; although the money's hardly enough for a house.'

'No, not for a house. Timber's dear up our way.'

'At least you'd repair the old one. And what about a horse? Have you got a horse?'

'Yes, but it's a feeble old thing.'

'So you'll need to buy a new horse. A first-rate horse. And a cow.... And some sheep. And some poultry, eh?'

'Ekh, don't mention it! Couldn't I set myself up fine!'

'You could, brother. And life would be like a song. I know a thing or two about such things myself. I had a nest of my own once. My father was one of the richest men in the village.'

Chelkash was scarcely rowing. The boat was tossed by the waves splashing mischievously against its sides, and it made almost no progress through the dark waters, now growing more and more playful. The two men sat there rocking and looking about them, each absorbed in his own dreams. Chelkash had reminded Gavrilla of his village in the hope of quieting the boy's nerves and cheering him up. He had done so with his tongue in his cheek, but as he taunted his companion with reminders of the joys of peasant life, joys which he himself had long since ceased to value and had quite forgotten until this moment, he gradually let himself be carried away, and before he knew it he himself was expounding on the subject instead of questioning the boy about the village and its affairs.

'The best thing about peasant life is that a man's free, he's his own boss. He's got his own house, even if it's a poor one. And he's got his own land – maybe only a little patch, but it's his. He's a king, once he's got his own land. He's a man to be reckoned with. He can demand respect from anybody, can't he?' he ended up with animation.

Gavrilla looked at him curiously, and he, too, became animated. In the course of their talk he had forgotten who this man was;

he saw in him only another peasant like himself, glued fast to the land by the sweat of many generations of forefathers, bound to it by memories of childhood; a peasant who of his own free choice had severed connections with the land and with labour on the land, for which he had been duly punished.

'True, brother. How very true! Look at you, now; what are you without any land? The land, brother, is like your mother; there's no forgetting it.'

Chelkash came back to his surroundings. Again he felt that burning sensation in his chest that always troubled him when his pride – the pride of a reckless dare-devil – was injured, especially if injured by someone he considered a nonentity.

'Trying to teach me!' he said fiercely.

'Did you think I meant what I said? Know your place, upstart!'

'You're a funny one,' said Gavrilla with his former timidity. 'I didn't mean you. There's lots of others like you. God, how many miserable people there are in the world! Homeless tramps.'

'Here, take over the oars,' snapped Chelkash, holding back the flood of oaths that surged in his throat.

Once more they exchanged places, and as Chelkash climbed over the bundles he had an irresistible desire to give Gavrilla a push that would send him flying into the water.

They did no more talking, but Gavrilla emanated the breath of the village even when he was silent. Chelkash became so engrossed in thoughts of the past that he forgot to steer, and the current turned the boat out to sea. The waves seemed to sense that this boat was without a pilot, and they played with it gleefully, tossing it on their crests and leaping in little blue flames about the oars. In front of Chelkash's eyes passed a kaleidoscope of the past, of the distant past, separated from the present by the gulf of eleven years of vagrancy. He saw himself as a child, saw his native village, saw his mother, a stout red-cheeked woman with kindly grey eyes, and his father, a stern-faced, red-bearded giant. He saw himself as a bridegroom, and he saw his bride, the plump black-eyed Anfisa with a mild, cheerful disposition and a long plait hanging down her back. Again he saw himself, this time as a handsome Guardsman; again his father, now grey-haired and stooped with labour; and his mother, wrinkled and bent to earth. He saw the reception the village gave him when his army service was over, and he recalled how proud his father had been to show off this healthy, handsome, bewhiskered soldier-son to the neighbours. Memory is the bane of those who have come to misfortune; it brings to life the very stones of the past, and adds a drop of honey even to the bitterest portion drunk at some far time.

It was as if a gentle stream of native air were wafted over Chelkash, bringing to his ears his mother's tender words, his father's earnest peasant speech and many other forgotten sounds; bringing to his nostrils the fragrance of mother-earth as it thawed, as it was new-ploughed, as it drew on an emerald coverlet of springing rye. He felt lonely, uprooted, thrown once and for all beyond the pale of that way of life which had produced the blood flowing in his veins.

'Hey, where are we going?' cried Gavrilla.

Chelkash started and glanced about with the alertness of a bird of prey.

'Look where we've drifted, damn it all. Row harder.'

'Daydreaming?' smiled Gavrilla.

'Tired.'

'No danger of getting caught with them things?' asked Gavrilla, giving the bundles a little kick.

'No, have no fear. I'll turn them in now and get my money.'

'Five hundred?'

'At least.'

'God, what a pile! If only I had it!

Wouldn't I play a pretty tune with it, just!'

'A peasant tune?'

'What else? I'd....'

And Gavrilla soared on the wings of his imagination. Chelkash said nothing. His moustache drooped, his right side had been drenched by a wave, his eyes were sunken and lustreless. All the hawkishness had gone out of him, had been wrung out of him by a humiliating introspection that even glanced out of the folds of his filthy shirt.

He turned the boat sharply about and steered it towards a black form rising out of the water.

Once more the sky was veiled in clouds and a fine warm rain set in, making cheerful little plopping sounds as its drops struck the water.

'Stop! Hold it!' ordered Chelkash.

The nose of the boat ran into the side of a barge.

'Are they asleep or what, the bastards?' growled Chelkash as he slipped a boat-hook into some ropes hanging over the side. 'Throw down the ladder! And the rain had to wait till this minute to come down! Hey, you sponges! Hey!'

'Selkash?' purred someone on deck.

'Where's the ladder?'

'Kalimera, Selkash.'

'The ladder, God damn you!'

'Oo, what a temper he's in tonight! Eloy!'

'Climb up, Gavrilla,' said Chelkash to his companion.

The next minute they were on deck, where three bearded, dark-skinned fellows were talking animatedly in a lisping tongue as they stared over the gunwale into Chelkash's boat. A fourth, wrapped in a long chlamys, went over to Chelkash and shook his hand without a word, then threw Gavrilla a questioning look.

'Have the money ready in the morning,' Chelkash said to him briefly. 'I'm going to take a snooze now. Come along, Gavrilla. Are you hungry?'

'I'm sleepy,' said Gavrilla. Five minutes later he was snoring loudly while Chelkash sat beside him trying on somebody else's boots, spitting off to one side and whistling a sad tune through his teeth. Presently he stretched out beside Gavrilla with his hands behind his head and lay there with his moustache twitching.

The barge rolled on the waves, a board creaked plaintively, the rain beat on the deck and the waves against the sides of the barge. It was all very mournful and reminded one of the cradle-song of a mother who has little hope of seeing her child happy.

Chelkash bared his teeth, raised his head, glanced about him, muttered something to himself and lay down again with his legs spread wide apart, making him look like a pair of giant scissors.

III

He was the first to wake up. He glanced anxiously about him, was instantly reassured, and looked down at Gavrilla, who was snoring happily, a smile spread all over his wholesome, sunburnt, boyish face. Chelkash gave a sigh and climbed up a narrow rope-ladder. A patch of lead-coloured sky peered down the hatchway. It was light, but the day was dull and dreary, as is often so in autumn.

Chelkash came back in a couple of hours. His face was red and his whiskers had been given a rakish twist. He was wearing a sturdy pair of high-boots, a leather hunting: jacket and breeches as a hunter wears. The outfit was not new, but in good condition and very becoming to him, since it filled out his figure, rounded off the edges and gave him a certain military air.

'Get up, puppy,' said he, giving Gavrilla a little kick.

Gavrilla jumped up only half-awake and gazed at Chelkash with frightened eyes, not recognizing him. Chelkash burst out laughing.

'Don't you look grand!' said Gavrilla with a broad grin at last. 'Quite the gentleman.'

'That don't take us long. But you're a lily-livered fellow if there ever was one. How many times were you about to pass out last night?'

'You can't blame me; I'd never been on a job like that before. I might have lost my soul.'

'Would you do it again, eh?'

'Again? Only if – how shall I put it? What would I get for it?'

'If you got, let's say, two smackers?'

'You mean two hundred rubles? Not bad. I might.'

'And what about losing your soul?'

'Maybe I wouldn't lose it after all,' grinned Gavrilla.

'You wouldn't lose it, and you'd be made for the rest of your life.'

Chelkash laughed gaily.

'Well, enough of joking; let's go ashore.'

And so they found themselves in the boat again, Chelkash steering, Gavrilla rowing. Above them stretched a solid canopy of grey clouds; the sea was a dull green and it played joyfully with the boat, tossing it up on waves that had not yet grown to any size, and throwing handfuls of pale spray against its sides. Far up ahead could be glimpsed a strip of yellow sand, while behind them stretched the sea, chopped up into coveys of white-caps. Behind them, too, were the ships – a whole forest of masts back there to the left, with the white buildings of the port as a background. A dull rumble came pouring out of the port over the sea, mingling with the roar of the waves to form fine strong music. And over everything hung a thin veil of fog that made all objects seem remote.

'Ekh, it'll be something to see by nightfall!' exclaimed Chelkash, nodding out to sea.

'A storm?' asked Gavrilla as he ploughed powerfully through the waves with his oars. His clothes were soaked with wind-blown spray.

'Uh-huh,' said Chelkash.

Gavrilla looked at him inquisitively.

'Well, how much did they give you?' he asked at last, seeing that Chelkash had no intention of broaching the subject.

'Look,' and Chelkash pulled something out of his pocket and held it out.

Gavrilla's eyes were dazzled by the sight of so many crisp bright bank-notes.

'And here I was thinking you had lied to me! How much is it?'

'Five hundred and forty.'

'Phe-e-w!' gasped Gavrilla, following the course of the notes back to the pocket with greedy eyes. 'God! If only I had that much money!' and he gave a doleful sigh.

'You and me'll go on a big spree, mate,' cried Chelkash ecstatically. 'We'll paint the town red. You'll get your share, never fear. I'll give you forty. That enough, eh? Give it straight away if you want me to.'

'All right, I'll take it if you don't mind.'

Gavrilla was shaking with anticipation.

'Ekh, you scarecrow you! "I'll take it!" Here, go ahead and take it. Take it, damn it all. I don't know what to do with so much money. Do me a favour and take some of it off my hands.'

Chelkash held out several notes to Gavrilla, who let go of the oars to clutch them in trembling fingers and thrust them inside his shirt, screwing up his eyes as he did so and taking in great gulps of air as if he had just scalded his throat. Chelkash watched him, a squeamish smile on his lips. Once more Gavrilla picked up the oars and began to row nervously, hurriedly, with his eyes cast down, like a man who has just had a bad fright. His shoulders and ears were twitching.

'You're a greedy bloke. That's no good. But what's to be expected? – you're a peasant,' mused Chelkash.

'A man can do anything with money!' exclaimed Gavrilla in a sudden flare of excitement. And then hurriedly, incoherently, chasing his thoughts and catching his words on the fly, he drew the contrast between life in the village with money and without it. Honour, comfort, pleasure!

Chelkash followed him attentively, his face grave, his eyes narrowed thoughtfully. From time to time he would give a pleased smile.

'Here we are!' he interrupted Gavrilla's tirade.

The boat was caught on a wave that drove it into the sand.

'Well, this is the end. But we've got to pull the boat up good and high so that it don't get washed away. Some people will come for it. And now it's good-bye. We're about ten versts from town. You going back to town?'

Chelkash's face was beaming with a sly and good-natured smile, as if he were contemplating something very pleasant for himself and very unexpected for Gavrilla. He thrust his hand into his pocket and rustled the notes there.

'No – I'm not going. I'm – I'm—' Gavrilla stammered as if choking.

Chelkash looked at him.

'What's eating you?' he said.

'Nothing.' But Gavrilla's face turned first red, then grey, and he kept shifting on his feet as if he wanted to throw himself at Chelkash or do something else of insuperable difficulty.

Chelkash was nonplussed by the boy's agitation. He waited to see what would come of it.

Gavrilla broke into laughter that sounded more like sobbing. His head was hanging, so that Chelkash could not see the expression of his face, but he could see his ears going from red to white.

'To hell with you,' said Chelkash with a disgusted wave of his hand. 'Are you in love with me, or what? Squirming like a girl. Or maybe you can't bear to part with me? Speak up, spineless, or I'll just walk off.'

'You'll walk off?' shrieked Gavrilla.

The deserted beach trembled at the shriek, and the ripples of yellow sand made up by the washing of the waves seemed to heave. Chelkash himself started. All of a sudden Gavrilla rushed towards Chelkash, threw himself at his feet, seized him round the knees and gave him a tug. Chelkash staggered and sat down heavily in the sand; clenching his teeth, he swung up his long arm with the hand closed in a tight fist. But the blow was intercepted by Gavrilla's pleadings, uttered in a cringing whisper:

'Give me that money, there's a good fellow! For the love of Christ give it to me. What do you need with it? Look, in just one night – in one single night! And it would take me years and years. Give it to me. I'll pray for you. All my life. In three churches. For the salvation of your soul. You'll only throw it to the winds, while I? I'll put it in the land. Give it to me! What is it to you? It comes so easy. One night, and you're a rich man. Do a good deed once in your life. After all, you're a lost soul; there's nothing ahead of you. And I'd – oh what wouldn't I do with it! Give it to me!'

Chelkash – frightened, dumbfounded, infuriated – sat in the sand leaning back on his elbows; sat without a word, his eyes boring into this boy whose head was pressed against his knees as he gasped out his plea.

At last Chelkash jumped to his feet, thrust his hand into his pocket and threw the notes at Gavrilla.

'Here, lick it up!' he cried, trembling with excitement, with pity and loathing for this greedy slave. He felt heroic when he had tossed him the money.

'I was going to give you more anyway. Went soft last night thinking of my own village. Thought to myself: I'll help the lad. But I waited to see if you'd ask for it. And you did, you milksop, you beggar, you. Is it worth tormenting yourself like that for money? Fool. Greedy devils. No pride. They'd sell themselves for five kopeks.'

'May Christ watch over you! What's this I've got? Why, I'm a rich man now!' squealed Gavrilla, twitching all over in ecstasy and hiding the money inside his shirt. 'Bless you, my friend. I'll never forget you. Never. And I'll have my wife and children say prayers for you, too.'

As Chelkash heard his joyful squeals and looked at his beaming face distorted by this paroxysm of greed, he realized that, thief and drunk that he was, he would never stoop so low, would never be so grasping, so lacking in self-pride. Never, never! And this thought and this feeling, filling him with a sense of his own freedom, made him linger there beside Gavrilla on the shore of the sea.

'You've made me a present of happiness,' cried Gavrilla, snatching Chelkash's hand and pressing it against his own face.

Chelkash bared his teeth like a wolf but said nothing.

'And just to think what I almost did!' went on Gavrilla. 'On the way here I thought – to myself – I'll hit him – you, that is – over the head – with an oar – bang! – take the money – and throw him – you, that is – overboard. Who'd ever miss him? And if they found his body – nobody'd bother to find out who did it and how. He's not worth making a fuss over. Nobody needs him. Nobody'd go to the trouble.'

'Hand over that money!' roared Chelkash, seizing Gavrilla by the throat.

Gavrilla wrenched away once, twice, but Chelkash's arm wound about him like a snake. The sound of a shirt ripping, and – there was Gavrilla flat on his back in the sand, his eyes popping out of his head, his fingers clutching the air, his feet kicking helplessly. Chelkash stood over him lean, erect, hawk-like, his teeth bared as he gave a hard dry laugh, his whiskers twitching nervously on his sharp bony face. Never in all his life had he been wounded so cruelly, and never had he been so furious.

'Well, are you happy now?' he laughed, then turned on his heel and set off in the direction of the town. Before he had gone five steps Gavrilla arched himself like a cat, sprang to his feet, swung out with his arm and hurled a big stone at him.

'Take that!'

Chelkash let out a grunt, put his hands to his head, staggered forward, turned round to Gavrilla, and fell on his face in the sand. Gavrilla was frozen with fear. Chelkash moved one leg, tried to lift his head, stretched out, trembling like a harp string. Then Gavrilla ran for all he was worth, ran out into the dark space where a shaggy black cloud was hanging over the fog-enshrouded steppe. The waves rustled as they scurried up the sand, mingled with the sand for a brief moment, scurried back again. The foam hissed and the air was filled with spray.

It began to rain. At first it came down in single drops, but soon turned into a torrent that came pouring out of the sky in thin streams. These streams wove a net of watery threads that enveloped the whole expanse of the steppe, the whole expanse of the sea. Gavrilla was swallowed up in it. For a long time nothing was to be seen but the rain and the long figure of the man laying in the sand at the edge of the sea. Then Gavrilla came swooping like a bird out of the darkness. When he reached Chelkash he fell on his knees beside him and tried to lift him up. His hand came in contact with something warm and red and sticky. He shuddered and started back, with a wild expression on his white face.

'Get up, brother, get up!' he whispered in Chelkash's ear above the noise of the rain.

Chelkash opened his eyes and gave Gavrilla a little push.

'Go away,' he whispered hoarsely.

'Brother! Forgive me! It was the devil's doings,' whispered Gavrilla trembling as he kissed Chelkash's hand.

'Go away. Leave me.'

'Take this sin off my soul. Forgive me, brother.'

'Away! Go away! Go to hell!' Chelkash suddenly cried out and sat up in the sand. His face was white and angry, his eyes were hazy and kept closing as if he were sleepy. 'What else do you want? You've done what you wanted to do. Go away. Get out!' He tried to give the grief-stricken Gavrilla a kick, but he could not and would have collapsed again had not Gavrilla put an arm round his shoulders. Chelkash's face was on a level with Gavrilla's. Both faces were white and dreadful to see.

'Bah!' And Chelkash spat into the wide-open eyes of his assistant.

Gavrilla humbly wiped his face on his sleeve.

'Do what you want to me,' he whispered. 'I won't say a word. Forgive me, in the name of Christ.'

'Scum. Can't even do your dirty work like a man,' cried Chelkash scathingly as he slipped his hand inside his jacket and ripped off a piece of shirt with which he silently bound his head, grinding his teeth from time to time. 'Have you taken the money?' he asked through his teeth.

'I haven't, brother. And I won't. I don't want it. Nothing but bad luck comes of it.'

Chelkash thrust his hand into a pocket of his jacket, pulled out the pile of notes, peeled off a hundred-ruble one, put it back into his pocket, and threw the rest at Gavrilla.

'Take it and go away.'

'I won't, brother. I can't. Forgive me what I've done.'

'Take it, I say,' roared Chelkash, rolling his eyes fearfully.

'Forgive me. I can't take it if you don't,' said Gavrilla humbly, falling at Chelkash's feet in the rain-drenched sand.

'That's a lie. You will take it, you scum,' said Chelkash with conviction. Pulling up his companion's head by the hair, he thrust the money under his nose.

'Take it. Take it. You didn't work for nothing. Don't be afraid, take it. And don't be ashamed that you almost killed a man. Nobody would hunt you down for killing a man like me. They'd even say thank you if they found out. Here, take it.'

Seeing that Chelkash was laughing, Gavrilla's heart grew lighter. He clutched the money.

'And do you forgive me, brother? Don't you want to do that for me?' he begged tearfully.

'My beloved friend,' replied Chelkash in the same vein, as he got up and stood swaying on his feet. 'What's there to forgive? Nothing to forgive. Today you get me; tomorrow I get you.'

'Ah brother, brother,' sighed Gavrilla disconsolately, shaking his head.

Chelkash stood in front of him with an odd smile on his face. The rag on his head, which had gradually been getting redder, resembled a Turkish fez.

The rain had become a downpour. The sea gave a low roar, the waves hurled themselves savagely at the shore.

The two men were silent.

'Well, good-bye,' said Chelkash mockingly as he turned to go.

He staggered, his legs were shaking, and he held his head as if afraid of losing it.

'Forgive me, brother,' pleaded Gavrilla once more.

'That's all right,' said Chelkash coldly, setting off.

He stumbled away, holding his head with his left hand, pulling gently at his dark moustache with his right.

Gavrilla stood watching him until he disappeared in the rain which kept coming down in fine endless streams, enveloping the steppe in impenetrable steel-grey gloom.

Then he took off his wet cap, crossed himself, looked at the money in his hand, heaved a deep sigh of relief, hid the money in his shirt, and strode off firmly down the shore in the opposite direction to that taken by Chelkash.

The sea growled as it hurled its huge waves on the sand, smashing them to foam and spray. The rain lashed at the water and the land. The wind howled. The air was filled with a roar, a howl, a murmur. The rain cut off sight of sea and sky.

Soon the rain and the spray washed away the red spot on the sand where Chelkash had lain, washed away the footsteps of Chelkash, washed away the footsteps of the youth who had walked so bravely down the beach. And not a sign was left on this deserted shore to testify to the little drama enacted here by these two men.

SONG OF THE FALCON

(tr. Margaret Wettlin)

THE BOUNDLESS SEA, LAPPING lazily where the shore-line ran, slumbering motionless in the distance, was steeped in blue moonlight. Soft and silvery, it merged at the horizon with the blue of the southern sky and slept soundly, mirroring the transparent fabric of fleecy clouds that also hung motionless, veiling, but not concealing, the golden tracery of the stars. The sky seemed to be bending down to the sea, trying to catch what the restless waves were whispering as they washed languidly over the shore.

The mountains, covered with wind-broken trees, hurled their jagged peaks into the blue wastes above, where their harsh contours were softened by the warm and caressing darkness of the southern night.

The mountains were gravely contemplative. Their dark shadows lay like confining garments upon the surging green waves, as if they wished to stay the tide, to silence the ceaseless plashing of the water, the sighing of the foam – all sounds violating the mysterious silence which flooded the scene, as did the silvery blue radiance of a moon not yet emerged from behind mountain peaks.

'Al-lah ak-bar!' came softly from the lips of Nadir Ragim ogly, an aged Crimean herdsman – tall, white-haired, tanned by southern sun – a lean and wise old man.

He and I were lying in the sand beside a huge rock draped in shadow and overgrown by moss – a sad and sombre rock that had broken away from its native mountain. One side of it was festooned with seaweed and water plants which seemed to bind it to the narrow strip of sand between sea and mountains. The flames of our camp-fire lighted the shore-side, and their flicker sent shadows dancing upon its ancient surface, scarred by a network of deep cracks.

Ragim and I were boiling some fish we had just caught, and we were both in a mood that made everything seem lucid, inspired, accessible to the understanding; our hearts were light and innocent and the only thing we wanted to do was lie here and dream.

The sea lapped at the shore, the sound of the waves so gentle that they seemed begging to warm themselves at our fire. Now and then the even hum of the surf was interrupted by a higher and more playful note: that would be one of the bolder waves creeping to our very feet.

Ragim lay facing the sea, his elbows dug into the sand, his head in his hands, gazing thoughtfully into the shadowy distance. His sheepskin hat had slipped to the back of his head, and a fresh sea breeze fanned his high forehead covered with fine lines. He made philosophical observations, unconcerned as to whether I listened or not, as if he were talking to the sea.

'A man who serves God faithfully goes to heaven. And one who does not serve God or the Prophet? Maybe he's out there – in that foam. Maybe those silver spots on the water are him. Who knows?'

The dark and heaving sea grew brighter, and patches of moonlight were scattered haphazardly over its surface. The moon had slipped out from behind the shaggy mountain-tops and was now dreamily pouring its radiance on the shore, on the rock beside which we were lying, and on the sea, which rose to meet it with a little sigh.

'Ragim, tell me a story,' I said to the old man.

'What for?' he asked, without turning his head.

'Oh, just because I enjoy listening to your stories.'

'I've told you all of them. I don't know any more.'

He wanted to be coaxed, and I coaxed him.

'If you want me to, I'll sing you a song,' he consented.

I was only too glad to listen to one of his old songs, and so he began reciting in a singsong voice, trying to preserve the cadence of the ancient melody.

I

High in the mountains crawled a Snake, and it came to rest in a misty gorge looking down on the sea.

High in the sky shone the sun, and the breath of the mountains rose hot in the sky, and the waves down below broke loud on the rocks.

And swift through the gorge, through the darkness and mist, flowed a river, up-turning the stones in its rush to the sea.

Crested with foam, vigorous, hoary, it cut through the rook and plunged to the sea with an angry roar.

Suddenly a Falcon with blood on its wings and a wound in its breast fell out of the sky, fell into the gorge where the Snake lay coiled.

It uttered a cry as it struck the earth and lay beating its wings on the rock in despair.

The Snake was frightened and darted away, but soon it saw that the bird was doomed, that the bird would die in a minute or two.

So back it crawled to the wounded bird and tauntingly hissed in its ear:

'So soon must thou die?'

'So soon must I die,' said the Falcon, sighing. 'But oh, I have lived! I have tasted of happiness, fought a good fight! I have soared in the sky! Never shalt thou, poor thing, see the sky as have I!'

'The sky? What is that? Why, nothing at all. Could I crawl in the sky? Far better this gorge – so warm and so damp.'

Thus said the Snake to the Falcon, the lover of freedom. And it laughed in its heart at the Falcon's brave words.

And it thought to itself: what matters it whether one flies or one crawls? The end is the same: all will lie in the earth, all to dust will return.

All of a sudden the Falcon up-lifted its head and swept the dark gorge with a lowering glance.

Water came oozing from cracks in the rock, and the air of the gorge smelt of death and decay.

With a mighty effort the Falcon cried out in sorrow and longing:

'Ah, to soar in the sky, to soar once again!... I would capture the foe... crush his head to my breast... make him choke on my blood.... Oh, the joy of the struggle!'

Thought the Snake: it must really be fine to live in the sky if it wrings such a cry from the Falcon!

And it said to the Falcon, the lover of freedom: 'Crawl out to the cliff's edge and throw thyself over. Perhaps thy wings will carry thee still, and again thou shalt soar in the sky.'

A tremor passed over the Falcon. It gave a proud cry and crawled out on the cliff, seeking a hold in the slime.

And on reaching the edge it spread wide its wings, drew a deep breath, and, with a flash of its eyes, plunged into space.

Swift as a stone fell the Falcon, scattering feathers, tearing its wings as it fell.

A wave caught it up, washed it of blood, wrapped it in foam, and carried it down to the sea.

Mournful the cry of the waves of the sea as they broke on the face of the cliff. And gone was the bird – lost to sight in the vast expanse of the sea.

II

For long the Snake lay coiled in the gorge, pondering the death of the bird, pondering its love of the sky.

And it glanced into space, where dreams are born to comfort the restless heart.

'What did it see, that hapless Falcon, in emptiness – space without end? Why should such birds rob others of peace with their passion for soaring? What is revealed in the sky? All this can I learn in a single flight, be it ever so brief.'

Thus having spoken, it coiled itself tighter, leaped into space, and flashed, a dark streak, in the sun.

But never shall those born to crawl, learn to fly. Down on the rocks fell the Snake, but not to its death did it fall. It laughed, and it said:

'So this is the joy of the flight: the joy of the fall! Oh, foolish birds! Unhappy on earth, which they know not, they would climb to the sky and live in its throbbing expanses. But what is the sky but an emptiness? Light in abundance, but nothing to sustain the body. Why, then, such pride? And why such contempt? To hide from the world their mad aspirations, their failure to cope with the business of life? Ridiculous birds! Never again will your words deceive me. For now I know all. I have seen the sky. I have mounted, explored it; and out of the sky have I fallen, though not to my death. All the stronger has grown my faith in myself. Let them live with illusions who love not the earth. I have found out the truth. Never again shall I heed the birds' challenge. Born of the earth, I am earthly.'

So saying, it coiled on a stone, full of pride in itself.

The sea was shining, a dazzle of light, and fiercely the waves beat the shore.

In their leonine roar rang the song of the Falcon. Trembled the rocks from the blows of the sea; trembled the sky from the notes of the song:

'We sing a song to the madness of daring!

'The madness of daring is the wisdom of life. Oh, Falcon undaunted! Thou hast shed precious blood in the fight with the foe, but the time will yet come when the drops of thy blood will glow like sparks in the gloom of life and fire brave hearts with love of freedom and light.

'Thou hast paid with thy life. But thou shall live on in the songs of the brave, a proud challenge to struggle for freedom and light!

'We sing a song to the madness of daring!'

… Silent are the opalescent reaches of the sea. Softly sing the waves lapping the shore, and I, too, am silent as I gaze into the distance. Now there are more silvery patches of moonlight on the water.… Our kettle is humming quietly.

One of the waves outdistances its brothers and gives a mocking little cry as it reaches for Ragim's head.

'Get back! Where do you think you're going?' cries Ragim, waving his hand, and the wave rolls back obediently.

I find nothing funny or startling in Ragim's personification of the wave. Everything about us is exceptionally alive, gentle and soothing. The sea is calm, and one feels power in the cool breath it wafts towards mountain peaks still charged with the heat of the day. In golden letters upon the dark blue background of the sky the stars have traced a solemn message, something enchanting the soul and disturbing the mind with the sweet expectation of a revelation.

Everything is drowsing, but with tense awareness, as if in another moment all objects would shake off their slumber and lift their voices in a choir of unutterably sweet harmony. This harmony would speak of the mysteries of life, would explain them to the mind and then extinguish the mind like a phantom flame and whisk the soul up into the blue spaces of the night where the delicate tracery of the stars sings the same divine music of revelation.

A MITE OF A GIRL

(tr. Margaret Wettlin)

'JUST A MITE OF a girl she was, stranger.'

Every time I recall this phrase, two pairs of old and feeble eyes smile at me through the years – smile with a soft and tender smile full of love and compassion; and I hear two cracked voices impressing on me in identical tones that she was 'just a mite of a girl.'

And I am made happy and hopeful by this remembrance, the best of all those relating to those ten months I spent tramping the winding roads of this my native land – a land so vast and sorrowful.

On my way from Zadonsk to Voronezh I overtook two pilgrims, an old man and an old woman. Both of them seemed to be over a hundred years old, so slowly and haltingly did they walk, so painfully did they lift their feet out of the scorching dust of the road. There was an illusive something in their dress and their faces that led one to assume they had come a long way.

'All the way on foot from Tobolskaya Gubernia,[1] with God's help,' said the old man in confirmation of my assumption.

---

1 A far province in Siberia to which political prisoners were exiled by the tsarist government. – Tr.

As we walked along, the old woman looked at me with kindly eyes that had once been blue and added with a sigh and a benign smile:

'All the way from the X Factory in the village of Lysaya, my old man and me.'

'Aren't you very tired?'

'Not very. We can still make our way, still crawl on, by the grace of God.'

'Did you make a vow to come, or is it just an old-age pilgrimage?'

'We made a vow, stranger. We made a vow to the saints of the Kiev and the Solovki monasteries. A vow,' repeated the old man, and then, turning to his companion: 'Come mother, let's sit down and ease our bones a bit.'

'Let's,' said she.

And so we sat down in the shade of an old willow growing at the side of the road. The day was hot, the sky cloudless; before and behind us wound the road into the heat-hazy distance. It was a quiet lonely spot. On either side of the road stretched fields of sickly rye.

'They've sucked the earth dry,' said the old man, handing me a few stalks he had plucked.

We talked about the earth and about the cruel dependence of the peasants on its charity. The old woman sighed as she listened to us, and from time to time she would contribute a wise and knowing word.

'If she was alive, how she would strain her poor muscles in a field like that,' said the old woman suddenly, glancing round at the rows of stunted, shrivelled rye and the bald spots in the field where it did not grow at all.

'Ah, yes, she would have worn herself out,' said the old man, shaking his head.

There was a pause.

'Who are you talking about?' I asked.

The old man smiled good-naturedly.

'About a certain little lass,' he said.

'She was quartered on us. One of the gentlefolk,' sighed the old woman.

And then they both looked at me, and as if by mutual consent said in unison, slowly and plaintively:

'Such a mite of a girl she was!'

The odd way in which they said it went to my heart; the words sounded almost like a last rite intoned by these two faltering voices. And suddenly the old man and woman began to talk so quickly that they fairly took the words out of each other's mouths and kept me, who was sitting between them, turning my head from one to the other.

'A gendarme brought her to our village and turned her over to the elders. "Quarter her on someone," he said—'

'In other words, find her a home,' explained the old man.

'And they sent her to us.'

'You should have seen her – all red and shivering with cold.'

'Such a mite of a girl!'

'It made us cry to see her—'

'Lord, thinks us, to have sent such a one to such a place!'

'For what reason? For what offence?'

'It's from these parts she came—'

'The west, that is—'

'We put her up on the stove-bunk first—'

'Ours is a big stove and a warm one,' sighed the old woman.

'And then we gave her to eat.'

'How she laughed!'

'She had shining black eyes, like a mouse's—'

'She was like a mouse herself, so round and smooth.'

'When she felt better she began to cry. "Thank you, dears," she said.'

'And then how she did set the house on end!'

'How she did turn things upside down!' laughed the old man gleefully, screwing up his eyes.

'Went bouncing like a bail about our hut – here, there, everywhere, putting this in order, putting that in order. "The swills," says she, "are to go out to the pigs". "And she picks up the swill-tub herself, and then she slips, and plop! in go her arms up to the shoulder. My, oh my! What a sight!'

And both of them laughed till they coughed and had to wipe the tears from their eyes.

'And then the pigs—'

'Kissed them right on the snout!'

'"Out with the pigs, too!" says she. "The hut's no place for pigs!"'

'For a whole week she made order—'

'Worked both of us to a sweat—'

'Laughing and shouting and stamping her little feet—'

'And then all of a sudden going quiet and solemn—'

'As if she was going to die—'

'Bursting into tears and crying as if her heart would break. I'd fuss about her, wondering what could be the matter. Such a strange thing. And I'd cry myself, cry without knowing why. And I'd put my arms about her and there we'd be, both of us crying our eyes out—'

'As was only natural. After all, she was little more than a child—'

'And us all alone. One son in the army, the other in the gold-fields—'

'And her only seventeen years old—'

'Seventeen! No one would give her more than twelve!'

'Come now, that's stretching it a point, father. Twelve's stretching it.'

'And would you give her more? Would you, now?'

'Why, she was a ripe little piece. As for her being so little, is that to be held against her?'

'And am I holding it against her? Tut, tut!'

'You're not,' conceded the old woman good-naturedly.

Their quarrel over, they both grew silent.

'And what happened after that?' I asked.

'After that? Why, nothing, stranger,' sighed the old man.

'She died. Died of the fire-fever,' and two tears stole down the old woman's wrinkled cheeks.

'She died, stranger; only lived with us two years. Everybody in the village knew her. The village, did I say? Why, lots more knew her. She had learning and would sit in council with the elders. Sometimes she spoke sharp, but nobody minded. A clever one.'

'Ah, but it was her heart that counted. She had the heart of an angel. There was room in her heart for all our troubles, and she took them all to herself. She was a lady like any other from the town, with a velvet jacket and ribbons and shoes, and she read books and all that, but how she did understand us peasants! She knew all there was to know about us. "How did you learn it, dear?" "It's all written in the books," she would say. Fancy that! But why should she have cared? She ought to have got married and been a lady, and instead they sent her here, and – she died.'

'It was funny to see her teaching everybody. Such a tiny little thing, and teaching everybody so serious: you mustn't do this, you mustn't do that—'

'Oh, she had learning, indeed she did! And how she worried about everything, about everybody! If someone was sick, off she went to cure him; if someone was—'

'Her mind was wandering when she died; she kept saying, "Mama, Mama," – so plaintive-like. We sent for the priest, thinking he might bring her back to us. But she didn't wait for him, the darling; she passed away.'

Tears streamed down the old woman's face, and a feeling of beatitude came over me, as if these tears were being shed for me.

'The whole village gathered at our house, crowded into the yard, into the roadway, saying "What? Is it possible?" They loved her so.'

'And where else could such a lass be found?' sighed the old man.

'All the people gave her burial. And at Shrovetide her forty days were over, and it came to us: why should we not go on a pilgrimage to pray for her soul? And the neighbours, too, said why not indeed? Go, they said. You are free, with no work-bonds to hold you. Perhaps your prayers will be added to her account. And so we went.'

'You mean you have done this for her?' I asked.

'For her; for that blessed child. The dear Lord may hear our prayers, sinners though we be, and absolve her of sin. In the first week of Lent we set out, on a Tuesday it was—'

'For her!' I repeated.

'For her, stranger,' said the old man.

I wanted to hear them say again and again that it was just to pray for the soul of this girl they had come these thousands of versts. It struck me as being too wonderful to believe.

And so anxious was I to be convinced that it was only 'for her,' the little lass with the black eyes, that they had done this marvellous thing, that I suggested all sorts of other possible motives. But to my enormous satisfaction they convinced me there was no other.

'And have you really come all this way on foot?'

'Oh, dear no! Sometimes we ride. Ride for a day, then walk for a day. Labouring along, little by little. We're too old to go the whole way on foot. God sees how old we are. It would be different if it was her feet we walked on.'

And once more they interrupted each other in their eagerness to talk about her, a young girl whom fate had cast on such a distant shore, so far from home and mother, to die of the 'fire-fever.'

Two hours later we got up and went on our way. My thoughts were all about this girl, but try as I might I could not conjure up an image of her. And it was a hurtful thing to realize the feebleness of my imagination.

It is always hard for a Russian to imagine the good and the beautiful....

Soon we were overtaken by a Ukrainian driving a cart. He threw us a melancholy glance and lifted his cap in response to our bows.

'Climb in. I'll take you to the next village,' he called to the old couple.

They climbed in and were swallowed up in a cloud of dust. And I walked on in this cloud with my eyes on the cart that was taking away the old man and the old woman who had come thousands of versts to pray for the soul of a mite of a girl who had made them lovelier.

ONE AUTUMN NIGHT

ONCE IN THE AUTUMN I happened to be in a very unpleasant and inconvenient position. In the town where I had just arrived and where I knew not a soul, I found myself without a farthing in my pocket and without a night's lodging.

Having sold during the first few days every part of my costume without which it was still possible to go about, I passed from the town into the quarter called 'Yste,' where were the steamship wharves – a quarter which during the navigation season fermented with boisterous, laborious life, but now was silent and deserted, for we were in the last days of October.

Dragging my feet along the moist sand, and obstinately scrutinizing it with the desire to discover in it any sort of fragment of food, I wandered alone among the deserted buildings and warehouses, and thought how good it would be to get a full meal.

In our present state of culture, hunger of the mind is more quickly satisfied than hunger of the body. You wander about the streets, you are surrounded by buildings not bad-looking from the outside and – you may safely say it – not so badly furnished inside, and the sight of them may excite within you stimulating ideas about architecture, hygiene, and many other wise and high-flying subjects. You may meet warmly and neatly dressed folks

– all very polite, and turning away from you tactfully, not wishing offensively to notice the lamentable fact of your existence. Well, well, the mind of a hungry man is always better nourished and healthier than the mind of the well-fed man; and there you have a situation from which you may draw a very ingenious conclusion in favour of the ill fed.

The evening was approaching, the rain was falling, and the wind blew violently from the north. It whistled in the empty booths and shops, blew into the plastered window-panes of the taverns, and whipped into foam the wavelets of the river which splashed noisily on the sandy shore, casting high their white crests, racing one after another into the dim distance, and leaping impetuously over one another's shoulders. It seemed as if the river felt the proximity of winter, and was running at random away from the fetters of ice which the north wind might well have flung upon her that very night. The sky was heavy and dark; down from it swept incessantly scarcely visible drops of rain, and the melancholy elegy in nature all around me was emphasized by a couple of battered and misshapen willow-trees and a boat, bottom upwards, that was fastened to their roots.

The overturned canoe with its battered keel and the miserable old trees rifled by the cold wind – everything around me was bankrupt, barren, and dead, and the sky flowed with undryable tears.... Everything around was waste and gloomy... it seemed as if everything were dead, leaving me alone among the living, and for me also a cold death waited.

I was then eighteen years old – a good time!

I walked and walked along the cold wet sand, making my chattering teeth warble in honour of cold and hunger, when suddenly, as I was carefully searching for something to eat behind one of the empty crates, I perceived behind it, crouching on the ground, a figure in woman's clothes dank with the rain and clinging fast to her stooping shoulders. Standing over her, I watched to see what she was doing. It appeared that she was digging a trench in the sand with her hands – digging away under one of the crates.

'Why are you doing that?' I asked, crouching down on my heels quite close to her.

She gave a little scream and was quickly on her legs again. Now that she stood there staring at me, with her wide-open grey eyes full of terror, I perceived that it was a girl of my own age, with a very pleasant face embellished unfortunately by three large blue marks. This spoilt her, although these blue marks had been distributed with a remarkable sense of proportion, one at a time, and all were of equal size – two under the eyes, and one a little bigger on the forehead just over the bridge of the nose. This symmetry was evidently the work of an artist well inured to the business of spoiling the human physiognomy.

The girl looked at me, and the terror in her eyes gradually died out…. She shook the sand from her hands, adjusted her cotton head-gear, cowered down, and said:

'I suppose you too want something to eat? Dig away then! My hands are tired. Over there' – she nodded her head in the direction of a booth – 'there is bread for certain… and sausages too… That booth is still carrying on business.'

I began to dig. She, after waiting a little and looking at me, sat down beside me and began to help me.

We worked in silence. I cannot say now whether I thought at that moment of the criminal code, of morality, of proprietorship, and all the other things about which, in the opinion of many experienced persons, one ought to think every moment of one's life. Wishing to keep as close to the truth as possible, I must confess that apparently I was so deeply engaged in digging under the crate that I completely forgot about everything else except this one thing: What could be inside that crate?

The evening drew on. The grey, mouldy, cold fog grew thicker and thicker around us. The waves roared with a hollower sound than before, and the rain pattered down on the boards of that crate more loudly and more frequently. Somewhere or other the night-watchman began springing his rattle.

'Has it got a bottom or not?' softly inquired my assistant. I did not understand what she was talking about, and I kept silence.

'I say, has the crate got a bottom? If it has we shall try in vain to break into it. Here we are digging a trench, and we may, after all, come upon nothing but solid boards. How shall we take them off? Better smash the lock; it is a wretched lock.'

Good ideas rarely visit the heads of women, but, as you see, they do visit them sometimes. I have always valued good ideas, and have always tried to utilize them as far as possible.

Having found the lock, I tugged at it and wrenched off the whole thing. My accomplice immediately stooped down and wriggled like a serpent into the gaping-open, four-cornered cover of the crate whence she called to me approvingly, in a low tone:

'You're a brick!'

Nowadays a little crumb of praise from a woman is dearer to me than a whole dithyramb from a man, even though he be more eloquent than all the ancient and modern orators put together. Then, however, I was less amiably disposed than I am now, and, paying no attention to the compliment of my comrade, I asked her curtly and anxiously:

'Is there anything?'

In a monotonous tone she set about calculating our discoveries.

'A basketful of bottles – thick furs – a sunshade – an iron pail.'

All this was uneatable. I felt that my hopes had vanished.... But suddenly she exclaimed vivaciously:

'Aha! here it is!'

'What?'

'Bread... a loaf... it's only wet... take it!'

A loaf flew to my feet and after it herself, my valiant comrade. I had already bitten off a morsel, stuffed it in my mouth, and was chewing it....

'Come, give me some too!... And we mustn't stay here.... Where shall we go?' she looked inquiringly about on all sides.... It was dark, wet, and boisterous.

'Look! there's an upset canoe yonder...let us go there.'

'Let us go then!' And off we set, demolishing out booty as we went, and filling our mouths with large portions of it.... The rain grew more violent, the river roared; from somewhere or other resounded a prolonged mocking whistle – just as if someone great who feared nobody was whistling down all earthly institutions and along with them this horrid autumnal wind and us its heroes. This whistling made my heart throb painfully, in spite of which I greedily went on eating, and in this respect the girl, walking on my left hand, kept even pace with me.

'What do they call you?' I asked her – why I know not.

'Natasha,' she answered shortly, munching loudly.

I stared at her. My heart ached within me; and then I stared into the mist before me, and it seemed to me as if the inimical countenance of my Destiny was smiling at me enigmatically and coldly.

The rain scourged the timbers of the skiff incessantly, and its soft patter induced melancholy thoughts, and the wind whistled as it flew down into the boat's battered bottom through a rift, where some loose splinters of wood were rattling together – a disquieting and depressing sound. The waves of the river were splashing on the shore, and sounded so monotonous and hopeless, just as if they were telling something unbearably dull and heavy, which was boring them into utter disgust, something from which they wanted to run away and yet were obliged to talk about all the same. The sound of the rain blended with their splashing, and a long-drawn sigh seemed to be floating above the overturned skiff – the endless, labouring sigh of the earth, injured and exhausted by the eternal changes from the bright and warm summer to the cold misty and damp autumn. The wind blew continually over the desolate shore and the foaming river – blew and sang its melancholy songs....

Our position beneath the shelter of the skiff was utterly devoid of comfort; it was narrow and damp, tiny cold drops of rain dribbled through the damaged bottom; gusts of wind penetrated it. We sat in silence and shivered with cold. I remembered that I wanted to go to sleep. Natasha leaned her back against the hull of the boat and curled herself up into a tiny ball. Embracing her knees with her hands, and resting her chin upon them, she stared doggedly at the river with wide-open eyes; on the pale patch of her face they seemed immense, because of the blue marks below them. She never moved, and this immobility and silence – I felt it – gradually produced within me a terror of my neighbour. I wanted to talk to her, but I knew not how to begin.

It was she herself, who spoke.

'What a cursed thing life is!' she exclaimed plainly abstractedly, and in a tone of deep conviction.

But this was no complaint. In these words there was too much of indifference for a complaint. This simple soul thought according to her understanding – thought and proceeded to form a certain conclusion which she expressed aloud, and which I could not confute for fear of contradicting myself. Therefore I was silent, and she, as if she had not noticed me, continued to sit there immovable.

'Even if we croaked... what then...?' Natasha began again, this time quietly and reflectively, and still, there was not one note of complaint in her words. It was plain that this person, in the course of her reflections on life, was regarding her own case, and had arrived at the conviction that in order to preserve herself from the mockeries of life, she was not in a position to do anything else but simply 'croak' – to use her own expression.

The clearness of this line of thought was inexpressibly sad and painful to me, and I felt that if I kept silence any longer I was really bound to weep.... And it would have been shameful to have done this before a woman, especially as she was not weeping herself. I resolved to speak to her.

'Who was it that knocked you about?' I asked. For the moment I could not think of anything more sensible or more delicate.

'Pashka did it all,' she answered in a dull and level tone.

'And who is he?'

'My lover.... He was a baker.'

'Did he beat you often?'

'Whenever he was drunk he beat me.... Often!'

And suddenly, turning towards me, she began to talk about herself, Pashka, and their mutual relations. He was a baker with red moustaches and played very well on the banjo. He came to see her and greatly pleased her, for he was a merry chap and wore nice clean clothes. He had a vest which cost fifteen rubles and boots with dress tops. For these reasons she had fallen in love with him, and he became her 'creditor.' And when he became her creditor he made it his business to take away from her the money which her other friends gave to her for bonbons, and, getting drunk on this money, he would fall to beating her; but that would have been nothing if he hadn't also begun to 'run after' other girls before her very eyes.

'Now, wasn't that an insult? I am not worse than the others. Of course that meant that he was laughing at me, the blackguard. The day before yesterday I asked leave of my mistress to go out for a bit, went to him, and there I found Dimka sitting beside him drunk. And he, too, was half seas over. I said, 'You scoundrel, you!' And he gave me a thorough hiding. He kicked me and dragged me by the hair. But that was nothing to what came after. He spoiled everything I had on – left me just as I am now! How could I appear before my mistress? He spoiled everything... my dress and my jacket too – it was quite a new one; I gave a fiver for it... and tore my kerchief from my head.... Oh, Lord! What will become of me now?' she suddenly whined in a lamentable overstrained voice.

The wind howled, and became ever colder and more boisterous.... Again my teeth began to dance up and down, and she, huddled up to avoid the cold, pressed as closely to me as she could, so that I could see the gleam of her eyes through the darkness.

'What wretches all you men are! I'd burn you all in an oven; I'd cut you in pieces. If any one of you was dying I'd spit in his mouth, and not pity him a bit. Mean skunks! You wheedle and wheedle, you wag your tails like cringing dogs, and we fools give ourselves up to you, and it's all up with us! Immediately you trample us underfoot.... Miserable loafers!'

She cursed us up and down, but there was no vigour, no malice, no hatred of these 'miserable loafers' in her cursing that I could hear. The tone of her language by no means corresponded with its subject-matter, for it was calm enough, and the gamut of her voice was terribly poor.

Yet all this made a stronger impression on me than the most eloquent and convincing pessimistic books and speeches, of which I had read a good many and which I still read to this day. And this, you see, was because the agony of a dying person is much more natural and violent than the most minute and picturesque descriptions of death.

I felt really wretched – more from cold than from the words of my neighbour. I groaned softly and ground my teeth.

Almost at the same moment I felt two little arms about me – one of them touched my neck and the other lay upon my face – and at the same time an anxious, gentle, friendly voice uttered the question:

'What ails you?'

I was ready to believe that someone else was asking me this and not Natasha, who had just declared that all men were scoundrels, and expressed a wish for their destruction. But she it was, and now she began speaking quickly, hurriedly.

'What ails you, eh? Are you cold? Are you frozen? Ah, what a one you are, sitting there so silent like a little owl! Why, you should have told me long ago that you were cold. Come...lie on the ground... stretch yourself out and I will lie... there! How's that? Now put your arms round me?... tighter! How's that? You shall be warm very soon now.... And then we'll lie back to back.... The night will pass so quickly, see if it won't. I say... have you too been drinking?... Turned out of your place, eh?... It doesn't matter.'

And she comforted me.... She encouraged me.

May I be thrice accursed! What a world of irony was in this single fact for me! Just imagine! Here was I, seriously occupied at this very time with the destiny of humanity, thinking of the re-organization of the social system, of political revolutions, reading all sorts of devilishly-wise books whose abysmal profundity was certainly unfathomable by their very authors – at this very time. I say, I was trying with all my might to make of myself 'a potent active social force.' It even seemed to me that I had partially accomplished my object; anyhow, at this time, in my ideas about myself, I had got so far as to recognize that I had an exclusive right to exist, that I had the necessary greatness to deserve to live my life, and that I was fully competent to play a great historical part therein. And a woman was now warming me with her body, a wretched, battered, hunted creature, who had no place and no value in life, and whom I had never thought of helping till she helped me herself, and whom I really would not have known how to help in any way even if the thought of it had occurred to me.

Ah! I was ready to think that all this was happening to me in a dream – in a disagreeable, an oppressive dream.

But, ugh! it was impossible for me to think that, for cold drops of rain were dripping down upon me, the woman was pressing close to me, her warm breath was fanning my face, and – despite a slight odour of vodka – it did me good. The wind howled and raged, the rain smote upon the skiff, the waves splashed, and both of us, embracing each other convulsively, nevertheless shivered with cold. All this was only too real, and I am certain that nobody ever dreamed such an oppressive and horrid dream as that reality.

But Natasha was talking all the time of something or other, talking kindly and sympathetically, as only women can talk. Beneath the influence of her voice and kindly words a little fire began to burn up within me, and something inside my heart thawed in consequence.

Then tears poured from my eyes like a hailstorm, washing away from my heart much that was evil, much that was stupid, much sorrow and dirt which had fastened upon it before that night. Natasha comforted me.

'Come, come, that will do, little one! Don't take on! That'll do! God will give you another chance… you will right yourself and stand in your proper place again…and it will be all right.…'

And she kept kissing me… many kisses did she give me… burning kisses… and all for nothing.…

Those were the first kisses from a woman that had ever been bestowed upon me, and they were the best kisses too, for all the subsequent kisses cost me frightfully dear, and really gave me nothing at all in exchange.

'Come, don't take on so, funny one! I'll manage for you to-morrow if you cannot find a place.' Her quiet persuasive whispering sounded in my ears as if it came through a dream.…

There we lay till dawn.…

And when the dawn came, we crept from behind the skiff and went into the town.… Then we took friendly leave of each other and never met again, although for half a year I searched in every hole and corner for that kind Natasha, with whom I spent the autumn night just described.

If she be already dead – and well for her if it were so – may she rest in peace! And if she be alive… still I say 'Peace to her soul!' And may the consciousness of her fall never enter her soul… for that would be a superfluous and fruitless suffering if life is to be lived.…

THE OUTCASTS

(tr. Dora B. Montefiore and Emily Jakowleff)

I

THE HIGH STREET CONSISTS of two rows of one-storeyed hovels, squeezed close one against another; old hovels with leaning walls and crooked windows, with dilapidated roofs, disfigured by time, patched with shingles, and overgrown with moss; here and there above them rise tall poles surmounted with starling houses, whilst the roofs are shaded by the dusty green of pollard willows and elder bushes, the sole miserable vegetation of suburbs where dwell the poorest classes.

The windows of these hovels, their glass stained green with age, seem to watch each other with the shifty, cowardly glance of thieves. Up the middle of the street crawls a winding channel passing between deep holes, washed out by the heavy rain; here and there lie heaps of old, broken bricks and stones overgrown with weeds, the remains of the various attempts made from time to time by the inhabitants to build dwellings; but these attempts have been rendered useless by the torrents of stormwater sweeping down from the town above. On the hill nestle, amongst the luxuriant green of gardens, magnificent stone-built houses; the steeples of churches rise proudly towards the blue heavens, their golden crosses glittering in the sun.

In wet weather the town pours into this outlying suburb all its surface water, and in the dry weather all its dust, and this miserable row of hovels has the appearance of having been swept down at one of these moments by some powerful hand.

Crushed into the ground, these half-rotten human shelters seem to cover all the hill, whilst, stained by the sun, by the dust, and by the rains, they take on them the dirty nondescript colour of old decaying wood.

At the end of this miserable street stood an old, long, two-storeyed house, which seemed to have been cast out in this way from the town, and which had been bought by the merchant Petounnikoff. This was the last house in the row, standing just under the hill, and stretching beyond it were fields, ending at a distance of half a verst from the house in an abrupt fall towards the river. This large and very old house had a more sinister aspect than its neighbours; all its walls were crooked, and in its rows of windows there was not one that had preserved its regular form; whilst the remnants of the window panes were of the dirty green colour of stagnant water.

The spaces between the windows were disfigured with discoloured patches of fallen plaster, as if time had written the history of the house in these hieroglyphics. Its roof, sagging forwards towards the street, increased its pathetic aspect; it seemed as if the house were bowing itself towards the ground, and were humbly waiting for the last stroke of fate to crumble it into dust, or into a deformed heap of half-rotten ruins.

The front gates were ajar. One side, torn from its hinges, lay on the ground, and from the cracks between the boards sprang grass, which also covered the great desolate yard. At the farther end of this yard stood a low, smoke-blackened shed with an iron roof. The house itself was uninhabited, but in this mean shed, which had been a forge, was installed a common lodging-house or doss-house, kept by a retired cavalry officer, Aristide Fomitch Kouvalda.

Inside, this doss-house appeared as a long, dark den, lighted by four square windows and a wide door. The brick unplastered walls were dark with smoke, which had also blackened the ceiling. In the middle stood a large stove, round which, and along the walls, were ranged wooden bunks containing bundles of rubbish which served the dossers for beds. The walls reeked with smoke, the earthen floor with damp, and the bunks with sweat and rotten rags.

The master's bunk was on the stove, and those in its immediate neighbourhood were looked upon as places of honour, and were granted to the inmates who rejoiced in his favour and friendship. The master spent the greater part of the day seated at the door of the shed in a sort of arm-chair, which he had himself constructed of bricks, or else in the beerhouse of Jegor Vaviloff, just across the way, where Aristide dined and drank vodka.

Before starting the lodging-house, Aristide Kouvalda used to keep a servants' registry office in the town; and glancing farther back into his life, we should find he had had a printing establishment; and before the printing business, according to his own account, he lived – and 'lived, devil take it, well; lived as a connoisseur, I can assure you!'

He was a broad-shouldered man of about fifty, with a pock-marked face, bloated with drink, and a bushy, yellow beard. His eyes were grey, large, audaciously gay; he spoke with a bass voice, and almost always held between his teeth a German china pipe with a curved stem. When he was angry the nostrils of his red crooked nose would dilate wide, and his lips would quiver, showing two rows of large yellow teeth like those of a wolf. Long-handed and bow-legged, he dressed always in an old dirty military overcoat and a greasy cap with a red band, but without a peak; and in worn felt boots reaching to his knees. In the morning he was always in a state of drunken stupor, and in the evening he became lively. Drunk he never could be; for however much liquor he stowed away, he never lost his gay humour.

In the evening he might be seen seated in his brick arm-chair, his pipe between his teeth, receiving his lodgers.

'Who are you?' he would ask, on the approach of some ragged, depressed-looking individual, who had been turned out of the town for drunkenness or for some other reason.

The man would reply.

'Show me your papers, to prove that you are not lying!'

The papers were shown, if there were any forthcoming. The master would push them into his shirt, not caring to look at their contents.

'All right! For one night two kopecks; a week, ten kopecks; a month, twenty kopecks; go and take your place, but mind not to take anyone else's, or you will catch it. The people who live here are particular.'

The new-comer would ask him, 'Can one get tea, bread, and grub? Don't you sell them?'

'I sell only walls and roof, for which I pay the rogue Petounnikoff, the owner of this hole, five roubles a month,' Kouvalda would explain in a business-like tone. 'People who come to me are not used to luxury, and if you are in the habit of guzzling every day, there's a beershop just opposite. But you'd better get out of that bad habit as soon as possible, you skulker; you are not a gentleman born, then why do you want to eat? You had better eat yourself!'

For these and like speeches, uttered in a pretended severe voice, but always with a laugh in his eyes, and for his attention to his lodgers, Kouvalda was very popular among the outcasts of the town.

It sometimes happened that a former client would come into the doss-house, no longer ragged and down-trodden, but in more or less decent clothes, and with a cheerful face.

'Good-day, your honour; how are you?'

'All right; quite well; what do you want?'

'Don't you recognize me?'

'No, I don't.'

'Don't you remember last winter I spent a month with you, when you had a police raid and three were taken up?'

'Oh, my good fellow, the police often come under my hospitable roof!'

'And, good Lord! don't you remember how you cheeked the police officer?'

'Well, that will do with recollections; just say simply what you want.'

'Let me stand you something. When I lived with you, you were so' –

'Gratitude should be always encouraged, my friend, for we seldom meet with it. You must be a really good fellow, though I can't remember you; but I'll accompany you to the vodka shop with pleasure, and drink to your success in life.'

'Ah! you're always the same – always joking.'

'Well, what else can one do when one lives among a miserable set like you?'

Then they would go off, and often the former lodger would return staggering to the doss-house. Next day the entertainment would begin anew; and one fine morning the lodger would come to his senses, to find that he had drunk away all that he possessed.

'See, your honour! Once more I am one of your crew; what am I to do now?'

'Well, it's a position you can't boast about, but being in it, it's no use crying,' argued the captain. 'You must look at your position with equanimity, my friend, and not spoil life with philosophizing and reasoning. Philosophy is always useless, and to philosophize before the drink is out of one is inexpressibly foolish. When you are getting over a bout of drinking you want vodka, and not remorse and grinding of teeth. You must take care of your teeth, otherwise there will be none to knock out. Here are twenty kopecks; go and bring some vodka and a piece of hot tripe or lights, a pound of bread, and two cucumbers. When we get over our drink then we'll think over the state of affairs.'

The state of affairs would become clear in two or three days, when the master had nothing more left of the four or five roubles which had found their way into his pocket on the day of the return of the grateful lodger.

'Here we are, at the end of our tether!' the captain would say. 'Now, you fool, that we have drunk all we had, let us try to walk in the paths of sobriety and of virtue. As it is, how true is the saying, 'If one hasn't sinned, one can't repent; and if one hasn't repented, one can't be saved!' The first commandment we have fulfilled; but repentance is of no use, so let's go straight for salvation. Be off to the river and start work. If you are not sure of yourself, tell the contractor to keep your money back, or else give it to me to keep. When we've saved a good sum I'll buy you some breeches and what is necessary to make you look like a decent, tidy, working man persecuted by fate. In good breeches you will still stand a good chance. Now be off with you!'

The lodger went off to work on the towpath, down by the river, smiling to himself at the long, wise speeches of Kouvalda. The pith of the wisdom he did not understand, but watching the merry eyes, and feeling the influence of the cheerful spirit, he knew that in the discursive captain he had a friend who would always help him in case of need.

And, indeed, after a month or two of hard work, the lodger, thanks to the strict supervision of the captain, found himself in a pecuniary position which enabled him to rise a step above that condition into which he had fallen, thanks also to the kind assistance of the same captain.

'Well, my friend,' Kouvalda would say, critically inspecting his renovated acquaintance, 'here you are now with breeches and a coat. These matters are very important, believe me. As long as I had decent breeches I lived as a decent man in the town; but, damn it all! as soon as these fell to pieces, I fell also

in the estimation of mankind, and I had to leave the town and
come out here. People, you fool, judge by the outer appearance
only; the inner meaning is inaccessible to them, because of their
innate stupidity. Put that into your pipe and smoke it. – Pay
me half your debt if you like, and go in peace. Seek and you
will find.'

'How much, Aristide Fomitch, do I owe you?' the lodger would
ask confusedly.

'One rouble and seventy. You may give me the rouble or the
seventy kopecks, whichever you like now; and for the rest I'll
wait for the time when you can steal or earn more than you have
now.'

'Many thanks for your kindness,' replied the lodger, touched
by such consideration. 'You are – well, you are – such a good
soul; it's a pity that life has been so hard on you. You must have
been a proud sort of eagle when you were in your right place.'

The captain could not get on without grandiloquent phrases.
'What do you mean by being in my right place? Who knows
what his right place should be? Everyone wants to put his neck
into someone else's yoke. Judah Petounnikoff's place should be
in penal servitude, but he walks freely about the town, and is
even going to build a new factory. Our schoolmaster's place should
be by the side of a nice, fat, quiet wife, with half a dozen children
round him, instead of lying about drunk in Vaviloff's vodka shop.
Then there's yourself, who are going to look for a place as a
waiter or porter, whereas I know you ought to be a soldier. You
can endure much, you are not stupid, and you understand
discipline. See how the matter stands! Life shuffles us up like
cards, and it's only now and then we fall into our right places;
but when that does happen, it's not for long; we are soon shuffled
out again.'

Sometimes such farewell speeches would serve only as a preface
to a renewed friendship, which would start with a fresh booze,
and would end with the lodger being surprised to find that he

had nothing left, when the captain would again treat him, till both were in the same state of destitution.

These backslidings never spoilt the good understanding on either side. The aforementioned schoolmaster was amongst those friends who only got put on his feet in order to be knocked over again. He was intellectually the most on a level with the captain, and this was perhaps just the reason that, once having fallen to the doss-house, he could never rise again.

He was the only one with whom Aristide Kouvalda could philosophize, and be sure that he was understood. He appreciated the schoolmaster for this reason, and when his renovated friend was about to leave the doss-house, having again earned some money with the intention of taking a decent room in town, Aristide Kouvalda would begin such a string of melancholy tirades, that both would recommence drinking, and once more would lose all. In all probability Kouvalda was conscious of what he was doing, and the schoolmaster, much as he desired it, could never get away from the doss-house. Could Aristide Kouvalda, a gentleman by birth, and having received an education, the remnants of which still flashed through his conversation, along with a love of argument acquired during the vicissitudes of fortune – could he help desiring to keep by his side a kindred spirit? It is always ourselves we pity first. This schoolmaster once upon a time used to give lessons in a training school for teachers in a town on the Volga, but as the result of some trouble he was expelled; after that he became a clerk at a tanner's, and was forced, after a time, to leave that place as well; then he became a librarian in a private library, tried various other professions, and at length, having passed an attorney's examination, he began drinking, and came across the captain. He was a bald-headed man, with a stoop, and a sharp-pointed nose. In a thin, yellow face, with a pointed beard, glittered restless, sad, deep-sunk eyes, and the corners of his mouth were drawn down, giving him a depressed expression. His livelihood, or rather the means to get drunk, he earned by being a reporter on the local newspapers. Sometimes he would earn as much as fifteen roubles a week; these he would give to the captain, saying, 'This is the last of it! Another week of hard work, and I shall get enough to be decently dressed, and then – *addio, mio caro!*'

'That's all right; you have my hearty approbation. I won't give you another glass of vodka the whole week,' the captain would reply severely.

'I shall be very grateful. You must not give me a single drop.'

The captain heard in these words something approaching very near to a humble appeal, and would add still more severely, 'You may shout for it, but I won't give you any more.'

'Well, that's an end of it,' the teacher would sigh, and go off to his work. But in a day or two, feeling exhausted, fatigued, and thirsty, he would look furtively at the captain, with sad, imploring eyes, hoping anxiously that his friend's heart would melt. The captain would keep a severe face, uttering speeches full of the disgrace of weak natures, of the bestial pleasures of drunkenness, and other words applicable to the circumstances. To give him his due, it is right to add that he was sincere in his rôle of mentor and of moralist, but the patrons of his doss-house always inclined to be sceptical, and while listening to the scathing words of the captain, would say to each other with a wink, 'He's a sly one for knowing how to get rid of all responsibility himself! "I told you so; but you wouldn't listen to me; now blame yourself."'

'The gentleman is an old soldier; he doesn't advance without preparing a retreat.'

The schoolmaster would catch his friend in a dark corner, and holding him by his dirty cloak, trembling and moistening his parched lips with his tongue, would look into the captain's eyes with an expression so deeply tragic that no words could describe it.

'Can't you?' the captain would question sombrely.

The schoolmaster would silently nod, and then drop his head on his chest, trembling through all his long, thin body.

'Try one more day; perhaps you will conquer yourself,' proposed Kouvalda.

The schoolmaster would sigh and shake his head in a hopeless negative. When the captain saw that his friend's lean body was shaken with the thirst for poison, he would take the money out of his pocket.

'It's generally useless to argue with fate,' he would say, as if wishing to justify himself.

But if the schoolmaster held out the whole week, the farewell of the friends terminated in a touching scene, the end of which generally took place in Vaviloff's vodka shop.

The schoolmaster never drank all his money; at least half of it he spent on the children of the High Street. Poor people are always rich in children, and in the dust and ditches in this street might be seen from morning till night groups of torn, hungry, noisy youngsters. Children are the living flowers of the earth, but in the High Street they were like flowers faded before their time; probably because they grew on soil poor in nourishing qualities.

Sometimes the schoolmaster would gather the children round him, buy a quantity of bread, eggs, apples, nuts, and go with them into the fields towards the river. There they would greedily eat up all he had to offer them, filling the air around with merry noise and laughter. The lank, thin figure of the drunkard seemed to shrivel up and grow small like the little ones round him, who treated him with complete familiarity, as if he were one of their own age. They called him 'Philippe,' not adding even the title of 'uncle.' They jumped around him like eels, they pushed him, got on his back, slapped his bald head, and pulled his nose. He probably liked it, for he never protested against these liberties being taken. He spoke very little to them, and his words were humble and timid, as if he were afraid that his voice might soil or hurt them. He spent many hours with them, sometimes as plaything, and at other times as playmate. He used to look into their bright faces with sad eyes, and would then slowly and thoughtfully slink off into Vaviloff's vodka shop, where he would drink till he lost consciousness.

Almost every day when he returned from his reporting, the schoolmaster would bring back a paper from the town, and the outcasts would form a circle round him. As soon as they saw him coming, they would gather from the different corners of the yard, some drunk, some in a state of stupor, all in different stages of raggedness, but all equally miserable and dirty.

First would appear Alexai Maximovitch Simtzoff, round as a barrel; formerly a surveyor of forest lands, but now a pedlar of matches, ink, blacking, and bad lemons. He was an old man of sixty, in a canvas coat and a broad-brimmed crushed hat, which covered his fat red face, with its thick white beard, out of which peeped forth a small red nose, and thick lips of the same colour, and weak, running, cynical eyes. They called him 'Kubar,' a top, and this nickname well portrayed his round, slowly moving figure and his thick, humming speech.

Louka Antonovitch Martianoff, nicknamed Konetz, 'The End,' would come out of some corner, a morose, black, silent drunkard, formerly an inspector of a prison; a man who gained his livelihood at present by playing games of hazard, such as the three-card trick and thimble-rig, and by the display of other talents equally ingenious, but equally unappreciated by the police. He would drop his heavy, often ill-treated, body on the grass beside the schoolmaster, his black eyes glistening, and stretching forth his hand to the bottle, would ask in a hoarse bass voice –

'May I?'

Then also would draw near the mechanic Pavel Sontseff, a consumptive of about thirty. The ribs on his left side had been broken in a street row; and his face, yellow and sharp, was constantly twisted into a cunning, wicked smile. His thin lips showed two rows of black, decayed teeth, and the rags on his thin shoulders seemed to be hanging on a peg. They used to call him 'Scraps'; he earned his living by selling brooms of his own making, and brushes made of a certain kind of grass, which were very useful for brushing clothes.

Besides these, there was a tall, bony, one-eyed man with uncertain antecedents; he had a scared expression in his large, round, silent, and timid eyes. He had been three times condemned for thefts, and had suffered imprisonment for them. His name was Kisselnikoff, but he was nicknamed 'Tarass and a half' because he was just half the size again of his inseparable friend Tarass, a former church deacon, but degraded now for drunkenness and dissipation. The deacon was a short, robust little man with a broad chest and a round, matted head of hair; he was famous for his dancing, but more so for his swearing; both he and 'Tarass and a half' chose as their special work wood-sawing on the river-bank, and in their leisure hours the deacon would tell long stories 'of his own composition,' as he expressed it, to his friend or to anyone who cared to hear them. Whilst listening to these stories, the heroes of which were always saints, kings, clergy, and generals, even the habitués of the doss-house used to spit the taste of them out of their mouths, and opened wide eyes of astonishment at the wonderful imagination of the deacon, who would relate these shameless, obscene, fantastic adventures with great coolness, and with eyes closed in rapture. The imagination of this man was powerful and inexhaustible; he could invent and talk the whole day long, and never repeated himself. In him the world lost perhaps a great poet, and certainly a remarkable story-teller, who could put life and soul even into stones, by his foul but imaginatively powerful thought.

Besides these there was an absurd youth, who was called by Kouvalda 'The Meteor.' He once came to seek a night's lodging, and to the astonishment of all he never left. At first no one noticed him, for during the day he would go out to earn a livelihood, as did the rest, but in the evening he stuck closely to the friendly doss-house society. One day the captain asked him –

'My lad, what do you do in this world?'

The boy answered shortly and boldly, 'I? I'm a tramp.'

The captain looked at him critically. The lad had long hair, a broad, foolish face adorned with a snub nose; he wore a blue blouse without a belt, and on his head were the remains of a straw hat. His feet were bare.

'You are a fool!' said Aristide Kouvalda. 'What are you doing here? You are of no use to us. Do you drink vodka? No! And can you steal? Not that either? Well, go and learn all that, and make a man of yourself, and then come back.'

The lad smiled. 'No, I shan't; I'll stay where I am!'

'Why?'

'Because' –

'Ah! you're a meteor!' said the captain.

'Let me knock some of his teeth out,' proposed Martianoff.

'But why?' asked the lad.

'Because' –

'Well, then, I should take a stone and knock you on the head,' replied the boy respectfully.

Martianoff would have thrashed him if Kouvalda had not interfered. 'Leave him alone; he is distantly related to you, brother, as he is to all of us. You, without sufficient reason, want to knock his teeth out; and he, also without sufficient reason, wants to live with us. Well, damn it all! We all have to live without sufficient reason for doing so. We live, but ask us why; we can't say. Well, it's so with him, so let him be.'

'But still, young man, you had better leave us,' the schoolmaster intervened, surveying the lad with sad eyes.

The lad did not answer, but remained. At last they grew accustomed to him, and paid no attention to him, but he watched closely all that they said and did.

All the above-mentioned individuals formed the captain's bodyguard, and with good-natured irony he used to call them his 'Outcasts.' Besides these, there were five or six tramp rank-and-file in the doss-house; these were country-folk who could not boast of such antecedents as the outcasts, though they had undergone no less vicissitudes of fate; but they were a degree less degraded, and not so completely broken down. It may be that a decent man from the educated classes in town is somewhat above a decent peasant; but it is inevitable that a vicious townsman should be immeasurably more degraded in mind than a criminal from the country. This rule was strikingly illustrated by the inhabitants of Kouvalda's dwelling.

The most prominent peasant representative was a rag-picker of the name of Tiapa. Tall, and horribly thin, he constantly carried his head so that his chin fell on his breast, and from this position his shadow always assumed the shape of a hook.

One could never see his full face, but his profile showed an aquiline nose, projecting underlip, and bushy grey eyebrows. He was the captain's first lodger, and it was rumoured that he possessed large sums of money hidden somewhere about him. It was for this money that two years ago he had had his throat cut, since when he had been forced to keep his head so strangely bent. He denied having any money, and said that he had been struck with a knife for fun; and this accident had made it convenient for him to become a rag and bone picker, as his head was always necessarily bent forward towards the ground. When he walked about with his swaying, uncertain gait, and without his stick and bag, the badges of his profession, he seemed a being absorbed with his own thoughts, and Kouvalda, pointing at him with his finger, would say, 'Look out! there is the escaped conscience of Judah Petounnikoff, seeking for a refuge! See how ragged and dirty this fugitive conscience looks!'

Tiapa spoke with such a hoarse voice that it was almost impossible to understand him, and that was perhaps why he spoke little, and always sought solitude. Each time, when a new-comer, driven from the village, arrived at the doss-house, Tiapa at sight of him would fall into a state of angry irritation and restlessness.

He would persecute the miserable being with sharp, mocking words, which issued from his throat in an angry hiss; and he would set on him one of the most savage amongst the tramps, and finally threaten to beat and rob him himself in the night. He nearly always succeeded in driving out the terrified and disconcerted peasant, who never returned.

When Tiapa was somewhat appeased, he would hide himself in a corner to mend his old clothes or to read in a Bible, as old, as torn, as dirty as himself. Tiapa would come out of his corner when the schoolmaster brought the newspaper to read. Generally Tiapa listened silently to the news, sighed deeply, but never asked any questions. When the schoolmaster closed the newspaper, Tiapa would stretch out his bony hand and say –

'Give it here.'

'What do you want it for?'

'Give it; perhaps there is something written concerning us.'

'Concerning whom?'

'The village.'

They laughed at him, and threw the paper at him. He would take it and read those parts which told of corn beaten down by the hail; of thirty holdings being destroyed by fire, and of a woman poisoning a whole family; in fact, all those parts about village life which showed it as miserable, sordid, and cruel. Tiapa read all these in a dull voice, and emitted sounds which might be interpreted as expressing either pity or pleasure. On Sunday he never went out rag-picking, but spent most of his day reading his Bible, during which process he moaned and sighed. His book he always held resting on his chest, and he was angry if anyone touched it or interrupted his reading.

'Hullo, you magician!' Kouvalda would say; 'you don't understand anything of that; leave the book alone!'

'And you? What do you understand?'

'Well, old magician, I don't understand anything; but then I don't read books.'

'But I do.'

'More fool you!' answered the captain. 'It's bad enough to have vermin in the head. But to get thoughts into the bargain. How will you ever be able to live, you old toad?'

'Well, I have not got much longer to live,' said Tiapa quietly.

One day the schoolmaster inquired where he had learned to read, and Tiapa answered shortly –

'In prison.'

'Have you been there?'

'Yes, I have.'

'For what?'

'Because – I made a mistake. It was there I got my Bible. A lady gave it me. It's good in prison, don't you know that, brother?'

'It can't be. What is there good in it?'

'They teach one there. You see how I was taught to read. They gave me a book, and all that free!'

When the schoolmaster came to the doss-house, Tiapa had been there already a long time. He watched the schoolmaster constantly; he would bend his body on one side in order to get a good look at him, and would listen attentively to his conversation.

Once he began, 'Well, I see you are a learned man. Have you ever read the Bible?'

'Yes, I have.'

'Well, do you remember it?'

'I do! What then?'

The old man bent his whole body on one side and looked at the schoolmaster with grey, morose, distrustful eyes.

'And do you remember anything about the Amalekites?'

'Well, what then?'

'Where are they now?'

'They have died out, Tiapa – disappeared.'

The old man was silent, but soon he asked again –

'And the Philistines?'

'They've gone also.'

'Have they all disappeared?'

'Yes, all.'

'Does that mean that we shall also disappear as well?'

'Yes, when the time comes,' the schoolmaster replied, in an indifferent tone of voice.

'And to which tribe of Israel do we belong?'

The schoolmaster looked at him steadily, thought for a moment, and began telling him about the Cymri, the Scythians, the Huns, and the Slavs.

The old man seemed to bend more than ever on one side, and watched the schoolmaster with scared eyes.

'You are telling lies!' he hissed out, when the schoolmaster had finished.

'Why do you think I am lying?' asked the astonished schoolmaster.

'Those people you have spoken of, none of them are in the Bible!' He rose and went out, deeply insulted, and cursing angrily.

'You are going mad, Tiapa!' cried the schoolmaster after him.

Then the old man turned round, and stretching out his hand shook with a threatening action his dirty, crooked forefinger.

'Adam came from the Lord. The Jews came from Adam. And all people come from the Jews – we amongst them.'

'Well?'

'The Tartars came from Ishmael. And he came from a Jew!'

'Well, what then?'

'Nothing. Only why do you tell lies?'

And he went off, leaving his companion in a state of bewilderment. But in two or three days' time he approached him again.

'As you are a learned man, you ought at least to know who we are!'

'Slavs, Tiapa – Slavs!' replied the schoolmaster.

And he awaited with interest Tiapa's answer, hoping to understand him.

'Speak according to the Bible! There are no names like that in the Bible. Who are we, Babylonians or Edomites?'

The teacher began criticizing the Bible. The old man listened long and attentively, and finally interrupted him.

'Stop all that! Do you mean that among all the people known to God there were no Russians? We were unknown to God? Is that what you mean to say? Those people, written about in the Bible, God knew them all. He used to punish them with fire and sword; He destroyed their towns and villages, but still He sent them His prophets to teach them, which meant He loved them. He dispersed the Jews and Tartars, but He still preserved them. And what about us? Why have we no prophets?'

'Well, I don't know,' said the schoolmaster, trying in vain to understand the old man.

The old peasant put his hand on the schoolmaster's shoulder, rocking him gently to and fro whilst he hissed and gurgled as if swallowing something, and muttered in a hoarse voice –

'You should have said so long ago. And you went on talking as if you knew everything. It makes me sick to hear you. It troubles my soul. You'd better hold your tongue. See, you don't even know why we have no prophets. You don't know where we were when Jesus was on earth. And such lies too. Can a whole people die out? The Russian nation can't disappear; it's all lies. They are mentioned somewhere in the Bible, only I don't know under what name. Don't you know what a nation means? It is immense. See how many villages there are! And in each village look at the number of people; and you say they will die out. A people cannot die out, but a person can. A people is necessary to God, for they till the soil. The Amalekites have not died out; they are the French or the Germans. And see what you have been telling me. You ought to know why we don't possess God's favour; He never sends us now either plagues or prophets. So how *can* we be taught now?'

Tiapa's speech was terribly powerful. It was penetrated with irony, reproach, and fervent faith. He spoke for a long time, and the schoolmaster, who was as usual half drunk, and in a peaceful frame of mind, got tired of listening. He felt as if his nerves were being sawn with a wooden saw. He was watching the distorted body of the old man, and feeling the strange oppressive strength in his words. Finally he fell to pitying himself, and from that passed into a sad, wearied mood. He also wanted to say something forcible to old Tiapa, something positive, that might win the old man's favour, and change his reproachful, morose tone into one that was soft and fatherly. The schoolmaster felt as if words were rising to his lips, but could not find any strong enough to express his thought.

'Ah! You are a lost man,' said Tiapa. 'Your soul is torn, and yet you speak all sorts of empty fine words. You'd better be silent!'

'Ah, Tiapa!' sadly exclaimed the schoolmaster, 'all that you say is true. And about the people also. The mass of the people is immense! But I am a stranger to it, and it is a stranger to me. There lies the tragedy of my life! But what's to be done? I must go on suffering. Indeed there are no prophets; no, not any. And it's true I talk too much and to no purpose. I had better hold my tongue. But you mustn't be so hard on me. Ah, old man, you don't know! You don't know. You can't understand.'

Finally the schoolmaster burst into tears; he cried so easily and freely, with such abundant tears, that afterwards he felt quite relieved.

'You should go into the country; you should get a place as schoolmaster or as clerk. You would be comfortable there, and have a change of air. What's the use of leading this miserable life here?' Tiapa hissed morosely.

But the schoolmaster continued to weep, enjoying his tears.

From that time forth they became friends, and the outcasts, seeing them together, would say –

'The schoolmaster is making up to old Tiapa; he is trying to get at his money.'

'It's Kouvalda who has put him up to trying to find out where the old man's hoard is.'

It is very possible that their words were not in agreement with their thoughts; for these people had one strange trait in common – they liked to appear to each other worse than they really were.

The man who has nothing good in him likes sometimes to show himself in the worst light.

When all of them were gathered round the schoolmaster with his newspaper, the reading would begin.

'Now,' would say the captain, 'what does the paper offer us to-day? Is there a serial story coming out in it?'

'No,' the schoolmaster would reply.

'Your editor is mean. Is there a leading article?'

'Yes, there is one to-day. I think it is by Gouliaff.'

'Give us a taste of it! The fellow writes well. He's a cute one, he is!'

'The valuation of real estate,' reads the schoolmaster, 'which took place more than fifteen years ago, continues still to form a basis for present-day rating, to the great advantage of the town.'

'The rogues!' interjects Captain Kouvalda.

'"Still continues to form!" It's indeed absurd! It's to the advantage of the merchants who manage the affairs of the town that it should continue to form the basis, and that's why it does continue!'

'Well, the article is written with that idea,' says the school-master.

'Ah! is it? How strange! It would be a good theme for the serial story, where it could be given a spicy flavour!'

A short dispute arises. The company still listens attentively, for they are at their first bottle of vodka. After the leading article they take the local news. After that they attack the police news, and law cases. If in these a merchant is the sufferer, Aristide Kouvalda rejoices. If a merchant is robbed, all is well; it is only a pity they did not take more. If his horses ran away with him and smashed him up, it was pleasant to listen to, and only a pity that the fellow escaped alive. If a shopkeeper lost a lawsuit, that was a good hearing; the sad point was that he was not made to pay the expenses twice over.

'That would have been illegal,' remarks the schoolmaster.

'Illegal?' Kouvalda exclaims hotly. 'But does a shopkeeper himself act always according to the law? What is a shopkeeper? Let us examine this vulgar, absurd creature. To begin with, every shopkeeper is a moujik. He comes from the country, and after a certain time he takes a shop and begins to trade. To keep a shop one must have money, and where can a moujik or peasant get money? As everyone knows, money is not earned by honest labour. It means that the peasant by some means or other has cheated. It means that a shopkeeper is a dishonest peasant!'

'That's clever!' The audience shows its approbation of the orator's reasoning.

Tiapa groans and rubs his chest; the sound is like that which he makes after swallowing his first glass of vodka.

The captain is buoyant. They now begin reading provincial correspondence. Here the captain is in his own sphere, as he expresses it. Here it is apparent how shamefully the shopkeeper lives, and how he destroys and disfigures life. Kouvalda's speech thunders round the shopkeeper, and annihilates him. He is listened to with pleasure, for he uses violent words.

'Oh, if I could only write in newspapers!' he exclaims, 'I'd show the shopkeeper up in his right colours! I'd show he was only an animal who was temporarily performing the duties of man. I can see through him very well! I know him. He's a coarse fool with no taste for life, who has no notion of patriotism, and understands nothing beyond kopecks!'

'Scraps,' knowing the weak side of the captain, and delighting in arousing anger, would interpose –

'Yes, since the gentry are dying out from hunger, there is no one of any account left in the world.'

'You are right, you son of a spider and of a frog! Since the gentry have gone under no one is left. There are nothing but shopkeepers, and I hate them!'

'That's easy to see; for have they not trodden you under foot?'

'What's that to me? I came down in the world through my love of life, while the shopkeeper does not understand living. That's just why I hate him so, and not because I am a gentleman. But just take this as said, that I'm no longer a gentleman, but just simply an outcast, the shadow only of my former self. I spit at all and everything, and life for me is like a mistress who has deserted me. That is why I despise it, and am perfectly indifferent towards it.'

'All lies!' says 'Scraps.'

'Am I a liar?' roars Aristide Kouvalda, red with anger.

'Why roar like that?' says Martianoff's bass voice, coolly and gloomily. 'What's the use of arguing? Shopkeeper or gentleman, what does it matter to us?'

'That's just it, for we are neither fish, nor fowl, nor good red herring,' interposes Deacon Tarass.

'Leave him in peace, "Scraps,"' says the schoolmaster pacifically. 'What's the use of throwing oil on the fire?'

The schoolmaster did not like quarrels and noise. When passions grew hot around him his lips twitched painfully, and he unobtrusively tried to make peace; not succeeding in which, he would leave the company to themselves. The captain knew this well, and if he was not very drunk he restrained himself, not wishing to lose the best auditor of his brilliant speeches.

'I repeat,' he continued now, with more restraint – 'I repeat, that I see that life is in the hands of foes, not only of foes of the nobility, but foes of all that is noble; of greedy, ignorant people, who won't do anything to improve the conditions of life. Still,' argues the schoolmaster, 'merchants created Genoa, Venice,

Holland. It was the merchants, the merchants of England who won India. It was the merchants Stroganoff's' –

'What have I to do with those merchants? I am speaking of Judah Petounnikoff and his kind, with whom I have to do.'

'And what have you to do with these?' asked the schoolmaster softly.

'Well, I'm alive. I'm in the world. I can't help being indignant at the thought of these savages, who have got hold of life, and who are doing their best to spoil it!'

'And who are laughing at the noble indignation of a captain and an outcast!' interjects 'Scraps' provokingly.

'It's stupid, very stupid! I agree with you. As an outcast I must destroy all the feelings and thoughts that were once in me. That's perhaps true; but how shall we arm ourselves, you and I, if we throw on one side these feelings?'

'Now you are beginning to speak reasonably,' says the schoolmaster encouragingly.

'We want something different. New ways of looking at life, new feelings, something fresh, for we ourselves are a new phase in life.'

'Yes, indeed, that's what we want,' says the schoolmaster.

'What's the use of discussing and thinking?' inquires 'The End'; 'we haven't got long to live; I'm forty, you are fifty. There is no one under thirty among us. And even if one were twenty, one could not live very long in such surroundings as these.'

'And then again, what new phase are we? Tramps, it seems to we, have always existed in the world,' says 'Scraps' satirically.

'Tramps created Rome,' says the schoolmaster.

'Yes; that was so!' said the captain jubilantly. 'Romulus and Remus, were they not tramps? And we – when our time comes – we shall also create.'

'A breach of the peace!' interjects 'Scraps,' and laughs, pleased with his own wit.

His laugh is wicked, and jars on the nerves. He is echoed by Simtzoff, by the deacon, and by 'Tarass and a half.' The naïve eyes of the lad 'Meteor' burn with a bright glow, and his cheeks flush red. 'The End' mutters, in tones that fall like a hammer on the heads of the audience –

'All that's trash and nonsense, and dreams!'

It was strange to hear these people, outcasts from life, ragged, saturated with vodka, anger, irony, and filth, discussing life in this way.

For the captain such discussions were a feast. He spoke more than the others, and that gave him a chance of feeling his superiority. For however low a person may fall, he can never refuse himself the delight of feeling stronger and better off than the rest. Aristide Kouvalda abused this sensation, and never seemed to have enough of it, much to the disgust of 'Scraps,' 'The Top,' and the other outcasts, little interested in similar questions. Politics was with them the favourite topic. A discussion on the necessity of conquering India, and of checking England, would continue endlessly. The question as to the best means of sweeping the Jews off the face of the earth, was no less hotly debated. In this latter question the leader was always 'Scraps,' who invented marvellously cruel projects; but the captain, who liked always to be first in a discussion, evaded this topic. Women were always willingly and constantly discussed, but with unpleasant allusions; and the schoolmaster always appeared as women's champion, and grew angry when the expressions used by the others were of too strong a nature. They gave in to him, for they looked upon him as a superior being, and on Saturdays they would borrow money from him, which he had earned during the week.

He enjoyed besides many privileges. For instance, he was never knocked about on the frequent occasions when the discussions finished in a general row. He was allowed to bring women into the doss-house; and no one else enjoyed this right, for the captain always warned his clients –

'I'll have no women here! Women, shopkeepers, and philosophy have been the three causes of my ruin. I'll knock down anyone I see with a woman, and I'll knock the woman down as well. On principle, I would twist the neck of' –

He could have twisted anyone's neck, for in spite of his years he possessed wonderful strength. Besides, whenever he had a fighting job on, he was always helped by Martianoff. Gloomy and silent as the tomb in the usual way, yet on these occasions, when there was a general row on, he would stand back to back with Kouvaloff, these two forming together a destructive but indestructible engine. If Kouvalda was engaged in a hand-to-hand fight, 'The End' would creep up and throw his opponent on the ground.

Once when Simtzoff was drunk, he, without any reason, caught hold of the schoolmaster's hair and pulled a handful out. Kouvalda, with one blow of his fist, dropped Simtzoff unconscious, and he lay where he fell for half an hour. When the fellow came to his senses he was made to swallow the schoolmaster's hair, which he did for fear of being beaten to death.

Besides the reading of the newspaper, discussions, and laughter, the other amusement was card-playing. They always left Martianoff out, for he could not play honestly. After being several times caught cheating, he candidly confessed –

'I can't help cheating; it's a habit of mine.'

'Such things do happen,' corroborated Deacon Tarass. 'I used to have the habit of beating my wife every Sunday after mass; and, would you believe it, after she died I had such a gnawing feeling come over me every Sunday I can scarcely describe it. I got over one Sunday, but things seemed to go all wrong. Another Sunday passed, and I felt very bad. The third Sunday I could not bear it any longer, and struck the servant girl. She kicked up a row, and threatened to take me before a magistrate. Just imagine my position! When the fourth Sunday came I knocked her about as I used to do my wife; I paid her ten roubles down, and arranged that I should beat her as a matter of course until I married again.'

'Deacon, you are telling lies! How could you marry again?' broke in 'Scraps.'

'Well – I – she – we did without the ceremony. She kept house for me.'

'Had you any children?' asked the schoolmaster.

'Yes, five of them. One got drowned – the eldest. He was a queer boy. Two died of diphtheria. One daughter married a student, and followed him to Siberia. The other wanted to study in Petersburg, and died there; I am told it was consumption. Yes, five of them. We clergy are very prolific.'

And he began giving reasons for this, causing by his explanations Homeric laughter. When they were tired of laughing, Alexai Maximovitch Simtzoff remembered that he also had a daughter.

'She was called Lidka. Oh, how fat she was!' Probably he remembered nothing more, for he looked round deprecatingly, smiled, and found nothing more to say.

These people spoke but little of their past. They seldom recalled it, and if ever they did so, it was in general terms, and in a more or less scoffing tone. Perhaps they were right in treating their past slightingly, for recollections with most people have a tendency to weaken present energy, and destroy hope in the future.

On rainy days, and during dark, cold, autumn weather, these outcasts would gather in Vaviloff's vodka shop. They were habitués there, and were feared as a set of thieves and bullies; on one hand they were despised as confirmed drunkards, and on the other hand they were respected and listened to as superior people. Vaviloff's vodka shop was the club of the neighbourhood, and the outcasts were the intellectuals of the club.

On Saturday evenings, and on Sundays from early morning till night, the vodka shop was full of people, and the outcasts were welcome guests. They brought with them, amongst these inhabitants of the High Street, oppressed as they were by poverty and misery, a rollicking humour, in which there was something that seemed to brighten these lives, broken and worn out in the struggle for bread. The outcasts' art of talking jestingly on every subject, their fearlessness of opinion, their careless audacity of expression, their absence of fear of everything which the neighbourhood feared, their boldness, their dare-devilry – all this did not fail to please. Besides, almost all of them knew something of law, could give advice on many matters, could write a petition, or could give a helping hand in a shady transaction without getting into trouble. They were paid in vodka, and in flattering encomiums on their various talents.

According to their sympathies, the street was divided into two nearly equal parties. One considered that the captain was very superior to the schoolmaster: 'A real hero! His pluck and his intelligence are far greater!' The other considered that the schoolmaster outbalanced Kouvalda in every respect. The admirers of Kouvalda were those who were known in the street as confirmed drunkards, thieves, and scapegraces, who feared neither poverty nor prison. The schoolmaster was admired by those who were more decent, who were always hoping for something, always expecting something, and yet whose bellies were always empty.

The respective merits of Kouvalda and the schoolmaster may be judged of by the following example. Once in the vodka shop they were discussing the town regulations under which the inhabitants of the neighbourhood were bound to fill up the ruts and holes in the streets; the dead bodies of animals and manure were not to be used for this purpose, but rubble and broken bricks from buildings.

'How the devil am I to get broken bricks? I, who all my life have been wanting to build a starling house, and yet have never been able to begin?' complained in a pitiful voice Mokei Anissimoff, a seller of kringels[1] which were made by his wife.

---

1 A sort of white bread of a particular shape, which is very popular amongst the Russian peasantry.

The captain considered that he ought to give an opinion on the question, and thumped the table energetically to attract the attention of the company.

'Don't you know where to get bricks and rubble? Let's go all of us, my lads, into the town together and demolish the Town Hall. It's an old, good-for-nothing building, and your work will be crowned by a double success. You will improve the town by forcing them to build a new Town Hall, and you will make your own neighbourhood decent. You can use the Mayor's horses to draw the bricks, and you can take his three daughters as well; the girls would look well in harness! Or else you may pull down Judah Petounnikoff's house, and mend the street with wood. By the bye, Mokei, I know what your wife was using to-day to heat the oven for baking her kringels! It was the shutters from the third window, and the boards from two of the steps!'

When the audience had had its laugh out, and had finished joking at the captain's proposal, the serious-minded gardener Pavluguine asked –

'But, after all, captain, what's to be done? What do you advise us to do?'

'I – I advise you not to move hand or foot. If the rain destroys the street, let it. It isn't our fault.'

'Some of the houses are tumbling down already.'

'Leave them alone, let them fall! If they come down the town must pay damages, and if the authorities refuse, bring the matter before a magistrate. For just consider where the water comes from; doesn't it come down from the town? Well, that shows the town is to blame for the houses being destroyed.'

'They will say it's rain water.'

'But in the town the rain doesn't wash down the houses, does it? The town makes you pay rates and gives you no vote to help you claim your rights. The town destroys your life and your property, and yet holds you responsible for them. Pitch into the town on every side!'

And one half of the dwellers in the street, convinced by the radical Kouvalda, decided to wait till the storm-waters of the town had washed down their hovels.

The more serious half got the schoolmaster to write out an elaborate, convincing report for presentation to the town authorities. In this report, the refusal to carry out the town regulations was based on such solid reasons that the municipality was bound to take them into consideration. The dwellers in the street were granted permission to use the refuse left after the rebuilding of the barracks, and five horses from the fire brigade were lent to cart the rubbish. Besides this it was decided to lay a drain down the street.

This, added to other circumstances, made the schoolmaster very popular in the neighbourhood. He wrote petitions, got articles put into the papers. Once, for instance, the guests at Vaviloff's noticed that the herrings and other coarse food were not up to the mark, and two days later Vaviloff, standing at the counter with the newspaper in his hands, made a public recantation.

'It's quite just I have nothing to say for myself. The herrings were indeed rotten when I bought them, and the cabbage – that's also true – had been lying about too long. Well, it's only natural everyone wants to put more kopecks into his own pocket. And what comes of it? Just the opposite to what one hopes. I tried to get at other men's pockets, and a clever man has shown me up for my avarice. Now we're quits!'

This recantation produced an excellent effect on his audience, and gave Vaviloff the chance of using up all his bad herrings and stale cabbage, the public swallowing them down unheeding their ancient flavour, which was concealed with the spice of a favourable impression. This event was remarkable in two ways; it not only increased the prestige of the schoolmaster, but it taught the inhabitants the value of the Press.

Sometimes the schoolmaster would hold forth on practical morality.

'I saw,' he would say, accosting the house painter Jashka Turine, 'I saw, Jakoff, how you were beating your wife to-day.'

Jashka had already raised his spirits with two glasses of vodka, and was in a jovial mood. The company looked at him, expecting some sally, and silence reigned in the vodka shop.

'Well, if you saw it I hope you liked it!' said Jashka.

The company laughed discreetly.

'No, I didn't like it,' answered the schoolmaster; his tone of voice was suggestively serious, and silence fell on the listeners.

'I did what I could; in fact I tried to do my best,' said Jashka, trying to brave it out, but feeling he was about to catch it from the schoolmaster. 'My wife has had enough; she won't be able to get out of bed to-day.'

The schoolmaster traced with his forefinger some figures on the table, and whilst examining them said –

'Look here, Jakoff, this is why I don't like it. Let us go thoroughly into the question of what you are doing, and of what may be the result of it. Your wife is with child; you beat her yesterday all over the body; you might, when you do that, kill the child, and when your wife is in labour she might die or be seriously ill. The trouble of having a sick wife is not pleasant; it may cost you also a good deal, for illness means medicine, and medicine means money. If, even, you are fortunate enough not to have killed the child, you have certainly injured it, and it will very likely be born hunchbacked or crooked, and that means it won't be fit for work. It is of importance to you that the child should be able to earn its living. Even supposing it is only born delicate, that also will be an awkward business for you. It will be a burden to its mother, and it will require care and medicine. Do you see what you are laying up in store for yourself? Those who have to earn their living must be born healthy and bear healthy children. Am I not right?'

'Quite right,' affirms the company.

'But let's hope this won't happen,' says Jashka, rather taken aback by the picture drawn by the schoolmaster. 'She's so strong one can't touch the child through her. Besides, what's to be done? she's such a devil. She nags and nags at me for the least trifle.'

'I understand, Jakoff, that you can't resist beating your wife,' continued the schoolmaster, in his quiet, thoughtful voice. 'You may have many reasons for it, but it's not your wife's temper that causes you to beat her so unwisely. The cause is your unenlightened and miserable condition.'

'That's just so,' exclaimed Jakoff. 'We do indeed live in darkness – in darkness as black as pitch!'

'The conditions of your life irritate you, and your wife has to suffer for it. She is the one nearest to you in the world, and she is the innocent sufferer just because you are the stronger of the two. She is always there ready to your hand; she can't get away from you. Don't you see how absurd it is of you?'

'That's all right, damn her! But what am I to do? Am I not a man?'

'Just so; you are a man. Well, don't you see what I want to explain to you? If you must beat her, do so; but beat her carefully. Remember that you can injure her health and that of the child. Remember, as a general rule, it is bad to beat a woman who is with child on the breasts, or the lower part of the body. Beat her on the back of the neck, or take a rope and strike her on the fleshy parts of the body.'

As the orator finished his speech, his sunken dark eyes glanced at the audience as if asking pardon or begging for something. The audience was in a lively, talkative mood. This morality of an outcast was to it perfectly intelligible – the morality of the vodka shop and of poverty.

'Well, brother Jashka, have you understood?'

'Damn it all! there's truth in what you say.'

Jakoff understood one thing – that to beat his wife unwisely might be prejudicial to himself.

He kept silence, answering his friends' jokes with shamefaced smiles.

'And then again, look what a wife can be to one,' philosophizes the kringel-seller, Mokei Anissimoff. 'One's wife is a friend, if you look at the matter in the right light. She is, as it were, chained to one for life, like a fellow-convict, and one must try and walk in step with her. If one gets out of step, the chain galls.'

'Stop!' says Jakoff. 'You beat your wife also, don't you?'

'I'm not saying I don't, because I do. How can I help it? I can't beat the wall with my fists when I feel I must beat something!'

'That's just how I feel,' says Jakoff.

'What an existence is ours, brothers! So narrow and stifling, one can never have a real fling.'

'One has even to beat one's wife with caution,' humourously condoles someone.

Thus they would go on gossiping late into the night, or until a row would begin, provoked by their state of drunkenness, or by the impressions aroused by these conversations.

Outside the rain beats against the window and the icy wind howls wildly. Inside the air is close, heavy with smoke, but warm. In the street it is wet, cold, and dark; the gusts of wind seem to strike insolently against the window panes as if inviting the company to go outside, and threatening to drive them like dust over the face of the earth. Now and then is heard in its howling a suppressed moan, followed at intervals by what sounds like a hoarse, chill laugh. These sounds suggest sad thoughts of coming winter; of the damp, short, sunless days, and of the long nights; of the necessity for providing warm clothes and much food. There is little sleep to be got during these long winter nights if one has an empty stomach! Winter is coming – is coming! How is one to live through it?

These sad thoughts encouraged thirst among the dwellers in the High Street, and the sighs of the outcasts increased the number of wrinkles on their foreheads. Their voices sounded more hollow, and their dull, slow thought kept them, as it were, at a distance from each other. Suddenly amongst them there flashed forth anger like that of wild beasts or the desperation of those who are overdriven and crushed down by a cruel fate, or else they seemed to feel the proximity of that unrelenting foe who had twisted and contorted their lives into one long, cruel absurdity. But this foe was invulnerable because he was unknown.

Then they took to beating one another, and they struck each other cruelly, wildly. After making it up again they would fall to drinking once more, and drink till they had pawned everything that the easygoing Vaviloff would accept as a pledge.

Thus, in dull anger, in trouble that crushed the heart, in the uncertainty of the issue of this miserable existence, they spent the autumn days awaiting the still harder days of winter. During hard times like these Kouvalda would come to their rescue with his philosophy.

'Pluck up courage, lads! All comes to an end! – that's what there is best about life! Winter will pass and summer will follow; good times when, as they say, "even a sparrow has beer"!'

But his speeches were of little avail; a mouthful of pure water does not satisfy a hungry stomach.

Deacon Tarass would also try to amuse the company by singing songs and telling stories. He had more success. Sometimes his efforts would suddenly arouse desperate, wild gaiety in the vodka shop. They would sing, dance, shout with laughter, and for some hours would behave like maniacs. And then –

And then they would fall into a dull, indifferent state of despair as they sat round the gin-shop table in the smoke of the lamps and the reek of tobacco; gloomy, ragged, letting words drop idly from their lips while they listened to the triumphant howl of the wind; one thought uppermost in their minds – how to get more vodka to drown their senses and to bring unconsciousness. And each of them hated the other with a deadly, senseless hatred, but hid that hatred deep down in his heart.

II

Everything in this world is relative, and there is no situation which cannot be matched with a worse one.

One fine day at the end of September Captain Kouvalda sat, as was his custom, in his arm-chair at the door of the doss-house looking at the big brick building erected by the merchant Petounnikoff by the side of Vaviloff's vodka shop. Kouvalda was deep in thought.

This building, from which the scaffolding had not yet been removed, was destined to be a candle factory; and for some time it had been a thorn in the captain's side, with its row of dark, empty, hollow windows and its network of wood surrounding it from foundation to roof. Blood-red in colour, it resembled some cruel piece of machinery, not yet put into motion, but which had already opened its row of deep, greedy jaws ready to seize and gulp down everything that came in its way. The grey, wooden vodka shop of Vaviloff, with its crooked roof overgrown with moss, leaned up against one of the brick walls of the factory, giving the effect of a great parasite drawing its nourishment from it. The captain's mind was occupied by the thought that the old house would soon be replaced by a new one and the doss-house would be pulled down. He would have to seek another shelter, and it was doubtful if he would find one as cheap and as convenient. It was hard to be driven from a place one was used to, and harder still because a damned shopkeeper takes it into his head to want to make candles and soap. And the captain felt that if he had the chance of spoiling the game of this enemy of his he would do it with the greatest pleasure.

Yesterday, the shopkeeper, Ivan Andreevitch Petounnikoff, was in the yard of the doss-house with his son and an architect. They made a survey of the yard and stuck in pegs all over the place, which, after Petounnikoff had left, the captain ordered 'The Meteor' to pull up and throw away.

The shopkeeper was for ever before the captain's eyes – short, lean, shrivelled up, dressed in a long garment something between an overcoat and a kaftan, with a velvet cap on his head, and wearing long, brightly polished boots. With prominent cheek-bones and a grey, sharp-pointed beard; a high, wrinkled forehead, from under which peeped narrow, grey, half-closed, watchful eyes; a hooked, gristly nose and thin-lipped mouth – taken altogether, the merchant gave the impression of being piously rapacious and venerably wicked.

'Damned offspring of a fox and a sow!' said the captain angrily to himself, as he recalled some words of Petounnikoff's.

The merchant had come with a member of the town council to look at the house, and at the sight of the captain he had asked his companion in the abrupt dialect of Kostroma –

'Is that your tenant – that lunatic at large?'

And since that time, more than eighteen months ago, they had rivalled each other in the art of insult.

Yesterday again there had been a slight interchange of 'holy words,' as the captain called his conversations with the merchant. After having seen the architect off, Petounnikoff approached the captain.

'What, still sitting – always sitting?' asked he, touching the peak of his cap in a way that left it uncertain whether he were fixing it on his head or bowing.

'And you – you are still on the prowl,' echoed the captain, jerking out his lower jaw and making his beard wag in a way that might be taken for a bow by anyone not too exacting in these matters; it might also have been interpreted as the act of removing his pipe from one corner of his mouth to the other.

'I've plenty of money; that's why I'm always on the go. Money needs putting out, so I'm obliged to keep it moving,' says the shopkeeper in an aggravating voice to the other, screwing up his eyes slyly.

'Which means that you are the slave of money, and not money your slave,' replies Kouvalda, resisting an intense desire to kick his enemy in the stomach.

'It's all the same either way where money is concerned. But if you have no money!' – and the shopkeeper looked at the captain with bold but feigned compassion, while his trembling upper lip showed large, wolfish teeth.

'Anyone with a head on his shoulders and with a good conscience can do without it. Money generally comes when the conscience begins to grow a little out-at-elbows. The less honesty the more money!'

'That's true, but there are some people who have neither honesty nor money.'

'That describes you when you were young, no doubt,' said Kouvalda innocently.

Petounnikoff wrinkles his nose, he sighs, closes his narrow eyes, and says, 'Ah! when I was young, what heavy burdens I had to bear!'

'Yes, I should think so!'

'I worked! Oh, how I worked!'

'Yes, you worked at outwitting others!'

'People like you and the nobility – what does it matter? Many of them have, thanks to me, learnt to extend the hand in Christ's name.'

'Ah! then you did not assassinate, you only robbed?' interrupted the captain.

Petounnikoff turns a sickly green and thinks it is time to change the conversation.

'You are not an over polite host; you remain sitting while your visitor stands.'

'Well, he can sit down.'

'There is nothing to sit on.'

'There is the ground. The ground never rejects any filth!'

'You prove that rule, but I had better leave you, you blackguard!' says Petounnikoff coolly, though his eyes dart cold venom at the captain.

He went off leaving Kouvalda with the agreeable sensation that the merchant was afraid of him. If it were not so he would have turned him out of the doss-house long ago. It was not for the five roubles a month that the Jew let him remain on! … And the captain watches with pleasure the slowly retreating back of Petounnikoff, as he walks slowly away. Kouvalda's eyes still follow the merchant as he climbs up and down the scaffolding of his new building. He feels an intense desire that the merchant should fall and break his back. How many times has he not conjured up results of this imaginary fall, as he has sat watching Petounnikoff crawling about the scaffolding of his new factory, like a spider crawling about its net. Yesterday he had even imagined that one of the boards had given way under the weight of the merchant; and Kouvalda had jumped out of his seat with excitement – but nothing had come of it.

And to-day, as always, before the eyes of Aristide Kouvalda stands the great red building, so foursquare, so solid, so firmly fixed into the ground, as if already drawing from thence its nourishment. It seemed as if mocking the captain through the cold dark yawning openings in its walls. And the sun poured on its autumn rays with the same prodigality as on the distorted tumble-down little houses of the neighbourhood.

'But what if?' exclaimed the captain to himself, measuring with his eye the factory wall. 'What if?'

Aroused and excited by the thought which had come into his mind, Aristide Kouvalda jumped up and hastened over to Vaviloff's vodka shop, smiling, and muttering something to himself. Vaviloff met him at the counter with a friendly exclamation: 'How is your Excellency this morning?'

Vaviloff was a man of medium height, with a bald head surrounded by a fringe of grey hair; with clean-shaved cheeks, and moustache bristly as a toothbrush. Upright and active, in a dirty braided jacket, every movement betrayed the old soldier, the former non-commissioned officer.

'Jegor! Have you the deeds and the plan of your house and property?' Kouvalda asked hastily.

'Yes, I have.'

And Vaviloff closed his suspicious thievish eyes and scrutinized the captain's face, in which he observed something out of the common.

'Just show them to me!' exclaimed the captain, thumping on the counter with his fist, and dropping on to a stool.

'What for?' asked Vaviloff, who decided, in view of the captain's state of excitement, to be on his guard.

'You fool! Bring them at once!'

Vaviloff wrinkled his forehead, and looked up inquiringly at the ceiling.

'By the bye, where the devil are those papers?'

Not finding any information on this question on the ceiling, the old soldier dropped his eyes towards the ground, and began thoughtfully drumming with his fingers on the counter.

'Stop those antics!' shouted Kouvalda, who had no love for the old soldier; as, according to the captain, it was better for a former non-commissioned officer to be a thief than a keeper of a vodka shop.

'Well now, Aristide Kouvalda, I think I remember! I believe those papers were left at the law-courts at the time when' –

'Jegorka! stop this fooling. It's to your own interest to do so. Show me the plans, the deed of sale, and all that you have got at once! Perhaps you will gain by this more than a hundred roubles! Do you understand now?'

Vaviloff understood nothing; but the captain spoke in such an authoritative and serious tone that the eyes of the old soldier sparkled with intense curiosity; and saying that he would go and see if the papers were not in his strong box, he disappeared behind the door of the counter. In a few moments he returned with the papers in his hand, and a look of great surprise on his coarse face.

'Just see! The damned things were after all in the house!'

'You circus clown! Who would think you had been a soldier!'

Kouvalda could not resist trying to shame him, whilst snatching from his hands the cotton case containing the blue legal paper. Then he spread the papers out before him, thus exciting more and more the curiosity of Vaviloff, and began reading and scrutinizing them; uttering from time to time interjections in a meaning tone. Finally, he rose with an air of decision, went to the door leaving the papers on the counter, shouting out to Vaviloff –

'Wait a moment! Don't put them away yet!' Vaviloff gathered up the papers, put them in his cash box, locked it, felt to see that it was securely fastened. Then rubbing his bald head, he went and stood in the doorway of his shop. There he saw the captain measuring with his stride the length of the front of the vodka shop, whilst he snapped his fingers from time to time, and once more began his measurements – anxious but satisfied.

Vaviloff's face wore at first a worried expression; then it grew long, and at last it suddenly beamed with joy.

''Ristide Fomitch! Is it possible?' he exclaimed, as the captain drew near.

'Of course it's possible! More than a yard has been taken off! That's only as far as the frontage is concerned; as to the depth, I will see about that now!'

'The depth is thirty-two yards!'

'Well, I see you've guessed what I'm after. You stupid fool!'

'Well, you're a wonder, 'Ristide Fomitch! You've an eye that sees two yards into the ground!' exclaimed the delighted Vaviloff. A few minutes later they were seated opposite each other in

Vaviloff's room, and the captain was swallowing great gulps of beer, and saying to the landlord –

'You see, therefore, all the factory wall stands on your ground. Act without mercy. When the schoolmaster comes we will draw up a report for the law-courts. We will reckon the damages at a moderate figure, so that the revenue stamps shan't cost us too much, but we will ask that the wall shall be pulled down. This sort of thing, you fool, is called a violation of boundaries, and it's a stroke of luck for you! To pull a great wall like that down and move it farther back is not such an easy business, and costs no end of money. Now's your chance for squeezing Judah! We will make a calculation of what the pulling down will cost, taking into consideration the value of the broken bricks and the cost of digging out the new foundations. We will calculate everything, even the value of the time, and then, O just Judah, what do you say to two thousand roubles?'

'He won't give it!' exclaimed Vaviloff anxiously, blinking his eyes, which were sparkling with greedy fire.

'Let him try and get out of it! Just look, what can he do? There will be nothing for him but to pull it down. But look out, Jegor! Don't let yourself be worsted in the bargain. They will try and buy you off! Mind you don't let them off too easily! They will try and frighten you; don't you be afraid; rely on us to back you up!'

The captain's eyes burnt with wild delight, and his face, purple with excitement, twitched nervously. He had succeeded in arousing the greed of the gin-shop keeper, and after having persuaded him to commence proceedings as soon as possible, went off triumphant, and implacably revengeful.

That evening all the outcasts learnt the discovery that the captain had made, and discussed eagerly the future proceedings of Petounnikoff, representing to themselves vividly his astonishment and anger the day when he should have the copy of the lawsuit presented to him. The captain was the hero of the day.

He was happy, and all around were pleased. A heap of dark tattered figures lay about in the yard, talking noisily and eagerly, animated by the important event. All knew Petounnikoff, who often passed near them, blinking his eyes disdainfully, and paying as little attention to them as he did to the rest of the rubbish lying about in the yard. He was a picture of self-satisfaction, and this irritated them; even his boots seemed to shine disdainfully at them. But now the shopkeeper's pocket and his self-esteem were going to be hurt by one of themselves! Wasn't that an excellent joke?

Evil had a singular attraction for these people; it was the only weapon which came easily to their hands, and which was within their reach. For a long time now, each of them had cultivated within himself dim half-conscious feelings of keen hatred against all who, unlike themselves, were neither hungry nor ragged. This was why all the outcasts felt such an intense interest in the war declared by Kouvalda against the shopkeeper Petounnikoff. Two whole weeks the dwellers in the doss-house had been living on the expectation of new developments, and during all that time Petounnikoff did not once come to visit the almost completed building. They assured each other that he was out of town, and that the summons had not therefore yet been served upon him. Kouvalda raged against the delays of civil procedure. It is doubtful if anyone ever awaited the arrival of the shopkeeper so impatiently as did these tramps.

'He comes not, he comes not!
Alas! he loves me not!'

sang the Deacon Tarass, leaning his chin on his hand, and gazing with a comically sad expression up the hill.

But one fine day, towards evening, Petounnikoff appeared. He arrived in a strong light cart, driven by his son, a young man with red cheeks and wearing a long checked overcoat, and smoked blue spectacles. They tied up the horse; the son drew from his pocket a tape measure, gave one end of it to his father, and both of them silently, and with anxious expressions, began measuring the ground.

'Ah!' exclaimed triumphantly the captain.

All who were about the doss-house went and stood outside the gate watching the proceedings and expressing aloud their opinions on what was going forward.

'See what it is to have the habit of stealing! A man steals unconsciously, not intending to steal, and thereby risks more than he can gain,' said the captain, with mock sympathy; thereby arousing laughter among his bodyguard, and provoking a whole string of remarks in the same strain.

'Look out, you rogue!' at length exclaimed Petounnikoff, exasperated by these jibes. 'If you don't mind I'll have you up before the magistrate.'

'It's of no use without witnesses, and a son can't give evidence for a father,' the captain reminded him.

'All right; we shall see! Though you seem such a bold leader, you may find your match some day.'

And Petounnikoff shook his forefinger at him. The son, quiet and deeply interested in his calculations, paid no heed to this group of squalid figures, who were cruelly mocking his father. He never looked once towards them.

'The young spider is well trained!' remarked 'Scraps,' who was following the actions and the movements of the younger Petounnikoff.

Having taken all the necessary measurements, Ivan Andreevitch frowned, climbed silently into his cart, and drove off, whilst his son, with firm, decided steps, entered Vaviloff's vodka shop, and disappeared.

'He's a precious young thief! that he is. We shall see what comes of it!' said Kouvalda.

'What will come of it? Why, Petounnikoff junior will square Jegor Vaviloff!' remarked 'Scraps,' with great assurance, smacking his lips, and with a look of keen satisfaction on his cunning face.

'That would please you, perhaps?' asked Kouvalda severely.

'It pleases me to see human calculations go wrong!' explained 'Scraps,' blinking his eyes and rubbing his hands.

The captain spat angrily, and kept silence. The rest of them, standing at the gate of the tumbledown house, watched silently the door of the vodka shop. An hour and more passed in this silent expectation. At length the door opened, and young Petounnikoff appeared, looking as calm as when he had entered. He paused for a moment, cleared his throat, raised his coat collar, glanced at those who were watching his movements, and turned up the street towards the town.

The captain watched him till he was out of sight, and, turning towards 'Scraps,' smiled ironically and said –

'It seems, after all, as if you might be right, you son of a scorpion and of a centipede! You smell out everything that's evil. One can see by the dirty mug of the young rogue that he has got his own way! I wonder how much Jegor has screwed out of him? He's got something, that's sure! They're birds of a feather. I'm damned if I haven't arranged it all for them. It's cursed hard to think what a fool I've been. You see, mates, life is dead against us. One can't even spit into one's neighbour's face – the spittle flies back into one's own eyes.'

Consoling himself with this speech, the venerable captain glanced at his bodyguard. All were disappointed, for all felt that what had taken place between Vaviloff and Petounnikoff had turned out differently from what they had expected, and all felt annoyed. The consciousness of being unable to cause evil is more obnoxious to men than the consciousness of being unable to do good; it is so simple and so easy to do evil!

'Well! what's the use of sticking here? We have nothing to wait for except for Jegorka to stand us treat,' said the captain, glowering angrily at the vodka shop. 'It's all up with our peaceful and happy life under Judah's roof. He'll send us packing now; so I give you all notice, my brigade of *sans-culottes!*'

'The End' laughed morosely.

'Now then, gaoler, what's the matter with you?' asked Kouvalda.

'Where the devil am I to go?'

'That indeed is a serious question, my friend. But never fear, your fate will decide it for you,' said the captain, turning towards the doss-house.

The outcasts followed him idly.

'We shall await the critical moment,' said the captain, walking along with them. 'When we get the sack there will be time enough to look out for another shelter. Meanwhile, what's the use of spoiling life with troubles like that? It is at critical moments that man rises to the occasion, and if life as a whole were to consist of nothing but critical moments, if one had to tremble every minute of one's life for the safety of one's carcass, I'll be hanged if life wouldn't be more lively, and people more interesting!'

'Which would mean that people would fly at each other's throats more savagely than they do now,' explained 'Scraps,' smiling.

'Well, what of that?' struck in the captain, who did not care to have his ideas enlarged on.

'Nothing! nothing! It's all right – when one wants to get to one's destination quickly, one thrashes the horse, or one stokes up one's machine.'

'Yes, that's it; let everything go full speed to the devil. I should be only too glad if the earth would suddenly take fire, burst up, and go to pieces, only I should like to be the last man left, to see the others.'

'You're a nice one!' sneered 'Scraps.'

'What of that? I'm an outcast, am I not? I'm freed from all chains and fetters; therefore I can spit at everything. By the very nature of the life I lead now, I am bound to drop everything to do with the past – all fine manners and conventional ideas of people who are well fed, and well dressed, and who despise me because I am not equally well fed and dressed. So I have to cultivate in myself something fresh and new – don't you see – something you know which will make people like Judah Petounnikoff, when they pass by me, feel a cold shudder run down their backs!'

'You have a bold tongue!' sneered 'Scraps.'

'You miserable wretch!' Kouvalda scanned him disdainfully. 'What do you understand, what do you know? You don't even know how to think! But I have thought much, I have read books of which you would not have understood a word.'

'Oh, I know I'm not fit to black the boots of such a learned man! But though you have read and thought so much, and I have done neither the one nor the other, yet we are not after all so far apart.'

'Go to the devil!' exclaimed Kouvalda.

His conversations with 'Scraps' always finished in this way. When the schoolmaster was not about, the captain knew well that his speeches were only wasted, and were lost for want of understanding and appreciation. But for all that, he couldn't help talking, and now, having snubbed his interlocutor, he felt himself lonely amongst the others. His desire for conversation was not, however, satisfied, and he turned therefore to Simtzoff with a question.

'And you, Alexai Maximovitch, where will you lay your old head?'

The old man smiled good-naturedly, rubbed his nose with his hand, and explained –

'Don't know! Shall see by and by. I'm not of much account. A glass of vodka, that's all I want.'

'A very praiseworthy ambition, and very simple,' said the captain.

After a short silence Simtzoff added that he would find shelter more easily than the rest, because the women liked him.

This was true, for the old man had always two or three mistresses among the prostitutes, who would keep him sometimes for two or three days at a time on their scant earnings. They often beat him, but he took it stoically. For some reason or other they never hurt him much; perhaps they pitied him. He was a great admirer of women, but added that they were the cause of all his misfortunes in life. The close terms on which he lived with women, and the character of their relations towards him, were shown by the fact that his clothes were always neatly mended, and cleaner than the clothes of his companions. Seated now on the ground at the door of the doss-house amidst his mates, he boastfully related that he had for some time been asked by Riedka to go and live with her, but that he had till now refused, not wanting to give up the present company.

He was listened to with interest, mingled with envy. All knew Riedka; she lived not far down the hill, and only a few months ago she came out of prison after serving a second term for theft. She had formerly been a wet nurse; a tall, stout, strapping countrywoman, with a pock-marked face, and fine eyes, somewhat dulled by drink.

'The old rogue!' cursed 'Scraps,' watching Simtzoff, who smiled with self-satisfaction.

'And do you know why they all like me? Because I understand what their souls need.'

'Indeed?' exclaimed Kouvalda interrogatively.

'I know how to make women pity me. And when a woman's pity is aroused, she can even kill, out of pure pity! Weep before her, and implore her to kill; she will have pity on you, and will kill.'

'It's I who would kill!' exclaimed Martianoff, in a decided voice, with a dark scowl.

'Whom do you mean?' asked 'Scraps,' edging away from him.

'It's all the same to me! Petounnikoff – Jegorka – you if you like!'

'Why?' asked Kouvalda, with aroused interest.

'I want to be sent to Siberia. I'm tired of this stupid life. There one will know what to do with one's life.'

'H'm!' said the captain reflectively. 'You will indeed know what to do with your life there!'

Nothing more was spoken about Petounnikoff, nor of their impending expulsion from the doss-house. All were sure that this expulsion was imminent, was perhaps a matter of a few days only; and they therefore considered it useless to discuss the point further. Discussion wouldn't make it easier; besides, it was not cold yet, though the rainy season had begun. One could sleep on the ground anywhere outside the town.

Seated in a circle on the grass, they chatted idly and aimlessly, changing easily from one topic to another, and paying only just as much attention to the words of their companions as was absolutely necessary to prevent the conversation from dropping. It was a nuisance to have to be silent, but it was equally a nuisance to have to listen with attention. This society of the outcasts had one great virtue: no one ever made an effort to appear better than he was, nor forced others to try and appear better than they were.

The August sun was shedding its warmth impartially on the rags that covered their backs and on their uncombed heads – a chaotic blending of animal, vegetable, and mineral matter. In the corners of the yard, weeds grew luxuriantly – tall agrimony, all covered with prickles, and other useless plants, whose growth rejoiced the eyes of none but these equally useless people.

In Vaviloff's vodka shop the following scene had been going forward.

Petounnikoff junior entered, leisurely looked around, made a disdainful grimace, and slowly removing his grey hat, asked the landlord, who met him with an amiable bow and a respectful smile –

'Are you Jegor Terentievitch Vaviloff?'

'That's myself!' answered the old soldier, leaning on the counter with both hands, as if ready with one bound to jump over.

'I have some business to transact with you,' said Petounnikoff.

'Delighted! Won't you come into the back room?'

They went into the back part of the house, and sat down before a round table; the visitor on a sofa covered with oilcloth, and the host on a chair opposite to him.

In one corner of the room a lamp burnt before a shrine, around which on the walls hung eikons, the gold backgrounds of which were carefully burnished, and shone as if new. In the room, piled up with boxes and old furniture, there was a mingled smell of paraffin oil, of tobacco, and of sour cabbage. Petounnikoff glanced around, and made another grimace. Vaviloff with a sigh glanced up at the images, and then they scrutinized each other attentively, and each produced on the other a favourable impression. Petounnikoff was pleased with Vaviloff's frankly thievish eyes, and Vaviloff was satisfied with the cold, decided countenance of Petounnikoff, with its broad jaw and strong white teeth.

'You know me, of course, and can guess my errand,' began Petounnikoff.

'About the summons, I guess,' replied the old soldier respectfully.

'Just so! I'm glad to see that you are straightforward, and attack the matter like an open-hearted man,' continued Petounnikoff encouragingly.

'You see I'm a soldier,' modestly suggested the other.

'I can see that. Let us tackle this business as quickly and as straightforwardly as possible, and get it over.'

'By all means!'

'Your complaint is quite in order, and there is no doubt but that you have right on your side. I think it better to tell you that at once.'

'Much obliged to you,' said the soldier, blinking his eyes to conceal a smile.

'But I should like to know why you thought it best to begin an acquaintance with us, your future neighbours, so unpleasantly – with a lawsuit?' Vaviloff shrugged his shoulders, and was silent.

'It would have been better for you to have come to us, and we could have arranged matters between us. Don't you think so?'

'That indeed would have been pleasanter. But, don't you see? there was a little hitch. I didn't act altogether on my own. I was set on by someone else; afterwards I understood what would have been best, but it was too late then.'

'That's just it. I suppose it was some lawyer who put you up to it!'

'Something of that sort.'

'Yes, yes. And now you are willing to settle things out of court?'

'That's my great wish!' exclaimed the soldier. Petounnikoff remained silent for a moment, then glanced at the landlord and said in an abrupt, dry voice –

'And why do you wish it now, may I ask?' Vaviloff did not expect this question, and was not prepared for an immediate answer. He considered it an idle question, and shrugging his shoulders with a look of superiority, smiled sneeringly at Petounnikoff:

'Why? Well, it's easy to understand: because one must live with others in peace.'

'Come!' interrupted Petounnikoff, 'it isn't altogether that! I see you don't clearly understand yourself why it is so necessary for you to live in peace with us. I will explain it to you.'

The soldier was slightly surprised. This queerlooking young fellow in his check suit was holding forth to him just as Commander Rashkin used to do, who when he got angry would knock out three teeth at a time from the head of one of his troopers.

'It is necessary for you to live in peace with us because it will be profitable to you to have us as neighbours. And it will be profitable because we shall employ at least a hundred and fifty workmen at first, and more as time goes on. If a hundred of these on each weekly pay-day drink a glass of vodka, it means that during the month you will sell four hundred glasses more than you do at present. This is taking it at the lowest calculation; besides that, there's the catering for them. You don't seem a fool, and you've had some experience; don't you see now the advantage that our neighbourhood will be to you?'

'It's true!' said Vaviloff, nodding his head. 'I knew it.'

'Well then' –

The young merchant raised his voice.

'Oh! nothing. Let's arrange terms.'

'I'm delighted you make up your mind so promptly. I have here a declaration prepared in readiness, declaring that you are willing to stop proceedings against my father. Read it and sign it.'

Vaviloff glanced with round eyes at his interlocutor, with a presentiment that something exceedingly disagreeable was coming.

'Wait a moment. Sign what? What do you mean?'

'Simply write your name and your family name here,' said Petounnikoff, politely pointing out with his finger the place left for the signature.

'That's not what I mean – that is, I mean, what compensation will you give me for the land?'

'The land is of no use to you,' said Petounnikoff soothingly.

'Still it's mine!' exclaimed the soldier.

'To be sure. But how much would you claim?'

'Well, let's say the sum named in the summons. The amount is stated there,' suggested Vaviloff hesitatingly.

'Six hundred?' Petounnikoff laughed as if highly amused. 'That's a good joke!'

'I have a right to it! I can even claim two thousand! I can insist on your pulling down the wall; and that is what I want. That's why the sum claimed is so small. I demand that you should pull it down!'

'Go on with it then! We shall perhaps have to pull it down, but not for two or three years – not till you have been involved in heavy law expenses. After that we shall open a vodka shop of our own, which will be better than yours, and you will go to the wall! You'll be ruined, my friend; we'll take care of that. We might be taking steps to start the vodka shop at once, but we are busy just now, have got our hands full; besides, we are sorry for you. Why should one take the bread out of a man's mouth without a reason?'

Jegor Terentievitch clenched his teeth, feeling that his visitor held his fate in his hands. Vaviloff felt pity for himself, brought face to face as he was with this cold, mercenary, implacable person in his ridiculous check suit.

'And living so near us, and being on friendly terms with us, you, my friend, might have turned a pretty penny. We might have helped you also; for instance, I should advise you at once to open a little shop – tobacco, matches, bread, cucumbers, and so on. You'd find plenty of customers.'

Vaviloff listened, and not being a fool, understood that the best for him at present was to trust to the generosity of his enemy. In fact, he ought to have begun by that; and not being able any longer to conceal his anger and his humiliation, he burst out into loud imprecations against Kouvalda.

'Drunkard! Cursed swine – may the devil take him!'

'That's meant for the lawyer who worded your report?' asked Petounnikoff quietly, and added with a sigh: 'Indeed he might have served you a bad turn, if we hadn't taken pity on you!'

'Ah!' sighed the distressed soldier, letting his hands fall in despair. 'There were two of them – one started the business, and the other did the writing, the cursed scribbler!'

'How, a newspaper scribbler?'

'Well, he writes for the newspapers. They are both of them tenants of yours. Nice sort of people they are! Get rid of them; send them off for God's sake! They are robbers; they set everyone

152 MAXIM GORKY

in the street against each other; there is no peace with them; they have no respect for law or order. One has always to be on one's guard with them against robbery or arson.'

'But this newspaper scribbler, who is he?' asked Petounnikoff in an interested tone.

'He? He's a drunkard. He was a schoolteacher, and got turned away. He has drunk all he had, and now he writes for the newspapers, and invents petitions. He's a real bad 'un!'

'H'm-m! And it was he, then, who wrote your petition? Just so! Evidently it was he who wrote about the construction of the scaffolding. He seemed to suggest that the scaffolding was not built according to the by-laws.'

'That's he! That's just like him, the dog! He read it here, and was boasting that he would run Petounnikoff into expense!'

'H'm-m! Well, how about coming to terms?'

'To terms?' The soldier dropped his head and grew thoughtful. 'Ah! what a miserable dark existence ours is!' he exclaimed sadly, scratching the back of his head.

'You must begin to improve it!' said Petounnikoff, lighting a cigarette.

'Improve it? That's easy to say, sir! But we have no liberty! that's what is the matter. Just look at my life, sir. I'm always in terror, always on my guard, and have no freedom of action. And why is that? Fear! This wretch of a schoolmaster may write to the newspapers about me, he sets the sanitary authorities at me, and I have to pay fines. One has always to be on one's guard against these lodgers of yours, lest they burn, murder, or rob one! How can I stop them? They don't fear the police! If they do get clapped into prison, they are only glad; because it means free rations!'

'Well, we'll get rid of them if we come to terms with you,' Petounnikoff promised.

'And what shall the terms be?' asked Vaviloff, anxiously and gloomily.

'State your own terms.'

'Well, then, let it be the six hundred mentioned in the summons!'

'Wouldn't a hundred be enough?' said the trader, in a calm voice.

He watched the landlord narrowly, and smiling gently, added, 'I won't give a rouble more!'

After saying this he removed his spectacles, and began slowly wiping the glasses with his handkerchief. Vaviloff, sick at heart, looked at him, experiencing every moment towards him a feeling of greater respect. In the quiet face of young Petounnikoff, in his large grey eyes and prominent cheek-bones, and in his whole coarse, robust figure, there was so much self-reliant force, sure of itself, and well disciplined by the mind. Besides, Vaviloff liked the way that Petounnikoff spoke to him; his voice possessed simple friendly intonations, and there was no striving after effect, just as if he were speaking to an equal; though Vaviloff well understood that he, a soldier, was not the equal of this man.

Watching him almost with admiration, the soldier felt within himself a rush of eager curiosity, which for a moment checked all other feeling, so that he could not help asking Petounnikoff in a respectful voice –

'Where did you study?'

'At the Technological Institution. But why do you ask?' replied the other, smiling.

'Oh, nothing; I beg your pardon.'

The soldier dropped his head, and suddenly exclaimed in a voice that was almost inspired, so full was it of admiration and of envy, 'Yes! that's what education can do! Knowledge is indeed enlightenment, and that means everything! And we others, we are like owls looking at the sun. Bad luck to us! Well, sir, let us settle up this affair.'

And with a decided gesture he stretched out his hand to Petounnikoff, and said in a half choking voice –

'Let's say five hundred!'

'Not more than a hundred roubles, Jegor Terentievitch!'

Petounnikoff shrugged his shoulders, as if regretting not being able to give more, and patted the soldier's hairy hand with his large white one.

They soon clinched the bargain now, for the soldier suddenly started with long strides to meet the terms of Petounnikoff, who remained implacably firm. When Vaviloff had received the hundred roubles, and signed the paper, he dashed the pen on the table, exclaiming, 'That's done! Now I'll have to settle up with that band of tramps. They'll bother the life out of me, the devils!'

'You can tell them that I paid you all that you demanded in the summons,' suggested Petounnikoff, puffing out thin rings of smoke, and watching them rise and vanish.

'They'll never believe that! They are clever rogues; as sharp as' –

Vaviloff stopped just in time, confused at the thought of the comparison which almost escaped from his lips, and glanced nervously at the merchant's son. But this latter went on smoking, and seemed wholly engrossed with that occupation. He left soon after, promising Vaviloff, as he bade him good-bye, to destroy ere long this nest of noxious beings. Vaviloff watched him, sighing, and feeling a keen desire to shout something malicious and offensive at the man who walked with firm steps up the steep road, striding over the ruts and heaps of rubbish.

That same evening the captain appeared at the vodka shop; his brows were knit severely, and his right hand was firmly clenched. Vaviloff glanced at him deprecatingly.

'Well, you worthy descendant of Cain and of Judas! tell us all about it!'

'It's all settled!' said Vaviloff, sighing and dropping his eyes.

'I don't doubt it. How many shekels did you get?'

'Four hundred roubles down!'

'A lie! as sure as I live! Well, so much the better for me.

Without any more talking, Jegorka, hand me over 10 per cent, for my discovery; twenty-five roubles for the schoolmaster for writing out the summons, and a gallon of vodka for the company, with grub to match. Hand the money over at once, and the vodka with the rest must be ready by eight o'clock!'

Vaviloff turned green, and stared at Kouvalda with wide-open eyes.

'Don't you wish you may get it! That's downright robbery! I'm not going to give it. Are you in your senses to suggest such a thing, Aristide Fomitch? You'll have to keep your appetite till the next holiday comes round; things have changed, and I'm in a position not to be afraid of you now, I am!'

Kouvalda glanced at the clock.

'I give you, Jegor, ten minutes for your fool's chatter! Then stop wagging your tongue and give me what I demand! If you don't – then look out for yourself! Do you remember reading in the paper about that robbery at Bassoff's? Well, 'The End' has been selling things to you – you understand? You shan't have time to hide anything; we'll see to that; and this very night, you understand?'

''Ristide Fomitch! Why are you so hard on me?' wailed the old soldier.

'No more cackle! Have you understood? Yes or no?'

Kouvalda, tall and grey-headed, frowning impressively, spoke in a low voice, whose hoarse bass resounded threateningly in the empty vodka shop. At the best of times Vaviloff was afraid of him as a man who had been once an officer, and as an individual who had now nothing to lose. But at this moment he beheld Kouvalda in a new light; unlike his usual manner, the captain spoke little, but his words were those of one who expected obedience, and in his voice there was an implied threat Vaviloff felt that the captain could, if he chose, destroy him with pleasure. He had to give way to force, but choking with rage, he tried once more to escape his punishment. He sighed deeply and began humbly –

'It would seem the proverb is right which says, 'You reap what you sow.' 'Ristide Fomitch, I have lied to you! I wanted to make myself out cleverer than I really am. All I got was a hundred roubles.'

'Well! what then?' asked Kouvalda curtly.

'It wasn't four hundred as I told you, and that means' –

'It means nothing! How am I to know whether you were lying then or now? I mean to have sixty-five roubles out of you. That's only reasonable, so now.'

'Ah, my God! 'Ristide Fomitch. I have always paid you your due!'

'Come! no more words, Jegorka, you descendant of Judas!'

'I will give it to you, then, but God will punish you for this!'

'Silence, you scab!' roared the captain, rolling his eyes savagely. 'I am sufficiently punished by God already. He has placed me in a position in which I am obliged to see you and talk to you. I'll crush you here on the spot like a fly.'

And he shook his fist under Vaviloff's nose, and gnashed his teeth.

After he had left, Vaviloff smiled cunningly and blinked his eyes rapidly. Then two large tears rolled down his cheeks. They were hot and grimy, and as they disappeared into his beard, two others rolled down in their place. Then Vaviloff retired into the back room, and knelt in front of the eikons; he remained there for some time motionless, without wiping the tears from his wrinkled brown cheeks.

Deacon Tarass, who had always a fancy for the open air, proposed to the outcasts they should go out into the fields, and there in one of the hollows, in the midst of nature's beauties, and under the open sky, should drink Vaviloff's vodka. But the captain and the others unanimously scouted the deacon's ideas of nature, and decided to have their carouse in their own yard.

'One, two, three,' reckoned Aristide Fomitch, 'we are thirteen in all; the schoolmaster is missing, but some other waifs and strays are sure to turn up, so let's say twenty. Two cucumbers and a half for each, a pound of bread and of meat – that's not a bad allowance! As to vodka, there will be about a bottle each. There's some sour cabbage, some apples, and three melons. What the devil do we want more? What do you say, mates? Let us therefore prepare to devour Jegor Vaviloff; for all this is his body and his blood!'

They spread some ragged garments on the ground, on which they laid out their food and drink, and they crouched round in a circle, restraining with difficulty the thirst for drink which lurked in the eyes of each one of them.

Evening was coming on, its shadows fell across the foul, untidy yard, and the last rays of the sun lit up the roof of the half-ruined house. The evening was cool and calm.

'Let us fall to, brethren!' commanded the captain. 'How many mugs have we? Only six, and there are thirteen of us. Alexai Maximovitch, pour out the drink! Make ready! Present! Fire!'

'Ach – h!' They swallowed down great gulps, and then fell to eating.

'But the schoolmaster isn't here I I haven't seen him for three days. Has anyone else seen him?' said Kouvalda.

'No one.'

'That's not like him! Well, never mind, let's have another drink. Let's drink to the health of Aristide Kouvalda, my only friend, who, during all my lifetime has never once forsaken me; though, devil take it, if he had deprived me of his society sometimes I might have been the gainer.'

'That's well said,' cried 'Scraps,' and cleared his throat.

The captain, conscious of his superiority, looked round at his cronies, but said nothing, for he was eating.

After drinking two glasses the company brightened up; for the measures were full ones. 'Tarass and a half' humbly expressed a wish for a story, but the deacon was eagerly engaged discussing with 'The Top' the superiority of thin women over fat ones, and took no notice of his friend's words, defending his point of view with the eagerness and fervour of a man deeply convinced of the truth of his opinion. The naïve face of 'The Meteor,' who was lying beside him on his stomach, expressed admiration and delight at the suggestive words of the disputants. Martianoff, hugging his knees with his huge, hairy hands, glanced gloomily and silently at the vodka bottle, while he constantly made attempts to catch his moustache with his tongue and gnaw it with his teeth. 'Scraps' was teasing Tiapa.

'I know now where you hide your money, you old ogre!'

'All the better for you!' hissed Tiapa in a hoarse voice.

'I'll manage to get hold of it some day!'

'Do it if you can!'

Kouvalda felt bored amongst this set of people; there was not one worthy to hear his eloquence, or capable of understanding it.

'Where the devil can the schoolmaster be?' he said, expressing his thought aloud.

Martianoff looked at him and said –

'He will return.'

'I am certain he will come back on foot, and not in a carriage! Let us drink to your future, you born convict. If you murder a man who has got some money, go shares with me. Then, old chap, I shall start for America, make tracks for those lampas – pampas – what do you call them? I shall go there, and rise at length to be President of the United States. Then I shall declare war against Europe, and won't I give it them hot? As to an army, I shall buy mercenaries in Europe itself. I shall invite the French, the Germans, and the Turks, and the whole lot of them, and I shall use them to beat their own relations. Just as Ilia de Mouronetz conquered the Tartars with the Tartars. With money one can become even an Ilia, and destroy Europe, and hire Judah Petounnikoff as one's servant. He'd work if one gave him a hundred roubles a month, that he would, I'm sure. But he'd be a bad servant; he'd begin by stealing.'

'And besides, a thin woman is better than a fat one, because she costs less,' eagerly continued the deacon. 'My first deaconess used to buy twelve yards for a dress, and the second one only ten. It's the same with food.'

'Tarass and a half' smiled deprecatingly, turned his face towards the deacon, fixed his one eye on him, and shyly suggested in an embarrassed tone – 'I also had a wife once.'

'That may happen to anybody,' observed Kouvalda. 'Go on with your lies!'

'She was thin, but she ate a great deal; it was even the cause of her death.'

'You poisoned her, you one-eyed beggar!' said 'Scraps,' with conviction.

'No! on my word I didn't; she ate too much pickled herring.'

'And I tell you, you did! you poisoned her,' 'Scraps' repeated, with further assurance.

It was often his way, after having said some absurdity, to continue to repeat it, without bringing forward any grounds of confirmation; and beginning in a pettish, childish tone, he would gradually work himself up into a rage.

The deacon took up the cudgels for his friend.

'He couldn't have poisoned her, he had no reason to do so.'

'And I say he did poison her!' screamed 'Scraps.'

'Shut up!' shouted the captain in a threatening voice.

His sense of boredom was gradually changing into suppressed anger. With savage eyes he glanced round at the company, and not finding anything in their already half-drunken faces that might serve as an excuse for his fury, he dropped his head on his breast, remained sitting thus for a few moments, and then stretched himself full length on the ground, with his face upwards. 'The Meteor' was gnawing cucumbers; he would take one in his hand, without looking at it, thrust half of it into his mouth, and then suddenly bite it in two with his large yellow teeth, so that the salt juice oozed out on either side and wetted his cheeks. He was clearly not hungry, but this proceeding amused him. Martianoff remained motionless as a statue in the position he had taken, stretched on the ground and absorbed in gloomily watching the barrel of vodka, which was by this time more than half empty. Tiapa had his eyes fixed on the ground, whilst he masticated noisily the meat which would not yield to his old teeth. 'Scraps' lay on his stomach, coughing from time to time, whilst convulsive movements shook all his small body. The rest of the silent dark figures sat or lay about in various positions, and these ragged objects were scarcely distinguishable in the twilight from the heaps of rubbish half overgrown with weeds which were strewn about the yard. Their bent, crouching forms, and their tatters gave them the look of hideous animals, created by some coarse and freakish power, in mockery of man.

'There lived in Sousdal town
A lady of small renown;
She suffered from cramps and pains,
And very disagreeable they were ...'

sang the deacon in a low voice, embracing Alexai Maximovitch, who smiled back stupidly in his face. 'Tarass and a half' leered lasciviously.

Night was coming on. Stars glittered in the sky; on the hill towards the town the lights began to show. The prolonged wail of the steamers' whistles was heard from the river; the door of Vaviloff's vodka shop opened with a creaking noise, and a sound of cracking glass. Two dark figures entered the yard and approached the group of men seated round the vodka barrel, one of them asking in a hoarse voice –

'You are drinking?'

Whilst the other figure exclaimed in a low tone, envy and delight in his voice –

'What a set of lucky devils!'

Then over the head of the deacon a hand was stretched out and seized the bottle; and the peculiar gurgling sound was heard of vodka being poured from the bottle into a glass. Then someone coughed loudly.

'How dull you all are!' exclaimed the deacon. 'Come, you one-eyed beggar, let's recall old times and have a song! Let us sing *By the waters of Babylon.*'

'Does he know it?' asked Simtzoff.

'He? Why he was the soloist in the archbishop's choir. Come now, begin! *By – the – waters – of – Babylon.*'

The voice of the deacon was wild, hoarse, and broken, whilst his friend sang with a whining falsetto. The doss-house, shrouded in darkness, seemed either to have grown larger or to have moved its half-rotten mass nearer towards these people, who with their wild howlings had aroused its dull echoes. A thick, heavy cloud slowly moved across the sky over the house. One of the outcasts was already snoring; the rest, not yet quite drunk, were either eating or drinking, or talking in low voices with long pauses. All felt a strange sense of oppression after this unusually abundant feast of vodka and of food. For some reason or another it took longer than usual to arouse to-day the wild gaiety of the company, which generally came so easily when the dossers were engaged round the bottle.

'Stop your howling for a minute, you dogs!' said the captain to the singers, raising his head from the ground, and listening. 'Someone is coming, in a carriage!'

A carriage in those parts at this time of night could not fail to arouse general attention. Who would risk leaving the town, to encounter the ruts and holes of such a street? Who? and for what purpose?

All raised their heads and listened. In the silence of the night could be heard the grating of the wheels against the splashboards.

The carriage drew nearer. A coarse voice was heard asking –
'Well, where is it then?'

Another voice answered –

'It must be the house over there.'

'I'm not going any farther!'

'They must be coming here!' exclaimed the captain.

An anxious murmur was heard: 'The Police!'

'In a carriage? You fools!' said Martianoff in a low voice.

Kouvalda rose and went towards the entrance gates.

'Scraps,' stretching his neck in the direction the captain had taken, was listening attentively.

'Is this the doss-house?' asked someone in a cracked voice.

'Yes, it is the house of Aristide Kouvalda,' replied the uninviting bass voice of the captain.

'That's it, that's it! It's here that the reporter Titoff lived, is it not?'

'Ah! You have brought him back?'

'Yes.'

'Drunk?'

'Ill.'

'That means he's very drunk. Now then, schoolmaster, out with you!'

'Wait a minute. I'll help you; he's very bad. He's been two nights at my house; take him under the arms. We've had the doctor, but he's very bad.'

Tiapa rose and went slowly towards the gates. 'Scraps' sneered, and drank another glass.

'Light up there!' ordered the captain.

'The Meteor' went into the doss-house and lit a lamp, from which a long stream of light fell across the yard, and the captain, with the assistance of the stranger, led the schoolmaster into the doss-house. His head hung loose on his breast, and his feet dragged along the ground; his arms hung in the air as if they were broken. With Tiapa's help they huddled him on to one of the bunks, where he stretched out his limbs, uttering suppressed groans, whilst shudders ran through his body.

'We worked together on the same newspaper; he's been very unlucky. I told him, 'Stay at my house if you like; you won't disturb me'; but he begged and implored me to take him home, got quite excited about it. I feared that worrying would do him more harm, so I have brought him home; for this is where he meant, isn't it?'

'Perhaps you think he's got some other home?' asked Kouvalda in a coarse voice, watching his friend closely all the time. 'Go, Tiapa, and fetch some cold water.'

'Well now,' said the little man, fidgeting about shyly, 'I suppose I can't be of any further use to him.'

'Who? You?'

The captain scanned him contemptuously.

The little man was dressed in a well-worn coat, carefully buttoned to the chin. His trousers were frayed out at the bottom. His hat was discoloured with age, and was as crooked and wrinkled as was his thin, starved face.

'No, you can't be of any further use. There are many like you here,' said the captain, turning away from the little man.

'Well, good-bye then!'

The little man went towards the door, and standing there said softly –

'If anything happens let us know at the office; my name is Rijoff. I would write a short obituary notice. After all, you see, he was a journalist.'

'H – m – m! an obituary notice, do you say? Twenty lines, forty kopecks. I'll do something better, when he dies; I will cut off one of his legs, and send it to the office, addressed to you. That will be worth more to you than an obituary notice. It will last you at least three or four days; he has nice fat legs. I know all of you down there lived on him when he was alive, so you may as well live on him when he is dead.'

The little man uttered a strange sound, and disappeared; the captain seated himself on the bunk, by the side of the schoolmaster, felt his forehead and his chest, and called him by name –

'Philippe!'

The sound echoed along the dirty walls of the doss-house, and died away.

'Come, old chap! this is absurd!' said the captain, smoothing with his hand the disordered hair of the motionless schoolmaster. Then the captain listened to the hot gasping breath, noted the death-like, haggard face, sighed, and wrinkling his brows severely, glanced around. The lamp gave a sickly light; its flame flickered, and on the walls of the doss-house dark shadows danced silently.

The captain sat watching them and stroking his beard.

Tiapa came in with a bucket of water, placed it on the floor beside the schoolmaster's head, and taking hold of his arm held it in his hand, as if to feel its weight.

'The water is of no use!' said the captain in a hopeless voice.

'It's the priest he wants,' said the old rag-picker.

'Nothing's of any use,' replied the captain.

They remained a few moments silent, watching the school-master.

'Come and have a drink, old boy!'

'And what about him?'

'Can you do anything for him?'

Tiapa turned his back on the schoolmaster, and both returned to the yard, and rejoined the company.

'Well, what's going on?' asked 'Scraps,' turning his shrewd face round to the captain.

'Nothing out of the common. The man's dying,' the captain replied abruptly.

'Has he been knocked about?' asked 'Scraps,' with curiosity.

The captain did not answer, for at that moment he was drinking vodka.

'It's just as if he knew that we had something extra for his funeral feast,' said 'Scraps,' lighting a cigarette.

One of them laughed, and another sighed heavily, but on the whole the conversation of 'Scraps' and the captain did not produce much impression on the company; at least there were no apparent signs of trouble, of interest, or of thought. All had looked upon the schoolmaster as a man rather out of the common, but now most of them were drunk, and the rest remained calm and outwardly detached from what was going forward. Only the deacon evinced signs of violent agitation; his lips moved, he rubbed his forehead, and wildly howled –

'*Peace be to the dead!...*'

'Stop it!' hissed 'Scraps.' 'What are you howling about?'

'Smash his jaw!' said the captain.

'You fool!' hissed Tiapa. 'When a soul is passing, you should keep quiet, and not break the silence.'

It was quiet enough; in the cloud-covered sky, which threatened rain, and on the earth, shrouded in the still silence of an autumn night. At intervals the silence was broken by the snoring of those who had fallen asleep; by the gurgle of vodka being poured from the bottle, or the noisy munching of food. The deacon was muttering something. The clouds hung so low that it almost seemed as if they would catch the roof of the old house, and overturn it on to the outcasts.

'Ah! how one suffers when a dear friend is passing away!' stammered the captain, dropping his head on his chest.

No one answered him.

'He was the best among you all – the cleverest, the most honest. I am sorry for him.'

'*May – the – sa-i-nts – receive – him!* ... Sing, you one-eyed devil!' muttered the deacon, nudging his friend, who lay by his side half asleep.

'Will you be quiet!' exclaimed 'Scraps' in an angry whisper, jumping to his feet.

'I'll go and give him a knock over the head,' proposed Martianoff.

'What! are you not asleep?' exclaimed Aristide Fomitch in an extraordinarily gentle voice. 'Have you heard? Our schoolmaster is' –

Martianoff turned over heavily on his side, stood up, and glanced at the streams of light which issued from the door and windows of the doss-house, shrugged his shoulders, and without a word came and sat down by the side of the captain.

'Let's have another drop,' suggested Kouvalda.

They groped for the glasses, and drank.

'I shall go and see,' said Tiapa. 'He may want something.'

'Nothing but a coffin!' hiccoughed the captain.

'Don't talk about it!' implored 'Scraps' in a dull voice.

After Tiapa, 'The Meteor' got up. The deacon wanted to rise as well; but he fell down again, cursing loudly.

When Tiapa had gone, the captain slapped Martianoff's shoulder, and began to talk in a low voice.

'That's how the matter stands, Martianoff; you ought to feel it more than the rest. You were – but it's better to drop it. Are you sorry for Philippe?'

'No!' answered the former gaoler, after a short silence. 'I don't feel anything of that sort. I have lost the habit of it; I am so disgusted with life. I'm quite in earnest when I say I shall kill someone.'

'Yes?' replied the captain indifferently. 'Well, what then?… let's have another drop!'

'We are of no account; we can drink, that's all we can do,' muttered Simtzoff, who had just woke in a happy frame of mind. 'Who's there, mates? Pour out a glass for the old man!'

The vodka was poured out and handed to him.

After drinking it he dropped down again, falling with his head on someone's body.

A silence, as dark and as miserable as the autumn night, continued for a few moments longer. Then someone spoke in a whisper.

'What is it?' the others asked aloud.

'I say that after all he was a good sort of fellow; he had a clever head on his shoulders, and so quiet and gentle!'

'Yes; and when he got hold of money he never grudged spending it amongst his friends.'

Once more silence fell on the company.

'He is going!'

Tiapa's cry rang out over the captain's head.

Aristide Fomitch rose, making an effort to walk, firmly, and went towards the doss-house.

'What are you going for?' said Tiapa, stopping him. 'Don't you know that you are drunk, and that it's not the right thing?'

The captain paused and reflected.

'And is anything right on this earth? Go to the devil!' And he pushed Tiapa aside.

On the walls of the doss-house the shadows were still flickering and dancing, as if struggling silently with one another.

On a bunk, stretched out at full length, lay the schoolmaster, with the death-rattle in his throat. His eyes were wide open, his bare breast heaved painfully, and froth oozed from the corners of his mouth. His face wore a strained expression, as if he were trying to say something important and difficult; and the failure to say it caused him inexpressible suffering.

The captain placed himself opposite, with his hands behind his back, and watched the dying man for a moment in silence. At last he spoke, knitting his brows as if in pain.

'Philippe, speak to me! Throw a word of comfort to your friend. You know I love you; all the others are brute beasts. You are the only one I look upon as a man, although you are a drunkard. What a one you were to drink vodka, Philippe! That was what caused your ruin. You ought to have kept yourself in hand and listened to me. Was I not always telling you so?'

The mysterious all-destructive force, called Death, as if insulted by the presence of this drunken man, during its supreme and solemn struggle with life, decided to finish its impassive work, and the schoolmaster, after sighing deeply, groaned, shuddered, stretched himself out, and died.

The captain swayed backwards and forwards, and continued his speech. 'What's the matter with you? Do you want me to bring you some vodka? It's better not to drink, Philippe! restrain yourself. Well, drink if you like! To speak candidly, what is the use of restraining oneself? What's the use of it, Philippe?'

And he took the body by the leg and pulled it towards him.

'Ah! you are already asleep, Philippe! Well, sleep on. Good-night. To-morrow I'll explain it all to you, and I hope I shall convince you that it's no use denying oneself anything. So now, go to sleep, if you are not dead.'

He went out, leaving dead silence behind him; and approaching his mates exclaimed –

'He's asleep or dead, I don't know which. I'm a – little – drunk.'

Tiapa stooped lower still, and crossed himself. Martianoff threw himself down on the ground without saying a word. 'The Meteor' began sobbing in a soft, silly way, like a woman who has been ill-treated. 'Scraps' wriggled about on the ground, saying in a low, angry, frightened voice –

'Devil take you all! A set of plagues! Dead? ... what of that? Why should I be bothered with it? When my time comes I shall have to die too! just as he has done; I'm no worse than the rest!'

'That's right! that's it!' exclaimed the captain, dropping himself down heavily on the earth. 'When the time comes, we shall all die, just like the rest! Ha! ha! It doesn't much matter how we live; but die we shall, like the rest. For that's the goal of life, trust my word for it! Man lives that he may die. And he dies, and this being so, isn't it all the same what he dies of, or how he dies, or how he lived? Am I not right, Martianoff? Let's have another drink, and yet another, and another, as long as there is life in us.'

Rain began to fall. Thick, heavy darkness enshrouded the figures of the outcasts, as they lay on the ground in all the ugliness of sleep or of drunkenness. The streak of light issuing from the doss-house grew paler, flickered, and finally disappeared. Either the wind had blown the lamp out, or the oil was exhausted. The drops of rain falling on the iron roof of the doss-house pattered down softly and timidly. The solemn sound of a bell came at intervals from the town above, telling that the watchers in the church were on duty.

The metallic sound wafted from the steeple melted into the soft darkness, and slowly died away; but before the gloom had smothered the last trembling note, another stroke was heard, and yet another, whilst through the silence of the night spread and echoed the sad booming sigh of the bell.

The following morning Tiapa was the first to awake.

Turning over on his back, he looked at the sky; for this was the only position in which his distorted neck would allow him to look upwards.

It was a monotonously grey morning. A cold, damp gloom, hiding the sun, and concealing the blue depths of the sky, shed sadness over the earth.

Tiapa crossed himself, and leaning on his elbow looked round to see if there was no vodka left. The bottle was near, but it proved to be – empty. Crawling over his companions, Tiapa began inspecting the mugs. He found one nearly full, and swallowed the contents, wiping his mouth with his sleeve, and then shook the captain by the shoulder.

'Get up! Can't you hear?'

The captain lifted his head, and looked at Tiapa with dim, bloodshot eyes.

'We must give notice to the police! so get up.'

'What's the matter?' asked the captain in an angry, drowsy voice.

'Why, he's dead.'

'Who's dead?'

'Why, the learned man.'

'Philippe? Ah, yes, so he is!'

'And you had already forgotten!' hissed Tiapa reproachfully.

The captain rose to his feet, yawned loudly, and stretched himself till his bones cracked.

'Well, go and give notice.'

'No, I shan't go. I'm not fond of those gentry!' said Tiapa gloomily.

'Well, go and wake the deacon, and I'll go and see what can be done.'

'Yes, that's better. Get up, deacon!'

The captain entered the doss-house, and stood at the foot of the bunk where lay the schoolmaster, stretched out at full length; his left hand lay on his breast, his right was thrown backwards, as if ready to strike. The idea crossed the captain's mind that if the schoolmaster were to get up now, he would be as tall as 'Tarass and a half.' Then he sat down on the bunk at the feet of his dead friend, and recalling to his mind the fact that they had lived together for three long years, he sighed.

Tiapa entered, holding his head like a goat ready to butt. He placed himself on the opposite side of the schoolmaster, watching for a time his sunk, serene, and calm face; then hissed out –

'Sure enough he is dead; it won't be long before I go also.'

'It's time you did,' said the captain gloomily.

'That's so!' agreed Tiapa. 'And you also – you ought to die; it would be better than living on as you are doing.'

'It might be worse. What do you know about it?'

'It can't be any worse. When one dies, one has to deal with God; whilst here, one has to deal with men. And men, you know what they are.'

'That's all right, only stop your grumbling!' said Kouvalda angrily.

And in the half light of early dawn an impressive silence reigned once more throughout the doss-house.

They sat thus for a long time quietly, at the feet of their dead companion, occasionally glancing at him, but plunged both of them in deep thought. At length Tiapa inquired –

'Are you going to bury him?'

'I? No, let the police bury him.'

'Ah! now it's you who ought to do it! You took the share of the money due to him for writing the petition for Vaviloff. If you haven't enough I'll make it up.'

'Yes, I have his money, but I am not going to bury him.'

'That doesn't seem right. It's like robbing a dead man. I shall tell everyone that you mean to stick to his money!'

'You are an old fool!' said Kouvalda disdainfully.

'I'm not such a fool as all that, but it doesn't seem right or friendly.'

'Very well! just leave me alone.'

'How much money was there?'

'A twenty-five rouble note,' said Kouvalda carelessly.

'Come now! you might give me five out of that.'

'What a rogue you are, old man!' scowled the captain, looking blankly into Tiapa's face.

'Why so? Come now, shell out!'

'Go to the devil! I'll erect a monument to him with the money,'

'What will be the use of that to him?'

'I'll buy a mill-stone and an anchor; I'll put the stone on the tomb, and I will fasten the anchor to the stone with a chain. That will make it heavy enough.'

'What's that for? Why do you talk such nonsense?'

'That's no business of yours.'

'Never mind! I shall tell of you,' threatened Tiapa once more.

Aristide Fomitch looked vaguely at him and was silent. And once more there reigned in the doss-house that solemn and mysterious hush, which always seems to accompany the presence of death.

'Hark! They are coming,' said Tiapa.

And he rose and went out at the door.

Almost at the same moment there appeared the police officer, the doctor, and the magistrate. All three in turn went up to the body, and after glancing at it moved away, looking meanwhile at Kouvalda askance and with suspicion.

He sat, taking no notice of them, until the police officer asked, nodding towards the schoolmaster's body –

'What did he die of?'

'Ask him yourself. I should say from being unaccustomed' –

'What do you mean?' asked the magistrate.

'I say that, according to my idea, he died from being unaccustomed to the complaint from which he was suffering.'

'H'm! Yes. Had he been ill long?'

'It would be better to bring him over here; one can't see anything in there,' suggested the doctor in a bored voice. 'There may be some marks on him.'

'Go and call someone to carry him out!' the police officer ordered Kouvalda.

'Call them in yourself. I don't mind his staying here,' retorted the captain coolly.

'Be off with you,' shouted the police officer savagely.

'Easy there!' threw back Kouvalda, not stirring from his place, speaking with cool insolence and showing his teeth.

'Damn you!' roared the police officer, his face suffused with blood from suppressed rage. 'You shall remember this!' –

'Good-day to you, honourable gentlemen!' said the oily, insinuating voice of Petounnikoff, as he appeared in the doorway. Scrutinizing rapidly the faces of the bystanders, he suddenly stopped, shuddered, drew back a step, and taking off his cap, crossed himself devoutly. Then a vicious smile of triumph spread over his countenance, and looking hard at the captain, he asked in a respectful tone, 'What is the matter here? No one has been killed, I hope.'

'It looks like it,' answered the magistrate.

Petounnikoff sighed deeply, crossed himself again, and in a grieved tone said –

'Merciful heavens! That's what I always feared! Whenever I came here, I used to look in, and then draw back with fear. Then when I was at home, such terrible things came into my mind. God preserve us all from such things! How often I used to wish to refuse shelter any longer to this gentleman here, the head of this band; but I was always afraid. You see, they were such a bad lot, that it seemed better to give in to them, lest something worse should happen.' He made a deprecating movement with one hand, and gathering up his beard with the other, sighed once more.

'They are a dangerous set, and this gentleman here is a sort of chief of the gang – quite like a brigand chief.'

'Well, we shall take him in hand!' said the police officer in a meaning tone, looking at the captain with a vindictive expression. 'I also know him well.'

'Yes, my fine fellow, we are old pals,' agreed Kouvalda in a tone of familiarity. 'How often have I bribed you and the like of you to hold your tongues?'

'Gentlemen!' said the police officer, 'did you hear that? I beg you will remember those words. I won't forgive that. That's how it is, then? Well, you shan't forget me! I'll give you something, my friend, to remember me by.'

'Don't holloa till you are out of the wood, my dear friend,' said Aristide Fomitch coolly. The doctor, a young man in spectacles, looked at him inquiringly; the magistrate with an attention that boded no good; Petounnikoff with a look of triumph; whilst the police officer shouted and gesticulated threateningly.

At the door of the doss-house appeared the dark figure of Martianoff; he came up quietly and stood behind Petounnikoff, so that his chin appeared just above the merchant's head. The old deacon peeped from behind Martianoff, opening wide his small, swollen red eyes.

'Well, something must be done,' suggested the doctor.

Martianoff made a frightful grimace, and suddenly sneezed

straight on to the head of Petounnikoff. The latter yelled, doubled
up his body, and sprang on one side, nearly knocking the police
officer off his feet, and falling into his arms.

'There, you see now!' said the merchant, trembling and
pointing at Martianoff. 'You see now what sort of people they
are, don't you?'

Kouvalda was shaking with laughter, in which the doctor and
the magistrate joined; whilst round the door of the doss-house
clustered every moment more and more figures. Drowsy,
dissipated faces, with red, inflamed eyes, and dishevelled hair,
stood unceremoniously surveying the doctor, the magistrate, and
the police officer.

'Where are you shoving to?' said a constable who had accompanied the police officer, pulling at their rags, and pushing them
away from the door.

But he was one against many; and they, paying no heed to
him, continued to press forward in threatening silence, their
breath heavy with sour vodka. Kouvalda glanced first at them
and then at the officials, who began to show signs of uneasiness
in the midst of this overwhelmingly numerous society of unde-
sirables, and sneeringly remarked to the officials –

'Perhaps, gentlemen, you would like me to introduce you
formally to my lodgers and my friends. Say so if you wish it, for
sooner or later, in the exercise of your duties, you will have to
make their acquaintance.'

The doctor laughed with an embarrassed air; the magistrate
closed his lips firmly; and the police officer was the only one
who showed himself equal to the emergency; he shouted into
the yard –

'Sideroff, blow your whistle, and when they come, tell them
to bring a cart.'

'Well, I'm off,' said Petounnikoff, appearing from some
remote corner. 'You'll be kind enough, sirs, to clear out my
little shed to-day. I want to have it pulled down. I beg you to

make the necessary arrangements; if not, I shall have to apply to the authorities.'

In the yard the policeman's whistle was sounding shrilly; and round the doss-house door stood the compact crowd of its occupants, yawning and scratching themselves.

'So you don't want to make their acquaintance; that's not quite polite,' said Aristide Kouvalda, laughing.

Petounnikoff drew his purse from his pocket, fumbled with it for a few minutes, finally pulling out ten kopecks; he crossed himself and placed them at the feet of the dead man.

'God rest his soul! Let this go towards burying the sinful ashes.'

'How!' roared the captain. 'You! you! giving towards the burial? Take it back; take it back, I command you, you rogue! How dare you give your dishonest gains towards the burial of an honest man! I'll smash every bone in your body!'

'Sir!' exclaimed the alarmed shopkeeper, seizing the police officer imploringly by the elbow.

The doctor and the magistrate hurried outside, while the police officer shouted again loudly, 'Sideroff! Come inside here!'

The outcasts formed a barrier round the door of the doss-house, watching and listening to the scene with an intense interest which lighted up their haggard faces.

Kouvalda, shaking his fist over Petounnikoff's head, roared wildly, rolling his bloodshot eyes –

'Rogue and thief! take the coppers back! you vile creature; take them back, I tell you, or I'll smash them into your eyes! Take them back!'

Petounnikoff stretched out one trembling hand towards his little offering, whilst shielding himself with the other against Kouvalda's threatening fist, and said –

'Bear witness, you, sir, the police officer, and you, my good people.'

'We are not good people, you damned old shopkeeper!' was heard in the creaking tones of 'Scraps.'

The police officer, distending his face like a bladder, was whistling wildly, whilst defending Petounnikoff, who was writhing and twisting about in front of him, as if wishing to get inside the officer for protection.

'You vile thing! I'll make you kiss the feet of this dead body if you don't mind! Come here with you!'

And seizing Petounnikoff by the collar, Kouvalda flung him out of the door, as he would have done a kitten.

The outcasts moved on one side to make room for the merchant to fall; and he pitched forward, frightened and yelling at their feet.

'They are killing me! Murder! They have killed me!'

Martianoff slowly lifted his foot, and took aim at the head of the shopkeeper; 'Scraps,' with an expression of extreme delight, spat full into the face of Petounnikoff. The merchant raised himself on to his hands and knees, and half rolled, half dragged himself farther out into the yard, followed by peals of laughter. At this moment two constables arrived in the yard, and the police officer, pointing to Kouvalda, exclaimed in a voice of triumph –

'Arrest him! Tie him up!'

'Yes, tie him up tightly, my dears!' implored Petounnikoff.

'I defy you to touch me! I'm not going to run away! I'll go wherever I have to go,' said Kouvalda, defending himself against the constables, who approached him.

The outcasts dropped off one by one. The cart rolled into the yard. One or two ragged strangers, who had been called in, were already dragging the schoolmaster's body out of the doss-house.

'You shall catch it! just wait a bit!' said the police officer threateningly to Kouvalda.

'Well, captain, how goes it now?' jeered Petounnikoff, maliciously pleased and happy at the sight of his foe's hands being tied. 'Well, you are caught now; only wait, and you will get something warmer by and by!'

But Kouvalda was silent; he stood between the two constables, terrible and erect, and was watching the schoolmaster's body being hoisted into the cart. The man who was holding the corpse under the arms, being too short for the job, could not get the schoolmaster's head into the cart at the same moment as his legs were thrown in. Thus, for a second it appeared as if the schoolmaster were trying to throw himself head foremost out of the cart, and hide himself in the ground, away from all these cruel and stupid people, who had never given him any rest.

'Take him away!' ordered the police officer, pointing to the captain.

Kouvalda, without a word of protest, walked silent and scowling from the yard, and, passing by the schoolmaster, bent his head towards the body, without looking at it. Martianoff followed him, his face set like a stone.

Petounnikoff's yard emptied rapidly.

'Gee-up!' cried the driver, shaking the reins on the horse's back. The cart moved off, jolting along the uneven surface of the yard. The schoolmaster's body, covered with some scanty rags, and lying face upwards, shook and tumbled about with the jolting of the cart. He seemed to be quietly and peacefully smiling, as if pleased with the thought that he was leaving the doss-house, never to return – never any more. Petounnikoff, following the cart with his eyes, crossed himself devoutly, and then began carefully dusting his clothes with his cap to get rid of the rubbish that had stuck to them. Gradually, as the dust disappeared from his coat, a serene expression of contentment and of self-reliance spread over his face. Looking up the hill, as he stood in the yard, he could see Captain Aristide Fomitch Kouvalda, with hands tied behind his back, tall and grey, wearing a cap with an old red band like a streak of blood round it, being led away towards the town. Petounnikoff smiled with a smile of triumph, and turned towards the doss-house, but suddenly stopped, shuddering. In the doorway facing him stood a terrible old man, horrible to look at in the rags which covered his long body, with a stick in his hand, and a large sack on his back, stooping under the weight of his burden, and bending his head forward on his chest as if he were about to rush forward at the merchant.

'What do you want?' cried Petounnikoff. 'Who are you?'

'A man,' hissed a muffled, hoarse voice.

This hoarse, hissing sound pleased Petounnikoff, and reassured him.

'A man!' he exclaimed. 'Was there ever a man who looked like you?'

And moving on one side, he made way for the old man, who walked straight towards him, muttering gloomily –

'There are men of all sorts. That's just as God wills. Some are worse than I am, that's all – much worse than I am.'

The threatening sky looked down quietly at the dirty yard, and the trim little old man with the sharp grey beard, who walked about measuring and calculating with his cunning eyes. On the roof of the old house sat a crow triumphantly croaking, and swaying backwards and forwards with outstretched neck.

The grey lowering clouds, with which the whole sky was covered, seemed fraught with suspense and inexorable design, as if ready to burst and pour forth torrents of water, to wash away all that soiled this sad, miserable, tortured earth.

THE AFFAIR OF THE CLASPS

(tr. Vera Volkhovsky)

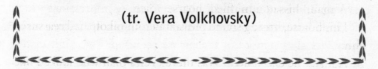

THERE WERE THREE OF us friends – Semka,[1] Kargouza, myself and Mishka,[2] a bearded giant with great blue eyes that perpetually beamed on everything and were always swollen from drink. We lived in a field beyond the town in an old tumbledown building, called for some reason 'the glass factory,' perhaps because there was not a single whole pane in its windows, and undertook all kinds of work, despising nothing; cleaned yards, dug ditches and sewers, pulled down old buildings and fences, and once even tried to build a henhouse. But in this we were unsuccessful. Semka, who was pedantically honest about the duties he took upon himself, began to doubt our knowledge of the architecture of hen-houses, and one day at noon, when we were all resting, took the nails that had been given out to us, two new planks, and the master's axe to the public-house. For this we lost our work, but as we possessed nothing no one demanded compensation.

We struggled on, living from hand to mouth, and all three of us felt a very natural and lawful dissatisfaction with our fate.

---

1 An abbreviation or diminutive of *Simon*, used to express intimacy or contempt. – Tr.
2 An abbreviation or diminutive of *Michael*, used to express intimacy or contempt. Bears are nicknamed Mishka in Russia. – Tr.

Sometimes this took an acute form, giving us a hostile feeling to all around us, and drawing us into somewhat riotous exploits provided for in the 'Statutes on Penalties inflicted by the Justices of the Peace'; but as a rule we were weighed down by a dull melancholy, anxiously preoccupied in the search of a meagre earning, and responded but feebly to all those impressions which we could not turn to material advantage. In our spare time – and there was always more of it than we required – we built castles in the air. Semka, the eldest and most matter-of-fact of us, was a thick-set, Penza-born peasant. He used to be a gardener, but, ruined by drink, as fate willed it, he struck at the town of K—— a year ago, on his way to the Nigny Fair, where he hoped somehow to 'get on.' His dreams, the embittered sceptic's, took a clear and definite form. He required but little.

'Damn my soul!'[3] he used to say, when we, lying on our empty stomachs on the ground, somewhere in the shade, beyond the town, tried to illumine our future, little by little, but insistently looking into its darkness.

'If I could just cut to Siberia. I'd make my way there, meet a good business-like man, apprentice myself to him directly. 'Take me, mate,' I'd say, 'to share your luck. Pals in prison, pals in hunger.' Then I'd polish off one or two little jobs with him. That would be something *like*. Ye-es.'

'Why should you go to Siberia particularly?' I asked him once.

'Why? It's there the real smart ones are, man. Lots of 'em – easy to find. But *here* – here you can't for the life of you find a good one. As for trying alone, you'd only go hang for nothing. Not used to it. Skill it wants – experience.'

Mishka could not express his dreams in words, but there was not the slightest doubt that he dreamed continually and persistently. You had but to look at his good-natured blue eyes, always gazing into space, at his gentle tipsy smile, constantly parting his

---

3 The Russian exclamation has no English equivalent. – Tr.

thick moustache and beard, which always contained some extraneous matter, such as bird's feathers, bits of straw, a shaving or two, breadcrumbs, pieces of eggshell, etc.; you had but to glance at his simple open face to see in him the typical peasant-dreamer. I had my dreams too, but the direction of my thoughts is even now interesting to no one but myself.

We had all three met in a night shelter a fortnight or so before the incident I want to describe, deeming it interesting. In a day or two we were friends – that is, went everywhere together, told each other our aims and wishes, divided everything that fell to one equally amongst us, and, in fact, made a tacit defensive and offensive alliance against Life, which treated us in an extremely hostile manner.

During the day we tried with great energy to find something to saw or take to pieces, to pull down, to dig, to carry, and, if such an opportunity occurred, at first set to work with a will.

But, perhaps because each of us in his heart thought himself destined for the fulfilment of higher-business than, for instance, the digging of cesspools, or cleaning them, which is still worse, I may add, for the information of those not initiated into that art, after some two hours of the work our ardour somewhat abated. Then Semka would begin to doubt its necessity.

'They dig a ditch... And what for? For *slops*. Why can't they just pour them out on the ground? "Won't do. They'll smell," they say. Get along with you! Slops smell! What stuff people do talk, just from having nothing to do. Now throw a salt cucumber[4] out. Why should it smell if it's a little one? It'll lie there a day or two, and there you are – it's gone, rotted away. If you throw a dead man out into the sun, now, he'll smell a bit, to be sure, for it's a big carcass.'

Such reasoning and conclusions on Semka's part considerably damped our ardour for work. And this was rather advantageous

---

4   A very common food in Russia. – Tr.

for us if the job was by the day, but if it was by the piece it invariably happened that we took our wages and spent them on food before the work was finished. Then we used to go to our employer to ask for a 'pribavka';[5] he generally told us to clear out, and threatened, with the help of the police, to make us finish the job already paid for. We argued that we could not work hungry, and more or less hotly insisted on the 'pribavka,' which in the majority of cases we got. Of course it was not exactly honourable, but really it was extremely advantageous, and it is not our fault if life is so clumsily arranged that the honourable and the advantageous nearly always clash. The wages disputes with our employers Semka always took upon himself, and really he conducted them with an artist's skill, detailing the proofs of his rights in the tones of a man worn out with work and exhausted by the burden of it.

Meanwhile Mishka looked on in silence, and blinked his blue eyes, smiling from time to time with his good-natured, kindly smile, as if he were trying to say something but could not summon up courage. He generally spoke very little, and only when half-seas-over was he capable of delivering something like an oration.

'Bratsi!'[6] he would then cry, smiling, and his lips twitched curiously, his throat grey husky, and he would cough for some time after the beginning of the speech, pressing his hand to his throat.

'W-e-ll?' would be Semka's impatient and ungracious encouragement.

'Bratsi! We live like dogs, we do. And worse even. And what for? Nobody knows. But I suppose by the will of God. Everything is done by His will – eh, bratsi? Well, then – So there ... it shows we deserve to live like dogs, for we are bad men. We're bad men, eh? Well, then – Now I say, serve 'em right, the dogs. Isn't it

---

5   Lit., 'an addition,' *i.e.* additional wage. – Tr.
6   Diminutive of 'brothers.' – Tr.

true what I say? So it shows it's for our sins. And we must put up with it, eh? Isn't it true?'

'Fool!' briefly and indifferently answered Semka to the anxious questioning of his comrade. And the other would penitently shrink up into himself, smile timidly, and fall silent, blinking his eyes, which he could scarcely keep open from drunken sleepiness.

Once we were in luck.

We were waiting for likely employers, elbowing our way through the market, when we came upon a small wizened old lady with a stern, wrinkled face. Her head shook, and on her beak-like nose hopped large spectacles with heavy silver rims; she was constantly putting them straight as her small, coldly glittering eyes gleamed out from behind them.

'You are free? Are you looking for work?' she asked us, when we all stared at her longingly. 'Very well,' she said, on receiving a quick and respectful answer in the affirmative from Semka. 'I want to have an old bath-house[7] pulled down, and a well cleaned. How much would you charge for it?'

'We should have to see, barynia, what sort of size your bath-house is,' said Semka, politely and reasonably. 'And the well too. They run different depths. Sometimes they are very deep.'

We were invited to look, and in an hour's time, already armed with axes and a lever, we were lustily pulling down the rafters of the bath-house, having agreed to take it to pieces and to clean the well for five roubles.[8] The bath-house stood in the corner of an old neglected garden. Not far from it, among some cherry trees, was a summer-house, and from the top of the bath-house we saw that the old lady sat reading in there, holding a large open book on her lap. Now and then she cast a sharp, attentive

---

7 In Russia private dwellings have separate bath-houses, built mostly of wood, and the baths are taken in somewhat the same manner as Turkish. – Tr.

8 A rouble is about two shillings. – Tr.

glance at us, the book on her lap moved, and its massive clasps, evidently of silver, shone in the sun.

No work is so rapid as the work of destruction. We zealously bustled about among clouds of grey, pungent dust, sneezing, coughing, blowing our noses, and rubbing our eyes every minute. The bath-house, half rotten, and old like its mistress, was soon crashing and falling to pieces.

'Now, mates, hard on it – ea-sy!' commanded Semka, and row after row of beams fell creaking to the ground.

'Wonder what book that is she's got. Such a thick one!' said Mishka, reflectively leaning upon his lever and wiping the sweat off his face with his palm. Immediately turned into a mulatto, he spat on his hands, raised the lever to drive it into a crack between two beams, drove it in, and added in the same reflective tone, 'Suppose it's the Gospels – seems to me it's too thick.'

'What's that to you?' asked Semka.

'To me? Why, nothing. I like to hear a book read – if it's a holy one. We had a soldier in the village, African his name was; he'd begin to reel off the psalms sometimes, just like a drum – fine.'

'Well?' Semka said again, busy making a cigarette.

'Well – nothing. Only it *was* fine! Couldn't understand it, still it's the Word of God – don't hear it in the street like. Can't understand it, still you feel it's a word for the soul.'

'Can't understand it, you say. Still you can see you're a blockhead,' said Semka, imitating him.

'I know you're always swearing at me,' sighed the other.

'How else can you talk to fools? They can't understand anything. Come on – let's have a go at this rotten plank.'

The bath-house was falling to pieces, surrounded by splinters and drowned in clouds of dust, which had even made the leaves of the nearest trees a light grey. The July sun mercilessly scorched our backs and shoulders. One could not tell from our faces, streaked with dust and sweat, to which precisely of the four coloured races we belonged.

'The book's got silver on too,' again began Mishka.

Semka raised his head and looked attentively in the direction of the summer-house.

'Looks like it,' he said shortly.

'Must be the Gospels, then.'

'Well, and what if it is?'

'Nothing.'

'Got enough and to spare of that stuff, my boy. If you're so fond of Holy Scripture you'd better go to her. Go to her and say, "Read to me a bit, grannie. For *we* can't get that sort of thing." Say, "*We* don't go to church, by reason of our dirtiness. But we've got souls too, all as they should be, in the right place." Go on – go along.'

'Truth, shall I?'

'Go on.'

Mishka threw down his lever, pulled his shirt straight, smeared the dust over his face with his sleeve, and jumped down from the bath-house.

'*She'll* give it you, devil of a fool, you,' mumbled Semka, smiling sceptically, but watching with extreme curiosity the figure of his comrade, making its way to the summer-house through the mass of dock-leaves.

Tall and bent, with bare, dirty hands, heavily lurching as he walked and catching the branches of the bushes now and then, he was moving clumsily forward, a confused, gentle smile on his face.

The sun glistened on the glasses of the old lady's spectacles and on their silver rims.

Contrary to Semka's supposition, she did not 'give it him.' We could not hear for the rustle of the foliage what Mishka was saying to her, but we presently saw him heavily sitting down at her feet, so that his nose almost touched the open book. His face was dignified and calm; we saw him blow on his beard, to try and get the dust off it, fidget, and at last settle down in an uncomfortable position, with his neck stretched out, expectantly watching the old lady's little shrivelled hands as they methodically turned over the leaves of the book.

'Look at him, the hairy dog! Got a fine rest for himself. Let's go too! He'll be taking it easy there, and we've got to do his work for him. Come on!'

In two or three minutes Semka and I were also sitting on the ground, one on each side of our comrade. The old lady did not say a word to us when we appeared, only looked at us attentively and sharply, and again began to turn over the leaves of the book, searching for something. We sat in a luxuriant green ring of fresh, sweet-smelling foliage, and above us was spread the kindly, soft, cloudless sky. Now and then came a light breeze, and the leaves began to rustle with that mysterious sound which always speaks to the heart, waking in it gentleness and peace, and turning the thoughts to something indefinite, yet dear to man, cleansing his soul from foulness, or, at any rate, making him forget it for a time and breathe freely, and, as it were, anew.

'"Paul, a servant of Jesus Christ,"' began the old lady's voice. Shaking and cracked from age, it was yet full of a stern and pompous piety. At its first sound Mishka energetically crossed himself.

Semka began fidgeting on the ground, trying to find a more comfortable position. The old lady cast a glance at him, but continued to read.

'"For I long to see you, that I may impart unto you some spiritual gift, to the end ye may be established – that is, that I with you may be comforted in you, each of us by the other's faith, both yours and mine."'

Semka, like the true heathen he was, gave a loud yawn. His comrade cast a reproachful glance at him from his blue eyes and hung his touzled head, all covered with dust. The old lady also looked at him severely without leaving off reading, and this somewhat abashed him. He wrinkled up his nose, looked sideways, and, evidently wishing to atone for his yawn, gave a long, pious sigh.

Several minutes passed quietly. The improving and monotonous reading acted as a sedative.

'"For the wrath of God is revealed against all ungodliness and"' –

'What do you want?' suddenly cried the old lady to Semka.

'O-oh … nothing. If you would kindly go on reading – I am listening!' he explained meekly.

'Why are you touching the clasp with your dirty great hand?' she said, in exasperation.

'I'm curious, for – it's such fine work, you see. And it's in my line. I understand locksmith work. So I just felt it.'

'Listen,' said the old lady drily. 'Tell me, what have I been reading about?'

'Why, certainly. I understand.'

'Well, tell me.'

'A sermon – so, of course, it's teaching on the faith and likewise on sin. It's very simple, all of it, and – all very true. Just takes hold of the soul – pinches it, like!'

The old lady shook her head sadly and looked round on us all with reproach.

'Lost souls you are – stones. Go back to work!'

'She – seems to be annoyed, mates,' observed Mishka, smiling penitently.

Semka scratched his back, yawned, and looking after the old lady, who, without turning round, was walking away down the narrow path, said reflectively –

'The clasps are silver, no mistake,' and he gave a broad smile, as if enjoying some pleasant prospect.

Having spent the night in the garden by the ruins of the bath-house, which we had finished pulling down that day, towards noon of the next we cleaned out the well, got soaked in the water, smeared all over with mud, and were sitting in the yard by the porch in the expectation of our wages, talking to each other and anticipating a good dinner and supper in the near future; to look farther ahead we none of us were inclined.

'Why the devil doesn't that old hag come?' said Semka impatiently, but in a low voice.

'Just listen to him!' said Mishka reproachfully, shaking his head. 'Now, what on earth is he swearing for? She's a real godly old lady. And he swears at her. What a disposition!'

'We are clever, aren't we? You great scarecrow!'

This pleasant and interesting conversation of friends was interrupted by the appearance of the old lady. She came up to us, and holding out her hand with the money in it said scornfully –

'There, take it and go along. I wanted to give you the wash-house planks to break up for firewood, but you are not worth it.'

Unhonoured with the task of breaking up the wash-house planks, which, however, we were not in need of now, we took the money in silence and went.

'Oh, you old she-devil!' began Semka, as soon as we were outside the gate. 'Did you ever? We're not worth it! You dead toad – you! There, go and screech over your book now!'

Plunging his hand into his pocket, he pulled out two bright metal objects and showed them to us in triumph.

Mishka stopped, stretching his neck towards Semka's uplifted hand.

'You've broken the clasps off?' he asked, astonished.

'That's it, mate. Silver! Get a rouble for them at least.'

'Well, I never! When did you do it? Hide them quick, out of harm's way!'

'I'll hide 'em all right.'

We continued our way up the street in silence.

'That's smart,' Mishka said to himself. 'Went and broke it off! Ye-es. But the book is a good book. The old lady will be offended with us very likely.'

'Why, no, mate, not she! She'll call us back and tip us,' joked Semka.

'How much do you want for them?'

'Lowest price – ninety kopeks.[9] Not a copper less. Cost more to me. Broke my nail over it – look.'

'Sell them to me,' said Mishka timidly.

'To you? Thinking of having 'em for studs? They'll make first-rate ones – just suit your lovely face they would!'

'No; truth – sell them to me!' And Mishka lowered his tone in supplication.

'Why, take 'em, I say. How much will you give?'

'Take. How much is there for my share?'

'Rouble twenty.'

'And how much do you want for them?'

'A rouble.'

'Make it less to oblige a mate.'

'Oh, you fool! What the devil do you want them for?'

'Never mind; you just sell them to me.'

At last the bargain was struck, and the clasps were transferred to Mishka for ninety kopeks.

He stopped and began turning them over in his hand, his touzled head bent low, carefully examining them with knit brows.

'Hang 'em on your nose,' suggested Semka.

'Why should I?' replied Mishka gravely. 'I'll take 'em back to the old lady. "Here, old lady," I'll say, "we just took these little things with us by mistake, so you put 'em on again," I'll say, "in their places – on that same book there." Only you've torn them out with the stuff; how can she fix them on now?'

'Are you actually going to take them back?' and Semka opened his mouth.

'Why, yes. You see a book like that – it ought to be all whole, you know. It won't do to tear off bits of it. The old lady will be

---

9 A penny is equal to four or five kopeks. – Tr.

offended, too. And she's not far from her grave. So I'll just – You wait for me a minute. I'll run back.'

And before we could hold him, he had disappeared round the street corner.

'There's a soft-boned fool for you. You dirty insect, you!' cried Semka in indignation, taking in the meaning of the occurrence and its possible consequences. And swearing for all he was worth, he began persuading me.

'Come on, hurry up! He'll do us. He's sitting there now, as like as not, with his hands tied behind him, and the old hag's sent for the policeman already. That's what philandering round with a ninny like that means. Why, he'll get you into jail for nothing at all. What a scoundrel! What foul-souled thing would treat his mate like this? Good Lord! That's what people have come to! Come on, you devil, what are you standing there for? Waiting? The devil wait for you and take you all, the scoundrels. Pah, you damned asses! Not coming? All right, then' –

Promising me something extraordinarily dreadful, Semka gave me a despairing poke in the ribs, and went off with rapid strides.

I wanted to know what was happening to Mishka and the old lady, and walked quietly towards her house. I did not think that I would incur any danger or unpleasantness.

And I was not mistaken.

Approaching the house, I looked through a chink in the board fence, and saw and heard the following: –

The old lady sat on the steps holding the clasps of her Bible, 'torn out with the stuff,' in her hand, and looked searchingly and sternly through her spectacles at Mishka's face, who stood with his back to me.

Notwithstanding the stern, hard gleam in her hard eyes, there were soft lines at the corners of her mouth now; it was clear that the old lady wanted to conceal a kindly smile – the smile of forgiveness.

From behind her back protruded three heads – two women's

– one red-faced, and tied up in a many-coloured handkerchief, the other uncovered, with a cataract in the left eye; over her shoulders appeared a man's face – wedge-shaped, with little grey side-whiskers and a crest of hair on the top. This face incessantly blinked and winked in a curious manner with both eyes, as if saying to Mishka –

'Cut, man! Run!'

Mishka mumbled, trying to explain.

'Such a rare book! says you're all beasts and dogs, you are. So I thought to myself – it's true, Lord. To tell the truth, we are godless scoundrels – miserable wretches. And then, too, I thought, barynia – she's an old lady; perhaps she's got but this one book for a comfort. Then the clasps – we wouldn't get much for them. But on the book now, they are a real thing. So I turned it over in my mind, and I said to myself, 'I'll go give the old lady some pleasure' – bring her this back. Then too, thanked be the Lord, we earned somewhat yesterday to buy our bread. Well, good afternoon to you, ma'am; I'll be going.'

'Wait a moment,' said the old lady. 'Did you understand what I read yesterday?'

'Did I? Why, no, how can I understand it? I hear it, that's so – and even then, *how* do I hear it? As if our ears were fit for the Word of God? We can't understand it. You hear it with your heart like, but the ear, it doesn't take it in. Goodbye to you, ma'am.'

'So – so!' drawled out the old lady. 'No, just wait a minute.'

Mishka sighed forlornly, so that you could hear him all over the yard, and moved his weight from one foot to the other like a bear. Evidently this explanation was growing very wearisome to him.

'Would you like me to read you some more?'

'M'm! my mates are waiting for me.'

'Never mind them. You are a good fellow. You must leave them.'

'Very well,' assented Mishka in a low voice.

'You will leave them? Yes?'

'I'll leave them.'

'That's a sensible fellow. You're quite a child. And look at you – a great beard, almost to your waist! Are you married?'

'A widower. My wife, she died.'

'And why do you drink? You are a drunkard, aren't you?'

'A drunkard, ma'am. I drink.'

'Why?'

'Why do I drink? Why, from foolishness. Being a fool, I drink. If a man had brains, would he go and ruin himself of his own accord?' said Mishka in a desolate tone.

'You are quite right. Then cultivate wisdom and get better. Go to church. Hear God's Word. In It is all wisdom.'

'That's so, of course,' almost groaned Mishka.

'I will read some more to you. Would you like it?'

'Just as you please, ma'am.' Mishka was weary to death.

The old lady got her Bible from somewhere behind her, found a place, and the yard was filled with her quavering voice:

'"Judge not, that ye be not judged, for with what judgement ye judge, ye shall be judged; and with what measure ye mete, it shall be meted unto you."'

Mishka gave his head a shake, and scratched his left shoulder.

'"Dost thou think to escape the judgement of God?"'

'Barynia!' began Mishka in a plaintive tone, 'let me go, for God's sake. I had better come some other time to listen. But now I'm real hungry, barynia. My stomach aches, even. We've had nothing to eat since last night.'

The barynia shut the door with a bang.

'Go along! Go!' sounded sharply and shortly through the yard.

'Thank you kindly.' And he almost ran to the gate.

'Unrepentant souls, hearts of beasts,' hissed in the yard behind him.

In half an hour we were sitting in an inn, having tea and kalatch.[10]

---

10 A circular roll made of hard dough. – Tr.

'It was as though she was driving a gimlet into me,' said Mishka, smiling at me with his good-natured eyes. 'I stood there, and thought to myself, oh my goodness! What on earth did I go for? Went for martyrdom. She might, like a sensible woman, have taken the clasps from me and let me go my way; but no, she begins a-talking. What queer people there are! You want to treat them honest, and they go on, at their own, all the time. I tell her straight. "There, barynia," I said, "here are your clasps. Don't blame me." And she says, "No," she says, "wait a bit – you tell me why you brought them back to me," and went ahead as if she was pulling the veins out of my body. I broke out into a sweat, with her talking even – truth I did.'

And he still smiled with that infinitely gentle smile of his.

Semka, sulky, ruffled, and moody, said to him gravely when he had ended his Odyssey –

'You'd better die outright, you precious blockhead, you! Or else to-morrow, with these fine tricks of yours, the flies or beetles will eat you up.'

'How you do talk! Come, let's have a glass. Drink to the ending of the affair!'

And we heartily drank to the ending of this queer affair.

MALVA

THE SEA LAUGHED.

It trembled at the warm and light breath of the wind and became covered with tiny wrinkles that reflected the sun in blinding fashion and laughed at the sky with its thousands of silvery lips. In the deep space between sea and sky buzzed the deafening and joyous sound of the waves chasing each other on the flat beach of the sandy promontory. This noise and brilliancy of sunlight, reverberated a thousand times by the sea, mingled harmoniously in ceaseless and joyous agitation. The sky was glad to shine; the sea was happy to reflect the glorious light.

The wind caressed the powerful and satin-like breast of the sea, the sun heated it with its rays and it sighed as if fatigued by these ardent caresses; it filled the burning air with the salty aroma of its emanations. The green waves, coursing up the yellow sand, threw on the beach the white foam of their luxurious crests which melted with a gentle murmur, and wet it.

At intervals along the beach, scattered with shells and sea weed, were stakes of wood driven into the sand and on which hung fishing nets, drying and casting shadows as fine as cobwebs. A few large boats and a small one were drawn up beyond high-water mark, and the waves as they ran up towards them seemed as if they were calling to them. Gaffs, oars, coiled ropes, baskets and barrels lay about in disorder and amidst it all was a cabin built of yellow branches, bark and matting. Above the general chaos floated a red rag at the extremity of a tall mast.

Under the shade of a boat lay Vassili Legostev, the watchman at this outpost of the Grebentchikov fishing grounds. Lying on his stomach, his head resting on his hands, he was gazing fixedly out to sea, where away in the distance danced a black spot. Vassili saw with satisfaction that it grew larger and was drawing nearer.

Screwing up his eyes on account of the glare caused by the reflection on the water, he grunted with pleasure and content. Malva was coming. A few minutes more and she would be there, laughing so heartily as to strain every stitch of her well-filled bodice. She would throw her robust and gentle arms around him and kiss him, and in that rich sonorous voice that startles the sea gulls would give him the news of what was going on yonder. They would make a good fish soup together, and drink brandy as they chatted and caressed each other. That is how they spent every Sunday and holiday. And at daylight he would row her back over the sea in the sharp morning air. Malva, still nodding with sleep, would hold the tiller and he would watch her as he pulled. She was amusing at those times, funny and charming both, like a cat which had eaten well. Sometimes she would slip from her seat and roll herself up at the bottom of the boat like a ball.

As Vassili watched the little black spot grow larger it seemed to him that Malva was not alone in the boat. Could Serejka have come along with her? Vassili moved heavily on the sand, sat up, shaded his eyes with his hands, and with a show of ill humour began to strain his eyes to see who was coming. No, the man rowing was not Serejka. He rows strong but clumsily. If Serejka were rowing Malva would not take the trouble to hold the rudder.

'Hey there!' cried Vassili impatiently.

The sea gulls halted in their flight and listened.

'Hallo! Hallo!' came back from the boat. It was Malva's sonorous voice.

'Who's with you?'

A laugh replied to him.

'Jade!' swore Vassili under his breath.

He spat on the ground with vexation.

He was puzzled. While he rolled a cigarette he examined the neck and back of the rower who was rapidly drawing nearer. The sound of the water when the oars struck it resounded in the still air, and the sand crunched under the watchman's bare feet as he stamped about in his impatience.

'Who's with you?' he cried, when he could discern the familiar smile on Malva's pretty plump face.

'Wait. You'll know him all right,' she replied laughing.

The rower turned on his seat and, also laughing, looked at Vassili.

The watchman frowned. It seemed to him that he knew the fellow.

'Pull harder!' commanded Malva.

The stroke was so vigorous that the boat was carried up the beach on a wave, fell over on one side and then righted itself while the wave rolled back laughing into the sea. The rower jumped out on the beach, and going up to Vassili said:

'How are you, father?'

'Iakov!' cried Vassili, more surprised than pleased.

They embraced three times. Afterwards Vassili's stupor became mingled with both joy and uneasiness. The watchman stroked his blond beard with one hand and with the other gesticulated:

'I knew something was up; my heart told me so. So it was you! I kept asking myself if it was Serejka. But I saw it was not Serejka. How did you come here?'

Vassili would have liked to look at Malva, but his son's rollicking eyes were upon him and he did not dare. The pride he felt at having a son so strong and handsome struggled in him with the embarrassment caused by the presence of Malva. He shuffled about and kept asking Iakov one question after another, often without waiting for a reply. His head felt awhirl, and he felt particularly uneasy when he heard Malva say in a mocking tone.

'Don't skip about – for joy. Take him to the cabin and give him something to eat.'

The father examined his son from head to foot. On the latter's lips hovered that cunning smile Vassili knew so well. Malva turned her green eyes from the father to the son and munched melon seeds between her small white teeth. Iakov smiled and for a few seconds, which were painful to Vassili, all three were silent.

'I'll come back in a moment,' said Vassili suddenly going towards the cabin. 'Don't stay there in the sun, I'm going to fetch some water. We'll make some soup. I'll give you some fish soup, Iakov.'

He seized a saucepan that was lying on the ground and disappeared behind the fishing nets.

Malva and the peasant followed him.

'Well, my fine young fellow, I brought you to your father, didn't I?' said Malva, brushing up against Iakov's robust figure.

He turned towards her his face framed in its curled blond beard, and with a brilliant gleam in his eyes said:

'Yes, here we are – It's fine here, isn't it? What a stretch of sea!'

'The sea is great. Has the old man changed much?'

'No, not much. I expected to find him more grey. He's still pretty solid.'

'How long is it since you saw him?'

'About five years. I was nearly seventeen when he left the village.'

They entered the cabin, the air of which was suffocating from the heat and the odour of cooking fish. They sat down. Between them there was a roughly-hewn oak table. They looked at each other for a long time without speaking.

'So you want to work here?' said Malva at last.

'I don't know. If I find something, I'll work.'

'You'll find work,' replied Malva with assurance, examining him critically with her green eyes.

He paid no attention to her, and with his sleeve wiped away the perspiration that covered his face.

She suddenly began to laugh.

'Your mother probably sent messages for your father by you?'

Iakov gave a shrug of ill humour and replied:

'Of course. What if she did?'

'Oh, nothing.'

And she laughed the louder.

Her laugh displeased Iakov. He paid no attention to her and thought of his mother's instructions. When she accompanied him to the end of the village she had said quickly, blinking her eyes:

'In Christ's name, Iakov say to him: "Father, mother is alone yonder. Five years have gone by and she is always alone. She is getting old." Tell him that, Iakov, my little Iakov, for the love of God. Mother will soon be an old woman. She's always alone, always at work. In Christ's name, tell him that.'

And she had wept silently, hiding her face in her apron.

Iakov had not pitied her then, but he did now. And his face took on a hard expression before Malva, as if he were about to abuse her.

'Here I am!' cried Vassili, bursting in on them with a wriggling fish in one hand and a knife in the other.

He had not got over his uneasiness, but had succeeded in dissimulating it deep within him. Now he looked at his guests with serenity and good nature; only his manner was more agitated than usual.

'I'll make a bit of a fire in a minute, and we'll talk. Why, Iakov, what a fine fellow you've grown!'

Again he disappeared.

Malva went on munching her melon seeds. She stared familiarly at Iakov. He tried not to meet her eyes, although he would have liked to, and he thought to himself:

'Life must come easy here. People seem to eat as much as they want to. How strong she is and father, too!'

Then intimidated by the silence, he said aloud:

'I forgot my bag in the boat. I'll go and get it.'

Iakov rose leisurely and went out. Vassili appeared a moment later. He bent down towards Malva and said rapidly with anger:

'What did you want to bring him for? What shall I tell him about you?'

'What's that to me? Am I afraid of him? Or of you?' she asked, closing her green eyes with disdain. Then she laughed: 'How you went on when you saw him. It was so funny!'

'Funny, eh?'

The sand crunched under Iakov's steps and they had to suspend their conversation. Iakov had brought a bag which he threw into a corner. He cast a hostile look at the young woman.

She went on munching her seeds. Vassili, seating himself on the wood-bin, said with a forced smile:

'What made you think of coming?'

'Why, I just came. We wrote you.'

'When? I haven't received any letter.'

'Really? We wrote often.'

'The letter must have got lost,' said Vassili regretfully. 'It always does when it's important.'

'So you don't know how things are at home?' asked Iakov, suspiciously.

'How should I know? I received no letter.'

Then Iakov told him that the horse was dead, that all the corn had been eaten before the beginning of February, and that he himself had been unable to find any work. Hay was also short, and the cow had almost perished from hunger. They had managed as best they could until April and then they decided that Iakov should join the father far away and work three months with him. That is what they had written. Then they sold three sheep, bought flour and hay and Iakov had started.

'How is that possible?' cried Vassili. 'I sent you some money.'

'Your money didn't go far. We repaired the cottage, we had to marry sister off and I bought a plough. You know five years is a long time.'

'Hum,' said Vassili, 'wasn't it enough? What a tale of woe! Ah, there's my soup boiling over!'

He rose and stooping before the fire on which was the saucepan, Vassili meditated while throwing the scum into the flame. Nothing in his son's recital had touched him particularly, and he felt irritated against his wife and Iakov. He had sent them a great deal of money during the last five years, and yet they had not been able to manage. If Malva had not been present he would have told his son what he thought about it. Iakov was smart enough to leave the village on his own responsibility and without the father's permission, but he had not been able to get a living out of the soil. Vassili sighed as he stirred the soup, and as he watched the blue flames he thought of his son and Malva. Henceforward, he thought, his life would be less agreeable, less free. Iakov had surely guessed what Malva was.

Meanwhile Malva, in the cabin, was trying to arouse the rustic with her bold eyes.

'Perhaps you left a girl in the village?' she asked suddenly.

'Perhaps,' he responded surlily.

Inwardly he was abusing Malva.

'Is she pretty?' she asked with indifference.

Iakov made no reply.

'Why don't you answer? Is she better looking than I, or no?'

He looked at her in spite of himself. Her cheeks were sunburnt and plump, her lips red and tempting and now, parted in a malicious smile, showing the white even teeth, they seemed to tremble. Her bust was full and firm under a pink cotton waist that set off to advantage her trim waist and well-rounded arms. But he did not like her green and cynical eyes.

'Why do you talk like that?' he asked.

He sighed without reason and spoke in a beseeching tone, yet he wanted to speak brutally to her.

'How shall I talk?' she asked laughing.

'There you are, laughing – at what?'

'At you—'

'What have I done to you?' he said with irritation. And once more he lowered his eyes under her gaze.

She made no reply.

Iakov understood her relations towards his father perfectly well and that prevented him from expressing himself freely. He was not surprised. It would have been difficult for a man like his father to have been long without a companion.

'The soup is ready,' announced Vassili, at the threshold of the cabin. 'Get the spoons, Malva.'

When she found the spoons she said she must go down to the sea to wash them.

The father and son watched her as she ran down the sands and both were silent.

'Where did you meet her?' asked Vassili, finally.

'I went to get news of you at the office. She was there. She said to me: "Why go on foot along the sand? Come in the boat. I'm going there.' And so we started."

'And – what do you think of, her?'

'Not bad,' said Iakov, vaguely, blinking his eyes.

'What could I do?' asked Vassili. 'I tried at first. But it was impossible. She mends my clothes and so on. Besides it's as easy to escape from death as from a woman when once she's after you.'

'What's it to me?' said Iakov. 'It's your affair. I'm not your judge.'

Malva now returned with the spoons, and they sat down to
dinner. They ate without talking, sucking the bones noisily and
spitting them out on the sand, near the door. Iakov literally
devoured his food, which seemed to please Malva vastly; she
watched with tender interest his sunburnt cheeks extend and his
thick humid lips moving quickly. Vassili was not hungry. He tried,
however, to appear absorbed in the meal so as to be able to watch
Malva and Iakov at his ease.

After awhile, when Iakov had eaten his fill he said he was
sleepy.

'Lie down here,' said Vassili. 'We'll wake you up.'

'I'm willing,' said Iakov, sinking down on a coil of rope. 'And
what will you do?'

Embarrassed by his son's smile, Vassili left the cabin hastily,
Malva frowned and replied to Iakov:

'What's that to you? Learn to mind your own business, my
lad.'

Then she went out.

Iakov turned over and went to sleep.

Vassili had fixed three stakes in the sand, and with a piece of
matting had rigged up a shelter from the sun. Then he lay down
fiat on his back and contemplated the sky. When Malva came up
and dropped on the sand by his side he turned towards her with
vexation plainly written on his face.

'Well, old man,' she said laughing, 'you don't seem pleased to
see your son.'

'He mocks me. And why? Because of you,' replied Vassili
testily.

'Oh, I am sorry. What can we do? I mustn't come here again,
eh? All right. I'll not come again.'

'Siren that you are! Ah, you women! He mocks me and you
too – and yet you are what I have dearest to me.'

He moved away from her and was silent. Squatting on the
sand, with her legs drawn up to her chin, Malva balanced herself

gently to and fro, idly gazing with her green eyes over the dazzling joyous sea, and she smiled with triumph as all women do when they understand the power of their beauty.

'Why don't you speak?' asked Vassili.

'I'm thinking,' said Malva.

Then after a pause she added:

'Your son's a fine fellow.'

'What's that to you?' cried Vassili, jealously.

'Who knows?'

He glanced at her suspiciously. 'Take care,' he said, menacingly, 'Don't play the imbecile. I'm a patient man, but I mustn't be crossed.'

He ground his teeth and clenched his fists.

'Don't frighten me, Vassili,' she said indifferently, without looking up at him.

'Well, stop your joking.'

'Don't try to frighten me.'

'I'll soon make you dance if you begin any foolishness.'

'Would you beat me?'

She went up to him and gazed with curiosity at his frowning face.

'One would think you were a countess. Yes, I would beat you.'

'Yet I'm not your wife,' said Malva, calmly. 'You have been accustomed to beat your wife for nothing, and you imagine that you can do the same with me. No, I am free. I belong only to myself, and I am afraid of no one. But you are afraid of your son, and now you dare threaten me.'

She shook her head with disdain. Her careless manner cooled Vassili's anger. He had never seen her look so beautiful.

'I have something else to tell you,' she went on. 'You boasted to Serejka that I could no more get along without you than without bread, and that I cannot live without you. You are mistaken. Perhaps it is not you that I love and not for you that I come. Perhaps I love the peace of this deserted beach. (Here she made a wide gesture with her arms.) Perhaps I love these lonely sands, with their vast stretch of sea and sky, and to be away from vile beings. Because you are here is nothing to me. If this were Serejka's place I should come here. If your son lived here, I should come too. It would be better still if no one were here, for I am disgusted with you all. But if I take it into my head one day – beautiful as I am – I can always choose a man, and one who'll please me better than you.'

'So, so!' hissed Vassili, furiously, and he seized her by the throat. 'So that's your game, is it?'

He shook her, and she did not strive to get away from his grasp, although her face was congested and her eyes bloodshot. She merely placed her two hands on the rough hands that were around her throat.

'Ah, now I know you!' Vassili was hoarse with rage. 'And yet you said you loved me, and you kissed me and caressed me? Ah, I'll show you!'

Holding her down to the ground, he struck her repeatedly with his clenched fist. Finally, fatigued with the exertion, he pushed her away from him crying:

'There, serpent. Now you've got what you deserved.'

Without a complaint, silent and calm, Malva fell back on her back, all crumpled, red and still beautiful. Her green eyes watched him furtively under the lashes, and burned with a cold flame full of hatred, but he, gasping with excitement and satisfied with the punishment he had inflicted, did not notice the look, and when he stooped down towards her to see if she was crying, she smiled up at him gently.

He looked at her, not understanding and not knowing what to do next. Should he beat her again? But his fury was appeased, and he had no desire to recommence.

'How you love me!' she whispered.

Vassili felt hot all over.

'All right! all right! the devil take you,' he said gloomily. 'Are you satisfied now?'

'Was I not foolish, Vassili? I thought you no longer loved me! I said to myself, "now his son is here he will neglect me for him."'

And she burst out laughing, a strange forced laugh.

'Foolish girl!' said Vassili, smiling in spite of himself.

He felt himself at fault, and was sorry for her, but remembering what she had said, he went on crossly:

'My son has nothing to do with it. If I beat you it was your own fault. Why did you cross me?'

'I did it on purpose to try you.'

And purring like a cat she rubbed herself against his shoulder.

He glanced furtively towards the cabin and bending down embraced the young woman.

'To try me?' he repeated. 'As if you wanted to do that? You see the result?'

'Oh, that's nothing!' said Malva, half closing her eyes. 'I'm not angry. You beat me only because you loved me. You'll make it up to me.'

She gave him a long look, trembled and lowering her voice repeated:

'Oh, yes, you'll make it up to me.'

Vassili interpreted her words in a sense agreeable to him.

'How?' he asked.

'You'll see,' replied Malva calmly, very calmly, but her lips trembled.

'Ah, my darling!' cried Vassili, clasping her close in his arms. 'Do you know that since I have beaten you I love you better.' Her head fell back on his shoulders and he placed his lips on her trembling mouth.

The sea gulls whirled about over their heads uttering hoarse cries. From the distance came the regular and gentle splash of the tiny waves breaking on the sand.

When, at last, they broke from their long embrace, Malva sat up on Vassili's knee. The peasant's face, tanned by wind and sun, was bent close to hers and his great blond beard tickled her neck.

The young woman was motionless; only the gradual and regular rise and fall of her bosom showed her to be alive. Vassili's eyes wandered in turn from the sea to this woman by his side. He told Malva how tired he was of living alone and how painful were his sleepless nights filled with gloomy thoughts. Then he kissed her again on the mouth with the same sound that he might have made in chewing a hot piece of meat.

They stayed there three hours in this way, and finally, when he saw the sun setting, Vassili said with a bored look:

'I must go and make some tea. Our guest will soon be awake.'

Malva rose with the indolent gesture of a languorous cat, and with a gesture of regret he started towards the cabin. Through her half-open lids the young woman watched him as he moved away, and sighed as people sigh when they have borne too heavy a burden.

Fifteen days later it was again Sunday and again Vassili Legostev, stretched out on the sand near his hut, was gazing out to sea, waiting for Malva. And the deserted sea laughed, playing with the reflections of the sun, and legions of waves were born to run on the sand, deposit the foam of their crests and return to the sea, where they melted.

All was as before. Only Vassili, who the last time awaited her coming with peaceful security, was now filled with impatience. Last Sunday she had not come; to-day she would surely come. He did not doubt it for a moment, but he wanted to see her as soon as possible, Iakov, at least, would not be there to embarrass them. The day before yesterday, as he passed with the other fishermen, he said he would go to town on Sunday to buy a blouse. He had found work at fifteen roubles a month.

Except for the gulls, the sea was still deserted. The familiar little black spot did not appear.

'Ah, you're not coming!' said Vassili, with ill humour. 'All right, don't. I don't want you.'

And he spat with disdain in the direction of the water.

The sea laughed.

'If, at least, Serejka would come,' he thought. And he tried to think only of Serejka. What a good-for-nothing the fellow is! Robust, able to read, seen the world – but what a drunkard! Yet good company. One can't feel dull in his company. The women are mad for him; all run after him. Malva's the only one that keeps aloof. No, no sign of her! What a cursed woman! Perhaps she's angry because I beat her.'

Thus, thinking of his son, of Serejka, but more often of Malva, Vassili paced up and down the sandy beach, turning every now and then to look anxiously out to sea. But Malva did not come.

This is what had happened.

Iakov rose early, and on going down to the beach as usual to wash himself, he saw Malva. She was seated on the bow of a large fishing boat anchored in the surf and letting her bare feet hang, sat combing her damp hair.

Iakov stopped to watch her.

'Have you had a bath?' he cried.

She turned to look at him, and glanced down at her feet: then, continuing to comb herself, she replied:

'Yes, I took a bath. Why are you up so early?'

'Aren't you up early?'

'I am not an example for you. If you did all I do, you'd be in all kinds of trouble.'

'Why do you always wish to frighten me?' he asked.

'And you, why do you make eyes at me?'

Iakov had no recollection of having looked at her more than at the other women on the fishing grounds, but now he said to her suddenly:

'Because you are so – appetizing.'

'If your father heard you, he'd give you an appetite! No, my lad, don't run after me, because I don't want to be between you and Vassili. You understand?'

'What have I done?' asked Iakov. 'I haven't touched you.'

'You daren't touch me,' retorted Malva.

There was such a contemptuous tone in her voice that he resented this.

'So I dare not?' he replied, climbing up on the boat and seating himself at her side.

'No, you dare not.'

'And if I touch you?'

'Try!'

'What would you do?'

'I'd give you such a box on the ear that you would fall into the water.'

'Let's see you do it.'

'Touch me if you dare!'

Throwing his arm around her waist, he pressed her to his breast.

'Here I am. Now box my ears.'

'Let me be, Iakov,' she said, quickly, trying to disengage herself from his arms which trembled.

'Where is the punishment you promised me?'

'Let go or take care!'

'Oh, stop your threats – luscious strawberry that you are!'

He drew her to him and pressed his thick lips into her sunburnt cheek.

She gave a wild laugh of defiance, seized Iakov's arms and suddenly, with a quick movement of her whole body threw herself forward. They fell into the water enlaced, forming a single heavy mass, and disappeared under the splashing foam. Then from beneath the agitated water Iakov appeared, looking half drowned. Malva, at his side swimming like a fish, eluded his grasp, and tried to prevent him regaining the boat. Iakov struggled desperately, striking the water and roaring like a walrus, while Malva, screaming with laughter, swam round and round him, throwing the salt water in his face, and then diving to avoid his vigorous blows.

At last he caught her and pulled her under the water, and the waves passed over both their heads. Then they came to the surface again both panting with the exertion. Thus they played like two big fish until, finally, tired out and full of salt water, they climbed up the beach and sat down in the sun to dry.

Malva laughed and twisted her hair to get the water out.

The day was growing. The fishermen, after their night of heavy slumber, were emerging from their huts, one by one. From the distance all looked alike. One began to strike blows on an empty barrel at regular intervals. Two women were heard quarrelling. Dogs barked.

'They are getting up,' said Iakov. 'And I wanted to start to town early. I've lost time with you.'

'One does nothing good in my company,' she said, half in jest, half seriously.

'What a habit you have of scaring people,' replied Iakov.

'You'll see when your father—'

This allusion to his father angered him.

'What about my father? I'm not a boy. And I'm not blind, either. He's not a saint, either; he deprives himself of nothing. If you don't mind I'll steal you from my father.'

'You?'

'Do you think I wouldn't dare?'

'Really?'

'Now, look you,' he began furiously, 'don't defy me. I—'

'What now?' she asked with indifference.

'Nothing.'

He turned away with a determined look on his face.

'How brave you are,' she said, tauntingly. 'You remind me of the inspector's little dog. At a distance he barks and threatens to bite, but when you get near him he puts his tail between his legs and runs away.'

'All right,' cried Iakov, angrily. 'Wait! you'll see what I am.'

Advancing towards them came a sunburnt, tattered and

muscular-looking individual. He wore a ragged red shirt, his trousers were full of holes, and his feet were bare. His face was covered with freckles and he had big saucy blue eyes and an impertinent turned-up nose. When he came up he stopped and made a grimace.

'Serejka drank yesterday, and today Serejka's pocket is empty. Lend me twenty kopeks. I'll not return them.'

Iakov burst out laughing; Malva smiled.

'Give me the money,' went on the tramp. 'I'll marry you for twenty kopeks if you like.'

'You're an odd fellow,' said Iakov, 'are you a priest?'

'Imbecile question,' replied Serejka. 'Wasn't I servant to a priest at Ouglitch?'

'I don't want to get married,' said Iakov.

'Give the money all the same, and I won't tell your father you're paying court to his queen,' replied Serejka, passing his tongue over his dry and cracked lips.

Iakov did not want to give twenty kopeks, but they had warned him to be on his guard when dealing with Serejka, and to put up with his whims. The tramp never demanded much, but if he was refused he spread evil tales about you or else he would beat you. So Iakov, sighing, put his hand in his pocket.

'That's right,' said Serejka, with a tone of encouragement, and he sat down beside them on the sand. 'Always do what I tell you and you'll be happy. And you,' he went on, turning to Malva – 'when are you going to marry me? Better be quick. I don't like to wait long.'

'You are too ragged. Begin by sewing up your holes and then we'll see,' replied Malva.

Serejka regarded his rents with a reproachful air and shook his head.

'Give me one of your skirts, that'll be better.'

'Yes, I can,' said Malva, laughing.

'I'm serious. You must have an old one you don't want.'

'You'd do better to buy yourself a pair of trousers.'

'I prefer to drink the money.'

Serejka rose and, jingling his twenty kopeks, shuffled off, followed by a strange smile from Malva.

When he was some distance away, Iakov said:

'In our village such a braggart would soon have been put in his place. Here, every one seems afraid of him.'

Malva looked at Iakov and replied, disdainfully:

'You don't know his worth.'

'There's nothing to know. He's worth five kopeks a hundred.'

She did not reply, but watched the play of the waves as they chased one after the other, swaying the fishing boat. The mast inclined now to right, now to left, and the bow rose and then fell suddenly, striking the water with a loud splash.

'Why don't you go?' asked Malva.

'Where?' he asked.

'You wanted to go to town.'

'I shan't go now.'

'Well, go to your father's.'

'And you?'

'What?'

'Shall you go, too?'

'No.'

'Then I shan't either.'

'Are you going to stay round me all day?'

'I don't want your company so much as that,' replied Iakov, offended.

He rose and moved away.

But he was mistaken in saying that he did not need her, for when away from her he felt lonely. A strange feeling had come to him after their conversation, a secret desire to protest against the father. Only yesterday this feeling had not existed, nor even to-day, before he saw Malva. Now it seemed to him that his father embarrassed him and stood in his way, although he was far away over the sea yonder, on a narrow tongue of sand almost invisible to the eye. Then it seemed to him, too, that Malva was afraid of the father; if she were not afraid she would talk differently. Now she was missing in his life while only that morning he had not thought of her.

And so he wandered for several hours along the beach, stopping here and there to chat with fishermen he knew. At noon he took a siesta under the shade of an upturned boat. When he awoke he took another stroll and came across Malva far from the fishing ground, reading a tattered book under the shade of the willows.

She looked up at Iakov and smiled.

'Ah, there you are,' he said, sitting down beside her.

'Have you been looking for me long?' she asked, demurely.

'Looking for you? What an idea?' replied Iakov, who was only just beginning to realize that it was the truth.

'Do you know how to read?' she asked.

'Yes – I used to, but I've forgotten everything.'

'So have I.'

'Why didn't you go to the headland to-day?' asked Iakov, suddenly.

'What's that to you?'

Iakov plucked a leaf and chewed it.

'Listen,' he said in a low tone and drawing near her. 'Listen to what I'm going to say. I'm young and I love you.'

'You're a silly lad, very silly,' said Malva, shaking her head.

'I may be a fool,' cried Iakov, passionately. 'But I love you, I love you.'

'Be silent! Go away!'

'Why?'

'Because.'

'Don't be obstinate.' He took her gently by the shoulders. 'Can't you understand?'

'Go away, Iakov,' she cried, severely. 'Go away!'

'Oh, if that's the tone you take I don't care a rap. You're not the only woman here. You imagine that you are better than the others.'

She made no reply, rose and brushed the dust off her skirt.

'Come,' she said.

And they went back to the fishing grounds side by side.

They walked slowly on account of the soft sand. Suddenly, as they were nearing the boats, Iakov stopped short and seized Malva by the arms.

'Are you driving me desperate on purpose? Why do you play with me like this?' he demanded.

'Leave me alone, I tell you,' she said, calmly disengaging herself from his grasp.

Serejka appeared from behind a boat. He shook his fist at the couple, and said, threateningly:

'So, that's how you go off together. Vassili shall know of this.'

'Go to the devil, all of you!' cried Malva. And she left them, disappearing among the boats.

Iakov stood facing Serejka, and looked him square in the face. Serejka boldly returned the stare and so they remained for a minute or two, like two rams ready to charge on each other. Then without a word each turned away and went off in a different direction.

The sea was calm and crimson with the rays of the setting sun. A confused sound hovered over the fishing ground. The voice of a drunken woman sang hysterically words devoid of sense.

In the dawn's pure light the sea still slumbered, reflecting the pearl-like clouds. On the headland a party of fishermen still only half awake moved slowly about, getting ready the rigging of their boat.

Serejka, bareheaded and tattered as usual, stood in the bow hurrying the men on with a hoarse voice, the result of his drunken orgy of the previous night.

'Where are the oars, Vassili?'

Vassili, moody as a dark autumn day, was arranging the net at the bottom of the boat. Serejka watched him and, when he looked his way, smacked his lips, signifying that he wanted to drink.

'Have you any brandy,' he asked.

'Yes,' growled Vassili.

'Good. I'll take a nip when they've gone.'

'Is all ready?' cried the fishermen.

'Let go!' commanded Serejka, jumping to the ground. 'Be careful. Go far out so as not to entangle the net.'

The big boat slid down the greased planks to the water, and the fishermen, jumping in as it went, seized the oars, ready to strike the water directly she was afloat. Then with a big splash the graceful bark forged ahead through the great plain of luminous water.

'Why didn't you come Sunday?' said Vassili, as the two men went back to the cabin.

'I couldn't.'

'You were drunk?'

'No, I was watching your son and his step-mother,' said Serejka, phlegmatically.

'A new worry on your shoulders,' said Vassili, sarcastically and with a forced smile. 'They are only children.' He was tempted to learn where and how Serejka had seen Malva and Iakov the day before, but he was ashamed.

'Why don't you ask news of Malva?' asked Serejka, as he gulped down a glass of brandy.

'What do I care what she does?' replied Vassili, with indifference, although he trembled with a secret presentiment.

'As she didn't come Sunday, you should ask what she was doing. I know you are jealous, you old dog!'

'Oh, there are many like her,' said Vassili, carelessly.

'Are there?' said Serejka, imitating him. 'Ah, you peasants, you're all alike. As long as you gather your honey, it's all one to you.'

'What's she to you?' broke in Vassili with irritation. 'Have you come to ask her hand in marriage?'

'I know she's yours,' said Serejka. 'Have I ever bothered you? But now Iakov, your son, is all the time dancing around her, it's different. Beat him, do you hear? If not, I will. You've got a strong fist if you are a fool.'

Vassili did not reply, but watched the boat as it turned about and made toward the beach again.

'You are right,' he said finally. 'Iakov will hear from me.'

'I don't like him. He smells too much of the village,' said Serejka.

In the distance, on the sea, was opening out the pink fan formed by the rays of the rising sun. The glowing orb was already emerging from the water. Amid the noise of the waves was heard from the boat the distant cry:

'Draw in!'

'Come, boys!' cried Serejka, to the other fishermen on the beach. 'Let's pull together.'

'When you see Iakov tell him to come here to-morrow,' said Vassili.

The boat grounded on the beach and the fishermen, jumping out, pulled their end of the net so that the two groups gradually met, the cork floats bobbing up and down on the water forming a perfect semicircle.

Very late on the evening of the same day, when the fishermen had finished their dinner, Malva, tired and thoughtful, had seated herself on an old boat turned upside down and was watching the sea, already screened in twilight. In the distance a fire was burning, and Malva knew that Vassili had lighted it. Solitary and as if lost in the darkening shadows, the flame leaped high at times and then fell back as if broken. And Malva felt a certain sadness as she watched that red dot abandoned in the desert of ocean, and palpitating feebly among the indefatigable and incomprehensible murmur of the waves.

'What are you doing there?' asked Serejka's voice behind her.

'What's that to you?' she replied dryly, without stirring.

He lighted a cigarette, was silent a moment and then said in a friendly tone:

'What a funny woman you are! First you run away from everybody, and then you throw yourself round everyone's neck.'

'Not round yours,' said Malva, carelessly.

'Not mine, perhaps, but round Iakov's.'

'It makes you envious.'

'Hum! do you want me to speak frankly?'

'Speak.'

'Have you broken off with Vassili?'

'I don't know,' she replied, after a silence. 'I am vexed with him.'

'Why?'

'He beat me.'

'Really? And you let him?'

Serejka could not understand it. He tried to catch a glimpse of Malva's face, and made an ironical grimace.

'I need not have let him beat me,' she said. 'I did not want to defend myself.'

'So you love the old grey cat as much as that?' grinned Serejka, puffing out a cloud of smoke. 'I thought better of you than that.'

'I love none of you,' she said, again indifferent and wafting the smoke away with her hand.

'But if you don't love him, why did you let him beat you?'

'Do you suppose I know? Leave me alone.'

'It's funny,' said Serejka, shaking his head.

Both remained silent.

Night was falling. The shadows came down from the slow-moving clouds to the seas beneath. The waves murmured.

Vassili's fire had gone out on the distant headland, but Malva continued to gaze in that direction.

* * *

The father and son were seated in the cabin facing each other, and drinking brandy which the youth had brought with him to conciliate the old man and so as not to be weary in his company.

Serejka had told Iakov that his father was angry with him on account of Malva, and that he had threatened to beat Malva until she was half dead. He also said that was the reason she resisted Iakov's advances.

This story had excited Iakov's resentment against his father. He now looked upon him as an obstacle in his road that he could neither remove nor get around.

But feeling himself of equal strength as his adversary, Iakov regarded his father boldly, with a look that meant: 'Touch me if you dare!'

They had both drunk two glasses without exchanging a word, except a few commonplace remarks about the fisheries. Alone amidst the deserted waters each nursed his hatred, and both knew that this hate would soon burst forth into flame.

'How's Serejka?' at last Vassili blurted out.

'Drunk as usual,' replied Iakov, pouring our some more brandy for his father.

'He'll end badly – and if you don't take care you'll do the same.'

'I shall never become like him,' replied Iakov, surlily.

'No?' said Vassili, frowning. 'I know what I'm talking about. How long are you here already? Two months. You must soon think of going back. How much money have you saved?'

'In so little time I've not been able to save any,' replied Iakov.

'Then you don't want to stay here any longer, my lad, go back to the village.'

Iakov smiled.

'Why these grimaces?' cried Vassili threateningly, and impatient at his son's coolness. 'Your father's advising you and you mock him. You're in too much of a hurry to play the independent. You want to be put in the traces again.'

Iakov poured out some more brandy and drank it. These coarse reproaches offended him, but he mastered himself, not wanting to arouse his father's anger.

Seeing that his son had drunk again, alone, without filling his glass, made Vassili more angry than ever.

'Your father says to you, "Go home," and you laugh at him. Very well, I'll speak differently. You'll get your pay Saturday and trot home to the village – do you understand?'

'I won't go,' said Iakov, firmly.

'What!' cried Vassili, and leaning his two hands on the edge of the table he rose to his feet. 'Have I spoken, yes or no? You dog, barking at your father! Do you forget that I can do what I please with you?'

His mouth trembled with passion, his face was convulsed, and two swollen veins stood out on his temples.

'I forget nothing,' said Iakov, in a low tone and not looking at his father. 'And you – have you forgotten nothing?'

'It's not your place to preach to me. I'll break every bone in your body.'

Iakov avoided the hand that his father raised over his head and a feeling of savage hatred arose in him. He said, between his clenched teeth:

'Don't touch me. We're not in the village now.'

'Be silent. I'm your father everywhere.'

They stood facing each other, Vassili, his eyes bloodshot, his neck outstretched, his fists clenched, panted his brandy-smelling breath in his son's face. Iakov stepped back. He was watching his father's movements, ready to ward off blows, peaceful outwardly, but steaming with perspiration. Between them was the table.

'Perhaps I won't give you a good beating?' cried Vassili hoarsely, and bending his back like a cat about to make a spring.

'Here we are equal,' said Iakov, watching him warily. 'You are a fisherman, I too. Why do you attack me like this? Do you think I do not understand? You began.'

Vassili howled with passion, and raised his arm to strike so rapidly that Iakov had no time to avoid it. The blow fell on his head. He staggered and ground his teeth in his father's face.

'Wait!' cried the latter, clenching his fists and again threatening him.

They were now at close quarters, and their feet were entangled in the empty sacks and cordage on the floor. Iakov, protecting himself as best he could against his father's blows, pale and bathed in perspiration, his teeth clenched, his eyes brilliant as a wolf's, slowly retreated, and as his father charged upon him, gesticulating with ferocity and blind with rage, like a wild boar, he turned and ran out of the cabin, down towards the sea.

Vassili started in pursuit, his head bent, his arms extended, but his foot caught in some rope, and he fell all his length on the sand. He tried to rise, but the fall had taken all the fight out of him and he sank back on the beach, shaking his fist at Iakov, who remained grinning at a safe distance. He shouted:

'Be cursed! I curse you forever!'

Bitterness came into Vassili's soul as he realized his own position. He sighed heavily. His head bent low as if an immense weight had crushed him. For an abandoned woman he had deserted his wife, with whom he had lived faithfully for fifteen years, and the Lord had punished him by this rebellion of his son. His son had mocked him and trampled on his heart. Yes, he was punished for the past. He made the sign of the cross and remained seated, blinking his eyes to free them from the tears that were blinding them.

And the sun went down into the sea, and the crimson twilight faded away in the sky. A warm wind caressed the face of the weeping peasant. Deep in his resolutions of repentance he stayed there until he fell asleep shortly before dawn.

The day following the quarrel, Iakov went off with a party to fish thirty miles out at sea. He returned alone five days later for provisions. It was midday when he arrived, and everyone was resting after dinner. It was unbearably hot. The sand burned his feet and the shells and fish bones pricked them. As Iakov carefully picked his way along the beach he regretted he had no boots on. He did not want to return to the bark as he was in a hurry to eat and to see Malva. Many a time had he thought of her during the long lonely hours on the sea. He wondered if she and his father had seen each other again and what they had said. Perhaps the old man had beaten her.

The deserted fisheries were slumbering, as if overcome by the heat. In the inspector's office a child was crying. From behind a heap of barrels came the sound of voices.

Iakov turned his steps in that direction. He thought he recognized Malva's voice, but when he arrived at the barrels he recoiled a step and stopped.

In the shade, lying on his back, with his arms under his head, was Serejka. Near him were, on one side, Vassili and, on the other, Malva.

Iakov thought to himself: 'Why is father here. Has he left his post so as to be nearer Malva and to watch her? Should he go up to them or not.

'So, you've decided!' said Serejka to Vassili. 'It's goodbye to us all? Well, go your way and scratch the soil.'

A thrill went through Iakov and he made a joyous grimace. 'Yes, I'm going;' said Vassili.

Then Iakov advanced boldly.

'Good-day, all!'

The father gave him a rapid glance and then turned away his eyes. Malva did not stir. Serejka moved his leg and raising his voice said:

'Here's our dearly beloved son, Iakov, back from a distant shore.'

Then he added in his ordinary voice:

'You should flay him alive and make drums with his skin.'

Malva laughed.

'It's hot,' said Iakov, sitting beside them.

'I've been waiting for you since this morning, Iakov. The inspector told me you were coming.'

The young man thought his voice seemed weaker than usual and his face seemed changed. He asked Serejka for a cigarette.

'I have no tobacco for an imbecile like you,' replied the latter, without stirring.

'I'm going back home, Iakov,' said Vassili, gravely digging into the sand with his fingers.

'Why,' asked the son, innocently.

'Never mind why, shall you stay?'

'Yes. I'll remain. What should we both do at home?'

'Very well. I have nothing to say. Do as you please. You are no longer a child. Only remember that I shall not get about long. I shall live, perhaps, but I do not know how long I shall work. I have lost the habit of the soil. Remember, too, that your mother is there.'

Evidently it was difficult for him to talk. The words stuck between his teeth. He stroked his beard and his hand trembled.

Malva eyed him. Serejka had half closed one eye and with the other watched Iakov. Iakov was jubilant, but afraid of betraying himself; he was silent and lowered his head.

'Don't forget your mother, Iakov. Remember, you are all she has.'

'I know,' said Iakov, shrugging his shoulders.

'It is well if you know,' said the father, with a look of distrust. 'I only warn you not to forget it.'

Vassili sighed deeply. For a few minutes all were silent.

Then Malva said:

'The work bell will soon ring.'

'I'm going,' said Vassili, rising.

And all rose.

'Goodbye, Serejka. If you happen to be on the Volga, maybe you'll drop in to see me.'

'I'll not fail,' said Serejka.

'Goodbye.'

'Goodbye, dear friend.'

'Goodbye, Malva,' said Vassili, not raising his eyes.

She slowly wiped her lips with her sleeve, threw her two white arms round his neck and kissed him three times on the lips and cheeks.

He was overcome with emotion and uttered some indistinct words, Iakov lowered his head, dissimulating a smile. Serejka was impassible, and he even yawned a little, at the same time gazing at the sky.

'You'll find it hot walking,' he said.

'No matter. Goodbye, you too, Iakov.'

'Goodbye!'

They stood facing each other, not knowing what to do. The sad word 'goodbye' aroused in Iakov a feeling of tenderness for his father, but he did not know how to express it. Should he embrace his father as Malva had done or shake his hand like Serejka? And Vassili felt hurt at this hesitation, which was visible in his son's attitude.

'Remember your mother,' said Vassili, finally.

'Yes, yes,' replied Iakov, cordially. 'Don't worry. I know.'

'That's all. Be happy. God protect you. Don't think badly of me. The kettle, Serejka, is buried in the sand near the bow of the green boat.'

'What does he want with the kettle?' asked Iakov.

'He has taken my place yonder on the headland,' explained Vassili.

Iakov looked enviously at Serejka, then at Malva.

'Farewell, all! I'm going.'

Vassili waved his hand to them and moved away. Malva followed him.

'I'll accompany you a bit of the road.'

Serejka sat down on the ground and seized the leg of Iakov, who was preparing to accompany Malva.

'Stop! where are you going?'

'Let me alone,' said Iakov, making a forward movement. But Serejka had seized his other leg.

'Sit down by my side.'

'Why? What new folly is this?'

'It is not folly. Sit down.'

Iakov obeyed, grinding his teeth.

'What do you want?'

'Wait. Be silent, and I'll think, and then I'll talk.'

He began staring at Iakov, who gave way.

Malva and Vassili walked for a few minutes in silence. Malva's eyes shone strangely. Vassili was gloomy and preoccupied. Their feet sank in the sand and they advanced slowly.

'Vassili!'

'What?'

He turned and looked at her.

'I made you quarrel with Iakov on purpose. You might both have lived here without quarrelling,' she said in a calm tone.

There was not a shade of repentance in her words.

'Why did you do that?' asked Vassili, after a silence.

'I do not know – for nothing.'

She shrugged her shoulders and smiled.

'What you have done was noble!' he said, with irritation.

She was silent.

'You will ruin my boy, ruin him entirely. You do not fear God, you have no shame! What are you going to do?'

'What should I do?' she said.

There was a ring of anguish, or vexation, in her voice.

'What you ought to do!' cried Vassili, seized suddenly with a fierce rage.

He felt a passionate desire to strike her, to knock her down and bury her in the sand, to kick her in the face, in the breast. He clenched his fists and looked back.

Yonder, near the barrels, he saw Iakov and Serejka. Their faces were turned in his direction.

'Get away with you! I could crush you!'

He stopped and hissed insults in her face. His eyes were bloodshot, his beard trembled and his hands seemed to advance involuntarily towards Malva's hair, which emerged from beneath her shawl.

She fixed her green eyes on him.

'You deserve killing,' he said

'Wait, someone will break your head yet.'

She smiled, still silent. Then she sighed deeply and said:

'That's enough! now farewell!'

And suddenly turning on her heels she left him and came back.

Vassili shouted after her and shook his fists. Malva, as she walked, took pains to place each foot in the deep impressions of Vassili's feet, and when she succeeded she carefully effaced the traces. Thus she continued on until she came to the barrels where Serejka greeted her with this question:

'Well, have you seen the last of him?'

She gave an affirmative sign, and sat down beside him. Iakov looked at her and smiled, gently moving his lips as if he were saying things that he alone heard.

'When will you go to the headland?' she asked Serejka, indicating the sea with a movement of her head.

'This evening.'

'I will go with you.'

'Bravo, that suits me.'

'And I, too – I'll go,' cried Iakov.

'Who invited you?' asked Serejka, screwing up his eyes.

The sound of a cracked bell called the men to work.

'She will invite me,' said Iakov.

He looked defiantly at Malva.

'I? what need have I of you?' she replied, surprised.

'Let us be frank, Iakov,' said Serejeka. 'If you annoy her, I'll beat you to a jelly. And if you as much as touch her with a finger, I'll kill you like a fly. I am a simple man.'

His face, all his person, his knotty and muscular arms proved eloquently that killing a man would be a very simple thing for him.

Iakov recoiled a step and said, in a choking voice:

'Wait! That is for Malva to—'

'Keep quiet, that's all. You are not the dog that will eat the lamb. If you get the bones you may be thankful.'

Iakov looked at Malva. Her green eyes laughed in a humiliating way at him and she fondled Serejka so that Iakov felt himself grow hot and cold.

Then they went away side by side and both burst out laughing. Iakov dug his foot deep in the sand and remained glued to the spot, his body stretched forward, his face red, his heart beating wildly.

In the distance, on the dead waves of sand, was a small dark human figure moving slowly away; on his right beamed the sun and the powerful sea, and on the left, to the horizon, there was sand, nothing but sand, uniform, deserted, – gloomy. Iakov watched the receding figure of the lonely man and blinked his eyes, filled with tears – tears of humiliation and painful uncertainty.

On the fishing grounds everyone was busy at work. Iakov heard Malva's sonorous voice ask, angrily:

'Who has taken my knife?'

The waves murmured, the sun shone and the sea laughed.

ON THE STEPPES

told by a tramp

(tr. Emily Jakowleff and Dora B. Montefiore)

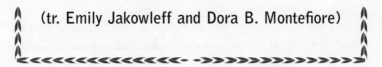

WE LEFT PEREKOPP IN the worst possible humour – hungry as wolves, and angry with the whole world. From early in the morning we had been trying to turn our talents and efforts to account, either by stealing or earning something, and when at length we were forced to the conclusion that neither one nor the other was likely to be crowned with success we made up our minds to push on... But where?... Just on, and on.... This was the unanimous but silent decision taken by us all; for we were ready to go on, in every sense of the word, along the path of life which we had already for some time been tramping. This decision was no less silent than the previous one, though it flashed forth from under the lowering gloom of our hungry eyes.

There were three of us; our acquaintanceship was of recent date. We dropped across one another in a vodka shop in Kherson, on the banks of the Dnieper.

One of us had been a soldier attached to the railway brigade, and later on took service as a platelayer on one of the Viesla lines; a red-haired, muscular man, with cold grey eyes; he could speak German, and had an extensive knowledge of prison life.

Folk like us don't care much to speak of their past life, having always more or less good reasons for not doing so; and all of us believed one another – at least apparently – for inwardly each of us had ceased to trust even himself.

The second one of the party was a shrivelled, dried up little man, with thin lips, always sceptically pursed up; and when he told us that he was a former student of Moscow University, the soldier and I took it as a matter of course.

As a matter of fact it was all the same to us whether he was a student, a spy, or a rogue. All that concerned us was that during our present acquaintanceship he was our equal; he was hungry, he enjoyed in towns the special attention of the police, and in villages was looked upon by the peasants with suspicion. He hated both town and village with the hatred of an impotent hunted hungry animal, and used to dream of a general vengeance on all and on everything. In a word, as regards his position amongst the chosen ones of nature, and the powerful ones of life, and as regards his disposition, he was one of us.

Misfortune is the strongest cement in the uniting of characters, even divergent ones; and we were all deeply convinced of our right to consider ourselves unfortunate.

The third was myself. From that natural modesty which has distinguished me from my earliest days, I shall not say a word about my own qualities; and not wishing to appear before you as a knave, I shall be silent on the subject of my faults. But as a clue to my character I shall allow myself to mention that I always considered myself as superior to the others, and continue to do so till the present day.

Well,… we left Perekopp, and were trudging along with nothing in view but bread, which we might beg of the shepherds, who seldom refused the petition of wayfarers.

I was walking abreast of the soldier, and the 'student' was striding behind us. Something that suggested the remains of a coat was hanging on his back. On his close cropped head, adorned with a striking variety of humps, rested composedly what was little more than a recollection of a broad-brimmed hat. His thin legs were clad in tight grey breeches, with variegated patches; to the soles of his feet he had bound with strips of rag torn from the linings of his clothes, the old uppers of a boot he had found on the road; this arrangement he called sandals, and he shuffled along in them, kicking up the dust as he went, and glancing from side to side with furtive eyes. The soldier wore a red shirt, which, according to his own account, was actually bought by himself in Kernoneff. Over this shirt he wore a thick wadded waistcoat; on his head, worn with a military cock, was a soldier's cap of indefinite colour, and on his legs hung loosely wide moujik trousers; he was barefooted.

I was dressed much in the same style, and was also barefooted.

We, trudged along... and on all sides of us stretched the immense boundless steppes, looking like a huge round flat black bowl, under the hot blue dome of a summer sky. The grey, dusty road cut through the distance like a broad stripe, whilst its baked surface burnt our feet. From time to time we came across bristly patches of freshly cut corn, which bore a strange resemblance to the soldier's stubbly cheeks. He stepped along, singing in a rather hoarse voice:

'The blessed resurrection,

We greet, and sing its praise...'

Whilst serving in the army he had performed the duties of a deacon in the garrison chapel, and knew an endless number of these sacred songs, to which he always had recourse whenever the conversation flagged.

Ahead of us, on the horizon, rose a delicate sky-line, steeped in tones that shaded from lilac to pale pink.

'These are evidently the Crimean hills,' said the 'student' in a dry voice.

'Hills?' exclaimed the soldier, 'It's too early in the day to see hills yet, my friend. Those are clouds, nothing but clouds. See how strange they look; they are of the colour of curdled milk and fruit.'

I hinted that it would be extremely agreeable if these clouds were in reality curdled milk and fruit. This suddenly aroused our hunger – the bane of our life.

'Damn it all!' cursed the soldier, spitting on one side. 'If we could but come across a living soul, but there isn't one… We shall have to do as the bears in the woods do, and suck our own paws.'

'I told you we ought to have kept to inhabited parts of the country,' said the 'student' didactically.

'You told us so,' exclaimed the soldier indignantly. 'All your learning is nothing but words. What inhabited places are there here? The devil only knows where they are.'

The 'student' pursed up his lips silently… the sun was setting… the clouds on the horizon were taking on them a variety of colours, indescribable in words… a mingled smell of earth and of salt arose from the ground… This dry and savoury smell increased our appetites more and more.

A gnawing feeling took possession of our stomachs – a strange and disagreeable feeling as if from all the muscles of our bodies the life juices were exuding, evaporating, and as if the muscles themselves were losing their elasticity. A pricking dryness filled the mouth and throat, the head grew dizzy, and now and again dark spots flashed and danced before the eyes. Sometimes these took the form of hot, steaming meats, sometimes of loaves of bread; fancy attaching to these 'silent visions of the past,' their own particular smells, and then it seemed as if a knife were being turned in the stomach. Still, on we went, sharing with each other the description of our impressions, and keeping a keen look-out on either side lest a flock of sheep might be seen, or listening for the squeaking creak of the Tartar's cart, carrying fruit to the Armenian market.

But the steppe was void and silent… On the eve of this unlucky day we three had eaten four pounds of rye bread and five watermelons; after which we walked forty versts... and, the expenses not, equalling the income, we fell asleep on the market-place of Perekopp, and awoke at the call of hunger.

The 'student' wisely advised us not to go to sleep, but to take advantage of the night for... business; ... but in respectable society it is not considered correct to speak of projects bearing on the violation of the rights of property, and, therefore I keep silence... I only wish to be truthful, but it is not in my own interests to be brutal. I know that people are growing more tender-hearted in these highly-cultivated days; and even when they take their neighbour by the throat, with the evident intention of throttling him, they try to do it with all the amiability in the world, and with the strict regard for etiquette proper to the circumstances. The experience that my own throat has undergone causes me to observe this advance in manners, and, with an agreeable feeling of deep conviction, I assert that everything in this world develops and becomes perfect. More especially is this wonderful process admirably proved by the annual growth of prisons, vodka shops and brothels.

Striving thus to swallow down the saliva of hunger, and making an effort to appease the tortures of the stomach by friendly talk, we tramped along the vast and silent steppes in the ruddy rays of the sunset, ... full of vague hope ... We watched the sun sinking quietly into the soft clouds, richly coloured by its rays, whilst behind us, and on either side, a bluish mist rising up from the steppes towards the sky veiled the gloomy landscape behind us.

'Come, mates, gather some fuel for a fire,' said the soldier, picking up a log from the ground. 'It seems as if we shall have to spend the night on the steppes... The dew is heavy... Take twigs, dung, anything you find.' We scattered on either side of the road, and began collecting dried weeds and anything else that would burn. Each time one of us stooped towards the earth the whole body seemed possessed with an intense desire to throw itself down full length, to lie there motionless and eat... eat

232 ǒ MAXIM GORKY

long… eat to repletion… and then fall asleep… Though it might be an eternal sleep… only to eat, and eat… to chew…. to feel a warm thick mash slowly sliding down the parched gullet into the starved, contracted stomach, aching with the desire to absorb something into itself.

'If we could but find some roots,' said the soldier. 'Eatable roots are sometimes to be found.'

But in the black, ploughed ground there were no roots to be had. The southern night came on suddenly, and the last ray of the sun had scarcely disappeared, when in the dark blue sky stars began to twinkle, and around us black shadows blended, narrowing the vast extent of the boundless steppes which swallowed us up.

'Brothers!' said the 'student' on the left in a low voice; 'there is… a man… lying down!'

'A man!' laughed the soldier, incredulously; 'what can a man be doing lying there?'

'Go and ask! Probably he has bread, if he has made up his mind to spend the night on the steppes,' exclaimed the 'student.'

The soldier looked in the direction indicated, and spitting resolutely, said –

'Come and see!'

Only the green, sharp eyes of the 'student' could discern that the dark heap which lay some hundred yards to the left of the road was a man.

We approached him quickly, striding over the heaps of ploughed ground and feeling that the aroused hope for food had sharpened the pangs of hunger; we had already got near, but the man did not move.

'Perhaps, after all, it's not a man' the soldier gloomily expressed the idea common to us all. But all doubt was at the same moment dispelled, for the heap on the ground suddenly began moving, and we saw that it was a real flesh-and-blood person, who knelt, stretching out his hand towards us.

He spoke in a dull shaky voice:

'Don't come nearer, or I shall shoot you.'

Through the misty air we heard the short, dry crack of a pistol. We stopped as if at a word of command, and for several seconds we were silent, taken aback by this uncourteous greeting.

'What a brute!' muttered the soldier.

'That he is,' answered the 'student' reflectively. 'He goes about with a revolver... one can see the sort of fellow he is.'

'I say!' shouted the soldier, having evidently taken a decision. The man did not change his position and remained silent.

'I say! ... whoever you are, We won't touch you; only give us some bread.... You're sure to have some... do, for Christ's sake! ... Damn... Damn...' the last words were uttered under his breath.

Still the man remained silent.

'Can't you hear' continued the soldier, trembling with rage and despair. 'Give us some bread! ... do! ... We won't go near you; throw it to us.'

'All right,' curtly answered the man.

If even he had added 'my dear brothers,' and if he had poured into these blessed words the most sacred and pure feeling they would not have touched us and humanized us so much as did this gruff and brief 'all right.'

'Don't be afraid of us, my good fellow,' continued the soldier, with a soft and ingratiating smile, which was lost on the stranger, who was still at least twenty paces distance from us, 'We are quiet people, travelling from Russia to the Kouban.... We were out of our reckoning in money matters, and have eaten everything off our backs ... This is the second day since we had a morsel in our mouths.'

'Here, catch!'... said the sympathizing man, swinging his arm forward. The black object flashed out, and fell near us on the ploughed ground. The 'student' rushed to catch it.

'Here, catch!... Here's some more... and some more!'

When the student had finished gathering up this strange alms, we found that it was four pounds of hard wheaten bread; it was soiled with earth and very stale; we paid little heed to the first fact, but the second gave us great pleasure. Stale bread is more satisfying than new bread, for it has less moisture in it.

'Here's for you... and for you... and for you'... The soldier divided busily the pieces... 'Stop! that isn't fair; let me take a bit off yours my friend, for the philosopher, for his share's not big enough.'

The 'student' put up with the loss of a few ounces of his bread without remonstrance. It fell to my share, and soon found its way into my mouth.

I began chewing it slowly with convulsive movements of the jaws, which seemed ready to crush even a stone. The contraction of the gullet gave me a sensation of keen delight, as did also the slow satisfaction of my hunger. Bit by bit the warm and indescribably delicious food found its way into the hot stomach and seemed there to be transformed into blood and brain. Joy, a strange, calm and vivifying joy, gradually warmed the heart at the same time as the stomach was being satisfied with food, and I fell into a half dreamy state. I forgot the cursed days of constant chronic hunger, and forgot also my companions, engrossed, for the time being, by the sensations I was experiencing.

But when with the palm of my hand I jerked the last crumbs of bread into my mouth, I felt I was still mortally hungry.

'That cursed dog over there, he has got some bacon left, and some sort of meat' ... growled the soldier, sitting on the ground opposite me, and rubbing his stomach with his hands.

'Yes, that's certain, for the bread smelt of meat ... And I believe he's got more bread left,' said the 'student,' whilst he added, in a low voice, 'If it were not for that revolver.'

'Who can he be, I wonder?'

'The chances are he's one of us.'

'Dog!' concluded the soldier.

We were sitting in a close group, and glancing askance towards the spot where crouched our benefactor with the revolver.

No sound came from his direction nor any sign of life.

Night was gathering around us its dark powers ... A deadly quiet reigned over the steppes... We could hear each other's breathing. From time to time was heard the distant melancholy whistle of the shrew mouse... The stars, the living flowers of the sky, glittered overhead... We were hungry.

I can say with pride that during this rather strange night I was neither worse nor better than my casual acquaintances. I suggested that we should get up and attack the man; not to hurt him, but to get hold of all the food he had with him. He may shoot ... well, let him... If he succeeds in hitting anyone, he can only hit one out of the three; and even if he should aim straight a bullet from a revolver would hardly kill.

'Come on!' said the soldier, jumping to his feet.

The 'student' rose more slowly.

We went off almost at a run.

The 'student' kept behind, and rather away from us.

'Come, mate!' exclaimed the soldier in a reproachful tone.

In front of us we heard a muttered threat, the sharp click of a trigger, a flash of fire, the report of a pistol.

'Missed!' exclaimed the soldier joyfully, jumping with a bound on to the man. 'Now, you devil! won't I give it you!'

The 'student' made a rush at the bag.

The 'devil' fell on his back, his arms flung out on the ground, and a choking sound in his throat.

'What the deuce does that mean?' exclaimed the astonished soldier, who had raised his foot prepared to kick the stranger.

'Could he have shot himself?... Hi!... you there!... Hi! Have you shot yourself, or what's the matter?'

'Meat!... some kinds of biscuits... and bread... plenty of everything, mates!' sounded the triumphant voice of the 'student.'

'Well curse you!... die if you like... let's come and eat, mates!' shouted the soldier.

I took the revolver out of the hand of the man, who lay now motionless, the choking sounds in his throat having ceased. In the barrel only one bullet remained.

Again we fell to and ate in silence.

The stranger lay by our side, also silent, and without moving a limb. We paid no heed to him.

Suddenly we heard uttered in a hoarse, trembling voice 'Dear friends... can you behave like this just for a piece of bread?'

A shudder ran through us, The 'student' choked himself with a piece of food, and bending forward, coughed loudly.

The soldier, having swallowed what was in his mouth, uttered curses.

'Hound... May you burst yourself! Did you think it was your skin we wanted? What use would that be to us, you fathead! You dirty coward – the idea of carrying arms, and shooting at people. Curses on you!'

He continued to curse and to eat by turns, which in no way interfered with the force of his expletives.

'Just wait till we've done eating! We'll be even with you, then,' was the 'student's' grim threat.

Then through the darkness of the night we heard loud sobs that frightened us.

'Friends... I didn't know. I fired because I was afraid... I am travelling from New Athon... to the government of Orel. Oh! dear me! The ague has got me! As soon as the sun sets my torture begins: It was the ague drove me away from Athon. I was a cabinetmaker there... that's how I earned my living. I've got a wife at home... Two little girls. It's three years... nearly four, since I saw them. Eat all there is, friends!'

'That's what we mean to do, without being asked,' said the 'student.'

'Gracious heaven! if only I had known that you were quiet, good people, I would never have fired!... but see friends... it was the steppes!... the night!... could I help it?... just think!'

He cried whilst he was speaking, or rather uttered a strange, trembling, terrified howl.

'Gammon!' interjected the soldier, disdainfully.

'He must have money about him,' suggested the 'student.'

The soldier screwed up his eyes, scanned him narrowly, and sneered.

'You're a sharp fellow... What I say is, let's have a fire, and go to sleep.'

'And what about him?' enquired the 'student.'

'Oh! devil take him!... we don't want to fry him, do we?'

'Why not?' nodded the 'student,' with his long, narrow head.

We went off to fetch the fuel which we had left at the place where we had been arrested by the shout of the cabinetmaker. We collected it again, and were soon sitting round a comfortable fire. It smouldered gently in the quiet windless night, and lit up the spot on which we were seated. We were getting sleepy, but we could still have eaten another supper.

'Friends!' called to us the cabinetmaker, he was lying a few steps away from us, and at times it seemed to me he was whispering something.

'Well' said the soldier.

'May I come near... to the fire? I'm not far from death's door; All my bones are full of pain!... Gracious heavens! I shall never reach home again.'

'Crawl in here!... said the 'student,' making room for him. The stranger crawled slowly towards the fire, as if afraid of losing on the way a leg or a hand. He was a tall, exceedingly emaciated man; his clothes hung terribly loosely on him, and his large dimmed eyes spoke of gnawing pain. His drawn face was bony, and even by the firelight showed an earthy, yellow, dead colour. He was shaking from head to foot, and aroused in us, a feeling of contemptuous pity. Stretching out to the fire his long thin hands, he rubbed his bony fingers, the joints of which bent stiffly and slowly. The sight of him became at last sickening and revolting.

'Why are you travelling on foot in this sort of state? Is it because you are so stingy?' asked the soldier gloomily.

'I was advised they told me not to travel by water... They said go by the Crimea... the air they told me was so good. And here am I, friends, unable to walk ... dying. I shall die alone on the steppes. The birds will eat my flesh... and no one will know. My wife ... my daughters... will await me. I wrote to them... I... told them.... And my bones will be washed by the rains of the steppes.'

And he howled with the dismal howl of a wounded wolf.

'Damn it all!' exclaimed the enraged soldier, jumping to his feet. 'What's all this about? You don't give us a chance of resting. If you're dying, just die, but be quiet about it. Who wants to bother about you? Just shut up that row!'

'Give him one over the head,' suggested the 'student.'

'Give us a chance of going to sleep,' said I, 'And if you want to stay near the fire, stop howling, for otherwise ... indeed.'

'Did you hear?' asked the soldier, angrily. 'If so, just remember. You think perhaps we are going to bother about you, after you have been slinging bread at our heads, and taking aim at us with your rotten pistol! You whining devil! Anyone in your place would...' And the soldier spat on one side with a gesture of disgust.

He stopped suddenly, and stretched himself full length on the ground. The 'student' had already settled himself to sleep. I had done the same. The terrified cabinetmaker shrunk together, and, creeping towards the fire, sat silently watching it. I was lying to the right of him, and I could hear his teeth chattering. The 'student' lay on the left, curled up in a heap, and seemed to have fallen asleep suddenly.

The soldier, with his hands behind his head, lay on his back, watching the sky. 'What a beautiful night... is it not?... just look at the stars! – And so warm!' After some minutes he added, speaking to me, 'Look at the sky... it's really more like a warm blanket than a sky! Oh! how I love this wandering life? Though it means sometimes cold and hunger… yet the freedom is worth everything. There is no master over one… one's own life is one's own… one can even do away with oneself, and no one dares say one nay. It's fine! See how angry and how famished I have been these last few days… and now, here am I, looking at the sky, with the stars twinkling above me, as if they were saying; "It's all right, Lakontine; continue to wander about the world, and don't let anyone get the better of you." Yes, and my heart and soul feel so happy. How are you now… what's your name… cabinetmaker? Don't be angry with me now, and don't fear me. It was so natural we should eat your bread, for you had some and we had none…. so, of course, we ate yours! And, fancy you firing at us! Don't you know that a bullet may hurt a fellow? I was very angry with you when you did that, and if you had not tripped up, I should have given you something to be going on with. And as for the bread – why to-morrow you will be at Perekopp, and can buy more… for you have plenty of money, I know. When did you pick up this ague?'

And for some time longer, the soldier's bass tones, and the trembling replies of the sick cabinetmaker sounded in my ears. The night, dark almost to blackness, fell thicker and darker on the earth, and the fresh scented night air tilled all one's lungs.

The fire gave forth a steady light, and an invigorating warmth… my eyelids grew gradually tired and drooped, and before my eyes something soft and beautiful seemed to hover.

'Up with you! Look sharp! Let's be off!'

With a feeling of fear I opened my eyes, and sprang to my feet assisted by the soldier, who dragged me up impetuously by the hand. 'Look sharp, I say? Let's be off!'

His face showed anxiety and fear.

I glanced around. The sun was rising, and its reddish ray was already lying on the motionless and livid face of the cabinetmaker.

His mouth was wide open, and his eyes protruded from the sockets, and seemed to glance upwards with a glassy look expressive of terror. The clothes on his body were torn, and lay in unnatural, tumbled disorder. There were no traces of the 'student.'

'What's the use of staring? Come along, don't you hear?' said the soldier meaningly, and dragging me along by the arm.

'Is he dead?" I asked, shivering with the chill air of the morning.

'Of course he is. If you were strangled, you would be dead?'

'Is he?… Has he been?… The student…' I exclaimed.

'Why, who else could it be? You don't think it was you or I who did it?… H'm… so much for a man of education! Finished off a man cleverly, he did, and left his mates in the lurch to stand the brunt of it. Had I known it yesterday, I would have killed the "student." I'd have done for him with one blow! A knock on the temple, and there would have been one rascal less in the world! Don't you see now what he has done? We've got to make off at once, so that no human eye shall be able to detect that we have been on the steppes! You see what I mean! In the first place they will find the cabinet-maker, and will see plainly that he has been strangled and robbed. Then all folk like us will be watched and questioned… "Where do you come from?….! Where did you sleep last night?" And then they will arrest us … Though you and I have nothing compromising on us. But there's the revolver in my shirt … that's awkward.'

'Throw it away,' I advised him.

'Throw it away? be replied thoughtfully; 'it's valuable… and perhaps after all we shan't be caught! No, I won't throw it away! worth three roubles. Ah with what pleasure I would put this bullet into our friend's ear!… I should like to know how much he grabbed… the dog!… How much do you think? … Damn it all!'

'As to the cabinetmaker's daughters – it all up with their chance of getting it!' said I.

'Daughters?... what daughters? Ah! Yes! Well, they will grow up; they are sure not to marry fellows like us; it's not to be thought of. Step; along quicker!... where shall we go?'

'I don't know, I'm sure. It's all the same.'

'No more do I... but as you say... it's all the same. Let's go towards the right, it must lead to the sea.'

So we went to the right.

I glanced back... Far behind us on the bare steppes rose a dark mound, lit up by rays of the morning sun.

'Are you looking to see if he has risen from the dead? No fear, he won't pursue us. That philosopher friend of ours was evidently a clever fellow; he did it neatly. A fine sort of mate he was! He's got us into a rare muddle!... Ah!... Ah!... I see that people are getting worse from year to year,' added the soldier despondingly.

The silent and deserted steppes, all inundated with the bright glow of the morning sun, stretched out around us, uniting at the horizon with the sky, suffused with such a clear caressing and soft light that everything black and evil seemed impossible amidst this immense space of free open land shut in with the blue dome of heaven.

'I feel empty still,' said my companion, twisting up a cigarette of coarse tobacco. 'What shall we get to eat to-day? Where shall we get it... and how?

'Ah... that's the question!'

Here the narrator, my neighbour in the next bed in the hospital, finished his story, adding: 'And this is all. My friendship with the soldier continued, and together we tramped to Kars. He was a good and very clever fellow, the real type of a vagabond tramp, I respected him. We travelled together as far as Asia Minor, and there we lost sight of each other.'

'And do you ever remember the cabinetmaker?' asked I.

'Yes, as you see, or, rather, as you have heard.'

'And... what do you feel about him?'

He laughed.

'Well, what is there for me to feel about him?… It was no more my fault what happened to him than it was your fault what has happened to me… For, in fact, no one is to blame for anything, for all of us are alike, beasts!'

HER LOVER

AN ACQUAINTANCE OF MINE once told me the following story.

When I was a student at Moscow I happened to live alongside one of those ladies whose repute is questionable. She was a Pole, and they called her Teresa. She was a tallish, powerfully-built brunette, with black, bushy eyebrows and a large coarse face as if carved out by a hatchet – the bestial gleam of her dark eyes, her thick bass voice, her cabman-like gait and her immense muscular vigour, worthy of a fishwife, inspired me with horror. I lived on the top flight and her garret was opposite to mine. I never left my door open when I knew her to be at home. But this, after all, was a very rare occurrence. Sometimes I chanced to meet her on the staircase or in the yard, and she would smile upon me with a smile which seemed to me to be sly and cynical. Occasionally, I saw her drunk, with bleary eyes, tousled hair, and a particularly hideous grin. on such occasions she would speak to me.

'How d'ye do, Mr. Student!' and her stupid laugh would still further intensify my loathing of her. I should have liked to have changed my quarters in order to have avoided such encounters and greetings; but my little chamber was a nice one, and there was such a wide view from the window, and it was always so quiet in the street below – so I endured.

And one morning I was sprawling on my couch, trying to find some sort of excuse for not attending my class, when the door opened, and the bass voice of Teresa the loathsome resounded from my threshold:

'Good health to you, Mr. Student!'

'What do you want?' I said. I saw that her face was confused and supplicatory.... It was a very unusual sort of face for her.

'Sir! I want to beg a favour of you. Will you grant it me?'

I lay there silent, and thought to myself:

'Gracious!... Courage, my boy!'

'I want to send a letter home, that's what it is,' she said; her voice was beseeching, soft, timid.

'Deuce take you!' I thought; but up I jumped, sat down at my table, took a sheet of paper, and said:

'Come here, sit down, and dictate!'

She came, sat down very gingerly on a chair, and looked at me with a guilty look.

'Well, to whom do you want to write?'

'To Boleslav Kashput, at the town of Svieptziana, on the Warsaw Road....'

'Well, fire away!'

'My dear Boles... my darling... my faithful lover. May the Mother of God protect thee! Thou heart of gold, why hast thou not written for such a long time to thy sorrowing little dove, Teresa?'

I very nearly burst out laughing. 'A sorrowing little dove!' more than five feet high, with fists a stone and more in weight, and as black a face as if the little dove had lived all its life in a chimney, and had never once washed itself! Restraining myself somehow, I asked:

'Who is this Bolest?'

'Boles, Mr. Student,' she said, as if offended with me for blundering over the name, 'he is Boles – my young man.'

'Young man!'

'Why are you so surprised, sir? Cannot I, a girl, have a young man?'

She? A girl? Well!

'Oh, why not?' I said. 'All things are possible. And has he been your young man long?'

'Six years.'

'Oh, ho!' I thought. 'Well, let us write your letter....'

And I tell you plainly that I would willingly have changed places with this Boles if his fair correspondent had been not Teresa but something less than she.

'I thank you most heartily, sir, for your kind services,' said Teresa to me, with a curtsey. 'Perhaps *I* can show *you* some service, eh?'

'No, I most humbly thank you all the same.'

'Perhaps, sir, your shirts or your trousers may want a little mending?'

I felt that this mastodon in petticoats had made me grow quite red with shame, and I told her pretty sharply that I had no need whatever of her services.

She departed.

A week or two passed away. It was evening. I was sitting at my window whistling and thinking of some expedient for enabling me to get away from myself. I was bored; the weather was dirty. I didn't want to go out, and out of sheer ennui I began a course of self-analysis and reflection. This also was dull enough work, but I didn't care about doing anything else. Then the door opened. Heaven be praised! Someone came in.

'Oh, Mr. Student, you have no pressing business, I hope?'

It was Teresa. Humph!

'No. What is it?'

'I was going to ask you, sir, to write me another letter.'

'Very well! To Boles, eh?'

'No, this time it is from him.'

'Wha-at?'

'Stupid that I am! It is not for me, Mr. Student, I beg your pardon. It is for a friend of mine, that is to say, not a friend but an acquaintance – a man acquaintance. He has a sweetheart just like me here, Teresa. That's how it is. Will you, sir, write a letter to this Teresa?'

I looked at her – her face was troubled, her fingers were trembling. I was a bit fogged at first – and then I guessed how it was.

'Look here, my lady,' I said, 'there are no Boleses or Teresas at all, and you've been telling me a pack of lies. Don't you come sneaking about me any longer. I have no wish whatever to cultivate your acquaintance. Do you understand?'

And suddenly she grew strangely terrified and distraught; she began to shift from foot to foot without moving from the place, and spluttered comically, as if she wanted to say something and couldn't. I waited to see what would come of all this, and I saw and felt that, apparently, I had made a great mistake in suspecting her of wishing to draw me from the path of righteousness. It was evidently something very different.

'Mr. Student!' she began, and suddenly, waving her hand, she turned abruptly towards the door and went out. I remained with a very unpleasant feeling in my mind. I listened. Her door was flung violently to – plainly the poor wench was very angry....I thought it over, and resolved to go to her, and, inviting her to come in here, write everything she wanted.

I entered her apartment. I looked round. She was sitting at the table, leaning on her elbows, with her head in her hands.

'Listen to me,' I said.

Now, whenever I come to this point in my story, I always feel horribly awkward and idiotic. Well, well!

'Listen to me,' I said.

She leaped from her seat, came towards me with flashing eyes, and laying her hands on my shoulders, began to whisper, or rather to hum in her peculiar bass voice:

'Look you, now! It's like this. There's no Boles at all, and there's no Teresa either. But what's that to you? Is it a hard thing for you to draw your pen over paper? Eh? Ah, and *you*, too! Still such a little fair-haired boy! There's nobody at all, neither Boles, nor Teresa, only me. There you have it, and much good may it do you!'

'Pardon me!' said I, altogether flabbergasted by such a reception, 'what is it all about? There's no Boles, you say?'

'No. So it is.'

'And no Teresa either?'

'And no Teresa. I'm Teresa.'

I didn't understand it at all. I fixed my eyes upon her, and tried to make out which of us was taking leave of his or her senses. But she went again to the table, searched about for something, came back to me, and said in an offended tone:

'If it was so hard for you to write to Boles, look, there's your letter, take it! Others will write for me.'

I looked. In her hand was my letter to Boles. Phew!

'Listen, Teresa! What is the meaning of all this? Why must you get others to write for you when I have already written it, and you haven't sent it?'

'Sent it where?'

'Why, to this – Boles.'

'There's no such person.'

I absolutely did not understand it. There was nothing for me but to spit and go. Then she explained.

'What is it?' she said, still offended. 'There's no such person, I tell you,' and she extended her arms as if she herself did not understand why there should be no such person. 'But I wanted him to be.... Am I then not a human creature like the rest of them? Yes, yes, I know, I know, of course.... Yet no harm was done to any one by my writing to him that I can see....'

'Pardon me – to whom?'

'To Boles, of course.'

'But he doesn't exist.'

'Alas! alas! But what if he doesn't? He doesn't exist, but he *might!* I write to him, and it looks as if he did exist. And Teresa – that's me, and he replies to me, and then I write to him again....'

I understood at last. And I felt so sick, so miserable, so ashamed, somehow. Alongside of me, not three yards away, lived a human creature who had nobody in the world to treat her kindly, affectionately, and this human being had invented a friend for herself!

'Look, now! you wrote me a letter to Boles, and I gave it to someone else to read it to me; and when they read it to me I listened and fancied that Boles was there. And I asked you to write me a letter from Boles to Teresa – that is to me. When they write such a letter for me, and read it to me, I feel quite sure that Boles is there. And life grows easier for me in consequence.'

'Deuce take you for a blockhead!' said I to myself when I heard this.

And from thenceforth, regularly, twice a week, I wrote a letter to Boles, and an answer from Boles to Teresa. I wrote those answers well.... She, of course, listened to them, and wept like anything, roared, I should say, with her bass voice. And in return for my thus moving her to tears by real letters from the imaginary Boles, she began to mend the holes I had in my socks, shirts, and other articles of clothing. Subsequently, about three months after this history began, they put her in prison for something or other. No doubt by this time she is dead.

My acquaintance shook the ash from his cigarette, looked pensively up at the sky, and thus concluded:

Well, well, the more a human creature has tasted of bitter things the more it hungers after the sweet things of life. And we, wrapped round in the rags of our virtues, and regarding others through the mist of our self-sufficiency, and persuaded of our universal impeccability, do not understand this.

And the whole thing turns out pretty stupidly – and very cruelly. The fallen classes, we say. And who are the fallen classes, I should like to know? They are, first of all, people with the same bones, flesh, and blood and nerves as ourselves. We have been told this day after day for ages. And we actually listen – and the devil only knows how hideous the whole thing is. Or are we completely depraved by the loud sermonizing of humanism? In reality, we also are fallen folks, and, so far as I can see, very deeply fallen into the abyss of self-sufficiency and the conviction of our own superiority. But enough of this. It is all as old as the hills – so old that it is a shame to speak of it. Very old indeed – yes, that's what it is!

TWENTY-SIX AND ONE

THERE WERE TWENTY-SIX OF us – twenty-six living machines, locked up in a damp cellar, where we patted dough from morning till night, making biscuits and cakes. The windows of our cellar looked out into a ditch, which was covered with bricks grown green from dampness, the window frames were obstructed from the outside by a dense iron netting, and the light of the sun could not peep in through the panes, which were covered with flour-dust. Our proprietor stopped up our windows with iron that we might not give his bread to the poor or to those of our companions who, being out of work, were starving; our proprietor called us cheats and gave us for our dinner tainted garbage instead of meat.

It was stifling and narrow in our box of stone under the low, heavy ceiling, covered with smoke-black and spider-webs. It was close and disgusting within the thick walls, which were spattered with stains of mud and mustiness.... We rose at five o'clock in the morning, without having had enough sleep, and, dull and indifferent, we seated ourselves by the table at six to make biscuits out of the dough, which had been prepared for us by our companions while we were asleep. And all day long, from morning till ten o'clock at night, some of us sat by the table rolling out the elastic dough with our hands, and shaking ourselves that we might not grow stiff, while the others kneaded the dough with water. And the boiling water in the kettle, where the cracknels were being boiled, was purring sadly and thoughtfully all day long; the baker's shovel was scraping quickly and angrily against the oven, throwing off on the hot bricks the slippery pieces of dough. On one side of the oven, wood was burning from morning till night, and the red reflection of the flame was trembling on the wall of the workshop as though it were silently mocking us. The huge oven looked like the deformed head of a fairy-tale monster. It looked as though it thrust itself out from underneath the floor, opened its wide mouth full of fire, and breathed on us with heat and stared at our endless work through the two black air-holes above the forehead. These two cavities were like eyes – pitiless and impassible eyes of a monster: they stared at us with the same dark gaze, as though they had grown tired of looking at slaves, and expecting nothing human from them, despised them with the cold contempt of wisdom. Day in and day out, amid flour-dust and mud and thick, bad-odoured suffocating heat, we rolled out the dough and made biscuits, wetting them with our sweat, and we hated our work with keen hatred; we never ate the biscuit that came out of our hands, preferring black bread to the cracknels. Sitting by a long table, one opposite the other – nine opposite nine – we mechanically moved our hands and fingers during the long hours, and became so accustomed to our work that we no longer ever followed the motions of our hands. And we had grown so tired of looking at one another that each of us knew all the wrinkles on the faces of the others. We had nothing to talk about, we were used to this and were silent all the time, unless abusing one another – for there is always something for which to abuse a man, especially a companion. But we even abused one another very seldom. Of what can a man be guilty when he is half dead, when he is like a statue, when all his feelings are crushed under the weight of toil? But silence is terrible and painful only to those who have said all and have nothing more to speak of; but to those who never had anything to say – to them silence is simple and easy.... Sometimes we sang, and our song began thus: During work someone would suddenly heave a sigh, like that of a tired horse, and would softly start one of those drawling songs, whose touchingly caressing tune always gives ease to the troubled soul of the singer. One of us sang, and at first we listened in silence to his lonely song, which was drowned and deafened underneath the heavy ceiling of the cellar, like the small fire of a wood-pile in the steppe on a damp autumn night, when the grey sky is hanging over the earth like a leaden roof. Then another joined the singer, and now two voices soar softly and mournfully over the suffocating heat of our narrow ditch. And suddenly a few more voices take up the song – and the song bubbles up like a wave, growing stronger, louder, as though moving asunder the damp, heavy walls of our stony prison.

All the twenty-six sing; loud voices, singing in unison, fill the workshop; the song has no room there; it strikes against the stones of the walls, it moans and weeps and reanimates the heart by a soft tickling pain, irritating old wounds and rousing sorrow.

The singers breathe deeply and heavily; someone unexpectedly leaves off his song and listens for a long time to the singing of his companions, and again his voice joins the general wave. Another mournfully exclaims, Eh! sings, his eyes closed, and it may be that the wide, heavy wave of sound appears to him like a road leading somewhere far away, like a wide road, lighted by the brilliant sun, and he sees himself walking there....

The flame is constantly trembling in the oven, the baker's shovel is scraping against the brick, the water in the kettle is purring, and the reflection of the fire is trembling on the wall, laughing in silence....And we sing away, with someone else's words, our dull sorrow, the heavy grief of living men, robbed of sunshine, the grief of slaves. Thus we lived, twenty-six of us, in the cellar of a big stony house, and it was hard for us to live as though all the three storeys of the house had been built upon our shoulders.

But besides the songs, we had one other good thing, something we all loved and which, perhaps, came to us instead of the sun. The second storey of our house was occupied by an embroidery shop, and there, among many girl workers, lived the sixteen-year-old chambermaid, Tanya. Every morning her little, pink face, with blue, cheerful eyes, leaned against the pane of the little window in our hallway door, and her ringing, kind voice cried to us: 'Little prisoners! Give me biscuits!'

We all turned around at this familiar, clear sound and joyously, kind-heartedly looked at the pure maiden face as it smiled to us delightfully. We were accustomed and pleased to see her nose flattened against the window-pane, and the small, white teeth that flashed from under her pink lips, which were open with a smile. We rush to open the door for her, pushing one another; she enters, cheerful and amiable, and holding out her apron. She stands before us, leaning her head somewhat on one side and smiles all the time. A thick, long braid of chestnut hair, falling across her shoulder, lies on her breast. We, dirty, dark, deformed men, look up at her from below – the threshold was four steps higher than the floor – we look at her, lifting our heads upwards, we wish her a good morning. We say to her some particular words, words we use for her alone. Speaking to her our voices are somehow softer, and our jokes lighter. Everything is different for her. The baker takes out a shovelful of the brownest and reddest biscuits and throws them cleverly into Tanya's apron.

'Look out that the boss doesn't see you!' we always warn her. She laughs roguishly and cries to us cheerfully:

'Good-by, little prisoners!' and she disappears quickly, like a little mouse. That's all. But long after her departure we speak pleasantly of her to one another. We say the very same thing we said yesterday and before, because she, as well as we and everything around us, is also the same as yesterday and before. It is very hard and painful for one to live, when nothing changes around him, and if it does not kill his soul for good, the immobility of the surroundings becomes all the more painful the longer he lives. We always spoke of women in such a manner that at times we were disgusted at our own rude and shameless words, and this is quite clear, for the women we had known, perhaps, never deserved any better words. But of Tanya we never spoke ill. Not only did none of us ever dare to touch her with his hand, she never even heard a free jest from us. It may be that this was because she never stayed long with us; she flashed before our eyes like a star coming from the sky and then disappeared, or, perhaps, because she was small and very beautiful, and all that is beautiful commands the respect even of rude people. And then, though our hard labour had turned us into dull oxen, we nevertheless remained human beings, and like all human beings, we could not live without worshipping something. We had nobody better than she, and none, except her, paid any attention to us, the dwellers of the cellar; no one, though tens of people lived in the house. And finally – this is probably the main reason – we all considered her as something of our own, as something that existed only because of our biscuits. We considered it our duty to give her hot biscuits and this became our daily offering to the idol, it became almost a sacred custom which bound us to her the more every day. Aside from the biscuits, we gave Tanya many advices – to dress more warmly, not to run fast on the staircase, nor to carry heavy loads of wood. She listened to our advice with a smile, replied to us with laughter and never obeyed us, but we did not feel offended at this. All we needed was to show that we cared for her. She often turned to us with various requests. She asked us, for instance, to open the heavy cellar door, to chop some wood. We did whatever she wanted us to do with joy, and even with some kind of pride.

But when one of us asked her to mend his only shirt, she declined, with a contemptuous sneer.

We laughed heartily at the queer fellow, and never again asked her for anything. We loved her; all is said in this. A human being always wants to bestow his love upon someone, although he may sometime choke or slander him; he may poison the life of his neighbour with his love, because, loving, he does not respect the beloved. We had to love Tanya, for there was no one else we could love.

At times some one of us would suddenly begin to reason thus: 'And why do we make so much of the girl? What's in her? Eh? We have too much to do with her.' We quickly and rudely checked the man who dared to say such words. We had to love something. We found it out and loved it, and the something which the twenty-six of us loved had to be inaccessible to each of us as our sanctity, and any one coming out against us in this matter was our enemy. We loved, perhaps, not what was really good, but then we were twenty-six, and therefore we always wanted the thing dear to us to be sacred in the eyes of others. Our love is not less painful than hatred. And perhaps this is why some haughty people claim that our hatred is more flattering than our love. But why, then, don't they run from us, if that is true?

Aside from the biscuit department our proprietor had also a shop for white bread; it was in the same house, separated from our ditch by a wall; the *bulochniks* (white-bread bakers), there were four of them, kept aloof, considering their work cleaner than ours, and therefore considering themselves better than we were; they never came to our shop, laughed at us whenever they met us in the yard; nor did we go to them. The proprietor had forbidden this for fear lest we might steal loaves of white bread. We did not like the *bulochniks*, because we envied them. Their work was easier than ours, they were better paid, they were given better meals, theirs was a spacious, light workshop, and they were all so clean and healthy – repulsive to us; while we were all yellow, and grey, and sickly. During holidays and whenever they were free from work they put on nice coats and creaking boots; two of them had harmonicas, and they all went to the city park; while we had on dirty rags and burst shoes, and the city police did not admit us into the park – could we love the *bulochniks*?

One day we learned that one of their bakers had taken to drink, that the proprietor had discharged him and hired another one in his place, and that the other one was a soldier, wearing a satin vest and a gold chain to his watch. We were curious to see such a dandy, and in the hope of seeing him we, now and again, one by one, began to run out into the yard.

But he came himself to our workshop. Kicking the door open with his foot, and leaving it open, he stood on the threshold, and smiling, said to us:

'God help you! Hello, fellows!'

The cold air, forcing itself in at the door in a thick, smoky cloud, was whirling around his feet; he stood on the threshold, looking down on us from above, and from under his fair, curled moustache, big, yellow teeth were flashing. His waistcoat was blue, embroidered with flowers; it was beaming, and the buttons were of some red stones. And there was a chain too. He was handsome, this soldier, tall, strong, with red cheeks, and his big, light eyes looked good – kind and clear. On his head was a white, stiffly-starched cap, and from under his clean apron peeped out sharp toes of stylish, brightly shining boots.

Our baker respectfully requested him to close the door; he did it without haste, and began to question us about the proprietor. Vieing with one another, we told him that our 'boss' was a rogue, a rascal, a villain, a tyrant, everything that could and ought to be said of our proprietor, but which cannot be repeated here. The soldier listened, stirred his moustache and examined us with a soft, light look.

'And are there many girls here?' he asked, suddenly.

Some of us began to laugh respectfully, others made soft grimaces; someone explained to the soldier that there were nine girls.

'Do you take advantage?'... asked the soldier, winking his eye.

Again we burst out laughing, not very loud, and with a confused laughter. Many of us wished to appear before the soldier just as clever as he was, but not one was able to do it. Someone confessed, saying in a low voice:

'It is not for us....'

'Yes, it is hard for you!' said the soldier with confidence, examining us fixedly. 'You haven't the bearing for it... the figure – you haven't the appearance, I mean! And a woman likes a good appearance in a man. To her it must be perfect, everything perfect! And then she respects strength.... A hand should be like this!' The soldier pulled his right hand out of his pocket. The shirt sleeve was rolled up to his elbow. He showed his hand to us.... It was white, strong, covered with glossy, golden hair.

'A leg, a chest, in everything there must be firmness. And then, again, the man must be dressed according to style.... As the beauty of things requires it. I, for instance, I am loved by women. I don't call them, I don't lure them, they come to me of themselves.' He seated himself on a bag of flour and told us how the women loved him and how he handled them boldly. Then he went away, and when the door closed behind him with a creak, we were silent for a long time, thinking of him and of his stories. And then suddenly we all began to speak, and it became clear at once that he pleased every one of us. Such a kind and plain fellow. He came, sat awhile and talked. Nobody came to us before, nobody ever spoke to us like this; so friendly....And we all spoke of him and of his future successes with the embroidery girls, who either passed us by, closing their lips insultingly, when they met us in the yard, or went straight on as if we had not been in their way at all. And we always admired them, meeting them in the yard, or when they went past our windows – in winter dressed in some particular hats and in fur coats, in summer in hats with flowers, with coloured parasols in their hands. But thereafter among ourselves, we spoke of these girls so that had they heard it, they would have gone mad for shame and insult.

'However, see that he doesn't spoil Tanushka, too!' said the baker, suddenly, with anxiety.

We all became silent, dumbfounded by these words. We had somehow forgotten Tanya; it looked as though the soldier's massive, handsome figure prevented us from seeing her. Then began a noisy dispute. Some said that Tanya would not submit herself to this, others argued that she would not hold out against the soldier; still others said that they would break the soldier's bones in case he should annoy Tanya, and finally all decided to look after the soldier and Tanya, and to warn the girl to be on guard against him.... This put an end to the dispute.

About a month went by. The soldier baked white bread, walked around with the embroidery girls, came quite often to our workshop, but never told us of his success with the girls; he only twisted his moustache and licked his lips with relish.

Tanya came every morning for the biscuits and, as always, was cheerful, amiable, kind to us. We attempted to start a conversation with her about the soldier, but she called him a 'goggle-eyed calf,' and other funny names, and this calmed us. We were proud of our little girl, seeing that the embroidery girls were making love to the soldier. Tanya's relation toward him somehow uplifted all of us, and we, as if guided by her relation, began to regard the soldier with contempt. And we began to love Tanya still more, and meet her in the morning more cheerfully and kind-heartedly.

But one day the soldier came to us a little intoxicated, seated himself and began to laugh, and when we asked him what he was laughing at he explained: 'Two had a fight on account of me... Lidka and Grushka.... How they disfigured each other! Ha, ha! One grabbed the other by the hair, and knocked her to the ground in the hallway, and sat on her.... Ha, ha, ha! They scratched each other's faces.... It is laughable! And why cannot women fight honestly? Why do they scratch? Eh?'

He sat on the bench, strong and clean and jovial; talking and laughing all the time. We were silent. Somehow or other he seemed repulsive to us this time.

'How lucky I am with women, eh? It is very funny! Just a wink and I have them!'

His white hands, covered with glossy hair, were lifted and thrown back to his knees with a loud noise. And he stared at us with such a pleasantly surprised look, as though he really could not understand why he was so lucky in his affairs with women. His stout, red face was radiant with happiness and self-satisfaction, and he kept on licking his lips with relish.

Our baker scraped the shovel firmly and angrily against the hearth of the oven and suddenly said, sarcastically:

'You need no great strength to fell little fir-trees, but try to throw down a pine....'

'That is, do you refer to me?' asked the soldier.

'To you....'

'What is it?'

'Nothing.... Too late!'

'No, wait! What's the matter? Which pine?'

Our baker did not reply, quickly working with his shovel at the oven. He would throw into the oven the biscuits from the boiling kettle, would take out the ready ones and throw them noisily to the floor, to the boys who put them on bast strings. It looked as though he had forgotten all about the soldier and his conversation with him. But suddenly the soldier became very restless. He rose to his feet and walking up to the oven, risked striking his chest against the handle of the shovel, which was convulsively trembling in the air.

'No, you tell me – who is she? You have insulted me.... I?... Not a single one can wrench herself from me, never! And you say to me such offensive words.'... And, indeed, he looked really offended. Evidently there was nothing for which he might respect himself, except for his ability to lead women astray; it may be that aside from this ability there was no life in him, and only this ability permitted him to feel himself a living man.

There are people to whom the best and dearest thing in life is some kind of a disease of either the body or the soul. They make much of it during all their lives and live by it only; suffering from it, they are nourished by it, they always complain of it to others and thus attract the attention of their neighbours. By this they gain people's compassion for themselves, and aside from this they have nothing. Take away this disease from them, cure them, and they are rendered most unfortunate, because they thus lose their sole means of living, they then become empty. Sometimes a man's life is so poor that he is involuntarily compelled to prize his defect and live by it. It may frankly be said that people are often depraved out of mere weariness. The soldier felt insulted, and besetting our baker, roared:

'Tell me – who is it?'

'Shall I tell you?' the baker suddenly turned to him.

'Well?'

'Do you know Tanya?'

'Well?'

'Well, try.'...

'I?'

'You!'

'Her? That's easy enough!'

'We'll see!'

'You'll see! Ha, ha!'

'She'll....'

'A month's time!'

'What a boaster you are, soldier!'

'Two weeks! I'll show you! Who is it? Tanya! Tfoo!'...

'Get away, I say.'

'Get away,... you're bragging!'

'Two weeks, that's all!'

Suddenly our baker became enraged, and he raised the shovel

against the soldier. The soldier stepped back, surprised, kept silent for awhile, and, saying ominously, in a low voice: 'Very well, then!' he left us.

During the dispute we were all silent, interested in the result. But when the soldier went out, a loud, animated talk and noise was started among us.

Someone cried to the baker:

'You contrived a bad thing, Pavel!'

'Work!' replied the baker, enraged.

We felt that the soldier was touched to the quick and that a danger was threatening Tanya. We felt this, and at the same time we were seized with a burning, pleasant curiosity – what will happen? Will she resist the soldier? And almost all of us cried out with confidence: 'Tanya? She will resist! You cannot take her with bare hands!'

We were very desirous of testing the strength of our godling; we persistently proved to one another that our godling was a strong godling, and that Tanya would come out the victor in this combat. Then, finally, it appeared to us that we did not provoke the soldier enough, that he might forget about the dispute, and that we ought to irritate his self-love the more. Since that day we began to live a particular, intensely nervous life – a life we had never lived before. We argued with one another all day long, as if we had grown wiser. We spoke more and better. It seemed to us that we were playing a game with the devil, with Tanya as the stake on our side. And when we had learned from the *bulochniks* that the soldier began to court 'our Tanya,' we felt so dreadfully good and were so absorbed in our curiosity that we did not even notice that the proprietor, availing himself of our excitement, added to our work fourteen *poods* (a *pood* is a weight of forty Russian pounds) of dough a day. We did not even get tired of working. Tanya's name did not leave our lips all day long. And each morning we expected her with especial impatience. Sometimes we imagined that she might come to us – and that she would be no longer the same Tanya, but another one.

However, we told her nothing about the dispute. We asked her no questions and treated her as kindly as before. But something new and foreign to our former feelings for Tanya crept in stealthily into our relation toward her, and this new *something* was keen curiosity, sharp and cold like a steel knife.

'Fellows! Time is up to-day!' said the baker one morning, commencing to work.

We knew this well without his calling our attention to it, but we gave a start, nevertheless.

'Watch her!... She'll come soon!' suggested the baker. Some one exclaimed regretfully: 'What can we see?'

And again a lively, noisy dispute ensued. To-day we were to learn at last how far pure and inaccessible to filth was the urn wherein we had placed all that was best in us. This morning we felt for the first time that we were really playing a big game, that this test of our godling's purity might destroy our idol. We had been told all these days that the soldier was following Tanya obstinately, but for some reason or other none of us asked how she treated him. And she kept on coming to us regularly every morning for biscuits and was the same as before. This day, too, we soon heard her voice:

'Little prisoners! I've come....'

We hastened to let her in, and when she entered we met her, against our habit, in silence. Staring at her fixedly, we did not know what to say to her, what to ask her; and as we stood before her we formed a dark, silent crowd. She was evidently surprised at our unusual reception, and suddenly we noticed that she turned pale, became restless, began to bustle about and asked in a choking voice:

'Why are you... such. . .'

'And you?' asked the baker sternly, without taking his eyes off the girl.

'What's the matter with me?'

'Nothing....'

'Well, quicker, give me biscuits....'

She had never before hurried us on....

'There's plenty of time!' said the baker, his eyes fixed on her face.

Then she suddenly turned around and disappeared behind the door.

The baker took up his shovel and said calmly, turning towards the oven:

'It is done, it seems!... The soldier!... Rascal!... Scoundrel!'...

Like a herd of sheep, pushing one another, we walked back to the table, seated ourselves in silence and began to work slowly. Soon someone said:

'And perhaps not yet.'...

'Go on! Talk about it!' cried the baker.

We all knew that he was a clever man, cleverer than any of us, and we understood by his words that he was firmly convinced of the soldier's victory.... We were sad and uneasy. At twelve o'clock, during the dinner hour, the soldier came. He was, as usual, clean and smart, and, as usual, looked straight into our eyes. We felt awkward to look at him.

'Well, honourable gentlemen, if you wish, I can show you a soldier's boldness,'... said he, smiling proudly. 'You go out into the hallway and look through the clefts.... Understand?'

We went out and, falling on one another, we stuck to the cleft, in the wooden walls of the hallway, leading to the yard. We did not have to wait long.... Soon Tanya passed with a quick pace, skipping over the plashes of melted snow and mud. Her face looked troubled. She disappeared behind the cellar door. Then the soldier went there slowly and whistling. His hands were thrust into his pockets, and his moustache was stirring.

A rain was falling, and we saw the drops fall into plashes, and the plashes were wrinkling under their blows. It was a damp, grey day – a very dreary day. The snow still lay on the roofs, while on the ground, here and there, were dark spots of mud. And the snow on the roofs, too, was covered with a brownish, muddy coating. The rain trickled slowly, producing a mournful sound. We felt cold and disagreeable.

The soldier came first out of the cellar; he crossed the yard slowly, stirring his moustache, his hands in his pockets – the same as always.

Then Tanya came out. Her eyes…her eyes were radiant with joy and happiness, and her lips were smiling. And she walked as though in sleep, staggering, with uncertain steps. We could not stand this calmly. We all rushed toward the door, jumped out into the yard, and began to hiss and bawl at her angrily and wildly. On noticing us she trembled and stopped short as if petrified in the mud under her feet. We surrounded her and malignantly abused her in the most obscene language. We told her shameless things.

We did this not loud but slowly, seeing that she could not get away, that she was surrounded by us and we could mock her as much as we pleased. I don't know why, but we did not beat her. She stood among us, turning her head one way and another, listening to our abuses. And we kept on throwing at her more of the mire and poison of our words.

The colour left her face. Her blue eyes, so happy a moment ago, opened wide, her breast breathed heavily and her lips were trembling.

And we, surrounding her, avenged ourselves upon her, for she had robbed us. She had belonged to us, we had spent on her all that was best in us, though that best was the crusts of beggars, but we were twenty-six, while she was one, and therefore there was no suffering painful enough to punish her for her crime! How we abused her! She was silent, looked at us wild-eyed, and trembling in every limb. We were laughing, roaring, growling. Some more people ran up to us. Some one of us pulled Tanya by the sleeve of her waist.…

Suddenly her eyes began to flash; slowly she lifted her hands to her head, and, adjusting her hair, said loudly, but calmly, looking straight into our eyes:

'Miserable prisoners!'

And she came directly toward us, she walked, too, as though we were not in front of her, as though we were not in her way. Therefore none of us were in her way, and coming out of our circle, without turning to us, she said aloud, and with indescribable contempt:

'Rascals!... Rabble!'...

Then she went away.

We remained standing in the centre of the yard, in the mud, under the rain and the grey, sunless sky....

Then we all went back silently to our damp, stony ditch. As before, the sun never peeped in through our windows, and Tanya never came there again!....

WAITING FOR THE FERRY

(tr. Dora B. Montefiore and Emily Jakowleff)

AS MY HOODED SLEIGH jolted across the confines of the wood, and we came out on to the open road, a broad, dull-hued horizon lay stretched out before us. Isaiah stood up on the coach-box, and, stretching forward his neck, exclaimed –

'Devil take it all! It seems to have started already!'

'Is that so?'

'Yes; it looks as if it were moving.'

'Drive on, then, as fast as you can, you scoundrel!'

The sturdy little pony, with ears like a donkey and coat like a poodle dog, jumped forward at the crack of the whip; then stopped short suddenly, stamping its feet and shaking its head with a sort of injured look.

'Come! I'll teach you to play tricks!' shouted Isaiah, pulling at the reins.

The clerk, Isaiah Miakunikoff, was a frightfully ugly man of about forty years of age. On his left cheek and under his jaw grew a sandy beard; while on his right cheek there was an immense swelling which closed up one eye and hung down to his shoulder in a kind of wrinkly bag. Isaiah was a desperate drunkard, and something of a philosopher and a satirist. He was taking me to see his brother, who had been a fellow-teacher with me in a village school, but who now lay dying of consumption. After five hours' travelling, we had scarcely done twenty versts, partly because the road was bad, and partly because our fantastic steed was a cross-grained brute. Isaiah called it every name he could lay his tongue to – 'a clumsy brute,' 'a mortar,' 'a mill-stone,' etc. – each of which epithets seemed to express equally well one or other of the inward or outward characteristics of the animal. In the same way one comes across at times human beings with similar complex characters, so that whatever name one applies to them seems a fitting one. Only the one word 'man' seems inapplicable to them.

Above us hung a heavy, grey, clouded sky. Around us stretched enormous snow-covered fields, dotted with black spaces, showing where the snow was thawing. In front of us, and three versts ahead, rose the blue hills of the mountain range through which flowed the Volga. The distant hills looked low under the leaden, lowering sky, which seemed to crush and weigh them down. The river itself was hidden from our sight by a hedge of thick tangled bushes. A south wind was blowing, covering the surfaces of the little pools with quivering ripples; the air seemed full of a dull, heavy moisture; the water splashed under the horse's feet. A spirit of sadness seemed diffused over everything visible, as if Nature were wearied with waiting for the bright sun of spring, and as if she were dissatisfied with the long absence of the warm sun-rays, without which she was melancholy and depressed.

'The flood-tide in the river will stop us!' cried Isaiah, jumping up and down on the coach-box. 'Jakoff will die before we get there; then our journey will have been a useless torment of the flesh. And even if we do find him alive, what will be the good of it all? No one should force himself into the presence of the dying at the moment of death; the dying person should be left alone, so that his thoughts may not be distracted from the consideration of the needs of his soul, nor his mind turned from the depths of his own heart to the contemplation of trifles. For we, who are alive, are in fact nothing but trifles and of no use to one who is dying.... It is true that our customs demand that we should remain near them; but if we only would make use of the brains in our heads instead of the brains in our heels, we should soon see that this custom is good neither for the living nor for the dying, but is only an extra torment for the heart. The living ought not to think of death, nor remember that it is waiting somewhere for them; it is bad for them to do so, for it darkens their joys. Holloa! you stock! Move your legs more briskly! Look alive!'

Isaiah spoke in a monotonous, thick, hoarse voice, and his awkward, thin figure, wrapped in a clumsy, ragged, rusty armiah, rocked heavily backwards and forwards on the coach-box. Now and again he would jump up from his seat, then he would sway from side to side, then nod his head, or toss it backwards. His broad-brimmed black hat – a present from the priest – was fastened under his chin with tapes, the floating ends of which were blown into his face by the wind. With his hat slouched forward over his eyes, and his coat-tails puffed out behind by the wind, he shook his queer-shaped head, and jumped and swore, and twisted about on his seat. As I watched him, I thought how much needless trouble men take about most insignificant things! If the miserable worm of small commonplace evils had not so much power over us, we might easily crush the great horrible serpent of our serious misfortunes!

'It's gone!' exclaimed Isaiah.

'Can you see it?'

'I can see horses standing near the bushes. And there are people with them!' Isaiah spat on one side with a gesture of despair.

'That means there is no chance of getting across?'

'Oh, we shall manage to get over somehow! Yes, of course we shall get over, when the ice has gone down stream, but what are we to do till then? That's the question now! Besides, I'm hungry already; I'm too hungry for words! I told you we ought to have had something to eat. 'No, drive on!' Well, now you see I have driven on!'

'I'm as hungry as you are! Didn't you bring something with you?'

'And what if I have forgotten to bring something?' replied Isaiah crossly.

Looking ahead over his shoulders, I caught sight of a landau, drawn by a troika, and a wicker char-a-banc with a pair of horses. The horses' heads were turned towards us, and several people were standing near them; one, a tall Russian functionary with a red moustache, and wearing a cap with a scarlet band, the badge of Russian nobility. The other man wore a long fur coat.

'That's our district judge, Soutchoff, and the miller Mamaieff,' muttered Isaiah, in a tone that denoted respect. Then, addressing the pony, he shouted, 'Whoa, my benefactor!'

Then, pushing his hat to the back of his head, he turned to the fat coachman standing near the troika, and remarked, 'We are too late, it seems; eh?'

The coachman glanced with a sulky look at Isaiah's egg-shaped head, and turned away without deigning to reply.

'Yes, you are behindhand,' said the miller, with a smile. He was a short, thick-set man, with a very red face and cunning, smiling eyes.

The district judge scanned us from under his full eyebrows, as he leant against the foot-board of his carriage, smoked a cigarette, and twisted his moustache. There were two other people in the group – Mamaieff's coachman, a tall fellow with a curly head, and a miserable bandy-legged peasant in a torn sheepskin overcoat swathed tightly round him. His figure seemed bent into the chronic position of a low bow, which at the present moment was evidently meant for us. His small, shrunk face was covered with a scanty grey beard, his eyes were almost hidden in his wrinkled countenance, and his thin blue lips were drawn into a smile, expressive at one and the same time of respect and of derision, of stupidity and of cunning. He was sitting in an ape-like attitude, with his legs drawn up under his body; and, as he turned his head from side to side, he followed each one of us closely with his glance, without showing his own eyes. Through the many holes of his ragged sheepskin bunches of wool protruded, and he produced altogether a singular impression – an impression of having been half masticated before escaping from the iron jaws of some monster, who had meant to swallow him up.

The high sandy bank behind which we were standing sheltered us from the blasts of wind, though it concealed the river from our view.

'I am going to see how matters stand yonder,' said Isaiah, as he started climbing up the bank.

The district judge followed him in gloomy silence; and finally the merchant and myself, with the unhappy-looking peasant, who scrambled on his hands and feet, brought up the rear. When we had all reached the top of the bank we all sat down again, looking as black and as gloomy as a lot of crows. About three or four arshines away from us, and eight or nine below us, lay the river, a broad blue-grey line, its surface wrinkled and dotted with heaps of broken ice. These little heaps of ice had the appearance of an unpleasant scab, moving ever slowly forward with an indomitable force lying hidden under its furtive movement. A grating, scraping sound was heard through the raw, damp air.

'Kireelka!' cried the district judge.

The unhappy-looking peasant jumped to his feet, and pulling off his hat, bowed low before the judge; at the same time placing himself in a position which gave him the appearance of offering his head for decapitation.

'Well, is it coming soon?'

'It won't detain your honour long; it will put in directly. Just see, your honour: this is the way it comes. At this rate it can't help getting in in time. A little higher up there is a small headland; if it touches that, all will be right. It will all depend on that large block of ice. If that gets fixed in the passage by the headland, then all is up, for the ferry will get squeezed in the narrow passage, and all movement will be stopped.'

'That's enough! Hold your tongue!'

The peasant closed his lips with a snap, and was silent.

'Devil take it all!' cried the judge indignantly. 'I told you, you idiot, to send two boats over to this side, didn't I?'

'Yes, your honour, you did,' replied the peasant, with an air of having deserved blame.

'Well, and why did you not do so?'

'I hadn't time, because it went off all of a sudden.'

'You blockhead!' replied the judge; then turning to Mamaieff, 'These stupid asses can't even understand ordinary language!'

'Yes, that's true; but then they're nothing but peasants,' sneered Manaieff, with an ingratiating smirk. 'They're a silly race – a dull set of wooden blockheads; but let us hope that this renewed energy of the Zemstvo, this increase of schools, this enlighten- ment, this education' –

'Schools! Oh yes, indeed! Reading – rooms, magic lanterns! A fine story! I know what it all means. But I'm no enemy to education, as you know yourself. And I know by experience that a good whipping educates quicker and better than does anything else. Birch rods cost the peasant nothing, whereas education strips him bare to the skin, and causes him more suffering than can any rod. Up to the present time education has brought nothing but ruin to the peasant. That's my opinion. I don't, however, object to their being taught; I only say wait a little.'

'That's it!' exclaimed the merchant, in a tone of voice that denoted thorough agreement. 'It would really be better to wait a little; times are hard for the peasants just now. Failing harvests, sickness and disease, their unfortunate weakness for strong drinks, all these things undermine their prosperity, and then, on the top of this, they pile schools and reading-rooms! What's to be done for the peasant under such circumstances? There is nothing to be done for him, believe me.'

'Yes; nobody knows that better than you do, Nitrita Pavlovitch,' remarked Isaiah. His tone was firm but scrupulously polite, and he sighed devoutly as he spoke.

'I should think so, indeed! Haven't I been seventeen years among them? As for education, my opinion is this: if education is given at the proper time it's all right, then it may benefit people. But if – excuse the expression – I have an empty belly, I don't want to learn anything except, maybe, how to rob and steal.'

'No, indeed, there's no good at all in education!' exclaimed Isaiah, assuming an expression of good-natured respect.

Mamaieff glanced at him, and drew in his lips.

'There's a peasant for you, that fellow Kireelka!' cried the judge, turning to us with something almost of solemnity in his face and in his voice. 'Just look at him, please. He is anything but an ordinary peasant – he is a rare sort of animal! During the fire on board the steamer *Gregory* this ragamuffin, this gnat, rescued without anyone's assistance six persons. It was late autumn then; for four long hours he laboured in peril of his life, soaked to the skin, for rain was coming down in torrents. When he had rescued six lives, he quietly disappeared; they looked for him everywhere, for they wanted to recompense him, to give him a medal for his bravery; and at last they found him, stealing away to hide himself in the dark woods. He has always managed his affairs well; he has been thrifty; he drove his young daughter-in-law into her grave; his old wife beats him sometimes with logs of wood; he is a drunkard, and at the same time he is pious. He sings in the church choir, and he possesses a fine beehive with good swarms of bees; added to all this, he is a great thief! Once a barge got stopped here, and he was caught stealing; he had carried off three bags of plums. You see what a curious character he is!'

This speech made us all turn our attention to the clever peasant, who stood in front of us with eyes cast down, and sniffing vigorously. His gaze was fixed on the elegant shoes of the district judge, and two suggestive little wrinkles played round the corner of his mouth, though his lips were firmly closed, and his face was void of all expression.

'Come, let us examine him. Tell us, Kireelka, what benefits are to be derived from learning to read?'

Kireelka sighed, moved his lips, but no word escaped from them.

'Come now, you can read!' continued the judge, in a more imperative tone. 'You must know whether learning to read has made it easier for you to live or not!'

'That depends upon circumstances,' said Kireelka, dropping his head still lower on his breast.

'But you must tell us something more definite than that. You can read and write, so you surely can say whether you gain any benefit by it?'

'Benefit, well perhaps. But no, I think there is more; that is, if we look upon it in the right light, those who teach us may gain something by it.'

'What can they gain by it? And who do you mean by "they"?'

'Well, I mean the teachers, or maybe the Zemstvo, or somebody.'

'You stupid creature! But I ask you about yourself; for you personally, is it of any use?'

'That is just as you wish, your honour.'

'How just as I wish?'

'Why, to be sure, just as you wish. You see, you are our masters.'

'Be off with you!'

The ends of the judge's moustache quivered, and his face grew very red.

'Well, you see, he has said little, but I think you are well answered. No, gentlemen, the time is not yet ripe for teaching the peasant his A B C; he must be thoroughly disciplined first. The peasant is nothing but a vicious child; that is what he is.

Nevertheless, it is of him that the foundations are made. Do you understand? He is the groundwork, the base of the pyramid of the State. If that base should suddenly begin to shake, do you not understand what serious disorder might be produced in the State?'

'That's quite true,' reflected Mamaieff. 'Certainly the foundations ought to be kept strong.'

As I also was interested in the cause of the peasants, I, at this point, joined in the conversation, and in a short time all four of us were hotly and eagerly deciding the future of the peasantry. The true vocation of every individual seems to be to lay down rules for his neighbour's conduct; and those preachers are in the wrong who declare that we are all egoists; for in our altruistic aspirations to improve the human race, we forget our own shortcomings; and this may account for the fact that much of the evil of the world is concealed from us. We continued thus to argue, whilst the river wound its serpentine course in front of our eyes, swishing against the banks with its cold grey scales of ice.

In the same way our conversation twisted and wound like an angry snake, that flings itself now on one side, and now on the other, in the endeavour to seize its prey, which nevertheless continues to escape. And the cause of all our talk, the peasant himself, who sat there, at no great distance from us, on the sandy bank, in silence, and with a countenance wholly devoid of expression – who was he, and what was he?

Mamaieff again took up the conversation.

'No, he is not such a fool as you say; he is not really stupid; it's not so easy to get round him.'

The district judge seemed to be losing his temper. 'I don't say he is a fool; I say he is demoralized!'

'Pray don't misunderstand me. I say he has no control over himself. No control such as it is necessary to exercise over children – that is where the root of the evil lies.'

'And with all due deference, I beg to think that there is nothing wrong with him! He is one of the Great Maker's children, like all of us; but, I must apologize perhaps for mentioning it, he is tormented out of his senses. I mean, bad government has deprived him of all hope for the future.'

It was Isaiah who spoke in a suave, respectful voice, smiling softly, and sighing all the time. His eyes were half closed, as if he feared to look straight at anyone; but the swelling on the side of his head seemed to be overflowing with laughter, ready to burst into loud mirth, but not daring to do so. 'I for my part urge that there is nothing the matter with the peasant but hunger. Only give him enough good food, and he would soon be everything we I could desire.'

'You believe he is starved!' exclaimed the judge irritably. 'In the devil's name, what makes you think so?'

'To me it seems quite clear.'

'For goodness' sake, do tell me! Why, fifty years ago, he did not know what hunger meant. He was then well fed, healthy, humble – h'm! I did not mean that exactly. I meant to say – I – I – myself am hungry just now! And hungry – devil take him! – because of his stupidity. Come now, what do you think of that? I had given orders for the boats to be sent over here to wait for me. Well, when I get here, there sits Kireelka, just as if nothing were the matter. No, really, they are a dreadful set of idiots, I assure you. I mean they have not the least respect or the least obedience for the commands of those who are set in authority over them.'

'Well, it would be a good thing if we could get something to eat,' said Mamaieff in a melancholy voice.

'Ah, it would indeed!' sighed Isaiah.

Suddenly all four of us, who a few moments before had been snarling irritably at each other over our argument, grew silent, feeling suddenly united by the common pangs of hunger, felt in common. We all turned towards poor Kireelka, who grew confused under our gaze, and began dragging at his hat.

'Whatever have you done with that boat – eh?' Isaiah asked him reproachfully.

'Well, supposing the boat had been here, you couldn't have eaten it,' replied Kireelka, with a hangdog look on his face, which made us all turn our backs on him.

'Six mortal hours have I been sitting here!' ejaculated Mamaieff, taking out his gold watch and looking at it.

'There now, you see!' angrily exclaimed the judge, twisting his moustache. 'And this wretch says there will be a block in the ice directly, and I want to know if we shall get off before that – eh?'

It almost appeared as if the judge imagined that Kireelka had some power over the river, and considered that he was entirely to blame for our long delay. However that might be, the judge's question set all poor Kireelka's muscles in motion. He crawled to the very edge of the bank, shaded his eyes with his hand, and with a troubled look on his face tried to peer out into the distance. His lips moved, and he spasmodically kicked out one leg, as if he were trying either to work a spell or to utter some inaudible commands to the river.

The ice was moving slowly down in an ever more compact mass, the grey-blue blocks ground against each other with a grating sound as they broke, cracked, and split into small fragments, sometimes showing the muddy waters below, and then once again hiding them from view. The river had the appearance of some enormous body eaten by some terrible skin disease, as it lay spread out before us, covered with scabs and sores; while some invisible hand seemed to be trying to purify it from the filthy scales which disfigured its surface. Any minute it seemed to us we might behold the river, freed from its bondage, and flowing past us in all its might and beauty, with its waves once more sparkling and gleaming under the sunlight, which, piercing the clouds, would cast bright, joyful glances earthwards.

'They will be here soon now, your honour!' exclaimed Kireelka in a cheerful voice. 'The ice is getting thinner there, and they are just at the headland now.'

He pointed with his cap, which he held in his hand, into the distance, where, however, I could see nothing but ice.

'Is it far from here to Olchoff?'

'Well, your honour, by the nearest way it would be about five versts.'

'Devil take it all! A-hem. I say, have you got anything with you? Potatoes or bread?'

'Bread? Well, yes, your honour, I have got a bit of bread with me, but as for potatoes – no – I haven't any; they didn't yield this year.'

'Well, have you got the bread with you?'

'Yes, here it is, inside my shirt.'

'Faugh! Why the devil do you put it into your pazoika?'

'Well, there isn't much of it – only a pound or two; and it keeps warmer there.'

'You fool! I wish I had sent my man over to Olchoff; he might have got some milk or something else there; but this idiot kept on saying, "Very so-on, very so-on!" The devil! how vexing it all is!'

The judge continued to twist his moustache angrily, but the merchant cast longing glances in the direction of the peasant's pazoika. This latter stood with bowed head, slowly raising his hand towards his shirt front. Isaiah meanwhile was making signs to him. When he caught sight of them he moved noiselessly towards my friend, keeping his face turned to the judge's back.

The ice was still gradually diminishing, and already fissures showed themselves between the blocks, like wrinkles on a pale, bloodless face. The play of these wrinkles seemed to give various expressions to the river, all of them alike cold and pensive, though sometimes sad or mocking, or even disfigured by pain. The heavy, damp mass of clouds overhead seemed to look down on the movements of the ice with a stolid, passionless expression. The grating of the ice blocks against the sand sounded now like a frightened whisper, awakening in those who listened to it a feeling of despondency.

'Give me a bit of your bread,' I heard Isaiah say in a low whisper.

At the same moment the merchant gave a grunt, and the judge called out in a loud, angry voice, 'Kireelka, bring the bread here!' The poor peasant pulled off his cap with one hand, whilst with the other he drew the bread out of his shirt, laid it on his cap, and presented it to the judge, bending and bowing low, like a court lackey of the time of Louis XV. Taking the bread in his hand, the judge examined it with something like a look of disgust, smiled sourly, and turning to us, said –

'Gentlemen, I see we all aspire to the possession of this piece of bread, and we all have a perfectly equal right to it – the right of hungry people. Well, let us divide equally this frugal meal. Devil take it! it is indeed a ludicrous position we are in! But what else is there to do? In my haste to start before the road got spoiled – Allow me to offer you' –

With this he handed a piece of the bread to Mamaieff. The merchant looked at it askance, cocked his head on one side, measured with his eye the piece of bread, and bolted his share of it. Isaiah took what was left and gave me my share of it. Once more we sat down side by side, this time silently munching our – what shall I call it? For lack of a better word to describe it, I suppose I must call it bread. It was of the consistency of clay, and it smelt of sheepskin, saturated with perspiration, and with the stale odour of rotten cabbage; its flavour no words could express! I ate it, however, as I silently watched the dirty fragments of the river's winter attire float slowly past.

'Now this is what they call bread!' said our judge, looking reproachfully at the sour lump in his hand. 'This is the Russian peasant's food! He eats this stuff while the peasants of other countries eat cheese, good wheaten bread, and drink wine. There is sawdust, trash, and refuse of all sorts in this bread; and this is our peasant's food on the eve of the twentieth century! I should like to know why that is so?'

As the question seemed addressed to the merchant, he sighed deeply, and meekly answered, 'Yes, it's not very grand food – not attractive!'

'But I ask you why, sir?' demanded the judge.

'Why? I suppose because the land is exhausted, if I may say so.'

'Ahem! Nonsense, no such thing! All this talk about exhausted land is useless; it's nothing but a fancy of the statisticians.'

On hearing this remark Kireelka sighed deeply, and crushed his hat down on his head.

'You tell me now, my good fellow, how does your land yield?' said the judge.

'Well, that depends. When the land is healthy it yields – well, as much as you can want.'

'Come, now, don't try to get out of it! But give a straight answer. Does your land give good crops?'

'If – that is – then—'

'Don't lie!'

'If good hands work it, why, then, it is all right.'

'Ah-ha! Do you hear that? Good hands! There it is! No hands to work the land! And why? What do we see? Drunkenness and slackness, idleness, sloth. There is no authority over the peasants. If they happen to have a bad crop one year, well, then, the Zemstvo comes at once to their aid, saying, "Here is seed for you; sow your land, my friend. Here is bread; eat it, my good friend." Now I tell you, this is all wrong! Why did the land yield good harvests up till 1861? Because when the crops were not good the peasant was brought before his master, who asked him, "How did you sow? How did you plough?" and so on. The master then gave him some seed, and if the crops were then not good the peasant answered for it with a scarred back. His crops after that were sure to be good. Whereas, now he is protected by the Zemstvo, and has lost his capacity for work. It's all because there is no master over him to teach him to use his senses!'

'Yes, that's just it. The proprietors knew well how to make their serfs work!' said Mamaieff, with assurance. 'They could make what they liked out of the moujiks!'

'Musicians, painters, dancers, actors!' eagerly interrupted the judge; 'they made them whatever they liked!'

'That's quite true. I well remember when I was a boy how our Count's house-servant was taught to mimic everything he heard.'

'Yes, that was so.'

'Indeed, he learnt to mimic everything, not only human or animal sounds, but even the sound of the sawing of wood, the breaking of glass, or anything else. He would blow out his cheeks and make whatever sound was commanded. The Count would say, "Feodka, bark like vixen – like Catcher!" And Feodka did it. That was how they were taught then. Nowadays a good sum of money might be earned by such tricks!'

'The boats are coming!' shouted Isaiah.

'At last! Kireelka, my horses! No, stop a moment; I will tell the coachman myself.'

'Well, let's hope our waiting has come to an end,' said Mamaieff, with a smile of relief.

'Yes, I suppose it has come to an end.'

'It's always like that in life; one waits, and waits; and at last what one was waiting for arrives. Ha! ha! ha! All things in this world come to an end.'

'That's a comfort, at any rate,' said Isaiah.

Two long objects were to be seen moving along near the opposite bank.

'They are coming nearer,' said Kireelka, as he watched them.

The judge watched him from the corner of his eye.

'Do you still drink as much as you used to?' he asked the peasant.

'If I have a chance, I drink a glass.'

'And do you still steal firewood in the forest?'

'Why should I do that, your honour?'

'Come, tell the truth!'

'I never did steal wood,' replied Kireelka, shaking his head deprecatingly.

'What was it I condemned you for, then?'

'It's true you condemned me.'

'What was it for, then?'

'Why, your honour, you see, you are put in authority over us; you have a right to condemn us.'

'Ah! I see you are a cunning rascal! And you do not steal plums from the barges either, when they are detained; do you?'

'I only tried that once, your honour.'

'And that once you were caught! Wasn't that so? Ha! Ha! Ha!'

'We are not accustomed to that sort of work. That's why I was caught.'

'Well, you had better get a little practice at it; hadn't you? Ha! Ha! Ha!'

'He! He! He!' echoed Mamaieff, laughing also.

The peasants on board the boat pushed away with large iron bars the ice which impeded its course; and, as they drew nearer, we could hear them shouting to each other. Kireelka, putting his hands to his mouth, stood up and shouted back to them, 'Steer for the old willow!'

Then he hurried down the bank towards the river, almost tumbling head over heels in his haste. We quickly followed him, and were soon on board; Isaiah and I going in one boat, whilst the judge and Mamaieff went in the other.

'All right, my men!' said the judge, taking off his hat and crossing himself.

The two men in his boat crossed themselves devoutly, and once more started pushing away the ice-blocks which pressed against the sides of the boat.

But the blocks continued to strike the sides of the boat with an angry crashing sound; the air struck cold as it blew over the water. Mamaieff's face turned livid, and the judge, with knitted brow and with a look of intense anxiety, watched the current which was driving enormous blue-grey heaps of ice against the boats. The smaller pieces grated against the keel with a sound of sharp teeth gnawing through the wooden planks.

The air was damp and full of noises; our eyes were anxiously fixed on the cold, dirty ice – so powerful and yet so helpless. Through the various noises around us I suddenly distinguished the voice of someone shouting from the shore, and glancing in the direction of the sound I saw Kireelka standing bareheaded on the bank behind us. There was a twinkle in his cunning grey eyes as he shouted in a strange, hoarse voice, 'Uncle Anthony, when you go to fetch the mail mind you don't forget to bring some bread for me! The gentry have eaten my loaf of bread whilst they were waiting for the ferry; and it was the last I had!'

COMRADES

I

THE BURNING SUN OF July shone blindingly down on Smolkena, flooding its old huts with liberal streams of bright sunshine. There was a particularly large quantity of sunlight on the roof of the Starosta's[1] hut, not so long ago re-roofed with smoothly-planed, yellow, fragrant boards. It was Sunday, and almost the whole population of the village had come out into the street thickly grown over with grass and spotted here and there with lumps of dry mud. In front of the Starosta's house, a large group of men and women were assembled; some were sitting on the mound of earth round the hut, others were sitting on the bare ground, others were standing. The little children were chasing each other in and out of the groups, to an accompaniment of angry rebukes and slaps from the grown-ups.

The centre of this crowd was a tall man, with large drooping moustaches. To judge from his cinnamon brown face, covered with thick, grey bristles, and a whole network of deep wrinkles – judging from the grey tufts of hair forcing their way from

---

1 Chief of a village community.

under his dirty straw hat, this man might have been fifty years of age. He was looking on the ground, and the nostrils of his large and gristly nose were trembling, and, when he raised his head to cast a glance at the window of the Starosta's house, his large, melancholy, almost sinister eyes became visible; they were deep sunk in their orbits, and his thick brows cast a shadow over their dark pupils. He was dressed in the brown shabby under-coat of a lay-brother, scarcely covering his knees, and was girt about with a cord. There was a satchel across his shoulder, in his right hand he held a long stick with an iron ferrule, his left was thrust into his bosom. Those around him regarded him suspiciously, jeeringly, with contempt, and finally with an obvious joy that they had succeeded in catching the wolf before he had done mischief to the fold. He had come walking through the village, and, going to the window of the Starosta, had asked for something to drink. The Starosta had given him some *kvas*,[2] and entered into conversation with him. But contrary to the habit of pilgrims, the wayfarer had answered very unwillingly. Then the Starosta had asked him for his documents, and there were no documents forthcoming. And they had detained the wayfarer and had determined to send him to the local magistrate. The Starosta had selected as his escort the village *Sotsky*,[3] and was now giving him directions in the hut, leaving the prisoner in the midst of the mob.

As if fixed to the trunk of a willow tree, there the prisoner stood, leaning his bowed back against it. But on the staircase of the hut appeared a purblind old man with a foxy face and a grey, wedge-shaped beard. Gradually his booted feet descended the staircase, step by step, and his round stomach waggled solidly beneath his long shirt. From behind his shoulder protruded the bearded, four-cornered face of the Sotsky.

---

2   A sour popular Russian drink.
3   The Starosta's deputy.

'You understand then, my dear Efimushka?' inquired the Starosta of the Sotsky.

'Certainly, why not? I understand thoroughly. That is to say, I, the Sotsky of Smolkena, am bound to conduct this man to the district magistrate – and that's all.' The Sotsky pronounced his speech staccato, and with comical dignity for the benefit of the public.

'And the papers?'

'The papers? They are stored away safely in my breast-pocket.'

'Well, that's all right,' said the Starosta approvingly, at the same time scratching his sides energetically.

'God be with you, then,' he added.

'Well, my father, shall we stroll on then?' said the Sotsky to the prisoner.

'You might give us a conveyance,' replied the prisoner.

The Starosta smiled.

'A con-vey-ance, eh? Go along! Our brother the wayfarer here is used to lounging about the fields and villages, and we've no horses to spare. You must go on your own legs, that's all.'

'It doesn't matter, let us go, my father!' said the Sotsky cheerfully. 'Surely you don't think it is too far for us? Twenty versts at most, thank God! Come, let us go, 'twill be nothing. We shall do it capitally, you and I. And when we get there you shall have a rest.'

'In a cold cellar,' explained the Starosta.

'Oh, that's nothing,' the Sotsky hastened to say; 'a man when he is tired is not sorry to rest even in a dungeon. And then, too, a cold cellar – it is cooling after a hot day – you'll be quite comfortable in it.'

The prisoner looked sourly at his escort; the latter smiled merrily and frankly.

'Well, come along, honoured father! Good-bye, Vasil Gavriluich! Let's be off!'

'God be with you, Efimushka. Be on your guard!'

'Be wide-awake!' suggested some young rustic out of the crowd to the Sotsky.

'Do you think I'm a child, or what?' replied the Sotsky.

And off they went, sticking close to the huts in order to keep in the strip of shadow. The man in the cassock went on in front, with the slouching but rapid gait of an animal accustomed to roaming. The Sotsky, with his good stout stick in his hand, walked behind him.

Efimushka was a little, undersized mujik but strongly built, with a broad, good-natured face framed in a rough, red straggling beard beginning a little below his bright grey eyes. He always seemed to be smiling at something, showing, as he did so, his healthy yellow teeth, and wrinkling his nose as if he wanted to sneeze. He was clothed in a long cloak, trussed up in the waist so as not to hamper his feet, and on his head was stuck a dark green, brimless cap, drawn down over his brows in front, and very much like the forage cap of his prisoner.

His fellow-traveller walked along without paying him the slightest attention, just as if he were unconscious of his presence behind him. They went along by the narrow country path, zigzagged through a billowy sea of rye, and the shadows of the travellers glided along the golden ears of corn.

The mane of a wood stood out blue against the horizon; to the left of the travellers fields and fields extended to an endless distance, in the midst of which lay villages like dark patches, and behind these again lay fields and fields, dwindling away into a bluish mist.

To the right, from the midst of a group of willows, the spire of a church, covered with lead, but not yet gilded over, pierced the blue sky; it glistened so in the sun that it was painful to look upon. The larks were singing in the sky, the cornflowers were smiling in the rye, and it was hot – almost stifling. The dust flew up from beneath the feet of the travellers.

Efimushka began to feel bored. Naturally a great talker, he

could not keep silent for long, and, clearing his throat, he suddenly burst forth with two bars of a song in a falsetto voice.

'My voice can't quite manage the tune, burst it!' he said, 'and I could sing once upon a time. The Vishensky teacher used to say, "Come along, Efimushka," and then we would sing together. A capital fellow he was too!'

'Who was he?' growled the man in the cassock.

'The Vishensky teacher …'

'Did he belong to the Vishensky family?'

'Vishensky is the name of a village, my brother. And the teacher's name was Pavel Mikhailivich. A first-rate sort the man was. He died three years ago.'

'Young?'

'Not thirty.'

'What did he die of?'

'Grief, I should say.'

Efimushka's companion cast a furtive glance at him and smiled.

'It was like this, dear man. He taught and taught for seven years at a stretch, and then he began to cough. He coughed and coughed and he grew anxious. Now anxiety you know is often the beginning of vodka drinking. Now Father Aleksei did not love him, and when he began to drink Father Aleksei sent reports to town, and said his and that, the teacher had taken to drink, it was becoming a scandal. And in reply other papers came from the town, and they sent another teacher-fellow too. He was lanky and bony, with a very big nose. Well, Pavel Mikhailivich saw that things were going wrong. He grew worried and ill. They sent him straight from the schoolroom to the hospital, and in five days he rendered up his soul to God. That's all.'

For a time they went on in silence. The forest drew nearer and nearer to the travellers at every step, growing up before their very eyes and turning from blue to green.

'We are going to the forest, eh?' inquired the traveller of Efimushka.

We shall hit the fringe of it; it is about a verst and a half distant now. But, eh? what? You're a nice one, too, my worthy father. I have my eye upon you!'

And Efimushka smiled and shook his head.

'What ails you?' inquired the prisoner.

'Nothing, nothing! Ah, ha! We are going to the forest, eh?' says he. 'You are a simpleton, my dear man. Another in your place would not have asked that question, that is, if he had had more sense. Another would have made straight for the forest, and then...

'Well!'

'Oh, nothing, nothing. I can see through you, my brother. Your idea is a thin reed in my eyes. No, you had better cast away that idea, I tell you, so far as that forest is concerned. We must come to an understanding, I see, you and I. Why, I would tackle three such as you, and polish you off singly with my left hand. Do you take me?'

'Take you? I take you for a fool!' said the prisoner curtly and expressively.

'Ah, ha! I've guessed what you were up to, eh?' said Efimushka triumphantly.

'You scarecrow! What do you think you've guessed?' asked the prisoner with a wry smile.

'Why, about the wood... I understand... I mean that when we came to the wood you meant to knock me down – knock me down, I say, and bolt across the fields or through the wood. Isn't that so?'

'You're a fool!' and the enigmatic man shrugged his shoulders. 'Come now, where could I go?'

'Where? Why where you liked; that was your affair.'

'But where?' Efimushka's comrade was either angry, or really wished to hear from his escort where he might have been expected to go.

'I tell you, wherever you chose,' Efimushka explained quietly.

'I have nowhere to run to, my brother, nowhere!' said his companion calmly.

'Well, well!' exclaimed his escort incredulously, and even waved his hand. 'There's always somewhere to run to. The earth is large. There is always room for a man on it.'

'But what do you mean? Do you really want me to run away, then?' inquired the prisoner curiously, with a smile.

'Go along! You are really too good! Is that right now? You run away, and instead of you someone else is put into gaol! I also should be locked up. No, thank you. I've a word to say to that.'

'You are a blessed fool, you are... but you seem a good sort of mujik too,' said Efimushka's comrade with a sigh. Efimushka did not hesitate to agree with him.

'Exactly, they do call me blessed sometimes, and it is also true that I am a good mujik. I am simple minded, that's the chief cause of it. Other folks get on by artfulness and cunning, but what is that to me? I am a man all by myself in the world. Deal falsely – and you will die; deal justly – and you will die all the same. So I always keep straight, it is greater.'

'You're a good fellow!' observed his companion indifferently.

'How! Why should I make my soul crooked when I stand here all alone? I'm a free man, little brother. I live as I wish to live, I go through life and am a law to myself....Well, well! But, say! what do they call you?'

'What? Well – say Ivan Ivanov.'

'So! Are you of a priestly stock or what?'

'No.'

'Really? I thought you were of a priestly family.'

'Because I am dressed like this, eh?'

'It's like this. You've all the appearance of a runaway monk or of an unfrocked priest. But then, your face does not correspond. By your face I should take you for a soldier. God only knows what manner of man you are,' and Efimushka cast an inquisitive look upon the pilgrim. The latter sighed, readjusted his hat, wiped his sweating forehead, and asked the Sotsky:

'Do you smoke?'

'Alas! crying your clemency! I do, indeed, smoke.'

He drew from his bosom a greasy tobacco-pouch, and, bowing his head, but without stopping, began stuffing the tobacco into the clay pipe.

'There you are, then, smoke away!' The prisoner stopped, and bending down to the match lighted by his escort, drew in his cheeks. A little blue cloud rose into the air.

'Well, what may your people have been? City people, eh?'

'Gentry!' said the prisoner curtly, spitting aside at an ear of corn already enveloped by the golden sunshine.

'Eh, eh! Very pretty! Then how do you come to be strolling about like this without a passport?'

'It is my way!'

'Ah, ha! A likely tale! Your gentry do not usually live this wolf's life, eh? You're a poor wretch, you are!'

'Very well – chatter away!' said the poor wretch drily.

Yet Efimushka continued to gaze at the passportless man with ever-increasing curiosity and sympathy, and shaking his head meditatively, continued:

'Ah, yes! How fate plays with a man if you come to think of it? Well, it may be true for all that; I know that you are a gentleman, for you have such a majestic bearing. Have you lived long in this guise?'

The man with the majestic bearing looked grimly at Efimushka, and waving him away as if he had been an importunate tuft of hair, 'Shut up!' said he, 'you keep on like an old woman!'

'Oh, don't be angry!' cried Efimushka soothingly.

I speak from a pure heart; my heart is very good.'

'Then you're lucky. But your tongue gallops along without stopping, and that is unlucky for me.'

'All right! I will shut up, maybe – indeed, it would be easy to shut up if only a man did not want to hear your conversation. And then, too, you get angry without due cause. Is it my fault that you have taken up the life of a vagabond?'

The prisoner stood still and clenched his teeth so hard that the sharp corners of his cheek-bones projected, and his grey bristles stood up like a hedgehog's. He measured Efimushka from head to foot with screwed-up eyes, which blazed with wrath.

But before Efimushka had had time to observe this play of feature, he had once more begun to measure the ground with broad strides.

A shade of distraught pensiveness lay across the face of the garrulous Sotsky. He looked upwards, whence flowed the trills of the larks, and whistled in concert between his teeth, beating time to his footsteps with his stick as he marched along.

They drew nearer to the confines of the wood. There it stood, a dark, immovable wall – not a sound came from it to greet the travellers. The sun was already sinking, and its oblique rays coloured the tops of the trees purple and gold. A breath of fragrant freshness came from the trees, the gloom and the concentrated silence which filled the forest gave birth to strange sensations.

When a forest stands before our eyes, dark and motionless, when it is all plunged in mysterious silence, and every single tree seems to be listening intently to something – then it seems to us as if the whole forest were filled with some living thing which is only hiding away for a time; and you wait expectantly for some thing immense and incomprehensible to the human understanding to emerge the next moment, and speak in a mighty voice concerning the great mysteries of nature and creation.

II

On arriving at the skirts of the wood Efimushka and his comrade resolved to rest, and sat down on the grass round the trunk of a huge oak. The prisoner slowly unloosed his knapsack from his shoulder, and said to the Sotsky indifferently, 'Would you like some bread?'

'Give me some, and I'll show you,' said Efimushka, smiling.

And they began to munch their bread in silence. Efimushka ate slowly, sighing to himself from time to time, and gazing about the fields to the left of him; but his comrade, altogether absorbed in the process of assimilation, ate quickly, and chewed noisily, with his eyes fixed steadily on his morsel of bread. The fields were growing dark, the ears of corn had already lost their golden colouring, and were turning a rosy yellow; ragged clouds were creeping up the sky from the south-west, and their shadows fell upon the plain – fell and crept along the corn towards the wood, where sat the two dusty human figures. And from the trees also shadows descended upon the earth, and the breath of these shadows wafted sorrow into the soul.

'Glory be to Thee, O Lord!' exclaimed Efimushka, gathering up the crumbs of his piece of bread from the ground, and licking them off the palm of his hand.

'The Lord hath fed us; no eye beheld us. And if any eye hath seen, unoffended it hath been. Well, friend, shall we sit here a little while? How about that cold dungeon of ours?'

The other shook his head.

'Well, this is a very nice place, and has many memories for me. Over there used to be the mansion of Squire Tuchkov ...'

'Where?' asked the prisoner quickly, turning in the direction indicated by a wave of Efimushka's hand.

'Over there, behind that rising land. Everything around here belongs to them. They were the richest people hereabouts, but after the emancipation they dwindled.... I also belonged to them once. All of us hereabouts belonged to them. It was a great family. The squire himself, Alexander Nikietich Tuchkov was a colonel. There were children, too, four sons; I wonder what has become of them now? Really folks are carried away like autumn leaves by the wind. Only one of them, Ivan Alexandrovich, is safe and sound – I am taking you to him now – he is our district magistrate. He is old already.'

The prisoner laughed. It was a hollow, internal sort of laugh – his bosom and his stomach were convulsed, but his face remained immovable, and through his gnashing teeth came hollow sounds like sharp barks.

Efimushka shuddered painfully, and, moving his stick closer to his hand, asked: 'What ails you? Is anything the matter?'

'Nothing – or, at any rate, it is all over now,' said the prisoner, spasmodically, but amicably, but go on with your story.'

'Well, that's how it is, you see. The Tuchkov Squires used to be something here, and now there are none left. Some of them died, and some of them came to grief, and now never a word do you hear of them – never a word. There was one in particular who used to be here. The youngest of the lot…they called him Victor…Vic.… He and I were comrades. In the days when the emancipation was promulgated, he and I were lads fourteen years old. Ah, what a fine young chap he was – the Lord be good to his dear little soul! A pure stream, if ever there was one! flashing along and gurgling merrily all day long. I wonder where he is now? Alive or already no more?'

'Was he such a frightfully good fellow as all that?' inquired Efimushka's fellow-traveller quietly.

'That he was!' exclaimed Efimushka, 'handsome, with a head of his own, and such a good heart! Ah, thou pilgrim man, good heart alive, he was a ripe berry if you like! If only you could have seen the pair of us in those days! Aye, aye, aye! What games we did play! What a merry life was ours! raspberries la la[4]! "Efimka!" he would cry, "let us go a-hunting!" He had a gun of his own – his father gave it to him on his name-day – and he let me carry it for him; and off we went to the woods

---

4 Equivalent to 'beer and skittles.'

for a whole day – nay, for two, for three days! When we came home, he had an imposition, and I had a whacking. Yet, look you! the next day he would say, "Efimka! shall we go after mushrooms?" Thousands of birds we killed together. And as for mushrooms, we gathered poods[5] of them! And the butterflies and cockchafers he caught, and stuck them on pins in little boxes! And he taught me my lessons, too. "Efimka," said he, "I'll teach you." And he went at it hammer and tongs. "Come, begin," says he; "say A," and I roared "A-a-a!" How we laughed. At first I looked upon it as a joke. What does a boor want with reading and writing? But he persuaded me. "Come, you little fool," says he, "the emancipation was given to you that you might learn. You must learn your letters in order to know how to live and where to seek for justice." Of course, children heard their parents speak like that in those days, and began to talk the same way themselves. It was all nonsense, of course. True learning is in the heart, and it is the heart that teaches the right way. So he taught me, you see! How he made me stick to it! He gave me no rest, I can tell you. What torments! "Vic," I said, "I can't learn my letters. It's not in me. I really can't do it." Oh, how he pitched into me. Sometimes he thrashed it into me with a whip – but teach me he would! "Oh, be merciful," I'd cry. "Learn, then," he would say. Once I ran away from him – regularly bolted – and there was a to do. He searched for me all day with a gun; he would have shot me. He said to me afterwards, "If I had met you that day," said he, "I should have shot you"; that's what he said! Ah, he was so fierce! Fiery, unbending, a genuine master. He loved me, and he had a soul of flame. Once my papa scored my back with the birch rod, and when Vic saw it he rushed off to our hut, and there was a scene, my brother! He was all pale and trembling, clenched his fists, and went after my father into his bedroom. "How dare you do

5 A pood – 40 lb.

it?" he asked. Papa said, "But I'm his father." "Father, eh? Very well, father! I cannot cope with you single-handed, but your back shall be the same as Efimka's." He burst into tears after these words, and ran away. And what do you say to this, my father? He was as good as his word. Evidently he said something to the manor house servants about it. For one day my father came home groaning, and began to take off his shirt, but it was sticking to his back! My father was very angry with me at that time. "I've suffered all through you," he said. "You're a sneak, the squire's sneak." And he gave me a sound hiding. But he was wrong about my being the squire's sneak. I was never that. He might have let it alone.'

'No, you were never that, Efim!' said the prisoner with conviction, and he trembled all over, 'that's plain. You could not become a lickspittle,' he added hastily.

'Ah, he was a one!' exclaimed Efimushka, 'and I loved him. Ah, Vic, Vic! Such a talented lad, too. Everyone loved him; it was not only I. He spoke several languages. I don't remember what they were. It's thirty years ago. Ah! Lord, Lord! Where is he now? Well, if he be alive, he is either in high places … or else he's in hot water. Life is a strange distracting thing! It seethes and seethes, and makes a pretty brew of the best of us! And folks vanish away; it is pitiful, to the last gasp it is pitiful!' Efimushka sighed heavily, and his head sank upon his breast. For a moment there was silence.

'And are you sorry for me?' asked the prisoner merrily. There was no doubt about his merry way of asking; his whole face was lit up by a good and kindly smile.

'You're a rum 'un!' exclaimed Efimushka; one cannot but pity you of course! What are you, if you come to think of it? Wandering about as you do, it is plain that you have nothing of your own in the earth – not a corner, not a chip that you can call your own. Maybe, too, you carry about with you some great sin – who knows what you are? In a word, you're a miserable creature.'

'So it is,' answered the prisoner.

And again they were silent. The sun had already set, and the shadows were growing thicker. In the air there was a fresh smell of earth and flowers and sylvan humidity. For a long time they sat there in silence.

'However nice it may be to stay here we must still be going. We have some eight versts before us. Come now, my father, let us be going!'

'Let us sit a little longer,' begged 'the father.' Well, I don't care, I love to be about the woods at night myself. But when shall we get to the district magistrate? He will blow me up, it is late.'

'Rubbish. He won't blow you up.'

'I suppose you'll say a little word on our behalf, eh?' remarked the Sotsky with a smile.

'I may.'

'Oh – ai!'

'What do you mean?'

'You're a joker. He'll pepper you finely.'

'Flog me, eh?'

'He's cruel! And quick to box one's ears, and at any rate you'll leave him feeling rather shaky.'

'Well, well, we'll make it all right with him,' said the prisoner confidently, at the same time giving his escort a friendly tap on the shoulder.

This familiarity did not please Efimushka. At any rate he, after all, was the person in authority, and this blockhead ought not to have forgotten that Efimushka carried his copper plaque of office on his bosom.

Efimushka rose to his feet, took up his stick, drew forth his plaque, let it hang openly on the middle of his breast, and said, severely:

'Stand up! Let's be off!'

'I'm not going,' said the prisoner.

Efimushka was flabbergasted. Screwing up his eyes, he was

silent for a moment, not understanding why this prisoner should suddenly have taken to jesting.

'Come, don't make a pother, let's be going!' he said somewhat more softly.

'I am not going,' repeated the prisoner emphatically.

'Why not?' shrieked Efimushka, full of rage and amazement.

'Because I want to pass the night here with you. Come! let us light a fire!'

'I let you pass the night here? I light a fire here by your side, eh? A pretty thing, indeed!' growled Efimushka. Yet at the bottom of his soul, he was amazed. The man had said, I won't go! but had shown no signs of opposition, no disposition to quarrel, but simply lay down on the ground and that was all. What was to be the end of it?

'Don't make a row, Efim!' advised the prisoner coolly.

Efimushka was silent again, and, shifting from leg to leg as he stood over the prisoner, regarded him with wide-open eyes. And the latter kept looking at him and looking at him and smiling. Efimushka fell a-pondering as to what he ought to be doing next.

And how was it that this vagabond, who had been so surly and sullen all along, should all at once have become so gentle? Wouldn't it be as well to fall upon him, twist his arms, give him a couple of whacks on the neck, and so put an end to all this nonsense? And with as severely an official tone as he could command, Efimushka said:

'Come, you rascal, stir yourself! Get up, I say! And I tell you this, I'll make you trot along then, never fear! Do you understand? Very well! Look! I am about to strike.'

'Strike me?' asked the prisoner with a smile.

'Yes, you; what are you thinking about, eh?'

'What! would you, Efimushka Gruizlov, strike me, Vic Tuchkov?'

'Alas! you are a little wide of the mark, you are,' cried Efimushka in astonishment; 'but who are you, really? What sort of game is this?'

'Don't screech so, Efimushka! It is about time you recognized me, I think,' said the prisoner, smiling quietly and regaining his feet; 'how do you find yourself, eh?'

Efimushka bounded back from the hand extended to him, and gazed with all his eyes at the face of his prisoner. Then his lips began to tremble, and his whole face puckered up.

'Victor Alexandrovich – is it really and truly you?' he asked in a whisper.

If you like I'll show you my documents, or better still, I'll call to mind old times. Let's see – don't you recollect how you fell into the wolf's lair in the Ramen sky fir-woods? Or how I climbed up that tree after the nest, and hung head downwards for the fun of the thing? Or how we stole the plums of that old Quaker woman Petrovna? And the tales she used to tell us?'

Efimushka sat down on the ground heavily and laughed awkwardly.

'You believe me now, eh?' asked the prisoner, and he sat down alongside of him, looked him in the face, and laid a hand upon his shoulder. Efimushka was silent. It had grown absolutely dark around them. In the forest a confused murmuring and whispering had arisen. Far away in the thickest part of the wood the wail of a night-bird could be heard. A cloud was passing over the wood with an almost perceptible motion.

'Well, Efim, art thou not glad to meet me? Or art thou so very glad after all? Ah – holy soul! Thou hast remained the child thou wert wont to be.

'Efim? Say something, my dear old paragon!'

Efimushka cleared his throat violently, 'Well, my brother! Aye, aye, aye!' and the prisoner shook his head reproachfully. 'What's up, eh? Aren't you ashamed of yourself? Here are you, in your fiftieth year, and yet you waste your time in this wretched sort of business. Chuck it!' and, putting his arm round the Sotsky's shoulder, he lightly shook him. The Sotsky laughed a tremulous sort of laugh, and at last he spoke, without looking at his neighbour.

'What am I? I'm glad, of course... And you to be like this? How can I believe it? You and... such a business as this! Vic – and in such a plight! In a dungeon... without passports... living on crusts of bread... without tobacco.... Oh, Lord!... Is this a right state of things? If I were like that for instance...and you were even a Sotsky... even that would be easier to bear! And now how will it end? How can I look you in the face? I had always a joyful recollection of you... Vic... as you may think.... Even then my heart ached. But now! Oh, Lord! Why, if I were to tell people, they wouldn't believe it.'

He murmured these broken phrases, gazing fixedly at his feet, and clutching now his bosom and now his throat with one hand.

'There's no need to tell folks anything about it. And pray cease... it is not your fault, is it? Don't be disquieted about me. I've got my papers. I didn't show them to the Starosta because I didn't want to be known about here. Brother Ivan won't put me in quod; on the contrary, he will help to put me on my legs again. I'll stay with him a bit, and you and I will go out hunting again, eh...? You see how well things are turning out.'

Vic said these words soothingly in the tone used by grown-up people when they would soothe spoilt children. The moon emerged from the forest to meet the advancing cloud, and the edge of the cloud, silvered by her rays, assumed a soft opal tint. In the corn the quails were calling; somewhere or other a land rail rattled. The darkness of the night was growing denser and denser.

'And this is all really true,' began Efimushka softly. 'Ivan Alexandrovich will be glad to see his own brother and you, of course, will begin your life again. And this is really so.... And we will go hunting again.... Only 'tis not altogether as it was. I dare say you have done some deeds in the course of your life. And it is – ah, what is it?'

Vic Tuchkov laughed.

'Brother Efimushka, I have certainly done deeds in my life and to spare.... I have run through my share of the property. I have not succeeded in the service, I have been an actor, I have been a timber trade clerk, after that I've had a troupe of actors of my own... and after that I've gone quite to the dogs, have owed debts right and left, got mixed up in a shady affair. Ah! I've been everything – and lost everything.'

The prisoner waved his hand and smiled good humouredly.

'Brother Efimushka, I am no longer a gentleman. I am quite cured of that. Now you and I will live together. Eh! what do you say?'

'Nothing at all,' said Efimushka with a stifled voice; 'I'm ashamed, that's all. Here have I been saying to you all sorts of things... senseless words, and all sorts of rubbish. If it were a mujik I could understand it.... Well, shall we make a night of it here? I'll make a fire.'

'All right! Make it!'

The prisoner stretched himself at full length on the ground, face upwards, while the Sotsky disappeared into the skirt of the wood, from whence speedily resounded the crackling of twigs and branches. Soon Efimushka reappeared with an armful of fire-wood, and in a few moments a fiery serpent was merrily creeping along a little hillock of dry branches.

The old comrades gazed at it meditatively, sitting opposite each other, and smoking their one pipe alternately.

'Just like it used to be,' said Efimushka sadly.

'Only times are changed,' said Tuchkov.

'Well, life is stronger than character. Lord, how she has broken you down.'

'It is still undecided which of the two will prevail – she or I,' laughed Tuchkov.

For a time they were silent.

'Oh, Lord, Vic! How lightly you take it all!' exclaimed Efimushka bitterly.

'Certainly! Why not? What has been is gone for ever!' observed Tuchkov philosophically.

Behind them arose the dark wall of the softly whispering forest, the bonfire crackled merrily; all around them the shadows danced their noiseless dance, and over the plain lay impenetrable darkness.